PRAISE FOR

THE ELECTRIC CHURCH

"Bullets and black comedy."
—SFSite.com

"Exhilarating."
—*The Guardian* (UK)

"A dark future of high tech
and low dreams."
—*Library Journal Review*

"First-rate piece of science
fiction entertainment."
—SFSignal.com

"*A gritty cyberpunk masterpiece.*"
—Blogcritics.com

"Dark and evocative."
—3FFWorld.com

"A rollicking sci-fi
adventure."
—CHUD.com

"One of the genre's most
promising newcomers."
—*Booklist*

BY JEFF SOMERS

The Electric Church
The Digital Plague
The Eternal Prison

THE
DIGITAL
PLAGUE

JEFF SOMERS

www.orbitbooks.net

New York   London

Copyright © 2008 by Jeff Somers
Excerpt from *The Eternal Prison* copyright © 2008 by Jeff Somers
All rights reserved. Except as permitted under the U.S. Copyright Act of 1976, no part of this publication may be reproduced, distributed, or transmitted in any form or by any means, or stored in a database or retrieval system, without the prior written permission of the publisher.

Orbit
Hachette Book Group
237 Park Avenue
New York, NY 10017
Visit our website at www.orbitbooks.net

Orbit is an imprint of Hachette Book Group. The Orbit name and logo are trademarks of Little, Brown Book Group Limited.

Printed in the United States of America

Originally published in trade paperback, May 2008
First mass market edition, December 2009

10 9 8 7 6 5 4 3 2

To Danette
My darling, more than I deserve, sometimes more
than I can handle, everything I need.

I

DAY ONE: I KNEW THE MECHANICS OF DEATH BETTER THAN ANYONE

I was going to have to kill a whole lot of people.

"Keep walking, Avery."

I didn't like how he kept calling me *Avery* in that distorted voice, like he knew me. It made me nervous. It was one thing to be sold out by someone in your own organization and sent into a fucking ambush; chances were, when you got sold on a bounty, you were just entering a startling gauntlet of upsells. Eventually you discovered the original bounty had been laid out by some Chinese gangster halfway around the fucking world. And I was big money these days: Avery Cates, cop killer.

This is what happened when you were successful in the System: you wore a target.

It was cold, a strong wind pushing a metallic smell up my nose with prejudice. I estimated ten or twelve people around me, though only two had spoken so far. Both sounded like they were using a digital morpher to mask their voices, which made me wonder if I knew the pieces of shit who'd sold me out. Anger, green and corrosive, bubbled inside me. I didn't work with anyone I didn't know, so a friend had sold me out, and it made me *angry*. If I'd been psionic—even a tiny, microscopic little bit—I would have been able to burn off the blindfold with my thoughts. As it was I was listening, trying to pick up clues. For when I came back and killed every last one of them.

That *Avery* stuck in my head.

I didn't know how long I'd been unconscious—one second I'd been on Hudson Street, pale sun fighting its way through the scummy clouds, yellowed acidic snow crunching beneath my feet, and then an explosion behind my eyes, red and yellow and orange. When I came to, I was on a hover, blindfolded, my hands bound in rubber bracelets. I knew the buyers were heavy hitters because of the hover—a ride like that took money and plenty of it. That made me feel better; if I was going to be fucking sold like cargo, I at least wanted it to be serious people. People I wouldn't feel bad about killing later.

I tried to walk steadily, but the ground was uneven and I kept tripping. The world was an endless howling wind that pressed against me, making me lean into it, panting with effort, and the icy ground beneath me crunching like tiny bird bones as I walked. I had no idea where we were; there were buildings, judging from the echoes, but no people. The suburbs of Manhattan didn't lack for Ghost Cities, so that didn't really narrow it down. Go an hour or so in any direction and you would find empty towns filled with collapsing buildings and riot damage. Gangs of Wilders sometimes took them over and tried to start permanent settlements, but the cops were pretty good about stamping that shit out, and so every year the countryside got bigger and those monuments to pre-Unification got smaller.

In case anyone was watching, I kept a smirk on my face. You had to keep up appearances. If my file hadn't been cleared by Dick Marin, Director of SSF Internal Affairs and pretty much the biggest ballkicker in the System these days, I probably would have been number two on the System Security Force's Most Wanted List, right behind the legendary — and probably dead — Cainnic Orel. You couldn't be the SSF's number two and get scared every time you found yourself blindfolded — it looked bad. Besides, I knew it was only a matter of time before my people found me; a transmitter chip under the skin of my right hand would lead them here. The only question was, would my people get here before I was sold off to the next outfit?

My people were mainly Belling — older than he'd been when he'd helped me on the Squalor job, but still the best Gunner I'd ever seen — and Gleason, who was just a kid but who'd proven herself to me a dozen times already. She did things the way I wanted them done, because she'd learned everything from me. They'd grab up some muscle, of course, but I didn't care about the muscle. Belling and Gleason were pretty much my people in total.

"Stop, Avery."

I stopped and beamed my invisible smile around. I started to say something, but my throat filled with phlegm and I had to hack up a warm mass of it onto the ground. "Stop talking to me like you know me," I finally managed.

"We are old friends, Avery," the voice responded. I was

trying to catch the rhythms, the beats and pauses he used, see if it tugged at a memory. "Kneel, please."

I turned slowly until I thought I was facing the voice. "Give me a hint."

There was a scrape and the dry sound of fabric, and I flinched a second too late as something resembling a cannonball in heft and weight slammed into my stomach. I went down on my knees as requested, overbalanced, and landed face-first in sharp, iced-over snow. I lay there trying to breathe but just sort of twitching like a dying fish.

"Thank you, Avery," the voice continued, calm and electronically blurry. "Pull him up."

Someone was moving toward me, and then there was a fist in the fabric of my coat — a good coat, expensive — that hauled me upright. I hung there, limp, struggling to get my burning lungs back into motion.

"A hint? Avery Cates, the king of fucking New York, right? How many people have you killed?"

Fifty-four, I thought. *Personally.*

"I know you keep count, Avery. But how many have you simply destroyed, leaving them shattered, ruined? So many, right, Avery? More than you even admit to. More than you even *know* about, since some of us were simply never noticed. You couldn't pick me out of the multitude."

Slowly, I was able to pull a thin thread of cold air into my lungs. My head pounded with a fuzzy, painful pulse, as if an artery had burst and my brain was filling up with blood. I'd bitten my tongue when I'd gone down, and the salty rust taste of blood was making me nauseous. And then I went still and cold, because the frozen muzzle of a gun had been placed against my forehead. Revenge shriveled up inside me and faded away. I could hear birds in the air, a multitude of calls. I'd never heard so many birds in my life.

"For all these things, Avery, you deserve to die."

Everything had changed. These weren't swaggering assholes trying to throw a scare into me, this wasn't just shipping a fat payday out to some bigger fish. I was used to the threat of instant, unforeseen death—every day of my life. Having it brought right up under my nose so I could smell it was shocking, though, and I froze up.

Behind my blindfold I closed my eyes. *There are better ways to die,* I thought, my heart pounding. I'd lived longer than I'd ever imagined, and I felt like I'd been tired for most of it, always scrubbing along on no sleep, scrabbling. I found a part of me, small but distinct, was suddenly happy. The wind leaned against me, making a hollow noise. The snow on my face burned slightly, and I'd be red there for a few days. The gun pressed into my skin and hurt, and I found myself leaning into it, pressing against it, like digging at a scab.

I guessed my people weren't going to be in time.

"This is not an execution, Avery," the voice continued. "This is an assassination. Not yours. But an assassination none the fucking less."

I was ready for it. I would not speak. I clenched my jaws and held my eyes tightly closed, trying to clear my mind and think, but there was nothing to do. I was bound and blind and there were at least ten people around me. I knew the mechanics of death better than anyone, and I was caught in the gears. This was the System, after all; a day hadn't gone by that I couldn't remember death there with me, just walking along. From my father's dirty, foul-smelling hospital room right before Unification, when there'd been separate countries and half a chance for a decent life, to this moment, death was always there. Except for the Monks, and Dick Marin. And even their batteries had to run out sometime.

Almost hidden by the wind, I heard distant hover displacement.

"Give me his neck," the voice said.

A new set of hands—hard, cold hands encased in creaking leather gloves—took me by the hair and chin and bent my head painfully to the left. There was an endless moment of silence as I knelt there, held in place by two pairs of strong hands, thinking *Do it, do it, just fucking do it.* Something stabbed into my neck like a fragment of glass being dragged along my jugular, a pain that went on and on. Then something cold was being pumped into me, a cold I could feel as it traveled in my blood, like a worm wriggling in my papery veins.

I'd gritted my teeth so hard they ached. I hadn't said a word. The fragment of glass was dragged back again and then was gone.

"Good-bye, Avery," the voice said. "And don't worry: when it is over, you will be punished again. He has told me how this will end. And He is never wrong."

The two pairs of hands vanished simultaneously, and I toppled over onto my side. My neck throbbed, and although it was fading, I could still feel the cold lump moving through me, warming as it went. I thought that if it didn't warm up enough before it hit my heart or brain I'd be dead, a shock aneurysm flooding me with black, smothering blood.

The hover displacement was louder now, and I could

hear my kidnappers beating retreat. I flipped myself back up onto my knees, grit and sharp-edged stones biting through my pants into my skin, and stayed that way, the snow lightly burning my skin, my hands numb from the bracelets, listening to the heavy boots crunching in the snow and the hover getting closer, until the displacement started to beat against me, invisible fists. The ground shuddered beneath me as the hover settled home, the engines cutting off abruptly and leaving me, for a moment, with just the wind and my own ragged breathing. Blood, warm and wet, trickled down my neck and soaked into the fabric of my shirt.

I made fists with my hands as I heard the hover's hatch snap open. I worked my mouth up and down, trying to maintain control over myself. I'd been close to death a dozen times. Hell, I'd *been* dead for a brief time in London all those years ago.

I was *angry*.

"Chief?" I heard Gleason call out. She'd come a long way from a skinny kid who liked to play with knives. She'd been one of our first recruits when Belling and I had returned from London, rich, traumatized, and already marked for death by Dick Marin and his System Cops. "Chief, you okay?"

I heard their feet packing down the snow. I was shaking with the rage that had filled me, adrenaline tearing through my veins. I thought that if I wanted, I could snap the restraints with just a twitch. Whoever these fuckers were, they'd had their chance. They'd had me on my knees, hands bound, and for some reason they'd walked away. I didn't know what they'd done to me, but I wasn't going to forget and I wasn't going to count my fucking blessings.

"Keep your eyes open," I heard Belling shout, his smooth voice agitated. "Fucking amateurs."

"Hold on," Gleason said into my ear. I could smell her, a clean, nice smell, and felt her tugging at the rubber bracelets, and then heard the familiar *snick* of one of her blades. Gleason liked knives. Refused to carry a gun, saying that guns were for shitheads, for street soldiers downtown. She could throw a properly balanced, custom-made knife from across the room, in the dark, and kill you every single time. I remembered when Glee had been this skinny little girl, almost fucking mute. Now I couldn't shut her up, usually.

A tug and my hands were free, the bracelets snapping away into the air. I stood and whirled, tearing the blindfold from my face. I paused for a moment, blinking in the bright, white sunlight. We were in a city, all right, standing in front of a church. Around us, the city was a deserted field of rubble, with buildings jutting up here and there like broken teeth. The ground around the church had been cleared and was a clean, uniform off-white, a sheet of frozen snow. The fucking church was enormous; broken, pitted steps rising up to a set of empty doorways. Above the doors was a gaping hole, a few ragged spikes of old stone still jutting up. The sheer weight of the thing beat at me in pulses, as if it had been eroded from softer rocks around it by acid rain and pollution.

"Where the hell are we?" I asked, struggling for breath and control. Without a word, Glee moved her shoulder under my arm and took some of my weight, her long red hair fanning out in the wind. I allowed her to without even thinking about it—anyone but Gleason I'd have twisted their arm back behind them. With Glee, I leaned down and let her help me stumble about.

"Newark, Avery," Gleason said, looking around. "You okay?"

Newark. Newark wasn't even a city anymore; it was a blast crater that happened to have a few dozen buildings still standing here and there. For years it had been a backwater for criminals and independent sorts who fled the cities proper to escape the System Cops and the crowds and, ever since the Monk Riots, whatever Monks who'd managed to hang on to control of themselves and avoid the SSF cleanup. A surprising number were almost sane.

I felt in my pockets and found my cigarette case and gun, right where they were supposed to be—my captors had been so confident they'd left me my weapon. As I shook out a cigarette and stuck it between my dry, chapped lips, the anger inside me swelled until I thought I'd start vibrating. I was Avery Cates. I'd killed fifty-four people. I'd killed Dennis Squalor and destroyed the Electric Church, crawling around beneath Westminster Abbey and leaving a half dozen dead friends in my wake. I'd been betrayed by Dick Marin, the fucking unofficial emperor of the whole damn System, but I'd survived and even put a bullet in his artificial, avatar face. I was Avery fucking Cates, and they'd left me my *weapon*.

I turned to face the hover. Belling was standing in front of it, glaring at everything as if personally affronted—which he should be, since he'd been in charge of my security. I could see Candy, fat and dark, peering at me from inside the cabin, which meant Glee had grabbed whoever was available. I liked Candida—she had a round face that was always laughing, and she hadn't screwed me yet—but she was useless in a fight.

Belling gave me his stern face, humorless and terrifying. "What are we doing, Avery?"

I lit my cigarette and sent a cloud of blue smoke into the dirty air. I turned and started walking for the hover, the kid acting as a crutch.

"We're going to crack some heads," I said. "Get Pick on the horn and start him digging into the grapevine. Send someone over to Marcel and buy out a contract for information—have him get the word out, a million yen to anyone who gets us next to whoever the fuck did this." Marcel, fat and lazy on his throne in his ancient hotel, hadn't moved under his own power in years and thought way too much of himself, but he could get shit done, for the right price. "Take a fucking head count and let me know if anyone's out of place. Glee and I are gonna do our bad-cop worse-cop routine and milk some of my straight contacts. Reach out to whatever System Pigs like taking our money and see if they have any information. Let New York know that Avery Cates is fucking pissed off, and things are going to get hot."

I was a big fucking deal these days.

"Okay, okay," Glee said. "Avery—you sure you're okay? Your neck is kind of—"

She sounded a little shaky. I hissed into her ear, clutching her to me to conceal the fact that I was suddenly hot and dizzy. "I am not fucking okay, kid. I was fucking *sold out*. I was on my *knees*. I had a rod in my *goddamn ear*. I am angry, Glee. I am not okay." As we neared the hover, the two guards hastily stepped aside, their eyes on the horizon. I let her help me put one leg up into the cabin and turned back to the kid, putting a numb hand on her shoulder. Gleason was on a very short list of people I thought I could trust. As I spoke my eyes shifted up and over her to look at Belling, who'd turned to regard me, hands in his coat pockets. No one would ever trip up Belling like that, I thought. "Get us up in the air and get to work. I want to know who the fuck did this, and I want to know *fast*." I looked around the shattered remnants of the city. "I am going to have to kill a lot of people."

II

DAY THREE: EAR TO EAR, FAT MAN

"Now, don't worry," I said. "She won't hurt you."

Out of the corner of my eye, I could see with some pride that Glee kept her face impassive, aping the hardassed stare I'd tried to teach her. The other woman in the elevator with us was gorgeous, but I'd found that everyone who lived above Thirty-fifth Street or so was beautiful. Beautiful had gotten boring. Who knew how old she was, either; everyone uptown seemed to be a uniform twenty-five, unless they were hauling garbage or scuttling along at your feet, trying to shine your shoes before you got wise and told them to get the hell away from you. *Twenty-five* had gotten boring, too. She was blond and blue-eyed because blond and blue eyes were in this season, and her waist was ridiculously, comically narrow, giving her a wasp shape that gave me a bellyache.

When I looked at her, she flinched. I winked.

We were gliding down from the rooftop hover dock to the seventy-fifth floor, where the government had seen fit to lease space for the Regional Office of Waste Disposal. Recently the civil government had been spreading its wings, eating into the System Pigs' budgets and taking back some of the jobs traditionally done by the SSF. Word was the cops weren't happy about it. Technically any citizen of the System had access to local government offices, appointments appreciated but not required—all very friendly. The funny thing was, buildings like this one didn't have any street access at all—you had to take a hover to the roof and worm your way down. It was a neat way to keep the riffraff out without having to post so much as a sign.

The elevator smelled like the Wasp, a pleasant mix of cigarette smoke and perfume that always made me think of women, especially the high-end hookers down on Bleecker Street, fifty thousand yen just to chat them up. Gleason was spit-shined, her long red hair pulled back in a neat tail, her face scrubbed clean. She wore the hell out of the black suit and coat, although the coat was long for her and pooled around her boots. She looked older than her fifteen years, her face bland and her eyes murderous. I felt a strange sense of pride, looking at her.

"Quit it, Avery," she said softly. "You're giving me the heebies."

I turned back to face the doors of the elevator. The collar of my shirt was scratching me and my neck throbbed, the tiny wound on its side refusing to heal and still leaking pus. As we sank, I considered the well-hidden security camera embedded in the cab ceiling and calculated its coverage, deciding that it didn't really afford any hiding spots at all.

At the eightieth floor, the doors snapped open and the

elevator's shell spoke softly around us: *Eightieth floor, thank you. Eightieth floor, thank you.* The Wasp edged her way toward the doors, her bright, clear eyes—a little wider and rounder, I thought, than was natural—locked on me. For some reason, even in an expensive suit, forty thousand yen of synthetic fabric itching me something fierce, I still made people nervous. It might have been the wound on my neck. Or maybe it was just the blood under my fingernails.

As the doors snapped shut again, Glee cleared her throat thickly and dragged one of her sleeves across her nose. Spitting a glob of something green and thick onto the cab floor, she grimaced.

"I don't know what I picked up," she muttered, her voice a little hoarse, "but it fucking *sucks*." The deep voice and the suit made her look older, and I didn't like it.

I sighed. "Mind your manners," I said. We were playing a role, and eyes were on us.

She grinned a little. "Uh-oh. Avery's embarrassed. Avery's *mortified*."

I couldn't help smiling a little. Gleason always got to me. "Fuck you, kid."

She dragged her sleeve across her nose again. "Tell me why we're visiting the fucking *Waste Disposal* office again?"

The doors snapped open to reveal a long hallway carpeted in a deep, green pile, the walls a uniform white. Identical doors lined the sides, each marked with a small plastic sign. Cloudy white bubbles on the ceiling housed cameras that tracked us. You couldn't take a piss uptown without being monitored. There was no smell to the air at all. I never got used to the scrubbed air.

"We're here, little one," I said as we stepped out of the cab, "because I have a burning need to know who in fuck thought they could snatch me off the street and fuck with me. I have a good asset here."

"Ooh, Avery's angry. Avery's *pissed off.*" She kept pace with me as we walked down the hall. The first-name bullshit had started a few weeks ago, and I was letting it ride for a while, see if she figured out that it was a liberty before I had to smack the lesson into her. "In the Department of Waste Disposal?"

Glee didn't get uptown much and was used to a more direct approach to things. "Everybody's got shit to get rid of, kid," I said, stopping in front of one of the doors. "And it all goes through here at one point or another." The door snapped open and I pushed her in ahead of me.

The door admitted us into a tiny reception area, the carpet sucking at my feet as we let the door shut behind us. The Droid behind the white for-show desk was vaguely humanoid, with a feminine torso, an oval head, and two spindly arms. When you got close you could see it was attached to the desk and was just a visual aid for the office's shell.

"*Welcome to the Office of Waste Disposal, North American Department, Local Office Five-five-six,*" the shell breathed gently around us. "*Do you have an appointment?*"

I paid it no attention, stepping around the desk and striding down a shorter hallway lined with unmarked doors. At the third one on our left I turned and stopped, smiling into the tiny camera mounted in it, Glee hidden behind me. After we stood there for a few seconds the door whisked open; I took hold of Glee's arm and pulled her in with me quickly, the door zooming back into place a second or so after she'd cleared the threshold.

"Hello, Reggie," I said, smiling in what I hoped passed for friendliness. "Due for another treatment, I see."

The office was so small Glee and I had to stand very close to each other, hips touching. A foot or so in front of us was a tiny desk with no obvious way for anyone to get around it, and entombed behind the desk was a fat, dark-haired man in his shirtsleeves. He was wedged in behind the desk so tightly it made me feel uncomfortable in sympathy. A half-burned cigarette dangled just below his pencil-thin mustache, its smoke sucked up aggressively into the crank air and never even reaching my nose. A paper-thin screen between us displayed several smaller boxes of information just inches from his face. As I spoke he started forward and gestured violently, the screen going opaque in an instant.

"Hell, Avery, you scared the shit out of me," he gasped. "Who the fuck is this?" His tiny little eyes were buried in flesh, but I could see them roam up and down Glee's body, pausing blatantly at chest level. I clenched my jaw and pushed my hands into my coat pockets. Glee just stared down at him, her cheeks red and her forehead a little damp.

"This is my associate," I said. I gestured at the fat man. "This is Reggie, my contact here."

They stared at each other for another few seconds. Reggie liked to eat, and every year he had a fat-sucking procedure performed that shed two hundred pounds in an hour, followed by a series of skin-tightening treatments. These were expensive procedures, and in me—or, more precisely, my yen—Reg had found salvation. In January he was svelte and tanned, and then slowly expanded over the months until by December he was a goddamn beach ball.

"You're not supposed to bring anyone else with you," Reggie said slowly, his eyes settling lazily on Glee's chest again. "It's dangerous." He brightened without looking up at me. "Unless this is for *me?*"

I flared my nostrils and leaned forward to slap him lightly across the face, not hard enough to hurt. "Eyes on me, Reg," I said easily, stepping back. "Eyes on me."

He blinked and gave me a piggy little stare. "Fuck you, Avery. This is a bad time. You're not popular with certain people, you know, and the Optical Facial Scanners seem to be under the impression you've been seen on security cameras in government offices." He shrugged. "So I have to ask you to leave."

I ignored this, pushing my hands into my pockets. "I need info on Newark, Reg. I took a little involuntary trip out there recently and I want to know who's got fingers in that trash heap, who's carting shit out there or from there, who's bribing you to let it happen."

He tried to lean back casually, lacing his hands behind his head, but his girth pushed his belly into his desk and made him grunt in discomfort. I noticed his cigarette was nearly all ash and watched in fascination, waiting for it to shake off. "I just told you, Avery, this isn't a good time."

I glanced at Glee, who looked back at me and shrugged. For a second I was aware of how grown-up and poised she'd become, apparently overnight. I looked back at Reg with my grin in place, calibrated to convey amusement. This fat piece of shit thought he was in charge. I realized

I could smell him, Reg's brand of sour sweat too much for scrubbers.

"Reggie, let's be friendly. Let's have a conversation, and when we're done you say, Ave, this one's on the house, on account of I was a fucking asshole when you showed up. And then I say, Shit, Reggie, I surprised you, so maybe you weren't in top form, and we part friends. Okay?"

He kept trying like hell to look relaxed even though it was obvious he was straining to hold his position. "Get out. What are you going to do, slap me again? You're unarmed, Avery. You didn't get through rooftop security with a gun." He raised his eyebrows. "You think stories about you scare me. Fuck off."

He was right, I didn't have a gun. Getting past security in a building containing even a pissant government agency could be done—anything could be done—but it was troublesome, and unnecessary.

"Glee," I said. She took a half step forward and snapped her arm out stiffly, a homemade bone blade leaping into her hand. I had a similar one in my boot. With practiced ease she whipped it across his face, producing a tiny red wound on the tip of his bulbous nose. She grinned down at him, her blue eyes wide and lit up.

"Ear to ear, fat man," she said, coughing wetly. "If Avery says so."

Reggie quivered, his loose skin rippling unnaturally as a tiny drop of bright red blood formed on his nose. His eyes moved from me to her and back again. Licking his lips, he squinted at me. "What, you're going to murder a government official in his fucking *office*, Avery?" He shook his head. "Never gonna happen."

I shrugged. "You've got ten seconds, Reggie, and we're gonna find out."

Next to me, Glee sighed softly, an excited, feminine sound. Reggie stared at her for a moment and then seemed to deflate like he was undergoing his fat-sucking process as we watched. "Fucking hell. You're still gonna pay me, right?"

"Reggie," I said, leaning forward and pulling my portable shell cube from one pocket, "we're just going to have to think on that."

Glum now, he accepted the cube and slid it into his desk unit, hands working deftly. Glee stepped back and leaned against the wall, a coughing fit racking her.

"Okay, okay," Reggie muttered, all business now, his thick-fingered hands moving quickly, his screen flashing through records. "Newark. Nothing officially in Newark, of course, so there won't be any front-line records — nothing so easy, eh?" He grinned at me in a flash, trying to be my friend again. "But there's always a record." Ash finally fell off his cigarette, leaving him with a burning stub in his mouth and a pile of soot on his belly. "If they're moving anything substantial to and from Newark, someone's got a record. You got a time frame? Any other parameters I can search on? If it's just WD records it'd be a few seconds, but if you want me to cross-check data points on the entire NE Department, it'll take a while."

I shrugged. "I've got time."

He nodded, sweat appearing on his brow. Behind me, Gleason had recovered and was completely silent, chewing her hair like she was ten again. For a few seconds there was no sound whatsoever, and I watched the smoke from Reggie's cigarette rising thinly from his mouth. When the red box appeared in the lower corner of his screen, I saw it immediately and tried to read the backwards text printed in it.

"Oh, shit," Reggie said just before the building shell cut in around us, a ridiculously soft-spoken artificial voice.

"Attention: By order of the Department of Public Health, New York Department, under Joint Council Resolution Eight-eight-nine-a, this building has been sealed. Please remain in your current location. Attention…"

It was strange to hear *Joint Council* in every announcement, since the JC was a bunch of mummified old corpses beneath London, their Undersecretaries the only legally incorporated government left in the System. Most of them had been appointed almost thirty years ago and had been running things since the council had tried for immortality and ended up crazy instead. Until Dick Marin had muscled in. Every time I heard the words *Joint Council* I thought of those dusty old men under Westminster Abbey and shooting Dick Marin in the face, knowing there were dozens of him waiting to step into the vacuum.

I glanced back at Glee, who had gone still, one end of her hair still in her mouth, her off-white blade perched under one fingernail. Her nose was running, and her expression had suddenly lost the cocky assurance of a moment ago. I winked. "Cops," I said, simply. I turned to smile down at Reggie. "Reg, I hope for your sake you didn't just sell me out." I leaned down to put my knuckles on his desk. "Because it will not go well for you."

He smiled at me, but it was such a cadaverous and hollow grin I chose not to be offended. "Shit, Avery," he said, sagging in his chair. "We're going to wish it was fucking *cops.*"

III

DAY THREE: GOOD LUCK WITH THE FOLKS FROM PUBLIC HEALTH

Making an effort to keep my adrenaline under control, I studied Reggie's face for a second or two and concluded that I saw real fear there, but whether it was because he was caught breaking some laws or because he was afraid I was about to have Gleason slit his throat, I couldn't tell. "Who's coming, then?"

"Aren't you listening? Public Health." His piggy little eyes danced on me and he reached up to take the last stub of cigarette from his mouth and toss it onto the floor. "But it doesn't matter what fucking *department*. It means Spooks, Avery. Psionics. The fucking Spooks have sealed the building. Oh, fuck *me*."

I turned and nodded at Glee. She turned and tried the door, but it didn't respond.

"It won't open," Reggie almost wailed. "The building's been *sealed*. Oh, fuck you, you fucking piece of trash. I'm fucking ruined."

I turned back to Reggie and pointed at the door.

"Open it up, Reg," I said.

He shrugged, a massive fleshquake that went on and on. "I can't, Avery — the building's *sealed*."

I nodded. I had a suspicion this would turn out to be System Pigs no matter what the shell announcement said, and if I was right that meant they were coming for *me*. "If I twist your nose, Reggie, I will break it. I won't really mean to, but it'll happen. You'll stain your shirt and, knowing you, probably piss your pants. And then you're going to hit the panic button wired into the door and let us out *anyway*. So save yourself the trouble."

Reggie looked at Glee, but didn't seem to like the blank expression on her face. I snapped my fingers under his nose, making him jump. "Damn, Reggie, you take your Health Department actions pretty fucking seriously, huh?"

He wiped a hand over his face. "You don't —"

I made a feint at his nose, and he slammed back against the strangling wall of his office.

"Tell me I don't understand again."

Keeping his eyes on me, he reached forward and gestured, fat hands moving with surprising delicacy through a complex series of positions. Behind us, the door opened with a *snick*. I scooped my portable shell from its dock and dropped it into my coat. "Good luck with the folks from Public Health, Reg," I said, turning. Glee spun with me and let me move ahead of her.

None of the other doors were open. I imagined people in each one, in their tiny offices, like beetles tied to pins. In the entryway, the Droid spun its blank oval head toward us in a creepy, doomed attempt to appear human. *"For your safety, please return to your office,"* it said, projecting its voice over the building shell. *"Your face has been scanned and transmitted to the System Security Force for reference. One citizen and one unknown. For your safety, please return to your office."*

Glee strode forward toward the entry door, but it didn't budge for her. "Don't bother," I said. "You've got to release each one separately." I started trying to replicate the gesture Reggie had made in his office. As I tried to will my hand into the right series of positions, I glanced up at Glee, who'd flashed out her blade again and stood ready, bouncing a little on the balls of her feet. She looked incredibly young, but then I'd been doing shank jobs in the street for food money when I'd been fifteen.

My third guess at the gesture snapped the office door open. Glee poked her head out into the hall and nodded, glancing back at me. "All clear." She looked pink and shiny, like something very hot was inside her, melting.

"Attention, HD lockdown violation on seventy-fifth floor," the building shell announced immediately. I pushed myself toward the door.

"Get back!" I shouted.

She spun to face me, walking backward into the hall, flipping the blade over her knuckles and back again. "Ooh, Avery is protective. Avery is a *father figure,*" she said, grinning. I lumbered as fast as I could at the doorway and slammed into her, knocking her down onto the floor and pinning her blade arm under one elbow. I looked up, panting, as she squirmed beneath me.

"Avery, what the *fuck?*"

The hallway was empty. Glee was frowning up at me, her face flushed, her hair matted damply to her forehead. I lifted my arm and thrust a finger under her nose.

"What the *fuck,* kid, is —"

A loud crash made us both whip our heads around in time to see ceiling panels drop to the floor as two plump spheres appeared from above.

"— Security Droids," I finished. "Get up slow and stay behind me."

"Citizen," the building shell boomed through the hallway, *"please lie facedown on the floor and await security personnel."*

I held a finger against my lips without looking away. "Pretty harmless. They just herd the taxpayers as long as the taxpayers don't do anything wonky. But you were never registered, kid — you're a blank, and they don't like blanks, okay? They will fire on you. And your blade won't do anything against them." I patted her cheek. "So stay behind me, okay?"

She nodded, nose runny, eyes wide. "Okay." She looked fifteen again.

"Citizen, please lie facedown on the floor and await security personnel."

I knew the Droids wouldn't fire on a citizen; they'd just browbeat me to death. I stood up and made sure I was between them and Glee. The Droids just floated, two gleaming black balls, emitting a soft, deep hum I could feel in my chest.

"The elevators," I said. "Slow. Stay behind me."

We scuttled awkwardly backward.

"Citizen, please lie facedown on the floor and await security personnel."

"Where do we go?" Glee whispered. "If the System Pigs are coming, they're coming down the elevators, right?"

I nodded. "Eleven eighty-five Sixth Avenue," I said over my shoulder, eyes on the humming Droids as they herded us, "is an old building, Glee. Built before fireproof materials."

I bumped into her and stopped. "Elevator," she said.

I grinned at the Droids. "And thus it has a standard public-access fire alarm system," I said, and gestured.

Immediately, a piercing alarm erupted like a solid thing all around us, and the building shell started talking over itself, first telling me to get on the floor and then announcing a fire emergency. Behind me, I heard the *whoosh* of the elevator doors as they opened, and every door in the hall snapped open at the same time.

"Fucking chaos," Glee said. "I fucking *love* it. Avery's a fucking *genius*."

I was loved and adored by adolescent girls everywhere.

I backed my way into the cab, the Droids following just a foot away. When I was barely inside I reached over and gestured, and the doors shut. The cab immediately started heading down.

"Where are we going?" Glee asked, grinning at me. I tried to keep my face straight, but I smiled back, feeling an unfamiliar and not unwelcome energy bristling inside me. I peered at the kid—she was so flushed and sweaty I worried for a moment that I'd missed something, that she'd gotten tagged somehow.

"In these old pre-Uni buildings," I said, "in the event of a fire they can't very well send you up to the roof to watch in horror while the building burns, kiddo. So they send you down to a bunker below street level." I'd gotten so used to giving Glee these little lessons I almost didn't notice I was doing it anymore. I got down on one knee and laced my hands together. "Come on, I'll give you a boost."

She squinted at me. "Where am I going? Why not just walk out of the bunker?"

I nodded. "Sure, if you want to get killed. Kid, they can see this elevator moving right now. If they're of a mind to intercept us, all they have to do is wait downstairs for us. So, we're going up."

She nodded dubiously, putting one old cracked boot into my hands and grabbing onto my shoulders for balance. I took a deep breath and hauled her up toward the maintenance hatch of the cab. "Up?" she said as she traced its lines with her fingers. "How far *up?* They invented elevators so we didn't have to, you know, *climb* and shit."

"Just the second floor," I said. "You lazy kid. We'll be able to make a jump from there."

With a soft *ooh,* she found the latch and the maintenance hatch released, hanging down and instantly forming a little ladder for us. A breeze rushed into the cab, making the stray strands of Glee's red hair whip around. She reached forward and pulled herself onto the ladder without waiting, and in a second had disappeared above me. I took a breath and followed her, emerging onto the top of the elevator just as it coasted to a stop, making us both dance a little to keep our balance. I looked around, squinting, and spied the maintenance ladder clinging precariously to the shaft wall behind Glee. I nodded at it, and she turned to examine it.

"This? You want us to climb *this?*" She looked back at me over her shoulder. "It's rusted. It looks like it's a hundred years old."

"It might be," I said. "Ladies first."

She made a face and I grinned. I was getting soft in my old age. This shit was almost fun. I knew I should be worried — I'd been betrayed, fucked with, and now might end my day with a bullet in the ear. I should be in a bad mood, but instead I was feeling…good.

Glee took hold of the ladder and started pulling herself up. I jumped up right behind her and followed to the next elevator bay.

"Pull this manual release lever?" she called down, and then pulled it without waiting. The outer elevator doors split open with a rusty scrape. Light and music and the hum of a crowd sifted into the shaft and fell on me like dust, weightless. She pulled herself across and up through the doors. I followed as quickly as I could, panting a little as I stretched myself, reaching for the handholds embedded in the ancient concrete.

"Avery's *fat*," Glee said breathlessly from the second floor. "Avery's fucking *huge*." Without transition she burst into a ragged coughing fit, croaking hoarsely.

I squirmed my way up onto the floor and stood, wiping my hands and looking around. The lobby was simple, a dark marble wall a few feet in front of us and a flickering, holographic image of a man in an old-fashioned formal suit, white tie and tails.

"Welcome to Umano," the holographic man said crisply, appearing to eye us up and down. "You do not have a reservation. Performing credit scan." After a moment, he brightened. "Welcome, Mr. Cates! And…guest." I couldn't tell if it was a true AI hologram or just a projection of an actor in a booth somewhere. "We do have several unfulfilled reservations, and I can seat you. Welcome to Umano."

Behind the hologram, the entryway seemed to appear out of the stone, thin lines outlining the doorway and getting thicker. A simple enough trick, but impressive looking. This was what people did with yen. I fucking hated being rich. It was exhausting. When you were broke you always thought money would make life easier, but it just gave you more shit to do.

We stepped forward and the world's greatest holographic man actually stepped aside to let us pass. We stepped through the doorway into the largest single room I'd ever seen. The hum of a hundred conversations going on simultaneously became loud, crushing against us. It looked like every load-bearing column in the whole floor had been removed somehow, and I had an image of the immense and *ancient* weight of the building above us. It smelled...*wonderful*. It smelled like *real food,* and my mouth watered.

To my surprise, an actual person carrying a menu was approaching us, looking tired and pissed off. She was of the usual indeterminate age, blond and blue-eyed, tall and, of course, beautiful. Her legs had been lengthened at some point by some butcher, and she walked up to us with a curious insectoid jerking.

"Welcome to Umano," she said as she approached. "My name is Mina and I will be your server this morning. Please follow me."

I blinked. I'd never heard of a restaurant that didn't use Droids — but that, I supposed, was the gimmick. If you were rich enough, you could afford to have live, actual human beings bring you your food.

As we stepped behind her into the dining room, I heard the second elevator doors open out in the lobby and started moving faster. The room sprawled around us, the whole opposite wall just glass and steel, the surrounding block on display. The tables and chairs were just white cubes—big cubes for the tables, smaller cubes for the seats. They looked like the most uncomfortable things ever devised.

I stepped around our waitress and grabbed Glee's arm, pushing her ahead of me. I heard the sudden silence of impending ruckus behind us, and we started to run, Glee coughing wetly as she struggled on ahead, the panes of glass temptingly close. Around us, I had the impression of people staring, of the hum getting smaller.

We made it to the windows, smacking into them and pushing our faces against the glass. The feeling of an alarmed and frightened crowd around us was exhilarating. As I'd expected, there was a huge garbage skid on the street below us—the restaurants always had nightly cart-aways. I slapped Glee's shoulder and we whirled to tear-ass along the window a few feet to position ourselves approximately above our soft—if disgusting—landing. Glee grinned at me, and I couldn't help grinning back. Landing in a load of rotting imported vegetables was going to be a great story, when she told it.

From behind, I heard a man's voice, deep and confident, almost completely devoid of any accent—its lack of accent becoming an accent itself. "Mr. Avery Cates!"

I stopped. One moment I was tearing ass, prepared to take up a chair, smash some glass, and make a jump—the next it seemed like a better idea to just *stop,* and I stumbled to a halt. Glee ran on a few feet and then spun, her face lit up with alarm, snot running from her nose.

"Avery," she said again. "What the fuck?"

Our eyes met and I pushed as hard as I could, trying to force myself into motion. "Fucking psionic," I panted. "A Pusher. Keep moving. Go!"

Two men and a woman—kids, really, pink and squeaky-clean—were walking toward me like they owned the place and had just remembered they'd left the lights on. They *smelled* like cops. They could have been triplets: all white, with dark hair, their faces round in every way—big round eyes that were going to make them look like babies their whole lives, round ears, their skulls globes on top of their necks. The girl was pretty until you realized she was just a female version of the boys. I wanted to turn and check on Glee but couldn't. The buzz of voices returned with a new urgency, and I could see people talking to the air, using implanted comm units.

"Avery Cates, I presume?" said the kid in the middle, shooting his cuffs and reaching into his jacket pocket, producing a leather wallet. When he flipped it open, he held it up close to my face, with the air of doing me a courtesy. A rainbow-colored hologram proclaimed him to be Richard Shockley, assistant to Undersecretary of the North American Department Calvin Ruberto, one of the shadowy men and women who'd been running things ever since the Joint Council had slipped away into digital senility.

I looked from his ID to his face but said nothing. He snapped the wallet shut and the hologram vanished.

"Mr. Cates," he said, "I have been asked to come here by Dr. Daniel Terries, director of Public Health, New York Department, to bring you uptown for a conversation." He spread his hands. "A conversation, only."

"Sorry, no," I said, bluffing out of habit. "My sense of

civic duty is a little lackluster these days. I've got business to attend to."

He turned to smile around at his two companions, who didn't look back at him, keeping their eyes on me. The girl was still staring at me, and I wished fervently that she would stop.

From behind, I heard a faint grunt, and Shockley's hand shot up. Glee's knife was suddenly suspended in the air between us, hovering as if gravity didn't apply. *A goddamn Telekinetic,* I thought. His eyes flicked over my shoulder for a second and my heart lurched. For a moment he stared and then flicked his hand out in a lazy, negligent gesture. I heard Glee scream, followed by the sound of shattering glass. I strained, hoping to hear her soft landing in the garbage, but couldn't.

The entire restaurant had gone silent. Dimly, I could hear the building shell repeating its warnings in the distance as a stale, stiff breeze buffeted me from behind. The outside air smelled rotten, sweet and fungoid. A wave of disgusted groans filled the air.

Shockley looked at me as the knife fell soundlessly to the carpet. "Mr. Cates," he said, laughing a little, as I found myself rising an inch or two off the floor. Our eyes met, and his were filled with mean humor, like a boy who delighted in pulling wings off flies. "I am afraid we insist."

IV

DAY THREE: I DIDN'T HAVE TIME FOR THIS. I HAD PEOPLE TO KILL.

Ears pounding with the muted howl of displacement, I sat across from the three of them and forced myself to look them in the eye. They were all psionics, I guessed, Shockley the Tele-K and at least one — the girl, I guessed — a Pusher, just like my old friend Kev Gatz had been. Back at the restaurant I'd had the sudden urge to do whatever they wanted me to do, and I'd climbed into a small government hover like it was stuffed with pre-Uni cigarettes and first-class gin. I kept myself still, legs crossed, a bland expression on my face: I was Avery Cates, and this shit did not impress me. I'd expected cops, but it looked like the tension between the Undersecretaries and the SSF had evolved a notch or two — if the government's first batch of psionic kids had graduated, I suspected the working truce between the civil service and the System Pigs was about to end. Fucking *psionics*. The System Pigs had been collecting psionics for years; whenever someone displayed any kind of uncanny ability, the next day the cops were there, filling out bullshit forms and taking the kid away. Leaving *receipts*. They were usually kids. If they made it to adulthood without getting nailed, like Kev had, they usually knew how to hide it.

I didn't like thinking about Kev. It always brought back the image of him stretched out, buried inside the old Electric Church complex.

Shockley had given the destination—a place on Fifty-second Street, not far from SSF Headquarters in the grim stone and steel tower everyone just called The Rock—and we'd ascended into silence. The hover had a disconcerting amount of glass; I could see New York passing by far beneath us, other hovers slipping between us and the ground. We were moving slowly, almost floating, with a deep vibration settling into the core of my body. It was dizzying and made my stomach lurch every time I glanced down. So I kept my eyes on Shockley's mean and tight ones. I imagined I could hear them drying out with a light sizzle, dust particles hitting like meteors and leaving microscopic scars behind.

I was free, though; no Push on my thoughts that I could detect, no invisible hand reaching out. I resisted the urge to test this every few seconds, forcing myself to remain still. They'd grabbed my guns, of course, but missed the blade in my boot. Definitely not cops. A System Pig would have shaken me upside down until everything had fallen out of my pockets.

"We will be at Dr. Terries's location in seven minutes," Shockley said suddenly, his eyes locked on me. "He has just a few questions for you. We appreciate your help."

I smiled blandly. If Shockley the Civil Servant wanted

to play a game, that was fine. The civil government and the cops had been at each other's necks ever since the Monk Riots—which I'd caused when I'd killed Dennis Squalor and brought down the Electric Church—as they struggled for supremacy. Even so I had no doubt that this little shit would consider it his duty to deliver me up to the System Police once I'd given my interview or whatever to Dr. Terries. Whoever the fuck *Dr. Terries* was. I didn't have any doubt that if I didn't get off this hover, and *soon*, I was a dead man, one way or another.

I looked past them into the cockpit. I could see the pilot, just a pair of shoulders in a blue jacket. Looking back at them, I recrossed my legs, laying one hand on my cracked, worn boot with my thumb and forefinger just above the hidden blade. I concentrated on slowing my breathing and heart rate.

"You could tell me what this Dr. Terries wants with me, and we'd all be able to bond over the intimacy," I suggested.

Shockley cocked his head. "You're a suspicious man, Mr. Cates."

"Last time I was scooped up into a hover, buddy, things didn't end too well for me."

He smiled, a tightening of the corners of his mouth that implied the exact opposite of humor. "Mr. Cates, do you know a woman named," he shut his eyes, "Candida Murrow?"

I squinted at him. I knew Candy. I saw her all the time down at Pick's, but I said nothing. The golden rule with cops—or fucking bureaucrats—was that you asked questions, you never answered them. The only question I had, really, was the identity of the piece of shit selling me out.

There was no way the fucking triplets here had found me through their superior investigative work and street contacts. Someone had fucked me.

I resisted the urge to reach up and touch the healing wound on my neck. Shockley opened his eyes. "Ms. Murrow—a fine, upstanding citizen, no doubt—was found dead late yesterday."

I blinked but didn't react. I hadn't heard. Big, happy Kenyan, enjoyed her work, her English theoretical at best, but useful. Or had been.

"She died in a very...unusual way. Looks viral—quite gruesome. Dr. Terries is director of Public Health, and he is concerned. She is a known associate of yours, Mr. Cates. You have an...organization." He said this as if the word tasted funny in his mouth. "Dr. Terries is concerned that others in your *organization* may be similarly...infected."

I gave him the bland smile again. "Never heard of Dr. Terries. I don't have a fucking health chip, Mr. Shockley."

He nodded. "Yes. When was the last time you had contact with Ms. Murrow, Mr. Cates? Dr. Terries is mainly concerned with her movements over the last few days."

I fidgeted; let them believe I was disconcerted, nervous. The tips of my fingers touched the top of the blade's handle, and I paused, taking my time. I still had a few minutes before we made it to our destination, and I would have only one chance at this, because the second after I moved they would leap on me: the Pusher would grab my mind and Shockley would be ready to toss me around just in case that failed. "I'm afraid I don't know Ms. Murrow."

Shockley smirked and glanced at the girl, and I knew my moment had come; they were going to start Pushing some cooperation into me. I sucked in the crank air and pinched the blade's handle between my thumb and forefinger.

As I leaped up, unfolding my legs and pushing off the seat, the blade slid from my boot, slicing my calf up a little as it did. I locked my eyes on the pilot's shoulder twenty feet or so away, cocked my arm back, and just as I felt the icy invisible fingers of Shockley's mind on me, I launched the blade across the cabin. It sank into the back of the pilot's neck, and he fell out of his seat as if he'd suddenly noticed gravity. With an explosive whine the hover flipped over, sending us crashing into the ceiling, which was now the floor.

The icy invisible hand disappeared.

I managed to duck my head under my arms and took the impact on my shoulders. There was a familiar wet cracking sound nearby, and as I launched myself at the tangle of well-dressed bodies I spotted the girl's head, bent at a bad angle, her eyes wide in shock. I wasn't going to have to worry about being Pushed anymore, at least.

The hover flipped again, an instant transformation. I managed to slap an arm under one of the seats and held on for just a moment, releasing myself to plummet the last few feet right onto Shockley's upturned face and neck. At the last moment he whipped both arms across his face and I stopped with a jerk, hung for a breathless second, and then rocketed back up to crash into the floor again, grunting as the rivets dug into my back and my skull bounced. I was pinned for a moment, but the hover obliged me again by suddenly yawing and losing altitude, rolling Shockley and his friend violently toward the cockpit.

I dropped at an angle, catching my chest on one set of seats, red pain shooting through my chest and straight into my head, as if a spike had been jammed up through one armpit. The hover yawed again, and I was tossed toward the rear, smacking into the flat wall there. I closed my eyes and flexed my hands, making sure I still had movement, and with a deep breath I pushed the pain aside and tried to clear my head. I grabbed onto the back of the row of seats and pulled myself up and forward. Hand over hand, I made my way toward the two men who were a jumble of limbs on the floor, hanging from seats. I clung to the seatback and reached down to roll Shockley over; he was unconscious, a blue and black welt on his forehead. The other man was groaning, feebly pulling at his coat, which was caught on a bolt in the floor, the tight fabric restricting his movements. I hit him hard against one temple, new pain shooting up through my arm, and he fell still.

The tearing, bending noise around me was hurting my ears as the hover's displacers fought against physics to keep us in the sky. The air had turned burned and smoky, scratching at my throat. I pushed myself upright, leaning hard against the seats, and just panted for a second or two, sweat streaming down my face, one side of me feeling like someone had shoved a particularly long and well-barbed piece of rusty metal between two ribs. The hover began to shake violently.

Moving carefully, I climbed my way to the cockpit, one heavy step at a time. The back of the hover seemed to have its own immense gravity, as if a black hole had erupted into being just behind the plate metal, sucking at me relentlessly. I couldn't get enough air into my lungs, and every step was an effort of immense proportions. When I clawed my way through the cockpit door, I hung there, straining, and stared out the windshield. A stupid smile spread over my face. We'd drifted wildly north; instead of the city beneath us there was the rubble-dotted wilderness of the northern island, old abandoned Inwood just one long riot scar. The Unification Riots had burned half of Manhattan to the ground, because the only people who'd thought welding the whole world under one government was a good idea were the folks who planned on running things afterward. No one had ever bothered to rebuild it, and I was about to ride this hover straight into the scar tissue at roughly a hundred miles an hour.

The smile remained on my face even though I wasn't feeling remotely humorous — it was like an alien thing on my face. I watched the ground approaching in deceptive slow motion and then glanced down at the pilot, lying in a shallow pool of blood on the floor up against the wall. I glanced back, twisting my head around to look at the triplets.

The whining noise of the displacers was ear-shredding.

I dived forward and took hold of the pilot's chair, my ribs lighting up into a wedge of fire stabbing into me. I let out a strangled yell and tore two fingernails pulling myself into the chair, where I was able to just go limp and let gravity and inertia press me back against the thin cushioning, panting in painful little hitches.

"This isn't fair," I muttered. I didn't have time for this. I had people to kill.

The displacers reached an almost silent crescendo so

loud my ears couldn't process it, and then, with a few hundred feet between me and the pitted bank of the river, they flatlined and went silent.

I could hear the wind howling as we tore through it. I breathed in tight, rapid snorts I couldn't hear. Scrabbling with bloodied fingers, I pulled the safety straps across my body and clicked in. Without warning, the ground wasn't coming in slow motion anymore—it was rushing up toward me faster than made sense.

Twenty feet up, I closed my eyes.

V

DAY THREE: KEEPING PANIC AT BAY WITH LIES AND CHEAP TRICKS

Thinking it was a bad idea, I opened my eyes anyway and blinked, feeling pain, one giant ache that stretched from my ass to my teeth. I tried to shift and stretch, but couldn't move my arms. A rain of tiny glass shards floated up away from me, scattering against the sky, as if the cracked and spidered edge of the world were just inches away. Shaking my head again, I snapped awake and tried to bend backward, but couldn't. An inch away from my right eye was a huge jagged hunk of glass, pointed straight at me. The thick windshield had shattered on impact; the nose of the hover was half buried in the dirt and snow, and I hung from the pilot's seat by the safety straps. The whole cabin smelled like blood, copper, and salt. Thin, bluish smoke wafted up toward me, stinging my eyes.

I turned my head, glass clinking down from hidden crannies, and there was the pilot himself, or at least half of him, lodged precariously between my seat and the floor.

He stared up at me with wide-open eyes that were startlingly green—bright and clear. I grimaced at him by way of apology and started trying to free my arms, which were pinned at my sides by the tight straps. As I moved, glass shards sprayed down, a dry sound. I kept stealing glances at the blade of glass just in front of me. One sudden drop and I'd be one of those beggars on Broadway, begging for yen. Or dead.

I didn't have time to be fancy, though; a hover crash was a noisy, messy thing, and the System Pigs were no doubt going to get around to it. And I didn't know if Shockley and his pal were dead or maybe coming to, irritated and able to slap me around without moving a muscle. My people were probably on their way again, tracing my implant, but I couldn't take the chance—I needed to get moving. Besides, once the fucking suits got you on their lists, they just kept coming at you, and I doubted it made any difference if they were cops or paper-pushers.

Everything hurt. I shut my eyes to get the distraction of the glass shard out of mind and concentrated on moving my arms. I had a little give, so I breathed out as hard as I could and strained my arm, my ribs creaking in outrage. Sweat popped out on my forehead and dripped down onto the control panel as I moved, finally popping free of the straps, my body dropping another inch in the process, the sharp point of the glass digging suddenly into my twitching eyelid.

I tasted blood in my mouth. I was fucking broken.

Keeping panic at bay with lies and cheap tricks, I turned my head, slicing a shallow gash into my eyelid, until the tip of the shard was planted against my temple. How this improved things escaped me. I opened my eyes, rolling them around spastically, blood dripping into my right one and making me wink madly. I flopped my arm around but couldn't locate the fucking clip on the safety strap. I rolled my eyes again and reached up for the glass shard, smacking at it, but the fucking thing was like a cockroach: it'd survived its own personal nuclear holocaust and saw no reason to give up the ghost now. It was as though it was welded in place.

I rolled my eyes again, breath sawing wetly in and out of my nose. My eyes fell on the dull, bloody handle of my blade sticking stiffly out of the pilot's neck. I reached out for it, my shoulder and elbow crackling as I stretched. My fingertips caressed the handle, so familiar, something I'd made in countless empty hours, standing in freezing shadows waiting for a mark, sitting in Pick's drinking on credit, passing hours or days trapped in a Safe Room while the System Pigs scanned and rescanned and fucking *re*scanned outside. With a final painful stretch, the jagged glass cutting a shallow wound across my cheek, I managed to get my thumb and forefinger on it and slowly pull the blade from the pilot's neck. Warm blood trickling down my face, I braced my feet against the control bank below me and manipulated the blade until it rested against the palm of my hand. I closed my eyes again, dragging air in through my clogged windpipe, and concentrated, trying to clear my mind, trying to find the edge of the strap by feel and then sawing at it, moving just my thumb and forefinger, tiny, purposeful movements.

Something above me started to groan and creak, a metallic sound. It wasn't encouraging.

I was good at clearing my mind, I had a trick for it. I imagined a clear sky, perfectly gray and scummed with clouds. I imagined it as super quiet — the sort of moment right before the city wakes up, that tiny window when everyone seemed to be passed out or asleep or finally dead, and it's just the wind and your own breathing and something clicking or whirring in the distance, hover displacement over Mogadishu, whatever. Nothing else could get in. Nothing else existed. It always worked, the sky eventually melting into a blank field, my hands and thoughts operating independently.

But now, trying to cut myself loose, I couldn't clear my head. It was full of people I'd killed.

They paraded through me in an endless loop, including the four people scattered and torn up around me. I wasn't completely sure that Shockley and his pal were dead, but it was a good bet, and if I hadn't stepped behind them in a dark room and put a bullet in their ear for yen, I'd killed them just the same. I saw every person I'd ever killed for money, picturing them at the moment my contract had been fulfilled: blown pupils, jagged flaps of skin with bone and yellowish fat clinging to them, piss and shit, and hands stretched out, pleading, hanging upside down from a fire escape. And then I saw myself with a hunk of glass jutting out of one side of my head, hanging from a strap. And then the slide show started again.

With a jerk the blade sliced the safety strap, my legs took my weight, and I was free. I carefully moved until I was out of the shard's path, and climbed down through the cockpit windshield, wriggling through glass and dirt up and out. Gasping, I crawled out of the shallow crater the hover had created and rolled onto my back, gasping, the snow burning my face. When I'd caught my breath, I sat up and looked around. I could see the city a few miles south of me, and on my right was the goddamn Hudson, flowing black and evil as always. Inwood, the desolate nothing north of Manhattan, had been part of the city before Unification and the Riots, but as far as I could remember it had been overgrown fields, broken pavement, and rubble. I struggled to my feet, head pounding with each movement. My arms were numb. After a moment, I found my cigarettes, crushed and damp, picked out the best of the bunch and lit it, sucking in harsh, tasteless smoke.

Coughing a glob of phlegm into the snow, I turned back to the hover. It was remarkably preserved, sticking up out of the ground in more or less one piece. The safety cage might even have saved everyone's life if I hadn't done my best to fuck them all up first. Flicking my cigarette away into the sloppy air, I climbed back up into the cockpit. Pushing the pilot's torso out of the way and getting blood all over my hands, I searched the bank of instruments in front of me and located the beacon unit, beaming our location and status back home every half second or so. Pulling myself up by the safety straps dangling down from the rear of the cockpit, I balanced myself and aimed a solid kick at the beacon unit, smashing it with the steel tip of my boot and sending a spark and whiff of ozone into the air. No need to make it easier for more fucking psionics to come by and toss me around.

Still hanging, I turned my head and glanced up into the cabin. All I could see was blood, and one remarkably shiny shoe jutting up into the air.

Carefully I set my feet on the control panel and put my weight on them, letting go of the safety straps. I located the satellite feed and tuned it to the low-frequency bands we used, frequencies that the cops and the government had abandoned. They were monitored, of course, so we didn't use them much and switched frequencies on an hourly basis. I searched my memory for the right frequency and dialed it up, getting the hollow sound of an open connection for my trouble.

"I need a ride," I said, sounding flat and hollow to myself. The silence absorbed my voice as if it had never been there.

"Who this?"

I didn't recognize the voice or its thick, muddy accent. "Where's Gleason?"

"Who *this?*"

I cursed softly, closing my eyes and praying for inner peace. "*This* is your fucking boss. You want to keep eating solid foods, put Gleason on the damn wire."

I waited. The hollow sound filled the cabin, which began to creak worryingly again. I started to get nervous; every moment I sat out here in the middle of goddamn nowhere was dangerous, and my people were usually too scared of me to jerk me off like this. Heads were going to have to roll, and the thought made me tired. I preferred to just coast on the stories of past atrocities.

The voice came back with a dry, shuffling sound. "Glee not here."

I blinked. "Where the fuck is she?"

There was another pause. "Glee dead. She dead."

I stared down at the console. For no apparent reason, the voice repeated itself. "She dead."

I felt nothing. For a moment I just squatted there, the hollow sound of the open connection around me, static and someone breathing. Gleason had come into Pick's just a kid, a fucking kid, and even as she developed into a dangerous woman I'd never stopped thinking of her as a kid. Dead. It was impossible.

My eyes watered and I clenched them shut. I would not *cry*. I saw her, twelve years old, caught red-handed with one grimy paw in my coat pocket. I'd lifted her up by the wrist until her round little face was level with mine.

"Ooh, you're fucking *scary*," she'd spat at me. "I'm *terrified*."

And then she'd jammed a small sharp blade into my belly, an inch deep, her whole little body quivering with the effort. She let out a cute, tiny grunt. Her eyes had flashed up to mine, eager. Behind her, I remembered Belling bursting into laughter, roaring at me.

I'd pulled her close as hot blood dripped down my belly, and I remembered her face going from savage triumph to wide-eyed terror with comical speed.

"I'm s-s-sorry," she sputtered. "I'm sorry!"

I remembered smiling. "You're sorry your knife is too small," I'd said, and she'd smiled back, her whole face transforming into something beautiful. And now she was gone. Opening my eyes, I silently added her to my total.

"Give me," I said, clearing my throat, "give me Belling."

There was another pause, the dim sound of voices conferring, and then: "He, too."

I blinked. I had the sudden urge to tear the feed out of the console, to rip up my fingers as I destroyed the whole goddamn cockpit. It was fucking impossible. I'd seen them both *hours* ago. They'd been breathing, talking. It was fucking *impossible*. Then I remembered Gleason at the restaurant, pink and sweating, looking terrible.

"What?" I managed to say evenly, making fists.

"He, too," the voice said. "He not here, the old man."

I punched my hand into the console, shooting pain up my arm. Knuckles aching, I did it again, smashing shards of plastic into the air. Fucking *Belling?* Belling was immortal.

"What do you mean," I gritted out, each word a separate effort, "he fucking *not here?*"

More conferring, and I wanted to reach through the feed and strangle whatever moron I had working for me. "Forget it," I said. "Repeat what I'm about to say or I will make a fucking *note* of you and I guarantee you will *regret* it. I need——"

I paused and cocked my head. A shiver of anxiety rippled through me, and I reached out and disconnected the connection. In the silence, there was no mistaking it: hover displacement, getting nearer.

Cops, I thought. "Fuck me," I muttered. "Looks like my ride is here."

VI

DAY THREE: ONE SMALL MOMENT OF HAPPINESS, WORTH IT

Horrified, I crouched in the ruined cockpit and took stock of my amazing situation: I'd been betrayed not once but twice by someone in my organization, my two key people were apparently, mysteriously, dead, I was unarmed, and I was surrounded by the dead bodies of official government representatives in the middle of flat wilderness that offered no hiding places.

I suddenly wished I was back in Newark. Blindfolded with a gun to my head sounded better than this shit, and Glee would still be there.

As the roar of the approaching hover grew steadily louder, I leaped up and pulled myself through the hatchway back into the cabin. The three bodies were jumbled together against one of the seats, blood smeared everywhere, eyes open and staring. I pulled myself up onto a seat and stared down at them for a moment, three more people who were dead simply because they'd met me. Reaching down, I smeared the still-warm blood onto my hand and began rubbing it onto myself, my face, my clothes, my hair. As the hover outside landed, kicking up a fine spray of dirty snow, I lay down between seats and pulled the nearest body, the girl, on top of me, put my head back, and stared up at the ceiling. There was always the chance they'd scan for heat signatures, but System Pigs could be arrogant and sloppy. They were still human.

Being a Gunner was about patience — all you did was wait. You waited in dark rooms for people to come home, you waited on busy streets for someone you'd only seen in blurry images to stroll by. You waited in perfect silence and you waited without moving, going mad, muscles twitching. I cleared my mind and fixed my eyes on a rivet in the ceiling of the hover, and waited.

Outside, there was a tangible tremor as the arriving hover settled onto the damp ground of the riverbank, and then silence. Immediately, I heard a cabin door sighing open, and two pairs of heavy feet hitting the ground.

"Control, this is Vaideeki Six-RR-Eight calling in a crashed hover. It's got a civvy tag, SFN-NY-Eighty-nine-a. Someone get on the wire and tell the DPH we've found one of their bricks."

The voice was smooth and unaccented, almost completely neutral, as if he'd learned English from aliens. I heard the heavy feet walking around.

"Copy that, control," the voice continued. "Tell the Spooks we'll secure their property until they find the fucking *time* to get here, and we'll breathe real shallow."

"What's up?" said a second voice, just as neutral but lower and rougher, a smoker.

"We have been officially advised that this is a quarantine site, Sanjay. The Department of Public Health thinks we might be in trouble."

"Fucking Spooks. Always doom and gloom from those freaks."

I could feel the girl's dissipating body heat on me and smelled her hair with each breath, my throat trying to close up and gag me to death. One of them stuck his head into the cockpit; I could see it as a tan blob out of the corner of my eye. The smell of pipe tobacco filled the air. I hadn't seen loose tobacco in years. My eyes were watering. I didn't dare blink, but watery eyes weren't good either—they'd notice, the fucking System Pigs knew death almost as well as I did. The hover began to shake and groan as he pulled himself up into the cockpit.

"Shit, look at this asshole," the first voice—Vaideeki—said from above me. "Should have been strapped in, buddy."

"You hear the Spooks are supposed to be reforming the army?" the second one shouted from outside. "Can you believe that? What the fuck do the Undersecretaries know about security, about breaking heads?"

"Forget it," Vaideeki said. "Tricky Dick won't *allow* that shit. Watch and see. That shit is going to blow up in their faces." The hover vibrated again as a second set of steel-tipped boots climbed into the cockpit from the other side.

"I got four more in the back," the second voice said. "A lot of blood. Looks like five for five, to me."

"Uh-huh," Vaideeki said. I wanted to get a good look at these two, at least keep them in sight, but I couldn't take the risk. My eyes burned, dust falling on them like invisible snow and drying them up, turning them yellow and brittle. "Something's off here, Sanjay. Look at the pilot. Why wasn't he strapped in?"

"Had generator trouble and got up to try something," Sanjay offered. I pictured him shrugging.

"Nah—think about it. You're sticking a brick through the air and you lose power, you lose steering, whatever. Do you leap out of your seat and go apeshit? All the controls are *designed* to be within reach from the chair—that's the point. You stay in the safety straps."

"All right, genius, you stay in the straps. This is some DPH idiot we're talking about. One of Ruberto's assholes. You're asking me if I think one of those shitheads might panic and fuck up? Hell yeah."

"Them, too? *All* of them, just deciding to have a fucking dance party while the hover's going down, hard? Get DPH on the wire. Find out what this hover was up to."

I heard the second cop talking into the air, implanted sensors transmitting his voice back to SSF HQ at The Rock. I swallowed slowly, almost choking and having to suppress an explosion of coughs that shook me silently, making my torso twitch. The girl wobbled slightly on top of me as I tried to get my body back under control.

I heard the first one, Vaideeki, pulling himself into the cabin, grunting with the effort. My eyes were tearing fiercely and it was getting hard to stop them from fluttering. I gripped the blade tightly as one of his boots came into my peripheral vision, just a huge blurry object that shoved at the girl's body on top of me, pushing her this way and that. I saw how it would unspool: he'd notice something—sweat seeping from my pores, the tears pooling in my eyes, the soft, barely-there rise and fall of my chest as I let air painfully slip slowly in and out of my burning, screaming lungs. Something; the System Pigs were too well trained to miss it all. He'd see something and pretend he hadn't, a tiny hesitation, maybe, the only sign that something had registered. He'd even turn away from me and take an easy step, saying something to his partner, and then he'd whirl, tearing his gun from its holster hanging low near his hip.

Maybe I'd even beat him. Maybe I'd flash the blade and sink it into his throat before he could get the shot off, or the shot would go wide as he staggered back in shock. And then what? And then I go for his gun, fast, pushing off the hundred pounds of dead fucking psionic and trying to snatch the auto from his slackening grip and come up ready to shoot before his partner — who I could only hope had been standing there with his mouth open and his dick in his hand while all this went on.

More probably, I thought with a rising edge of near panic, the second cop would blow my head off about five seconds before I could even locate him. *Most* probably, I wouldn't beat the first cop, and I'd just end up dead with nothing to show for it.

The second cop's voice burst into the cabin, so loud and sudden I almost jumped. "DPH isn't giving us shit. Says it's official business under Ruberto's paper, we need a fucking writ to get into it. You wanna call the Colonel?"

"Shit," Vaideeki muttered. "Fuck that. We'll put those pieces of shit down as *uncooperative* in the report and let it simmer. There's a reckoning coming for all of them, brother, mark my words."

His lower body came into view: purple pants, the crease razor sharp, a long leather coat that swirled around his ankles, the boots shiny but serious, the sort of boots you cracked ribs with. Purple fucking pants. I could see him slowly turning around, feet planted on the back of the last row of seats, like he was studying the cabin carefully, looking for hints.

"No shots," he said to himself.

The second cop grunted his way into the cabin, the hover shaking fiercely. "Whole thing's gonna fall over we keep pushing our way through it," he complained, letting loose a wet smoker's cough that started my own convulsions anew, my whole body quivering with the effort to keep from sputtering. I narrowed myself down, concentrating on the blade in my hand, gripping as tightly as I could, keeping my arm loose and ready to move. I pushed everything else out of my mind and got ready, forcing my stiff muscles to relax, to go slack, tracking the two cops as they moved awkwardly through the cabin. When the moment came, I wasn't going to waste any more time. I plotted how to throw the girl's corpse off me, where I could plant my foot to get good leverage, what I could hang on to for stability.

Suddenly, Vaideeki turned sharply, one arm shooting up. "Go ahead, Control," he said in his smooth, advertisement voice.

His partner continued to kick around the cabin, but you could tell from his movements that it was just for show, just to look busy. I wanted to stretch so badly I thought a bullet in the head might be worth it. This was how people ended up dying, I thought. It was a choice. You were lying there, suffering, fighting something, some black cancer in your gut or a bullet in your chest or a tumor like a rock in your brain, and you fought and fought until you couldn't fucking stand it any longer, and you just gave up and let go, for that one small moment of happiness, worth it, worth everything.

"Copy that, Control, on our way." Vaideeki half turned, legs spread awkwardly to keep his balance. "We got an all-hands situation midtown. Old Pennsylvania Hotel."

"What about this mess?"

Vaideeki started climbing down toward the cockpit. "Fuck, it's the DPH's brick. Let them come up here and clean it up. We've been ordered back into the city. You want to wire the King Worm and tell him no, you got higher *priorities?*"

"Shit, no," Sanjay muttered, following his partner.

"Fucking animals downtown," Vaideeki said as he planted one foot square on my upturned wrist, crushing it under his weight as he pulled himself over me. I almost stabbed him in the calf out of sudden reaction, pain shooting through me and lighting up all the other broken parts of me like a pinball hitting every damn bumper in sight. "What we need is a fucking natural disaster, clear everything out below Twenty-third. Don't know why we don't just go down there and clean that shit up."

"You said it," Sanjay agreed, and then Vaideeki's foot was off my arm, the pain burning down into the muscle, into the bone. Their voices faded as they went chatting through the cockpit and back out into the snow. I started to shake but kept my eyes open and fixed on the ceiling, tears leaking down into my hair. I kept as still as I could until I heard the displacers kick in, roaring into life, splitting my ears, the whole hover rocking gently in the field as they lifted off. I sat up and whimpered, moving every muscle spastically, dragging my sleeve across my watering eyes. I sat for a moment or two, stretching out, and then slowly climbed weakly to my feet and went back into the cockpit. I scanned the transmitter again, seeking out our frequencies, but on each and every one all I got was the hollow, empty sound.

I jumped down into the snow and turned to face south. *Well*, I thought, *this isn't the worst day I've ever had*. Hell, I'd been dead once, not so long ago, in a box pulled by a Monk. The city, distant, gleamed dully in the snowy light. I replaced the blade in my boot, pulled my coat around me, and started walking.

VII

DAY FOUR: IT SURE GAVE ME THE WARM FUZZIES

Energized somehow, I headed for the river's edge and hired one of an endless supply of skiffs, one hundred yen to get downtown without having to deal with SSF checkpoints or any of the upright citizens who lived above Twenty-third. We were barely afloat, me and two scrawny black girls who pulled on their oars like champions, water slopping over the edge and soaking into my pants. It smelled overpoweringly like fish, probably because only the crazies ate anything out of the toxic river, and even then only once. Neither one said a fucking word, just staring back at me while they worked. The entire boat felt slimy to the touch, like it was dry-rotting beneath us.

I stared back at the girls and thought about Glee. I should have done something. I should have done whatever it took, killed every last motherfucker in the place, torn the fucking building down around me—gotten her the fuck out of there. Every time I thought of her my whole body ached, but I kept coming back to her, to the sound of glass shattering.

I was near the old stadium in twenty minutes, wet and shivering and in an evil mood. The old stadium was started before Unification, back when the world had been divided into different nations, and had never been completed. It remained untouched on the river's edge, a bowl of concrete with a single huge letter *Y* attached to the facade, dangling by a rusty bolt. It was a huge squatter's paradise, always filled with the near permanent camps of pickpockets, snuff gangs, and other assorted nuisances, all banded together for protection. These were not the hardasses of the System; these were people who nibbled on the edges, who prospered by staying out of sight and avoiding direct light.

As we floated to the riverbank, no noise but the faint lapping of water and the soft grunts of the skinny girls, I could see the dim form of a tall, well-built man in a long coat, standing there burning a cigarette. I didn't have a gun on me, but I still had my blade, and I gripped it low in my palm and out of sight. So far today just about everything had gone wrong, and one more surprise would not, in fact, surprise me.

When the skiff was still a foot or two away from the bank, the figure spread his hands for me, his coat hanging open, in the international symbol for *not going to kill you.* I realized I knew him.

"Mistah Cates," he said, cocking his head at me, his huge and improbable hair swaying gently in the wind. "I'm here to be your fucking *valet* or some shit." Around us the soft sound of the water kept its own time. He was a tall black guy with the biggest goddamn Afro I'd ever

seen. It towered up from his triangular face and swayed in
the wind, a reddish-brown color.

"I remember you," I said, pointing at him. "Jabali, or
some shit like that. A Taker, out of Baltimore, right?"

He grinned and gave me a graceful little bow. "Charm
City, all right," he said. "Last few months I been hanging
about Pick's, and you gave me a couple odd jobs to do."
He squinted and scratched his head as I pulled myself
gracelessly from the damp skiff onto the deep mud of the
bank. "Your whatyacallit, the chip, in your hand, whatever, they saw you on the grid and shit, and I was the only
one still standing, so I was sent to escort you."

I panted my way up next to him and gestured for a
cigarette. Behind me, the girls paddled away wordlessly,
heading back up the river in search of another desperate
soul looking to get around Manhattan. As he fished for
his smokes I took the opportunity to look Jabali over. I'd
hired him a few times to track down a few people and
he'd done fair work. I'd used a lot of Takers in my time to
track people down; Gunners needed to know where their
contracts *were,* after all, before we could kill them.

I smiled at him as he flicked a lighter open for me,
keeping my eyes on him while I lit up. I could tell he was
terrified, and good thing; the System was all about your
image. All Jabali knew was that I'd killed a lot of people,
a lot of System Cops, and I'd never been touched. And I
was rich, and I worked with Canny Orel—or so rumor
had it. And here I was covered in dirt and blood after
word had gone out that I'd been snatched by the fucking
Department of Public Health of all things, and grinning
at him just like I would if I was in the mood to murder
someone in order to let off some steam.

Then Jabali offered me a wide, sloppy grin. "Well, Mistah Cates," he said, stressing the last syllable of *mister* to make it a little less a sign of respect, "what's your pleasure? Seeing as I'm your entire entourage this evening."

I grimaced. I couldn't fuck with someone this cheerful. I looked out into the night. The boat was already invisible, the two miserable girls gone. "Take me to Gleason," I said, swallowing. "I want to see her."

He looked away, embarrassed. "Shit, boss," he said, "I don't know. Better take you back to the bar, let brighter folks help you out."

I nodded, and we started walking east, skirting the stadium. There weren't a lot of people in the area, normally, aside from the squatters, but it felt unusually quiet. Even in this godforsaken area there were usually a few bums, a few pocket slicers looking to roll you, a couple of menacing Augment junkies trying to intimidate you long-range. As we ate up blocks we saw almost no one, little rainbow puddles of slick, oily melted snow everywhere.

I waited a few minutes, feeling like a coward. "How'd she die?" I finally managed, my heart pounding, my throat swollen.

He shrugged. "Something goin' around. A lot of people down at Pick's are coming down with it. It's fucking nasty." I kept my eyes grimly ahead, but saw him glance nervously at me as we walked. "Uh, she went fast, boss. When she came in, lookin' like a drowned rat and telling us how you got scooped uptown, she was pretty bad. Was like that for an hour or two, and then just got . . . worse." He shook his head. "Nasty." I saw him look back at me. "You know, boss, you maybe don't want to see her. You maybe shouldn't even come by Pick's, seeing as there's this shit going around. A bunch of people around the place come down sick. I started to think I was startin' to feel shitty, but I feel okay now." He grinned. "Take more than a little bug to take down Jabali. Jabali's got the *strength*."

I pictured Glee back at the restaurant. She'd looked a little sick, a little feverish. What the fuck killed you in a damn day? I tried to remember when I'd noticed her coughing, had it been the day before? Right after we'd gotten back from Newark. I reached up and touched the swollen spot on my neck, still refusing to heal up.

We walked the rest of the way in silence. By the time we were near Pickering's the streets felt almost normal again, with the usual crush of people moving discontentedly up and down the street, the smell of sweat pushing into everything. The Vids we passed on their high poles were silently beaming the news to us: a spontaneous peace demonstration had broken out in Tokyo celebrating the upcoming thirtieth anniversary of Unification. This complete with video footage of smiling Japanese holding signs and chanting. It sure gave me the warm fuzzies. Then a good-looking brunette was smiling far too widely as she silently informed us that fifty-five thousand people were assumed dead after a landslide in the slums of New Delhi. A square of video in the corner showed people screaming, intercut with some jackass Undersecretary making a speech that involved waving his arms quite a bit.

For a few steps I just contemplated the crowd, the spoiling blood of the System. There was a small commotion up the block, a sudden swirling of people that drew my eye. I opened my stance a little, getting my coat out of the way, and watched as a small hollow appeared in the stream of traffic, giving someone a lot of room. I just stared as he got nearer. Even without the blue-black bruises up and down his arms and on his face, one look told you this bastard was dead—he just hadn't realized it yet. He had that wasted-thin look, his skin yellowish and papery, stretched tight over his bones. He was tall, but walked with such a loopy, bent-over gait he looked shrunken. Blood, deep, deep red, was leaking from his nose and one corner of his mouth, meeting up as it trickled down his neck, forming one thick rope of death. The good news was, he didn't smell like sweat. The bad news was, he smelled like he'd been dead for a week, the reek crawling up your nostrils and clawing at you, making your eyes water.

"*Help me,*" he breathed, barely audible. "*Help me.*"

I watched him, unable to look away, something like slow-motion panic welling up inside me. Fifteen or twenty feet past me, he suddenly paused and collapsed, just going down on the spot as if someone had knocked his stick legs out from under him. He lay in a heap, convulsing for a few seconds as I stared, the System moving past him at a safe distance. He struggled up onto his elbows, panting and staring as if his goal was in sight, and choked up an incredible mass of red phlegm, thick and stringy. He seemed to steady after that, and for a moment I thought he might gather himself and climb back to his feet. Instead, he collapsed again and lay perfectly still. The crowd kept bubbling around him, some people turning to look, others just keeping their eyes straight ahead.

"That's how this shit works it," Jabali said quietly, tugging at my arm. "C'mon, boss. Bad luck to watch that shit."

Feeling sluggish, I let him pull me back into motion.

I'd been out of circulation for a day—a fucking *day*. I'd left with Glee and things had been as they always had. I came back and people were fucking *dead*. I felt like something was out of socket in my head and couldn't find its way back into place.

When we got to Pick's, the place went silent as we entered, the air warm and thick but smelling familiar, smoke and sawdust. It was only half full, and as we walked in the sound level wasn't the usual raucous blast but a lower hum, people talking quietly. The whole place seemed to turn as one and twist around to look at me for a moment and then look away, the low hum becoming whispers. Melody was behind the bar and stopped what she'd been doing to walk back toward us, a bottle of cloudy liquor in one fist, her face grim.

"Avery," she started to say, and then started coughing, a wet hack like she'd been smoking cartons of cigarettes steadily for days. With some effort she choked them down, red-faced. I waited patiently; I'd known Melody forever.

"In the back," she finally breathed. I nodded and started to turn for Pick's office but stopped when Melody reached out for me. "Avery!" she said, her face contorting. She wasn't a pretty girl. She was getting fatter, and somewhere in the last few years she'd lost a second tooth. This wasn't much of a burden to her, however, as she'd never been attractive to begin with and so didn't feel the loss. Seeing her eyes water was bizarre. I'd never seen Melody cry, not once. "Avery, Glendon's dead."

I froze. For a second Melody and I just looked at each other, probably the only people in the world who actually cared, beyond business, that Pickering was gone. That man had been so old he'd seemed immortal and unchanging, as ancient yesterday as he'd been the first time I'd seen him. I felt dizzy.

Without saying anything else I turned back toward the office, my hands balled into fists. I pushed through the sparse crowd roughly, and they all let me shove them, scrambling out of my way as I moved. If any one of them had been too slow, I would have broken a few arms. By the time I was within feet of the door the whole room seemed to have stood up and moved toward the walls, giving me a clear route. I gestured violently and the door sighed open. Slamming it into the wall, I stepped into the familiar gloom of Pick's office and stopped.

She was in the little bunk she'd used, too small for her once she'd started to grow. At least, I assumed it was her. Her face was mottled with dark, almost black bruises, and a small, wet-looking sore had erupted on her nose. Her chest looked like someone had cut a wedge out of it, a crater of scabby gore that seemed nearly to have consumed her shirt and thick hooded coat.

"Fucking hell," I whispered as I heard steps behind me and turned my head to find Jabali there, shutting the door carefully behind him.

"Keeps gettin' worse," he said. "She didn't look this bad a few hours ago. Keeps on keeping on, whatever this shit is, even after you're dead—no pity. Mel had us burn poor old Pick, you know? Said she didn't want him eaten up."

I looked back at Glee and forced myself to approach her. Her eyes were open and looked so normal, so clean and untouched, I didn't want to look at them. Standing over her, I reached down and pushed her eyes shut, flinching a little as I touched her cold flesh. I'd killed a lot of people. I'd killed a lot of people and not lost much sleep over it, but as I stared down at the kid I realized I was trembling. I touched her red hair, which seemed darker than I remembered against her suddenly pale skin. She was starting to smell, and I looked up at the ceiling, blinking and trying to control myself.

"Fucking *hell*," I muttered. I looked down at her again and startled—had her chest just...twitched? I stared down at her. I was losing my mind. I'd been hunted, crashed a hover, played dead, and now found out the only three people I could possibly have called friends were all dead, and not peacefully. I was losing my fucking mind.

I closed my eyes and ground my teeth, still trembling. "Burn her," I said quietly. "If this shit is still...spreading, then fucking burn her. Okay? Then get your shit together. We're heading back uptown." I turned and pushed past him, intending to drink until my hands stopped shaking. I scratched at the wound on my neck. *Newark,* I thought. "Someone in the Department of Public *Health* wanted to talk to me. So let's go talk."

VIII

DAY FIVE: YOU'VE JUST KILLED ME

Watching us, the two Crushers stood with their thumbs hooked into their belt loops, their uniforms sagging and wrinkled. One was a round, moon-faced Asian whose mouth worked absently in a constant chewing motion. The other was tall, pale, and rail thin, his pants too short for his legs, a thin, wispy beard shooting off his sharp chin. They slouched at the flimsy metal gate set up across Eighth Avenue and watched me approach with what they imagined were hardassed stares. The wind was a constant moan around us, dry and dustless, all the snow held in the gelatin-like yellow slush that clung to everything, making the world look rotted.

"Avery," the tall one said as Jabali and I stopped in front of them. I was wearing my Special Occasion suit, for when I needed to overawe my business partners with my wealth and material success. It was a little floppy in the arms and legs but close enough, and expensive looking. When going uptown to deal with civilians, it paid to look the part. I'd cleaned up Jabali as much as I could, which wasn't saying much, but he'd pass if he kept his mouth shut.

The checkpoints had gone up in record time overnight, and they'd drawn all the Crushers from the reserves, putting everyone on active duty. New York felt strange to me, thinned. Walking up Hudson Street in the morning there'd been elbow room to spare, and the people who were out pushing through fat flakes of acidic snow and the muffled, sound-eating air all seemed to move faster, scuttling as quickly through the street as they could. Rumors were already coming fast about a sickness, and people were staying indoors. I'd seen some dead bodies, too, just slumped here and there, looking like some wild animal had torn into them, the deep blue bruises on their necks and arms burst open, bloody, and no one willing to get near enough to them to move them off the street.

"Officer Stanley," I said to the skinny Crusher, nodding. "And Mongo."

The moon-man didn't react beyond a slow, deliberate blinking of his eyes. I raised an eyebrow at Officer Stanley. "The SSF isn't sparing any expense in recruiting, huh?"

Stanley turned his head and spat on the street, just a few inches away from my feet. "Pook can move pretty light on his feet, you give him a reason. You got business uptown, Avery? There's an Action Item about you from yesterday, you know."

I nodded, putting on the most serious face I could summon. "I have an appointment," I said. "You guys expecting trouble?"

There'd been a bug scare about thirteen years ago, I

remembered. Turned out to be the fucking Brazilian flu, just a few thousand people dead and those mostly on their last legs to begin with, but for a few days everyone hid inside and only came out with these ridiculous masks on, keeping their distance. I remembered negotiating a job from across the fucking street, shouting at my client because he wouldn't get any closer to me.

This felt worse. Names pushed through my head: *Candida Murrow, she died in a very... unusual way, Gleason, she dead, Wa too, Pickering*. Whatever this was, I was getting the feeling it had started with my people. With *me,* right around the time I'd been on my knees in Newark with a gun to my head and *not* shot. I'd done enough evil in my time, the cosmos had me on its list, no doubt. But why hadn't I gotten sick? Why wasn't *I* dead? This shit didn't make sense.

I remembered the distorted voice: *This is not an execution... this is an assassination. Not yours. But an assassination none the fucking less.*

"They don't tell us any fucking thing," Stanley said, hitching his pants up and giving Jabali the stinkeye for a bit. "We're just not supposed to let anyone through without a specific order from a Captain or above."

I nodded, looking around. "I need a pass."

He looked away from me, suddenly interested in something across the street. Jabali, who maybe wasn't the brightest guy in the world, had the common sense to shut the hell up and pretend to be deaf and dumb. "Fuck, Avery, you just come up here in the fucking open and—I'm not selling any passes today. You got an order, fine. Otherwise you turn around and go the fuck back to your shithole. Try again tomorrow."

My hands curled into fists and I recited my own personal Serenity Prayer. At least Stanley wasn't dumb enough to think he could cash in on my *Action Item* and bring me in himself. I scanned the street, so quiet I could hear the snow dissolving our boots and Moon-man's heavy mouth breathing. I counted eleven Crushers, not a drop of talent among them—especially Moon-man, who looked like he had to preplan every breath. I didn't doubt I could rush the barrier and make it, but I didn't need any manhunts up above Twenty-third Street, so I just shook my head. "I'll pay double."

Stanley pursed his lips.

"No bosses around," I said quickly. "You know me, Stanley. You know you will never hear from me on the way back across. It'll be like I was never here."

"Shit, Avery," he muttered, glancing at Jabali and taking a quick scan of the street again. "Double?"

I nodded. "The usual arrangement for payment. And we find our own way back."

Stanley shook his head, turning to spit. "Nothing's usual anymore. The fucking Worms have been up everyone's asses. Marin sees *everything*. I ain't gonna end up in some shithole like Chengara. Not for *you*."

I swore to myself. Officially, Dick Marin was director of Internal Affairs for the SSF—the King Worm. Before I'd killed Squalor for him, that's where his power had stopped, especially since he wasn't human anymore. He was a digitized intelligence operating through who knew how many mechanical avatars. You met Dick Marin in a room and he *looked* human enough, but he was just a remote-control Droid, with the real Marin, if that word meant anything, in a server somewhere. As such, there was low-level programming that controlled his behavior, and he'd been allowed to terrify only the System Pigs—who were all scared shitless of him, since he was the only person empowered to fuck with them.

But when I'd killed Squalor—when Marin had *manipulated* me into killing Squalor—he'd been able to declare a State of Emergency, and under his own obscure rules that had given him a much wider portfolio to work with. Officially, the Emergency continued, though you didn't hear about it much anymore. It bubbled in the background and allowed Marin to basically run the whole fucking System. A shadow emperor. He'd been closing his fist around everything ever since, and I was getting sick of it.

From what I'd heard, so were the Joint Council Undersecretaries, who should have benefited from events, too. Marin had had a free hand for years, but I'd heard rumors that the Undersecretaries were getting their shit together, and it promised to be an interesting time, assuming any of us survived.

One thing hadn't changed, though: yen ran the world and guys like Stanley had to grift a bit just to survive. "Double plus a bonus," I said, "for being flexible. We let it drift for now, and you touch me for it anytime you like. You know I'm good for it."

I had a reputation, and it came in handy sometimes.

"Fuck," he muttered, spinning around to see who was watching. "Fuck, fuck, fuck, fuck, *fuck*." He looked at me again and pulled on his little beard. "All right," he finally said, stepping aside and gesturing at Moon-man. "Open 'er up. Wait, wait a fucking sec," he muttered, pulling me close and miming examining me. "Just in case, let's at least look like you have a pass." I let him shove me around a bit, amused, because if any of the System Pigs *were* watching, he was pretty much going to get the shit beat out of him, or worse, no matter what kind of dumb show he put on. Finally, he patted me down and pushed me to the other side, grabbing Jabali by the lapels. Jabali didn't like it, but he took it. He was the sort of lifetime soldier who could hold his temper, and think twice—useful.

"All right, move," he growled, turning away. "Don't fucking dawdle."

I didn't pause for more conversation; Jabali and I stepped quickly through the barricade and kept walking, turning onto a side street as soon as we could. When the checkpoint had disappeared around the corner, Jabali cursed softly.

"Fucking hate sucking their dicks," he muttered. "Those assholes aren't worth shit."

I didn't say anything. Jabali was a Taker, and a good one; he'd tracked down Dr. Daniel Terries for me in just a few hours. But I'd been unable to discourage his tendency to think I gave a shit about what he thought.

While we walked, trying to approximate the alien gait of men without worries, I studied him, looking for any sign that he was sick or impaired in some way. The math was easy: Gleason had been sick a day and a half after we came back from Newark and dead in three. This shit didn't take time. He looked okay, though.

As we made our way uptown, the streets started to fill up a little, people better dressed and a little cheerier than I was used to, but not so different. The whole world was a fucking shit pyramid. Shit ran downhill and turned the wheel, kept things burning, but you had to have a lot of people trying to get out of the way of the shit or nothing much happened. These people were a little higher on the pyramid, maybe, but they were running for shelter just like the rest of us. They sure smelled better, although the mix of colognes and perfumes in the air made my head ache.

Jabali lumbered along next to me, looking like a hood. It was in his walk — you could put him in a decent suit, but the bastard still walked like a criminal — half cocky strut, half paranoid scuttle. But he looked healthy, normal. I had the strange feeling of everything being on pause, like that moment before a storm when you can feel the electricity in the air but nothing's started yet, and kept stealing glances at him, expecting to see a sudden bruise on his neck like I'd seen downtown.

He caught me looking at him and smiled nervously, his hair flopping about. "Feel like ev'ryone is staring at me, boss," he said, shrugging his coat on.

I nodded. A lot of people couldn't handle being uptown—you learned how to live a certain way, you learned to never take shit and never back off, to do your little dance every day, the toughest bastard in the room, any room, no matter what— and it was hard to try and act like a civilian. Some of us just couldn't do it. I knew real killers who wouldn't go past Twenty-third Street for anything because they couldn't stand the looks they got.

Terries lived around Fiftieth Street, real posh. As we humped up and across town, my skin started to crawl: everyone was clean, and styled, and the weirdest part was the fucking *hum of conversation*. Everyone was talking and making no effort to hide the fact, laughing, shouting. I'd never thought of downtown as quiet before. As we walked, it was like everyone was fucking shouting, and I was sweating, my hair standing on end. I made my living being fucking quiet. Noise equaled death, where I came from.

"Spare some yen?"

I started, one hand reaching for my piece before I caught myself. The Monk danced in front of me, limping on a damaged leg that had been repaired with a lead pipe welded at the knee. It wore a ragged suit of clothes, but its white plastic face was still perfect, clean and unmarred, floating like a moon in front of me. We were in an open area, the street widening out and making me dizzy with so much space. A church loomed up on our right, two sharp little spiky towers reaching for the sky, the three huge doors capped by triangular masonry. It was impossibly big, ancient stone wearing away under the weather, covered in bird shit and chipped to hell. I blinked stupidly as we walked past, herding the Tin Man ahead of us. Five or six other Monks sat on the church's steps, crouching, like birds.

I hadn't been this close to a Monk in years. It had put on the best smile it could manage, which wasn't much, and kept its balance magically as it hopped backward on its ruined leg. It looked from me to Jabali and back again, and I tensed up; the Monks were equipped with Optical Facial Recognition circuits, and back when they'd been hooked up to the Electric Church's net they'd been able to scan your face and come up with your name and any public information on you that was out there. The Electric Church was gone, but if they'd scanned you years ago, they still had the info, and sometimes a Monk would call you by name.

I looked past it at the wide, dizzying expanse of street

ahead of us. "Get the fuck out of my way," I growled. I was still acting my part. You never knew who might be paying attention.

It scuttled away and accosted someone behind us. I turned my head left and stared into the SSF hover yard, a big empty lot a block from The Rock where the cops kept a fleet of your standard hovers — small, two- or three-man units, not the big fat ones that could be stuffed with Stormers. A bunch of Crushers and officers were hanging around outside it, and some stared back at me as I walked. It was always bad to stare at the System Pigs. They didn't care for it and liked to teach lessons, but I couldn't make my head turn back. The hovers all looked scruffy and beat-up, sporting unmatched armor plating and evidence of rough handling. Not a single one looked new.

"Down here," Jabali said, gesturing to the right. I turned with him and we headed down the side street, away from The Rock, otherwise known as Cop fucking Central. Cop Central was a goddamn planet unto itself, four square city blocks of everything cop. It had its own gravity, and people like me wound up breaking up in its atmosphere if we got too close. The main tower was ancient and soared up above us, the tallest building in New York, with hovers landing and taking off from the roof all day long.

As we walked, I had to consciously adjust my pace, slowing down to an unconcerned roll while my heart pounded in my chest, pushing my acid blood around so it could slowly dissolve my bones. You stayed on the sidewalks, too, because of the pedicabs that were always barreling down the middle, shouting people out of the way, two or three fat fucks sitting in the back. As I stepped aside to let one skinny, exhausted bastard scamper past with his freight shouting at him to move his ass, I thought maybe I hadn't picked such a bad path after all. I might be royally fucked, but at least I wasn't *that* guy.

Jabali just grunted as we passed the spot. Dr. Daniel Terries lived in a narrow five-story building that looked as if it was held up by the buildings around it. I walked past it without turning my head. It was an old building—every building in New York was old—but it was obviously upgraded, reinforced, and outfitted with the standard amenities. We went around the block a few times, stealing glances as we passed, finally crossing the street and paying two hundred yen for two tiny coffee drinks from a stand. I put my back against a wall and looked at anything but the building, just getting snapshots as I turned my head this way and that, enjoying the goddamn hell out of my thimble of warm, brownish syrup.

There would be a shell system, of course, providing basic but useless security and valet services. An escalator, air system, Vid dish on the roof—middle-class luxury. I didn't expect to find much by way of real trouble getting in. It was crazy to break into a building just blocks away from Cop Central. Crazy was sometimes the best camouflage you could have.

"What now, boss?"

I shrugged. "We wait."

Waiting was the number one skill a Gunner could have. Half the stories you heard about Canny Orel involved him waiting heroic lengths of time, just being a statue in shadows, barely breathing. Going in didn't pay. Between the inadequate security shell and the expensive and equally useless inner security door, we'd lose precious seconds busting our way in, and Terries could make a run for it or maybe even call the cops—and since he was a government official, they might even come, though rumor had it the SSF and the civilian government had no love lost between them. No, we had to grab him off the street, and we had to do it clean and fast.

I just wanted to talk to the man, find out what he knew, without someone pressing their mental thumb into the soft spot in my brain. A Vid screen was located above the roof of a tall, skinny building with a burned-out top floor. I didn't think there was anywhere in New York you could stand and *not* be in view of a Vid; the fucking government was forever putting new ones up and swapping out the old ones for bigger versions with new features. You even found them inside buildings, in the oddest places. Silently, this one spelled out exciting news: the civilian government—which was the Undersecretaries, since the Joint Council they nominally served was just a bunch of defunct husks buried under London—had created, by decree, a reconstituted System Military, to be funded immediately. There hadn't been an army since Unification. Who needed an army? The dedicated and skilled members of our beloved System Security Force kept us snug, and we were one world now, without borders.

I lit a cigarette and ignored Jabali's longing look. I could wait if I had to. Not like a statue, but I doubted any of the stories we heard about Canny Orel were all that true. He'd probably killed a lot of people, but shit, killing people was easy. Killing a lot of them just made you ambitious.

I was halfway through the pack when Jabali nudged my shoulder, looking away down the block.

"There he is, boss. White hair, walking stick."

I squinted across the street and saw him—a tall, straight-backed man in a blue suit, a gnarled wooden walking stick in one hand. He wasn't that old, maybe a little older than me, but he looked healthy, his skin reddish and shining even from twenty feet away, his hair white, pure. He walked rapidly, staring down at a small hand-held device, and people instinctively got out of his way.

I gestured at Terries's house. "Get his door," I said, and launched myself into the crowd. Dodging pedicabs and perfumed men and women, I angled my way behind the good doctor and hurried to catch up with him. I slid my blade into my hand, the taped handle once again reassuring and solid. I thought of Gleason as I rushed the last two feet and stepped up close behind Terries, pushing the blade lightly against his back and putting my hand on his shoulder. Amateurs grabbed their marks around the neck or shoulders. It felt safer, having a big handful of your mark. But it gave them leverage on *you,* and if your mark had any talent at all, they'd flip you or roll you off them, spin you around, and stab *you* in the guts while you stared at them, wide-eyed, amazed. Best to stay separate from them.

He stiffened. "Don't stop," I said in a low voice. "Keep walking. See the man with the ridiculous hair by your door? He will fucking shoot you if you stop moving toward him."

To his credit, he recovered quickly and kept moving. "I don't carry credit dongles," he said.

"Fuck your credit dongles, Doc," I said, nodding at Jabali. "We just want to talk. Don't worry, I have it on good authority you *want* to talk to me."

"Yes?" The man's voice was almost melodious, almost soothing, even in a whisper. "And who are you?"

"Avery Cates, Doc," I said. "You sent some monkeys to collect me yesterday. Sorry I had to kill them all."

He stumbled a little, and a mean little flare of satisfaction lit up inside me for a second. "What's the matter, Doc? I thought you *wanted* to talk to me."

We reached his door, where Jabali was doing a creditable impression of a hardass. "Ah, Mr. Cates," Terries said softly, suddenly sounding old and frail. "You've just killed me."

IX

DAY FIVE: AVERY CATES, DESTROYER OF WORLDS

"Of course, you don't mind if I have a drink, Mr. Cates?"
Dr. Terries said, his voice flat. "And you'll have one, too."

Jabali glanced over his shoulder at me, and I nodded.
He stepped aside, and Terries stepped into his apartment
slowly, as if concentrating on each step. I watched him
cross to a glass bar near the big window that took up nearly
the entire back wall, a perfect view of The Rock, soaring
up out of the street. We could even see the tiny flecks of
hovers around its roof, Big Important People being ferried
to and from Cop Central. Terries pulled out three simple
tumblers and poured a clear liquid into each, two fingers
deep, and turned around with them in both hands.

"Vodka," he announced. "Real vodka. Good stuff."

I stared back at him, keeping my face blank, and he
smiled.

"Shall I take a sip from each, Mr. Cates? Do you imagine I have any reason to keep poisoned glasses in my home

against this possibility? I'm a scientist, for goodness' sake."

I shrugged. "This is the System, Dr. Terries," I said. "This is New York."

"Ah," he said, holding two glasses in one hand and lifting one to his lips, draining it with a wince. "I see." He placed the empty glass back on the bar and then carried the remaining glasses in each hand, stepping a few feet away from the bar and dropping into a comfortable black leather chair. He sat slumped down with his drinks in each hand.

I crossed to the bar. The whole place was decorated in leather and glass, black and clear. It was filled with light and the walls were clean, white—painfully white. I itched just looking around. This was what Dr. Terries did with money. This bullshit.

The bar was well stocked, though I didn't recognize most of the bottles. I began picking them up and removing the caps, sniffing experimentally. "You don't seem happy to see me, Dr. Terries."

"I have never been less happy in my life, Mr. Cates."

"I thought you wanted to see me. You sent a couple of Government Wonder Boys to grab me up."

There was a moment of silence. I'd found a bottle of gin, the familiar medicine smell cheering me. I took the bottle and turned to face the good doctor and paused; his face was ashen, collapsed.

"I should have known better," he murmured softly. I knew the tone of voice. There were only a few basic reactions when I showed up and pushed a gun into their ribs. Some people got angry, made threats they had no hope of ever carrying out. Some people got crafty, offered deals.

And some people just got tired, gave up, sat down, and let it happen. I'd always thought the last were the smarter ones, because I always knew there was no threat that would dissuade me, no deal I would take.

"You were supposed to have been brought to a secure location, Mr. Cates. In a reinforced cell, sealed off, airtight, following disaster protocol. I wasn't going to be within ten *feet* of you. But I should have known. You've killed so many people, for so long — of *course* you killed Mr. Shockley. Of *course* you killed everyone." He raised his gray eyes to me and almost smiled. I hated his face, hated the subtle expression on it. "You're *going* to kill everyone. Starting, apparently, with me."

I smiled and nodded, lifting the bottle and taking a long pull from it. Jabali stood like a good soldier, unmoving, attentive, blank. The gin was smooth, and I drank greedily, savoring the burn. "Well," I gasped as I swallowed and lowered the bottle, "I may not kill you. I just want to hear what you wanted to say. I want to know what's happening."

Terries drank off one more glass and then, without hesitation, drank off the third. He turned and set the glasses gently on the gleaming stone floor at his feet and sank back in the chair. "Mr. Cates, I am going to go out on a limb and guess that most everyone you spent the last few days with is now dead."

I blinked. I saw, out of the corner of my eye, Jabali look up sharply at me, but I didn't look at him. I hesitated; my instincts were to say nothing — this was about getting information from him, not giving information away. "Yes," I finally said, "but you can blame Shockley and company on me."

Terries shook his head, waving his hand at me dismissively. "That was an attempt to burn out the source, Mr. Cates. A desperate attempt at that. I knew I was sacrificing Mr. Shockley."

I took another pull from the bottle but suspected it would have no effect on me. My heart was pounding, every ligament and muscle tense.

"I'm a learned man, Mr. Cates," he suddenly said, closing his eyes. "While idiots like you were burning down the cities thirty years ago, I was doing advanced work that might have changed the world. I studied under Miles Amblen. I was doing *advanced work!*" He opened his eyes and stared at me, suddenly angry. "I've never seen anything like this before. I should have known it would be an animal like you who would destroy everything. You live in shit. You *eat* it, every day. It coats you and you spend your days wriggling through it."

I nodded. "A disease," I said. "A plague."

Terries barked a laugh. "A disease, he says." He looked at me, suddenly relaxed. "Mr. Cates, there is nothing natural about what is happening. Come! You are here. We have some hours before we are all dead. Let us use them. Maybe you can be useful after all. Or are you such an animal that all you know how to do is threaten and shoot?"

I clenched my teeth. "Dr. Terries—" I stopped myself. What was there to say? I shook myself and nodded. "Let's go."

He smiled and pulled himself from the chair slowly, as if exhausted. "I have a lab one level down. There is a private elevator. You may take whatever precautions you wish."

The elevator was white, too, and when the doors had

closed the seam disappeared expertly, creating the illusion of a sealed cube. I felt suddenly claustrophobic, and drank more gin in greedy, steady gulps. As I'd thought, I didn't feel a thing. When the doors suddenly split apart again, I was surprised.

The lab was better. It was a mess—well lit and surrounded by the same painfully white walls, but cluttered and stained, smelling of smoke. A massive work desk sported several huge video screens, each a few feet across, and Terries led us to them, gesturing them on with a complicated movement of his hand. He pointed at the center one.

"Mr. Cates," he said, "meet our plague."

I stared at the screen. For a moment I couldn't process what it was displaying. It was a blood sample, blown up to an immense magnification. Swimming in it, flitting quickly around the screen, were what at first glance looked like tiny little insects, multiple legs kicking and fluttering to propel them, tiny antennae waving softly. I blinked and leaned forward as Terries turned and walked away, hands clasped behind his back.

The insects glinted softly, shiny.

"What the *fuck*," I whispered.

"Mechanical, yes," Terries said without turning to look at us. "Robots, in a sense. Incredibly small, smaller than your red blood cells. Nanotechnology, extremely advanced. I don't know what lab in the System could even come close to something of this complexity. They are self-powered, contain fairly sophisticated processing units that give them a fair amount of flexibility, and—most amazingly, Mr. Cates—they are self-replicating. Each one can produce another copy of itself, using the body's own raw materials."

"That," Jabali muttered next to me, "is fucked up."

"They spread, Mr. Cates. Any human comes within about eight feet of someone infected with these, and they make the leap, through the air. They will hitch a ride on bodily excretions, the usual viral or bacterial vectors, and once a single microscopic unit enters the body, it begins replicating. Once there are enough units in the body, they begin...consuming." He turned back to us. I looked up at him, and he was smiling a terrible, cadaverous smile. He was a handsome man, his face finely etched, but he looked like a corpse taunting me. "They literally eat you from the inside out."

I thought of blue-black bruises that eventually burst.

"Someone *built* these?" I said, my voice a dry rasp. "Someone purposefully *built* these?"

Terries nodded. "Yes. Generally speaking, the infected are dead within a day or two, depending on their general health to begin with, size and mass, some other factors we haven't quantified yet." He shrugged. "It's spreading. We're taking steps, but..." He looked at me. "How many people did you pass on your way up here, Mr. Cates? A hundred? Two hundred?" He shook his head. "You've killed us."

Avery Cates, I thought, *Destroyer of Worlds.*

"Wait a second," Jabali said. "Killed *us?* As in, *me?*"

Terries nodded. "All of us."

I'd smelled a turning tide too many times before to ignore the obvious signs, so I reached across myself and drew my Roon, holding it pointed down at the floor but in plain sight. "Wait," I said. "Terries, why am I still alive?"

He blinked at me. "What?"

I was gripping the automatic so tightly my palm hurt. "Everyone I've been in contact with over the last few days is now dead. These things kill within days. I've seen people dead on the street, for fuck's sake." I remembered that peculiar feeling of well-being, on my knees, blindfolded but suddenly not worried about it, and that ruined voice saying *and don't worry: When it is over, you will be punished again.* "Why am I alive?"

Terries squinted at me for a moment and then transformed, life flowing back into his face. He threw up both hands. "Do not shoot!" he said, and turned away, running deeper into the lab.

A flash of panic ripped through me, and I brought the gun up, trying to keep Jabali in sight as I walked slowly around to follow. "Doc, don't fucking *do* that. Doc?" I met Jabali's eyes and paused. "You feel sick?" I said.

He stared back for a moment, and then swallowed. "Nah, boss. Guess I don't."

I nodded. "If you're thinking of shooting me in the back, Jabali, at least wait to feel something first, okay?"

He stared at me for a few moments more and then nodded, putting up his hands. "All right, boss. All right."

I nodded and turned away to follow Terries, but he was already striding back to me, holding a battered metal bin in both hands. "Roll up your sleeve, Mr. Cates," he panted, sounding suddenly excited.

"What?"

He slammed the bin down on the desk, making his video screens jump. One shut off with a pop. "Roll up your goddamn *sleeve,* Mr. Cates," he said, holding up a huge autohypo. "You're right: You are not sick. Let's find out *why.*"

X

DAY FIVE: A CLOUD OF DEATH AROUND ME

Needled by my instincts, which screamed out against exposing a vein to Dr. Terries, I sat with my naked arm outstretched. "If you cut me," I said conversationally, "I will hurt you. Just so we're clear."

From across the small table he'd unfolded in the middle of the lab, Terries nodded. "I understand, Mr. Cates. Believe me, I understand perfectly what someone like you is capable of."

With one hand already holding me by the wrist, he reached forward with the autohypo. I intercepted his arm with my free hand, clamping tightly around his forearm, probably causing him pain. He looked up at me with alarm.

"Are you implying I'm an animal again, Dr. Terries?"

His face registered several emotions, one after the other. I could have labeled them finely—the specific intensity of terror, the flavor of impotent rage, the flowchart of quick scheming—but I didn't bother. I'd made my point, and he put a rotten smile on his face and shook his head.

"Not at all, Mr. Cates!" he said quickly, making no move to free himself. He was sweating lightly. "I meant that with all respect. I am not a..." He paused to search for the perfect way to compliment me without seeming to kiss my ass. His face brightened pathetically. "I am not a *man of action,* yes? That is all I meant."

I gave him a grin, slight and humorless, and let go of his arm. I turned to Jabali. "Get that? We're *men of action.*"

Jabali looked like he didn't have any fucking clue what was going on, but he smiled anyway. "Shit, boss."

I was playing the role to the hilt because it was what Dr. Terries expected. From the moment I'd appeared behind him on the street, he'd pegged me as the typical downtown hooligan the Vids always portrayed: ignorant, violent, and greedy. And maybe I was, depending on the day, but for now it was just a way to keep Dr. Terries terrified, because if he suspected even for a moment that we didn't mean to kill him, he'd be impossible to deal with.

He swallowed and took a deep breath, putting his eyes on my inflated vein. Expertly, he jabbed the autohypo forward and I felt it pinch my skin, the pain melting away a second later as an automatic painkiller was administered. The clear chamber began to slowly fill with my blood, deep red.

"I've seen parts of your file," Terries said suddenly, glancing up at me and licking his lips. "Some of it is in the clear—not censored by Marin's office, I mean—and it makes for interesting reading."

I weighed whether or not to find this offensive and decided to let it pass without comment. It was good to be unpredictable. Kept the rubes terrified; people liked to learn the rules, because once you knew the rules you could manipulate the outcome. If there *were* no rules, it was best to keep your fucking arms and legs inside the safety cage.

"Did you really, uh, did you really interact with Dennis Squalor?" he went on, watching the autohypo do its work.

I nodded, keeping my face blank. I didn't like to think of the hours I'd spent under Westminster Abbey, hunting Squalor, killing Monks, and watching Kev Gatz die.

He waited another moment. "It's very exciting," he finally said, removing the autohypo cleanly and holding a small piece of gauze in place over the wound. "Squalor was a genius in his way. Did amazing work in cybernetics and Biological Systems Replacement. Would have won awards, had professorships, if . . . well," he smiled nervously, keeping his eyes down on the autohypo, "if he hadn't gone mad."

"You mean, if he hadn't tried to murder everyone and turn them into fucking Monks?"

He carried the autohypo over to a bank of equipment across the room, shadowed by a jumpy Jabali. "Well, of course . . . still, his accomplishments . . ."

"Would you like a lock of his hair, Doc? Get on with it."

"Very well, very well," he muttered, inserting the autohypo into a slot and ramming it home. A soft tone rang out and a small screen lit up, text streaming from top to bottom. Terries crouched down and stared at it. "You don't have a very healthy diet, Mr. Cates," he muttered absently. "And I would be concerned about your liver function if I were your physician. There—I can see the signatures of the nanobots. Yours are different, however; it's not entirely clear where the deviation is . . ."

His muttering died down to a whisper, and then he was gesturing at his equipment, his thin lips moving but making no sound. I lifted the gauze off my arm and peered under it experimentally, then tossed it onto the floor and began rolling my sleeve down.

"I've spent quite a bit of time working with this material remotely," Terries said suddenly. "Amazing tech. Far beyond anything I've seen anywhere else. Whoever developed this was a genius. So I'm familiar, you see, with the basic design. I can see where the examples in your blood deviate from the structures we've already cataloged, but it isn't clear why. Wait, there's a signal being emitted." He spun around on his stool to face me. "*Your* nanobots are *broadcasting*." He spun around again. "Two signals, actually. One is broad low power, one is narrow-beamed low power."

I took a deep breath. Techies. I hated working with them.

"I could do much better and faster work if I had more resources, Mr. Cates," he said suddenly, squinting at the screen. "I realize you do not trust me, thus your goon with the menacing air, but if I were in the Department's lab, we would—"

"You're doing fine, Doc," I said. I had no desire to get any closer to Cop Central.

"Very well. Perhaps I could at least call in some colleagues, trustworthy sorts—"

"Afraid not."

He worked in silence for a few moments. "Wait a second," he murmured, leaning forward. "Some of this is in cleartext…"

I stood up and walked over to him, squinting down at the equipment. "What is?"

"The narrow-beam signal," he said absently. "Looks like this is freelance work, and the technician signed his name in a signal that is beamed back to an originating point. Unbelievable arro—"

He went very still. It was the sort of stillness that brought all my instincts up, sniffing the air for a threat. "Well, I'll be *fucked*," he said in a conversational tone.

"Doc?"

He glanced up at me as if remembering I was there. He stared at me and then started to laugh, shaking his head and waving at the equipment. "Mr. Cates, I didn't realize you were Patient Fucking Zero. Is there anything left in that bottle?"

I looked back at the table and the bottle of gin I'd left there. "Sure," I said. "What's going on?"

He stood up and grinned around at me and Jabali, who glanced at his gun. I shook my head slightly, watching the good doctor walk unsteadily toward the table and pick up the bottle. He tipped it back and drank steadily for a few swallows, then put the bottle unsteadily back onto the table.

"Your nanobots are different, Mr. Cates. They are the *originators*. The builders. They do not attack your body, they simply build drones that are excreted through your pores to seek out hosts to infect. They are broadcasting a weak suppression field which keeps the drones dormant until they have exited your body, otherwise you would already be dead. If you died too soon, you might not infect enough people to achieve the tipping point, so the suppression field guaranteed that you would wander around for days, infecting as you went. Since the field actually has a range of a few feet—perhaps ten, at most—it also means that anyone near you for any length of time sees their own infection go dormant."

He started walking past the table, turning to look at me over his shoulder, smiling, grandfatherly. He was probably only five or ten years older than me. "You're the only reason I haven't started dying yet, Mr. Cates." He turned away and kept walking, gesturing blindly back toward Jabali. "Him, too! But if you move out of range, the nanobots inside me stop receiving the field and *wake up*—and start work."

I should have been paying attention to the older man, but my mind had gone blank. I pictured myself walking through the city, inches from people. Standing next to Gleason, next to Wa, shaking Pick's hand. Pick, who'd lived forever and might have lived another eternity, until I'd come along. I saw Glee, grinning at me. *Ooh, Avery's a father figure.* I swallowed something thick that had lodged in my throat. "You said," I managed to croak, "you said something about a second signal?"

I imagined a cloud of death around me.

"Yes!" Terries shouted from the other end of the lab, where he was rooting around in a cart of discarded equipment, cables, and mysterious black boxes. "It looks like a beacon signal, pinging a location in Europe, probably Paris by the looks of the EIP address, but I'd have to dig a little deeper to confirm that. I don't know what it could be for. We saw that in the other nanobots, the regular ones that all the victims to date have had. Same name embedded in it, too."

I nodded absently, my mind a second or two behind each word, trying to catch up. It was as if I was translating each word as I heard it, looking them up one at a time, everything coming to me in slow, lazy waves. Then I focused, staring at the doctor's back. "A name?"

"In cleartext no less! Taking credit for the work." He paused and looked over his shoulder at us, smiling, his teeth white and straight and perfect. "Taking credit for killing us all."

From outside and above us, there was a burst of deep, pounding static, and then a mellow, golden tone, the sound of all the Vid screens clearing their throats. Normally silent, with text crawls, all the newer Vids were equipped for sound and erupted into booming stereo whenever there was an important announcement.

"*Attention,*" boomed a generic male voice, pleasant and controlled. It reminded me of the Monks. "*By Emergency Decree under Charter regulation Six-six-ten, the System Security Force has declared a state of general emergency. All citizens are requested to remain inside their homes until further notice. Noncompliance will be met with force. Attention: By Emergency Decree under Charter Regulation Six-six…*"

The message repeated again and again, and we just stared at each other. A trickle of sweat made its way down my back, slow and itchy.

"This shit," Jabali said deliberately, "is beyond me."

I kept my eyes on Terries' back as he continued to rummage. "What was the name, Doc?" I wanted to know who'd done this to me. I remembered being on my knees, a cold gun against my skin, being told that I would be punished *again*. My hands twitched at my sides. I remembered, and I wanted revenge.

"Kieth," he said, reaching down into the bottom of the

cart. "Ty Kieth. Odd name, don't you think? But then those people are always *clever.* Always clever, and never *smart.*"

The name hung in the air. I knew Ty Kieth. I'd known Ty Kieth for years. He'd been there when I'd taken down the Electric Church, and he'd helped me build the beginnings of my organization in Manhattan, setting up security nets and communication systems. I knew the nose-wiggling, bald-headed bastard.

And I knew he wasn't who I was looking for. Ty Kieth was capable of a lot of things, but he would never have spent his time building something like this unless he'd been forced to—or been paid an awful lot of yen for his troubles. All Ty Kieth wanted to do was fiddle with shit in his lab in peace. When he'd left New York a few years before, there hadn't been any amount of money or begging that could convince him to stay: he'd had research to do.

Ty Kieth in Paris, I thought. Good enough for a start.

"Thank you, Doc," I said, waving Jabali forward. "I'm sorry I had to—"

The older man turned away from the cart, and I paused. He was holding a gun on us. It was bright and shiny, brand-new, and looked like it had never been fired before. It was a new Roon model; to my eye it looked like it cost about sixty thousand yen. I was the richest man I knew and I'd never seen a gun that expensive before.

Terries held it as if it might explode at any time, but he had his finger in the right place, so I chose to stay still and not take chances.

"I'm sorry, Mr. Cates," he said, smiling. "You're the only reason I'm not dying." He shrugged. "I can't let you *leave.*"

XI

DAY FIVE: A CERTAIN FREEDOM IN BEING COMPLETELY FUCKED

Deciding not to make things worse, I stayed still—besides, the doctor's gun was pointed at me. Jabali and I had more or less unconsciously followed your best practice and kept far apart, and now he took advantage of the gap by yanking out his own piece and covering the good doctor with it.

"Doc," he said, "don't pull a fucking rod unless you mean to use it. You don't mean to use it. That makes you a shithead."

Jabali glanced at me. I didn't look at him, but I gave a curt little shake of the head. I didn't want to kill the Doc; I was killing enough people on a daily basis as it was. The wail of the emergency Vid announcement continued to buzz around us, muffled by concrete and glass, and I put my hands up carefully.

Hesitation wasn't attractive in a Gunner. Hesitation got

you killed, and a feeling of unease filled me like black jelly.

"I'm sorry," Terries said smoothly, shrugging. He was used to being in charge, you could tell. He thought having the gun in his hand made him in charge again. A moment before he'd been shaken, hesitant, cowed, and now he was grinning at me as if one of us hadn't killed nearly sixty people, killed them while looking them in the eye. "If you walk out the door, I am on a rapid countdown to a horrible death."

"You have my blood sample," I pointed out. "You can work with that. You don't need me to work on this."

He nodded. "Perhaps, Mr. Cates. That's a small sample, though. And we don't know the behavior of these nanobots. Perhaps they are tuned to your biorhythmic signature and will revert if you are not within close proximity. Perhaps they go inert or self-destruct if they detect they are not in a live biological system." He shrugged. "Mr. Cates, letting you walk out of here would be akin to suicide."

"So, you want to just keep me pasted to your side for the foreseeable future?" I smiled. "What's next, asking me to tie myself up?"

Jabali snorted. Terries smiled, and when he started to move his free hand in a shell gesture all my instincts lit up like bright red alarms: Avery Cates, fucking moron. The lights went out. There were no windows in the lab, and the darkness was absolute. As adrenaline sizzled inside me, I let my legs just collapse under me, going limp, hitting the floor like a sack of shit. Two shots burped, the muzzle flashes bright as a strobe, showing me Jabali and Terries in a still life, all blue-gray.

I started crawling immediately, trying to be quiet. I had the floor plan of the lab in my head, mostly — what I'd seen, anyway. Not measured out, but I could bang against the walls. The floor smelled like disinfectant, and my breath was hot and sour around me as I pulled myself with my elbows, pushing with my knees. This was what I got for being fucking lazy and arrogant, put on the floor by a fucking civilian. This was what I got for hesitating.

"Mr. Cates," I heard Terries say, and then Jabali's gun exploded three times, fast, followed by shoes scraping on the floor and something heavy crashing over. Terries was learning fast that he wasn't really in charge. He was also learning the golden rule of gunfights: things only counted as advantages if they didn't make the situation worse for you, too.

I glanced up, eyes roving blindly, and saw the tiny glowing spots of the elevator buttons, very close. I fixed my position in my mind and started crawling toward it.

"You should know," Terries said, his actor's voice coming from behind me and to my right, where the table and screens were, "that I have a direct link to the SSF, and they are on their way. The alarm was tripped when we entered the lab."

I believed this. He was director of something or other, after all, someone who'd actually met Undersecretary Ruberto and probably the all-smiling, all-bullshitting avatar of Dick Marin. He'd had the juice to dispatch three psionics to the Library to gather me up; the cops probably did come when he called. At least, I was sure they did when there wasn't a general emergency demanding their attention.

I've killed my share of System Pigs, I wanted to say

back. *If you mentioned my name I'm sure they're fighting over who gets to respond.* I concentrated on not breathing too loudly and covering ground. When the glowing buttons loomed up directly above me, I put my back against the doors, forcing my burning lungs to work slowly, and reached up, seeking the call button. When I found it I pressed it gently. It lit up softly, and I flinched; against System Cops or anyone with talent, that would have been enough to bring a hail of gunfire my way, and I cursed myself silently for being a rusty asshole.

Nothing happened and I relaxed, pretty sure Terries hadn't noticed. Behind me, I felt the nearly silent humming operation of the elevator, and I held my gun firmly in my hand, aimed up at the ceiling, moving my eyes this way and that.

In the System—at least the parts of it that I lived in—all that mattered, all you really had, was your reputation. Two men went into a box, and one got killed and one climbed out, it doesn't matter if you were bloodied and beaten. It doesn't matter if you begged and bribed, wept and cursed inside that box—all that matters is that you lived and he died. That's all anyone ever remembered. And it didn't matter if you staggered home and climbed into a bottle, wept some more, and had the fucking shivers for a week straight—that shit didn't matter. He was dead and you'd survived, and thus you had a rep.

So far, everyone who'd ever come up against me had died. Sometimes it had been pure luck—a stumble, a distraction, a lucky shot. Sometimes I'd been able to cheat, get some inside information. Usually it was just that I had taken some time to recon my surroundings and knew where the hiding spots were, the geography of the place.

None of that mattered to the rep: on the streets I was just Avery Cates, who'd never been taken down, who'd left a long trail of dead bodies in his wake. And over time the space that formed around you on the street got bigger, and people got more spooked when you looked at them, and the number of people who wanted to kill you just to say they did it grew. And none of it meant a fucking thing, really, but it was all you ever had.

Sitting spread-eagled on the floor in the pitch darkness, I felt the crank air being pushed past me as the car descended and thought, *Fuck the rep—it's* good *to be lucky for a change.*

Now it was patience time again; I sat and regulated my breathing and waited for the elevator to arrive. I felt the car settling behind me and braced myself, ready to stay upright when the doors split open, eyes in the general area that Terries' voice had come from. Painful white light invaded the lab as the elevator doors opened, but I forced my eyes to search the glare for Terrics, finding him hiding behind his bank of monitors, his face a ruddy moon, his eyes squinted against the brightness. I noted the form of Jabali, off to my right and crouched down, and ignored him.

My hand came up automatically, training the gun on the good doctor, and immediately there was a movement behind me, fast and efficient, and something cold and metallic was pressed against the back of my head.

"Don't do it, shithead," the cop said quietly. "Or I'll tear off your legs and beat you over the head with them."

His breath was all around me for a second, warm and sweet, and I imagined thousands, millions of those tiny drones being pulled from me like an invisible wind, burrowing into him, setting his death in motion. Across the room Terries opened his eyes and blinked at me in shock, frozen for a moment. I picked the spot. A gap between two monitors that showed me his belly—a gut shot wasn't immediately lethal, but it was painful and incapacitating, useful when you wanted to put someone down without making a decision just yet. His head rose above the equipment like a red moon, coiffed and shaved, manicured, and I could kill him with a twitch if I wanted to.

My eyes found Jabali, who stood frozen in place, his gun half lowered. His eyes met mine and he extended two fingers from his grip on the automatic. Two cops behind me. Not much chance of putting them both on their asses with my smooth balletic moves. I put my eyes back on Terries. Everything had gone completely to shit so fast, I was still catching up. I knew I didn't deserve anything. I knew I was a bad man. But this was getting *ridiculous.*

There was a certain freedom in being completely fucked, though. I thought, *Avery Cates, Destroyer of Worlds,* and squeezed the trigger just as the cop behind me shoved the barrel of his gun viciously into the shallow skin on the back of my head, and my shot went wild. Terries dropped to the floor with a screech. I hadn't killed him, though, because he proceeded to scream and thrash around.

"You," the cop said, almost in my ear, "are a stupid little shit, huh?"

I closed my eyes and thought, *yep.* I heard the rustle of fabric and winced just before the butt of his gun.

XII

DAY SIX: I MIGHT EVEN *SURVIVE*

Emerging from gauzy semiconsciousness, I found I was trapped in a room with assholes.

There were two of them, big guys with permanent scabs on their knuckles and nicotine stains on the tips of their fingers. One was older, maybe thirty, balding and running to fat. He wore a purple suit that had been skillfully cut to hide his paunch, the fabric shimmering as he moved. He made a big show of removing his hat and jacket when he stepped into the room, and every time he left the room, which he'd done a dozen times already, he made a big show of putting them both back on again. It would have been amusing to watch if he hadn't spent all his time *in* the room beating the fucking tar out of me.

The other one was sitting on a table near the door of the Blank Room, eating cigarettes and watching. He looked like he was going to burst out of his suit, the shirt collar straining to contain the bulging veins and muscles of his neck. He had a stiff-looking shock of red hair that stood up from his head as if it hadn't been washed in a long time and bright green eyes that might have been augments, the way they shone at me in an unbroken stare. He chewed his tobacco steadily, hands clasped in his lap, legs dangling forgotten. He was wearing a simple black suit with shiny black shoes, thick soled and sturdy.

"The only reason you're still alive," Purple Suit wheezed, wiping sweat from his brow, "is because we haven't gotten permission to kill you yet."

One of my eyes was swollen shut, and my lips were split and rubbery. I nodded my head at him.

"Don't you fucking *nod,* you piece of shit—"

He was losing steam, so the kick he landed on my chest wasn't enough to knock me over. The chair I was tied to—a battered gray metal one—just skidded backward a few inches, leaving me sitting there gasping and heaving, a thin trickle of blood dripping from my mouth. Purple Suit put his hands on his knees and bent over, breathing heavily. He didn't look too good. Every ten or fifteen minutes he'd been leaving the room, leaving my sphere of influence, I thought, and each time he returned he looked worse. I imagined my little invisible drones eating away at him, a bit at a time, waking up each time he walked out the door and going to sleep again each time he returned.

Red just turned his head to spit and stared at me.

"Goin' out, Happ," Purple Suit said, wheezing and coughing.

"You okay?"

"Yeah, yeah. Just need a break. Watch him, okay?"

As Purple Suit went through his laborious dressing routine, coughing wetly the whole time until his round bald head was a fiery shade that was starting to resemble his suit, the other cop just stared at me. The whites of his eyes were bloodshot, thick angry veins. He hadn't left the room in two hours and looked healthy as a horse.

"I'll make sure no harm comes to him," he said tonelessly.

They'd scanned my face, of course, me and Jabali, and figured they'd hit the jackpot: Avery Cates, cop killer. Officially, I had no record, but every cop in New York—maybe the whole System—knew me. I'd come to in the Blank Room and it had been just these two ever since, Purple Suit tuning me up with standard SSF dedication to his job, Big Red sitting there and staring. I couldn't tell if he was enjoying it or not; he just stared. The room was featureless and silent, just me, a table, a chair, and two System Pigs who didn't even ask me any questions. They weren't beating *information* out of me, they were just *beating* me. I'd killed a lot of cops. Not as many as they thought I had, but enough.

I let my head drop onto my chest. They hadn't logged me in officially; they'd wanted me all to themselves for a while, and if my name had popped up on everyone's screen they'd have been forced to kick me upstairs. I would have floated above their level pretty quickly. So, I wasn't officially there. Anything might happen. Shit, I might even *survive*.

Big Red suddenly spoke. "How's it feel to have every single person within a mile of you want you dead?" he asked cheerfully, his face suddenly animating. His smile was terrible, too wide and too strong.

I moved my dry tongue over what was left of my lips, making them sting. "Normal," I croaked back, blowing bloody snot everywhere.

He nodded. "Don't worry. We won't kill you. We're going to beat you half to death, then nurse you tenderly back to health and well-being. Then we'll get two more guys in here to beat you half to death. We're going to start a club."

I struggled to breathe. My throat felt tight and flooded.

Big Red slid off the table and produced a single unfiltered cigarette from a pocket. He crushed it in his big hands and extracted a wad of tobacco from his palm and stuck it between his gums and cheek. "There's a new policy, you see, sent down from the fucking Mountain. The King Worm says, here's a list of people you can't kill, on pain of my wormy fucking boot up your quivering ass. So even though you're not really here, we hesitate: you can't take a shit without Dick Marin knowing what color it was and how often you grunted." He rubbed his hands clean, paper and tobacco dust falling to the floor. "Your friend, the haircut, isn't on any list, though. You can stop worrying about him."

I tried to close my eyes. My left one was already swollen shut, so there was no change, and my right one wouldn't close all the way. I hadn't known Jabali well, or for long. I added him to the list.

Big Red knelt down until his face was even with mine. His bright eyes bulged from their sockets, his angular face skeletal. His jacket hung open and I saw the glint of his holographic gold badge sizzling coldly in its little metal wallet and the black, lightless form of his gun in its holster, low under his shoulder.

"I'm Captain Nathan Happling, Mr. Cates," he said

softly. "And I'll be your personal tour guide through this experience."

I started to laugh, swallowed some blood, and began coughing, each spasm making me feel like my eyes were going to just pop out of my head and roll across the floor. I liked this guy.

I didn't know how long I'd been in the Blank Room; consciousness came and went. I'd been tuned up by System Pigs before, but never like this. Before, there'd been a point to it, information to be extracted, a lesson to be learned. This was just an endless beating. They didn't want anything from me, they didn't need me to do anything for them. I was a cop killer and they were happy to have me, unofficially, in their grasp.

I faded back as Purple Suit returned to the room, pale and glistening with a cold-looking sweat. He walked in stiffly, grimacing. Happling was back on the table, chewing away, his buggy eyes tracking his partner as he staggered toward me, leaving his coat on for a change.

"It's fucking pandemonium out there," he said, panting.

"Peace and quiet in here," Happling said. "You okay, Bob-O? You're looking a little under the weather."

"Fuck you, Happ," Purple Suit growled, standing in front of me. "I think——" he started to say, and then collapsed into a wave of heavy, thick coughs that kept him bent over double for a minute, his face filling with dark color. When he got himself back under control, he grunted and spat a glob of reddish, spongy phlegm onto the floor. We all stared at it for a moment.

"Bob-O," Happling said quietly. "Maybe you oughta take a break."

Purple Suit half turned toward Happling, then stiffened, his head bending to the side in an unnatural way as a choking noise hissed out of him. Then he collapsed, falling in a heap onto the floor. For a second both Happling and I just stared down at him.

"Uh-oh," Happling said softly, sliding off the table. "Bob-O's down." He crouched down near the other cop and glanced at me, one eyebrow up, his mouth twitching into an almost smile. "You didn't kill him...with your *mind,* did you?" he asked, and then exploded into raucous laughter, feeling up Bob-O for a pulse.

I revised my earlier impression: I was trapped in a room with an asshole and a fucking psycho. I concentrated on breathing through the rapidly narrowing aperture that had once been my mouth. When the door to the Blank Room flashed open again, I was almost happy — anything would be better than being trapped in this tiny, shielded space with Big Red Happling, guffawing over the soon-to-be-corpse of his partner.

For a moment she was framed in the doorway, a tiny, *tiny* black woman with skin so dark she looked burned, her hair a curly mass of reddish brown in a cloud around her face. Maybe my age, maybe younger, it was impossible to tell. I had the quick, confusing impression I'd seen her before, but fuck, I'd seen hundreds of cops and tried to forget each one as quickly as possible. She was pretty. Or would have been if the eyes set in that round, symmetrical face weren't the hardest eyes I think I'd ever seen.

"Captain," she bit off, sounding like the picture you'd find under *unamused* if you looked it up.

To my amazement Happling leaped to his feet. "Sir," he said, taking a step back.

"Oh, at ease, you jackass," she snapped. "What's wrong with him?"

Happling backed away from Purple Suit as if escaping something invisible. "He just collapsed, sir."

The woman's eyes were dark brown, giving the impression of dark holes in her face. They jumped from the body on the floor to me, and then to Happling, the expression on her face never changing. "Is he dead?"

Happling glanced down at Purple Suit and then back up at the wall across from him. "Not yet," he said, with just the barest hint of his spastic smile.

I ran my swollen tongue over my lips. "Who the hell are you?" It felt good to sass the cops; I had nothing much to lose on the deal. It wasn't as if they were going to give me credit for taking this shit like a man; after all, let me walk out of there alive.

She flicked those empty eyes at me and held them there for a moment, her whole body so perfectly still it made me nervous all over again—it was the sort of stillness that usually preceded violence. "Colonel Janet Hense," she finally said, stepping into the room and letting the door flash shut behind her. She was carrying a small, thin leather briefcase and was dressed in all black: smartly cut pants that looked good on her, a thick black turtleneck shirt, and a sumptuous-looking black leather jacket. Tossing the briefcase onto the table, she stared at Happling for a second or two, seconds he spent studying the far wall as if his life depended on figuring out what it was made of. Then she turned to me, reaching inside her jacket.

For a split second, I tensed, thinking, *Shit, the SSF calls in the big shots to put a bullet in your head.*

But it was just a tube of leather that twisted open to reveal a skinny, shiny metal flask and a metal disc.

"Drink, Mr. Cates?" Hense said, her blank eyes on me as her hands set about twisting and turning the pieces into an ersatz bar. "Gin. Real gin."

This was unexpected, and all my alarm bells sounded for a second. I doubted the Pigs routinely *poisoned* people in their Blank Rooms, and I reminded myself that I had nothing to lose anyway, so I forced myself to relax. "Got a straw?"

She'd twisted the disc into a cup and unscrewed the cap from the flask, and now she stared at me again for a moment. "Cut 'im loose," she said.

Happling visibly stuttered, his arms twitching and one foot shooting out before he stopped himself. He looked at her. "What?"

"Cut Mr. Cates loose," she said slowly, biting off each syllable, "so we can have a fucking drink like civilized people."

Happling hesitated for a second more, his big hands clenched and his throat working within the tight, painful-looking circle of his collar. Then he launched himself at me, a thin blade suddenly flashing out from one hand with a snap. He disappeared behind me and with a jerk my hands were free. My arms were completely numb, and my feet were still bound to the chair. I willed my arms to move, and they did, in a creepy way that seemed completely separate from me. Hense leaned forward and held the shiny cup out to me and I saw my alien hand reach up and take it. I held it in front of me, the smell of liquor very strong. I stared back at her, the cup shaking slightly in my grasp. I was aware of her smell: natural, a good, woman's smell.

She held up the flask, nodded, and tilted back a deep swallow. I shrugged inwardly and did my best, dashing the cup against my broken lips and getting most of the liquid inside my mouth. There was a moment of searing pain, and then the liquor made its way down my throat, where it bloomed in sudden warmth, the first good feeling I'd had in...hours? Days? Who the fuck knew.

Hense held out her hand and I returned the cup. She carefully crushed it back into its original form and re-placed everything inside the leather case, fastidious and precise. I watched her through my one squinted eye, wait-ing. In my experience, when System Pigs were nice to me it was a very bad sign of things to come. The last time one had offered me a drink, he'd almost cut off both my thumbs a few minutes later.

"We had an interesting conversation with DPH direc-tor Terrics about an hour ago," she said suddenly, her eyes fixed on the flask, her voice level. "When he came to in the hospital. He's concerned that he's going to die very soon, and his doctors seem to agree. He told us to find you, that you were the key to the sickness that's stirring up downtown. It took me a *long time* to locate you, how-ever, as several officers had taken you into custody and *not logged you in*."

Happling stood at attention, his eyes aimed up at the ceiling.

She let that marinate for a moment and then finished tying up her flask. "I have not passed this information on yet, for Captain Happling's sake. Tell me what's going on, Mr. Cates."

I cleared my throat and spat blood onto the floor. "I tried telling Tweedledum and Tweedledummer," I said, my throat burning as if I were exhaling gravel. "Twice."

For a second or two, we all contemplated Purple Suit.

"Tell me again," she suggested.

I told her again. I had it boiled down to a tight two-minute pitch by now. "As for you, take a look at Tweedledum. You get more than a few feet from me for any period of time, you're on a countdown to *that*." I raised my head, trying to blow some of the scabby mess out of my nose and clear the airway. A sudden crazy hope flared in me, and the word *survive* popped into my head again. "Look, take it to Marin. Tell Marin who you've got here. Tell him *why* I'm here." Dick Marin wouldn't pass up a chance to personally execute me, I didn't doubt, but he'd also take this shit seriously.

"Don't fucking tell me what to do," she said in a lazy, unconcerned tone. She looked at Happling and he looked at her, shrugging his eyebrows. Then she looked back at me. "A few feet away from you, huh? Terries didn't mention that. He just insisted you be brought to him for lab work. How fast?"

I shrugged. "Seems like it varies. I don't know why."

She nodded, taking a deep breath. "Captain Happling, take charge of Mr. Cates."

Happling nodded and strode around behind me. The chair tilted backward until I was looking up at his pale face. He grinned down at me and said in a bizarrely warm, friendly tone, "Hands in your pockets, buddy, okay?" and then, incredibly, he winked down at me. "If I see your hands, I break them."

He spun me around so he could drag me behind him,

and I heard the door flash open again. "Mr. Cates," Hense said briskly, "you are now my property. You will be within ten feet of me and Captain Happling at all times. If you try anything, we will shoot you dead and find out if you need to be alive to have this miraculous preserving effect on people."

"Colonel, sir," Happling said in a tentative, unhappy voice. "New directives on POIs state we're supposed—"

"Fuck the directive on Persons of Interest, Captain," Hense said coolly. "This man doesn't get more than ten feet away from me under any circumstances, understood?"

There were two or three beats of silence. "Understood, sir," Happling finally said.

When she spoke again, the harshness was gone for a second. "If what Terries and this piece of shit say is true, Nathan, we're dead if he gets more than a few feet away from us. Dead like your asshole partner back there. What do you think happens if we log Cates in? Do you think the fucking King Worm is going to let us tag along?"

Happling grunted. "I said *understood*."

The corridor beyond the Blank Room was empty and clinically white: clean and monochrome, the bright lights hurting my eyes. I counted fifteen lighting fixtures as I was dragged backward, and then the world tilted and I was pulled into an elevator. In the second before the doors snapped shut, I saw three fat drops of blood on the nice clean floor. This cheered me up for some unknown reason.

We rode in silence, the floors dropping away in a blur, until we had to be underground. None of us said anything. There was something wonderful about being securely bound, buried under endless tons of cops—I didn't have to make any decisions. Everything just flowed over me in an incomprehensible wave, keeping my head under.

When the elevator doors popped open, no one moved. Four System Cops blocked our way, all young men, jackets off, the sleeves of their uniformly white shirts rolled up even with their holsters, a cloud of cigarette smoke around them.

"Colonel Hense, *sir,*" said one in the middle, a pale, sweating man whose black hair was plastered to his forehead, his frame too slim and girlish to be a fucking cop. "With all due respect, why in *fuck* is Avery Cates still alive?"

XIII

DAY SIX: AND THE UNIVERSE SPUN ON

Raising one hand so she could stare down at her nails, the colonel spoke calmly. "Captain Happling, draw your weapon."

Behind me I heard the familiar sound of a gun being pulled.

"Who's feeling fast?" Happling said cheerfully. I could tell from his voice that he was smiling.

The four cops in front of us shifted uneasily, and I got the distinct feeling that Captain Happy behind me was the big cock in the room. The second biggest, I decided, considering the freezing wind blowing from the colonel's direction. The skinny, pale cop looked past me and didn't seem happy. "Hap, you know this shit is fucking wrong. That piece of crap is a cop killer. He should've been executed upon capture. What, you're gonna put him in the *system?* Fuck, Hap—the King Worm'll snap him up and he'll just disappear somewhere."

The King Worm. I'd always liked that name. Dick Marin, director of Internal Affairs, the de facto leader of the whole SSF. We hated the cops, the cops hated *their* cops. And the universe spun on.

"I do as I'm told, fellows," Happling responded. "In a second or two, the colonel's going to order you to step aside. You might gain some brownie points by doing so *now,* of your own free will."

It was amazing—there were four of them, each armed. The colonel remained stock-still, no weapon in sight. But the four cops blocking our way suddenly looked doubtful.

"Otherwise," Happling continued, "I'll be forced to kill you all, and I'll come out clean when I file the SIRs."

I wondered idly what the fuck an SIR was. The four cops stood there a moment longer, but I knew they'd move on. The energy had gone out of them; it was obvious none of them wanted to go up against Captain Happy or his boss. Their line broke, the three silent ones moving off, hands in pockets, sullen. The skinny one stood there a moment more, a faint layer of color coming into his face.

"This is bullshit, *sir,*" he said to Hense. "This is gonna come back on you."

No, I thought. *You'll be dead in two days.*

"If you have a misconduct charge," Hense said in the same level tone of voice she'd used when telling me she was going to kill me, "file it with the Worms and see what happens. I guarantee you'll be patrolling Chengara in hours. *Hours.* Continue to piss me off, Lieutenant, and you might have an accident one of these days."

The skinny cop looked worried, as if realizing he'd made an error. From behind me Happling's impossibly cheerful voice bubbled up and over me like laughing gas. "Now move along, you stupid prick, before she gets *really* annoyed."

The skinny cop hovered a final second or two, for pride's sake, and then turned to slink away. After a moment I was spun around and dragged out of the cab.

"Hands in pockets?" Happling said over me. "Good boy. We're going to be friends. Right up until I put a bullet in your fucking ear, you cop-killing piece of shit."

His cheerful tone was maybe the worst thing I'd ever heard in my life. I took some consolation from the thought that I was murdering every cop who came near me, in slow motion, by remote control. That warbly voice in Newark again, *This is an assassination. Not yours.*

The corridor was disappointingly similar to the last one: white, bright, spotless. As I glided along, the chair legs scraping loudly on the floor, cops glared back at me, all sorts of cops: big cops, short cops, fat cops, good-looking cops. I tried to smile but my mouth hurt, so I just stared back at them, imagining death. Then the world rotated again, and I glided backward into a lab. Glancing up, I saw LEVEL 4 TECH SERVICES painted in neat black letters on the door.

A Techie, I thought. The worst kind: a *cop* Techie.

The door snapped shut as I cleared the threshold, and I was left sitting there. Now that I'd gone ten minutes without a fist smashing into me, everything was aching and throbbing. I was a purplish blob of bruises and bleeding nanobots. After a moment, I was spun around to face a lab cluttered with equipment. It reminded me of Pick's old office, except with blindingly white light, white walls, and a lack of dust that was horrifying in its completeness.

Otherwise it was the same narrow lanes between piles of black boxes and circuit boards, looped wires, and other, less identifiable things.

We burrowed our way in deeper until I was swung around to face the inner sanctum of the lab. Techies everywhere were exactly the same: surrounded by crap, living their lives in the eye of a slow-moving storm of ruined tech. In the midst of the piles were two kids in gray SSF jumpsuits lounging on broken-down rolling chairs, wearing bizarre goggles that trailed thick cables connected to a monolithic black box. They both started and tore off the goggles, staring at us. One had a clean-shaven head that shone in the bright light; the other had a thick, dark beard and mustache blending into a dense head of hair, giving the impression of two small eyes peering out from behind a mask. The bald one leaped up, his shiny face turning red.

"What the fuck? Colonel, you know you can't just waltz in here without a ten-eighty-nine form and a precall from the fifteenth floor," he said in a nasally voice. "I'm going to have to—"

"Shut up," Hense said, snapping her fingers at Happling and pointing to a spot on the floor. I was dutifully dragged there, and the big cop took up his station next to me, his piece still in his huge, ham hand at his side, so near my face I could almost smell the fucking powder. He held it casually, his finger along the side. In my pockets my hands twitched, and I kept my eyes on it.

"Colonel," the skinny Techie continued, puffing out his chest, "I'll remind you of protocol. You're not my fucking boss. You're—"

Hense suddenly reached out and took hold of his nose,

and the kid started to squeal, crouching and doing a little dance under her tiny hand as she squeezed. Her empty eyes watched him for a moment—there was no joy in them, none of the usual System Pig arrogance and cruelty. They just stared down at the kid as he struggled to break free. She waited until he started to cry and then, with a snap of her wrist, she broke his nose and let him drop.

Smoothly, silently, her eyes flicked to the other kid, who was half crouched in his seat, frozen in shock. His pink tongue ran over his lips as he watched her carefully, as if he were tracking a wild animal.

I glanced at Happling's gun.

"Mr. Marko," Hense said in an even tone, "are you going to quote protocol at me?"

Marko shook his head so fast I imagined his beard making a *whoosh*ing sound in the still air. "No, no—never, Colonel, not me. I'm your man. What do you need?"

She hesitated as if considering the depth of his sincerity, and his face tightened as if he expected a slap. But she just gestured in my direction. "Take a blood sample and listen while I explain the situation."

He nodded and rubbed his hands together, staring at her blankly for a moment, and then started into motion. "Right! Yes, I'll take a blood sample...uh," he paused, peering uncertainly at me.

I grinned, imagining my teeth nice and bloody. "Don't worry," I said. "You're dead already."

"Go on, Mr. Marko," Hense said, sounding bored. "Mr. Cates will not molest you. Unless he wants to find out just how much pain a man can be in and still not be dead."

I tried to shrug my eyebrows, but wasn't sure what my face was doing, exactly, in response to my commands. I kept my eyes on the Techie, who stared back in obvious horror. "I think I already know, champ, but there's no margin in finding out *for sure,* is there?"

Marko blinked and dove for his workbench, where he scrabbled through a box of junk until he located an auto-hypo that looked exactly like the one Terries had used on me. Hense began running it all down for him, in clipped, impressive phrases that betrayed an organized, quick mind—she gave it to him in three or four horrifying sentences. Then he approached me like I was a wild animal on a long leash. I kept my eyes off him, looking first at his partner, who was slowly pulling himself from the floor, his nose strikingly crooked and his mouth and chin covered in dark blood, then at the colonel, who stared back at me with unblinking eyes, her arms crossed under her breasts.

Marko's hands were shaking as the autohypo smoothly sucked blood from my arm. When it *ding*ed softly, he yanked it out awkwardly and almost stumbled backward. He whirled around and disappeared into the maze of crap. His partner pulled himself onto a workbench and sat with his head in his arms, dripping blood onto the white floor and snuffling pathetically.

"Aw, c'mon," Happling said cheerfully. "Are you kidding me? You ain't hurt. Come here, I'll straighten that out for you with my thumbs, good as new."

The kid lifted his head to stare in horror at the big cop, which inspired a guffaw from the red-haired giant. I lifted my eyes from his gun just as he glanced down at me.

"Can you believe this kid?" he said, and then looked back at the Techie. "You know who this is, kid? This is Avery fucking Cates, cop killer. In other words, he's the one man in this room who needs to be worried about me. But look at 'im! The old bastard is free and easy. So why are you afraid of me?"

The Techie just stared. I let my eyes fall back on Happling's gun.

"Hell, it was *her* who snapped your nose, buddy, not me."

"That's enough, Captain."

I dropped my eyes quickly, studying the floor and the tiny pattern of blood droplets I'd produced there. After a moment, Happling said, "Yes, boss," in a tight, subdued voice.

I considered. Hense was keeping me off the grid because she didn't want to take the chance that what she'd been told was true, that she'd die quickly—and horribly—once I was out of sight, and the first thing her superiors would do if my name got put in the System was bundle me off somewhere. I could tell she was the sort of coldhearted bitch who would never lose a moment's sleep over putting one in my head, but she *needed* me, in a strange way.

Still, a feeling of freedom was singing inside me—I had nothing, *nothing* to lose. At the end of this little adventure, I was dead. There wasn't a fucking scenario that didn't end with me dead. I'd been here before. It was a good place. It clarified things.

The four of us sat in a tense silence for a while, Happling and Hense standing perfectly still, the other Techie from time to time moaning and snuffling back blood through what was left of his nose. When Marko returned, I saw him first and watched him make his way slowly back into the tiny clearing amid the mess.

"Mr. Marko?" Hense asked.

He nodded, staring at me, the expression on his face hard to pin down. It resembled the look of some of the hungry dogs that prowled the old stadium, hoping to snag a scrap or a slow-mover from some of the camps inside. I had the feeling Marko would gladly have slit my belly open and peered inside, just to satisfy his curiosity.

"You've got it right. I've never *seen* Tech like this. Ty Kieth—you know the name? Fuck, he's a legend. Totally unreliable, of course, but fuck, the man's gifted." He leaned toward me as if a strong wind were pushing him from behind. "I've never *seen* anything this elegant."

"Mr. Marko," Hense snapped. "You can confirm Dr. Terries's statements?"

He nodded again, slowly. "We're fucking dead, all right. The moment he's not in the room with us." A smile, wide and rapturous, spread across his face, his teeth shocking in the midst of the dark beard. "This is *amazing* work." He glanced at her. "I didn't have time for a thorough look. There's a lot going on there. But the basics are right."

He didn't spot the beacon, I thought. *Paris.* His buddy let out a long moan, but I couldn't tell if it was because of the news or his aching nose.

Hense nodded once, brisk. "Captain Happling, collect Mr. Cates. Marko and Jameson, grab your field gear. You're coming with me."

Marko nodded again, still staring at me. Happling didn't move. "Where we headed, boss?"

"The roof," she said, rubbing her temples. "We are leaving."

Suddenly the other Techie was back on his feet. "What? Colonel, you *cannot* remove him. This has to be kicked upstairs. This is a public health crisis, and if you won't—"

Hense's face clouded, her brows knitting together, and my belly tightened up just before she reached across herself, drew her shiny, chrome-plated Roon automatic, and shot him in the face.

None of us moved. She looked around at us. "I just saved that poor son of a bitch from a few hours of slow, painful dying," she said as if reading off a grocery list. She waited and then nodded, replacing her gun in its holster. "Captain?"

Happling hadn't moved. I knew I was dead, but I felt I owed Glee more than that. I could almost hear her: *Ooh, Avery's a martyr.* I owed her the bastards that had done this to her, just the same as if they'd blown her brains out. I owed her revenge. I took a deep breath and tore my hands from my pockets. I whipped my right hand out and had it, his gun, in my hand. I ripped it from his grasp and it seemed to settle into my grip of its own will.

But the big man was *fast.* Before I could do more, he'd moved, whirling and sending a solid kick against my chair, aiming for my balls but hitting the seat instead. I went sailing backward, toppling over, smacking my head against the floor. I heard him in the air and brought my arm around just in time to smack the barrel of his gun against his belly as he landed on me.

We both froze, panting. His breath smelled like ashes.

"Okay," I said, gasping. "Let's negotiate."

XIV

DAY SIX: I CAN'T IMAGINE WHAT IT IS YOU *DO* LIKE

"Shit, boss," Happling said between clenched teeth. "Permission to kill this son of a bitch?"

"Step back, Captain," Hense said immediately, not sounding particularly concerned.

Happling stayed put for a moment, his teeth bared, and then he straightened up and stepped back, cursing under his breath and thrusting his big hands into his pockets. I tried to keep both cops in sight. Hense was just standing there, the smallest thing in the room, arms still crossed as if she'd never dream of drawing her own weapon or raising a hand in anger.

In the sudden vacuum, Marko whispered, "You fucking shot him."

Hense unspooled one arm to gesture in my direction, a sculpted eyebrow going up. "Mr. Cates, you have the floor."

I didn't have much on my side, so I knew I was going

to have to start lying. "First off, I know you're not going to kill me, so stop threatening me."

Happling was staring down at the floor, face red and posture tense. I couldn't be sure, but it seemed likely he was making fists in his pockets. I'd make fists in my pockets, too, if I'd been made to look stupid like that. "How about we just *imply* great physical pain, then?" he said to the floor.

"Second," I said without waiting for more of a response, "you don't have all the information. Why do you think I've got these special nanos inside me? Because I'm fucking *patient zero.* I'm where it all started six days ago. You're going to carry me around like luggage, and you don't even know where to go. You've got a name, but do you think a lone underground Techie did this? Do your math, Colonel. Starting with me, this has been spreading outward steadily, right? Takes anywhere from a few hours to a few days to tear some poor asshole to pieces, right? The whole city's on the edge of a fucking breakdown. And after the city—what? You're a professional, Colonel, you know crowd control. Do you think you're going to be able to bottle this up? You're not even going to be able to keep this *downtown* for long."

She just stared at me, but something told me, some change in her aura or whatever signal she was beaming out from that cold lizard brain of hers, that I had her attention. "I know where we go," I said. "I know where we can find Ty Kieth. And I know where to go from there, too. Think about it," I finished. "You've got resources. I've got the information."

If her Techie had had more than five minutes to work, if Terries had managed to croak out everything he'd learned, I'd have nothing—but they hadn't. It was time to start playing the old familiar role of Avery Cates, the Gweat and Tewwible.

I took a chance and moved my eyes onto her, this slip of a woman, her dark skin looking like she would feel good, up close. "Colonel, we're *partners*."

Happling twitched his head and spat on the floor. "Nuts," he muttered.

Hense held up a hand and Happling went quiet again. I didn't look at the big man. He didn't count. The secret to Big Red Happling was his boss.

She regarded me silently for a few moments. I didn't like holding her gaze; she was one of those confident people who were absolutely certain that everything they did, they did for the right reasons. I was pretty sure Colonel Janet Hense never woke up sweating after a dream about all the people she'd killed, never had that nauseous feeling in the pit of her stomach that ate at her resolve like acid, had never lain panting in a muddy puddle somewhere, terrified and ready and willing to sell whatever she had just to guarantee her survival. Me, I was used to all three, and her steady, unblinking gaze was like fucking fire on my skin.

Then she nodded curtly. "Captain," she said slowly, still studying me. "Cut Mr. Cates loose. Let him keep the weapon."

Happling shivered, as if her words had released him from some invisible bond. I wondered, briefly, if she was a psionic, too, though she was too old. As far as I knew, the SSF had only started testing for and taking away psionic-positives about twenty years ago. I expected them all to be about the age the terrible DPH trio had been, midtwenties, kids.

"Boss," he said slowly, his voice low and steady, "that is a fucking bad idea. This guy is not just some informer, some asset. He's Avery Cates. He's a cop killer."

Hense didn't look at him; she was still looking at me, and I hadn't moved an inch. I didn't know why, but I was sure that if I moved too soon, everything was going to hell. So we kept staring at each other. "I'm not aware of any paperwork on Mr. Cates, Captain. As far as I am aware, his name does not appear in the database associated with any open investigations. He is," she said with just the hint of a smile, "the very model of a good citizen." She finally turned her head slightly to look at him. "And the SSF takes citizenship very seriously."

The sound of ten knuckles cracking simultaneously came from Happling's pockets. "Boss, you know as well as I do that Marin wiped his jacket, deleted him from the DB, years ago. Why? I don't know. You don't know. But since it was Marin, it fucking *sucked,* whatever it was. And this piece of shit has just been careful since then. This whole goddamn building is aching to put one in his ear. And you're telling me to *cut him loose* and to *let him keep my weapon.*"

Happling was quivering with rage, his whole body shaking slightly. Marko took a step backward, and I didn't blame him. I couldn't see Happling's face, but I'd seen big cops go fucking crazy before, and I knew it wasn't fun to watch.

Hense was now staring at Happling. "That was an order, Captain," she said evenly. "I don't see you obeying it."

He twitched. When he whirled to face me, I put the gun on him reflexively, the violence of his body language ringing all my alarms. He jerked his left arm out stiffly and the blade slid into his hand. He stormed over to me in four steps and I kept the gun on him, pointed at his face, until he was looming over me, face purple, the skin around his bulging eyes taut. When he moved, I almost pulled the trigger on him, it was so fast. But all he did was flash the blade down through the wires tying my ankles to the chair. Like my wrists, my ankles were cut deeply, blood soaking into my shoes.

He came up and pointed the blade at my nose. "Do something I don't like, Cates, and I will gut you."

"That's not fair," I said as he turned away. "I can't imagine what it is you *do* like." He hesitated for a moment and then resumed his spot on the floor, snapping the blade back into his sleeve. He shook himself and produced his pack of cheap cigarettes, shaking two out into one paw and crushing them without preamble.

"All right," Hense said as I experimentally pulled myself into a squatting position, dropping the gun into my coat pocket. "Now that we're all fast friends, let's get a few things straight. I am in charge here. Mr. Marko, I am pulling you into my portfolio on a rolling basis. If you have a problem with that, file an IA report and go through channels. In the meantime, do what I say. Captain Happling, I expect no bullshit from you."

"No, sir," he said, sounding tired.

She turned to me as I slowly stood up, feeling shaky, my head pounding. "Mr. Cates, where are we going?"

I shook my head. "One thing at a time, Colonel," I

said. "Get us moving, and I'll tell you where we're headed when we're airborne."

"Mr. Cates, as you just pointed out, we're not likely to kill you. You are, apparently, necessary for our survival."

I put a grin on my face, trying to look as nonchalant and unconcerned as possible for someone who was bruised and covered in his own crusted blood and worried he might have a concussion. "I also don't want to be carried around like luggage, Colonel."

"And if I gave you my word?"

I made my smile wider with some effort. "I knew a guy once, a small-fry shylock out of the Bronx, sold info to a pair of System Pigs for a few years. They gave him their word he'd have some consideration because he was helping them out. Then one day they show up, take him out back of his own fucking flop, and put a bullet in his head. Walked away laughing about it." I shrugged. "Fuck your word."

Happling turned on me, face purple again. "You fucking call any cop a *pig* again, you piece of shit, and I'll—"

"Gut me, I heard," I said, heart pounding. "How about we fucking *stipulate* that and we can stop repeating ourselves?"

He stared at me for another moment, breathing roughly through his nose, and then turned away again.

"Let's get moving," Hense said.

Marko cleared his throat. He was pale and so unhappy it was coming off him in soft, yellow waves. "Colonel, I—"

"Mr. Marko, I doubt there is anything I care less about than what you think. Grab whatever gear you think might be useful. We may be headed places without reliable power or communications, so try to think of that. You've got two minutes. Happ," she said, producing her gun in a clinical way and snapping it open to view the chamber. "I'm not going to have problems with you, am I?"

He shook his head. "No, sir," he said calmly.

"Good," she said, snapping the gun shut and reholstering it. "On our way up, we'll need to hit an armory closet, so think about where the most convenient one is. Mr. Cates," she said, turning to face me, "I will phrase all of my orders as requests and make a show of considering your opinions, and although you do not value it I give you my *word* you will be given fair warning when I decide your usefulness is at an end. Good enough?"

I shrugged. There wasn't anything to say to that. I had no intention of being anywhere near her when she decided my fucking usefulness was at a fucking end. I needed her to get across the ocean, to get me out of New York. Past that, they were all on their own, as far as I was concerned. She wasn't any better than me. At least I was going to get Glee's revenge, my revenge — which, it turned out, was the fucking world's revenge, too. The colonel was just keeping me near her to save her own life. I didn't doubt she would cut off my limbs and carry me around on her back like a gimp for the rest of our miserable lives, if it came to that.

Marko had started stuffing things into a large black duffel, looking shaky and completely freaked out as he stepped around his dead partner. His eyes were small and dark in the midst of his hairy face. "Why are we in such a rush, Colonel?" he managed to croak out as he scooped a handful of red plastic things into the maw of the bag. "This is pretty fucking irregular."

Hense nodded. "It's been an irregular couple of days, Mr. Marko. We need to get out of the city before this situation explodes."

Marko opened his unhappy mouth to reply just as a shrieking alarm split the air, honking urgently. It repeated three times and then a neutral, artificial voice boomed out of nowhere. I was getting sick and tired of shells making announcements.

"Attention, all SSF Personnel. By order of DIA Marin, Authorization Code One-Niner-Charlie-Alpha, this facility has been placed in lockdown. All personnel are ordered to remain where they are until further notice. All air traffic has been restricted and must be passed personally through DIA Marin's office. Please contact your COs for further information. Attention..."

As the message repeated, its volume slowly decreased. Marko looked around from under his thick eyebrows. "Looks like it's too late," he said.

XV

DAY SIX: PUMPING OUT DEATH FROM MY PORES, AND THINGS WERE STARTING TO LOOK UP

"Oh, fuck," Hense muttered, cocking her head a little. It was the first time I'd seen her even mildly irritated, and I found it strangely disconcerting. System Cops were not supposed to get fucking stymied. Doors opened magically for them; hovers appeared out of the ether to pick them up; scores of Stormers in their headachy Obfuscation Kit that mirrored their surroundings on the fly and made them almost invisible to the naked eye rained down at their command. System Cops did *not* mutter *fuck* like other jackasses who got themselves into a scrape.

She glanced at Marko. "Keep packing. We're moving in one minute. Happ," she said, glancing at him. "Guns."

His eyes bright sparks of unhappiness in his hairy face,

Marko nodded and turned immediately, stepping past me without a glance. I leaned back against the nearest pile of equipment and looked at the colonel. "Got a cigarette?" I said. I'd been able to afford them over the last few years and I'd gotten used to it. The alarm was now just a persistent whisper in the background—you could tune it in if you wanted, or ignore it.

Hense didn't look at me. She reached into one pocket and produced a dented tin holder, tossing it at me in a perfect little arc. I popped it open and found a small silver lighter and, to my delight, ten perfect little pre-Unification cancer sticks, thirty fucking years old but preserved somewhere by some wonderful genius, then sold on the black market for five thousand yen apiece. I took out three, stuck one in my mouth and two in my pocket. I lit up and snapped the tin shut, tossing it back to her without saying a word. She didn't look up as she snatched it from the air and stuffed it back into her pocket.

"Mr. Marko?" she snapped.

"One *minute*," he called back, and I gave the kid some credit. He'd just seen his fellow Techie get shot in the face. Now he was giving her attitude. He was either one of those brain-damaged geniuses who could decode algorithms in his head but didn't understand how to breathe without coaching, or he had bigger balls than I'd imagined. Either way, I downgraded his survival chances from *possible* to *doomed*. One of the System Pigs was going to end up strangling him.

He came bustling back from the depths of his lab, dragging the bulging duffel behind him. "You expect me to head into the field without H-cells? Like we're going to run shit off static electricity by rubbing our goddamn hands together?"

Hense swept out her arm. "After you, Mr. Marko," she

said with exaggerated politeness that should have scared the hell out of him.

I inhaled smoke as the kid walked past me, glaring. I toyed with the idea of making a sudden move to see how he'd react, but I was too old and too tired for stuff like that. Besides, the first rule of bullshit like this was *get on the Techie's good side*. Happling was the man to cower behind when things got thick, but more often than not things got thick while you were standing on the wrong side of a door you couldn't open, or a system that was tracking you. The Techies always saved your ass.

I glanced after Marko. *If they wanted to,* I thought, moving a molar around with my tongue.

The colonel was staring at me. "Any time, Mr. Cates."

I exhaled, the smoke almost blue and so thick it seemed to cling to the air, like a film. I wondered if my little microbots liked it or if it irritated them, if they were beaming home for permission to kill their host.

Hense launched herself toward the door. I fell in behind her tiny frame, burning my cigarette as fast as I could, filling myself with poison and smiling. Everything hurt, but it was a *good* hurt—it hurt because I was moving again.

Outside the lab, the corridor was deserted, hidden strobes flashing in perfect rhythm. Happling was stomping back down the hall toward us. "Fucking closets have all been sealed. My clearance is no good."

Hense just breezed past him, and we fell in behind her. Happling's huge form radiated frustration and unhappiness. All the doors were perfectly hidden, disappeared into the walls and giving the illusion that the hall, white and unmarked, was perpetual and perfect. After the bedlam of cops on our way down to the lab, the emptiness was eerie.

Hense led us around a corner to a spot on the wall outlined in red paint, without any identifying signage or other indication what it represented. She stepped close to the wall and paused.

"Fuck," she hissed. "Mine, too."

We stood there for a moment. "I don't want to know," Happling said slowly, "what kind of emergency restricts access to fucking *majors* and higher. There are what, three hundred majors in the whole goddamn *System?*"

"Mr. Marko," I said, burning my fingers as I dragged on the cigarette, burning it down to a nub. "Your turn to shine."

Hense ticked her head toward me but didn't look at me. "Mr. Marko," she said in a steady voice, "can you open this?"

Marko looked from her to Happling and then, in a moment of desperation, at *me*. I just flicked my cigarette at the floor and shrugged. "Colonel," he said, "do I have it right that you want me to vandalize SSF property?"

I expected an explosion. Happling did, too, the way he rocked forward on his feet. But the tiny black woman remained perfectly still. "Mr. Marko, we have to get out of this building. The longer we remain here, the better the chances that Mr. Catcs's presence will be discovered. Once that happens, they will remove him from our control. Once *that* happens, you, Captain Happling, and I will *die*. Do you understand that?"

Marko swallowed and glanced at me. "Yes."

Happling reached out lazily and smacked the Techie on the back of the head. "Then open the fucking locker, asshole, and stop wasting time."

Marko glared at Happling and rubbed his head but

dragged his duffel toward the wall. "That is *not* necessary, Captain," he complained, dropping the bag and kneeling down to unzip it. He rummaged inside it for a bit, finally pulling out a slender silver tool. He stood up and ran his fingers—long, thin fingers—against the wall, grunting when he found some invisible seam. He stepped back and brought the tool up, jamming it forward and into the wall with another grunt. There was a brief bluish spark and the wall opened like a flower, two panels swinging open in slow motion, revealing a surprisingly deep locker filled with weapons and ammunition—handguns, shotguns, shredding rifles, and grenades. He turned back to us, flipping the tool into the air and catching it. I gave him a grin. The fucking Techies ran the System. We were all there on sufferance.

Happling reached in and pulled two shredders off the rack and tossed one to Hense. Shredding rifles were serious shit—big and heavy, they fired huge fragmenting rounds, thousands per minute, making a whining, keening noise that made you want to cover your ears and shake your head until it stopped. They cut people into neat little pieces but were a bear to control. Even the Stormers rarely carried them. Hense hefted hers in her hands for a moment.

"Damn," I said. "Expecting trouble?"

No one answered me. They didn't offer me a shredder or more ammo for the Roon I'd appropriated. I watched Happling and Hense fill their pockets and a sturdy-looking satchel with clips, and then Happling swung the bag over his shoulder, immediately making it look tiny. Hense jerked her chin over her shoulder. "Let's go."

"Where to?" Happling asked, slamming one of the dense, bricklike clips into the shredder. "Nothing's gonna be cleared off the roof, boss."

"Street Field, First and Forty-eighth. Wait."

She looked me up and down. I surveyed myself with my good eye; the left one was slowly sealing itself. I was blood and spit and dust. Mostly blood.

"Give him your coat, Happ. He's going to attract eyes."

I smiled. "I'm pretty, I know."

Happling cursed and dropped the satchel. "Want me to give him a shave, too? A massage? My fucking gold badge?" He tore the heavy coat from his shoulders and tossed it at me. Snatching it out of the air, I pulled it on over my own coat. It went down to my ankles, but I rolled up the sleeves and it didn't look too bad.

Happling looked *bigger* out of the coat, his shoulder holster crowded by his arms. He squinted at me. "Nothing I can do about his face, boss. I think it's actually improved by the pounding, you ask me."

"Go," was all Hense said, her voice taut with that tone of command really dangerous cops had. Happling spun around, snatched up the bag, and we were off, hustling after the big man toward the elevators. I had to walk fast to keep up, feeling every cigarette I'd ever smoked.

"Elevators won't run for you," Happling said over his shoulder, "if the lockers rejected your badge."

Marko had fallen in beside me. "They'll run."

I turned to look at him. I loved the fucking Techies. "Now why," I said, just to make trouble, "would you have a vector set up for beating all these access restrictions, I wonder?"

His jaw tightened. "None of your business."

I nodded, feeling jolly. I was a valuable commodity, I had a bodyguard and a retinue, and I was going to Paris in fucking style. I was half blind, covered in my own blood and puke, pumping out death from my pores, and things were starting to look up.

Good as his word, Marko stepped forward as we approached the elevators, pulled a box about the size of his fist from his bag as it dropped to the floor, and fiddled with it, making various microgestures with his fingers. He frowned down at the box.

"*Fuck,* you have to be a goddamn *director level* to ride the fucking *elevators,*" he said, sounding astounded. I started to get the loose, heart-pounding feeling, complete with rust in my throat, that always preceded something bad. Marko continued to wave his long fingers over the brick. I moved my eyes from his slim frame to Happling's gorilla body and caught him staring murder at me with his fluorescent eyes. I lingered on him just long enough to show my balls and glanced up at the elevator's indicator lights.

"Take it easy, Mr. Marko," I said, rust flooding my mouth, hands clenching. "Looks like your job's half done. Someone's coming down to *us.*"

Hense's reaction was immediate. "Step aside, Mr. Marko," she spat, pulling her weapon as Happling dropped his bag of fun and did the same. I let them take up a crisscross position in front of the doors, their lines of fire carefully chosen.

"Boss," Happling said, sounding urgent.

"Not now," the colonel snapped.

Happling's jaw clenched. "*Now* is a good time to tell you," he gritted out as if chewing rocks, "that I'm not killing any cops."

XVI

DAY SIX: I'VE BEEN PROMOTED

For whatever obscure security reasons, the elevator indicator wasn't labeled; it was just a long string of LEDs sinking from the ceiling to the floor. The bottom three lit up red, one by one, dripping down toward us. I pulled my stolen Roon from my pocket and held it ready, but I was willing to let the two cops take the brunt of whatever was coming out of the cab. Marko pushed himself as flat as possible against the wall, clutching his bag of tricks to his chest and looking ready to shit his pants and run, in that order, at a moment's notice.

The bottom light glowed warmly and the doors snapped open, and it was difficult to stay still—after being beaten half to death in the Blank Room, my brain chemistry was running wild, dumping adrenaline and sleep into my blood—but I managed it with some effort.

The elevator was empty. We all stood still for a moment, thumbs up our asses. The adrenaline turned into vinegar inside me, curdling my stomach. I looked over at Marko, who had closed his eyes.

"You're one of those fucking geniuses I keep hearing about, aren't you?"

The kid opened his eyes one at a time and then visibly sagged, his whole body going jelly. He shut his eyes again and looked like he was going to throw up. I slipped my gun back into my pocket and stepped over to him, catching him under the armpits as his legs gave way.

"Deep breath," I said, trying to make my voice friendly. "You've had a rough hour or so."

He pushed at me weakly. "Fuck you," he said hoarsely.

I laughed and let him drop. "Ask the captain to tune you up a little," I said, turning away. "It's a wonderful fucking tonic."

"Shut up," Hense said in a distracted voice. "Good work, Mr. Marko. But we have to get moving."

"That was too easy," Marko said weakly, pulling himself up. "All I did was issue a standard reset and it just came. That shouldn't have worked."

"Why do it, then?"

He shrugged without looking at me. "It's always step one. Just in case it works."

Fucking Techies. I stood next to Happling and stared into the empty cab, white and clean. None of us moved.

"It's your fucking building," I said.

Out of the corner of my eye, I saw Hense turn to look at me, but I didn't look at her.

"Move," she spat, and stepped into the car. Happling followed, grabbing me by the shoulder and shoving me ahead of him.

"Mr. Marko!" Hense shouted.

The kid appeared in front of us, scratching at his beard. "I don't trust things I didn't make happen. Shit does not just happen."

I was standing behind him, but I could feel Happling's grin like a change in air pressure. "Kid, keep standing there like a piece of shit and I'll show you something else that does not *just happen*."

I imagined Happling's grin, feral, his teeth yellow. I could feel him next to me. He *wanted* to fuck the kid up. Marko sensed it, too, hustling into the elevator, looking around as if he expected it to sprout spikes from the ceiling and walls and start to contract on us.

Hense gestured hesitantly, but the elevator responded immediately, the doors snapping shut. "We're going out the back through the loading docks," she said. "They won't be abandoned, but they should be pretty sparse."

"Boss," Happling said slowly, not liking the taste of his words. "What if we get stopped? I'm not here to shoot cops."

"I thought that was what I was here for," I said, failing to match the big cop's amazing grin.

No one said anything to that. There was a momentary sick sense in my stomach, and then a light *ding* from the elevator.

"Happ, you're point. Marko and Cates after him." Hense turned those pretty, static eyes on me, making me regret my smart comments. I didn't want this woman to ever stare at me for any period of time. The feeling I'd seen her before swept through me like a flame, burning out as fast as it had come upon me. "Mr. Cates, try any bullshit and I will start investigating how badly you can be hurt without being killed."

She turned away before I could say anything back. "Happ," she said, "I won't order you to shoot cops. But if you obstruct *my* way out of here, I will shoot *you*. Understood?"

As the doors swooshed open, the big cop's jaws bunched, and then he was leading us out of the elevator. The kid was on his heels, looking terrified, and then me, a fake expression of bland disinterest in place. My game face. I was half blind, felt like something important had been broken inside me, and found myself in a building filled with people who would happily shoot me on sight—but I had to be Avery Cates. I was famous. I had to act like it.

We turned a corner of bald cinder blocks and were on the docks, where the grimy garbage hovers backed in every day to cart away tons and tons of garbage for dumping over in Jersey. It smelled like a toilet and all the concrete gleamed with an unhealthy shine. Loader Droids idled in the bay, humming softly, waiting for the next delivery or pickup. Weak daylight shone from the dock entrance a few dozen feet away. I could hear the Vids echoing an announcement in the distance, but I couldn't make out the words.

Behind us, the second elevator bay dinged softly.

The two cops whirled, Happling's satchel hitting the ground and Hense's coat swirling around her. I felt slow next to them, crouching and bringing my gun out, arm aching and head throbbing. Marko just stood there, a fucking target, blinking in confusion.

The second elevator split open and disgorged two men.

I recognized the first one; it had been only an hour or so since he'd expressed his disapproval of me outside the elevator, but I imagined I could already see signs of my little buggers eating away at him—circles under his eyes, a sheen of sweat like his body was trying to bake something out of itself. His dark hair was still plastered to his forehead as if he never thought to push it out of his eyes. He had put on his coat, and stepped forward with his hands in his pockets, shoulder holsters bulging under each arm. His tiny eyes were set close together, giving him a permanent squint.

"We're under lockdown orders, Colonel," he said in his weedy voice. "I'm shocked and dismayed to think you might disobey that command in order to smuggle a prisoner out of the building."

"I've been promoted," I said, smiling. "I've got this neat new coat and everything."

He pointed at me without looking at me. "Shut the fuck up, you fucking monkey. You think you got tuned up? You think you got hurt, your fucking rights violated? Asshole, we haven't begun *violating* you. How many cops have you killed?"

Thirty-three, I thought darkly. *Including the Stormers outside Westminster Abbey.* I kept my smile on my face, but my free hand formed a fist so hard my knuckles popped.

He licked his lips and shrugged. "You're not taking Cates out of the building, *sir.*"

His buddy was behind him, arms folded, a thick-chested guy with spindly legs that looked like they belonged to someone else. Neither of them moved for their guns. Hense and Happling relaxed a little, putting their weapons

up. They were going to stand there and piss on each other's shoes all fucking day, but no one was going to shoot.

I made a show of relaxing, too, letting my gun drop to
my side, out of immediate sight. I kept my one good eye
dancing from spot to spot.

"Do you idiots know what's happening here?" Hense
said levelly. "How you passed your CIS tests I'll never
fucking know, since you're dragging your goddamn
knuckles around bothering me. Lieutenant, get back
to your post or I'll break you down so hard you won't
just be reassigned to Chengara, you'll be serving *slop* at
Chengara."

The lieutenant's expression, which appeared to be
one thin beat per minute away from unconscious,
didn't change. I ran my eye over his friend, who was a
square-shaped kid, bloodshot eyes staring balefully at
Hense and Happling. No one was paying any attention
to me. Typical System Pigs—I was irrelevant. I was just
a shithead from the street they'd get around to shooting
when it fucking suited them. I cleared my mind, imagining snow, thick yellowed drifts of it falling silently, that
nothing could penetrate.

"Colonel, I think I speak for all of us, every cop in this
building, when I say *go fuck yourself.* You've broken a
dozen SSF regs just by not posting Cates to the system.
Now you're taking him from the building without posting
him. These are Class A violations, Colonel, as far as the
Worms are concerned. You're going to get burned for this
as it is, and I think if anyone has to worry about—"

Feeling peaceful, I took my moment. It didn't require
any theatrics or fancy moves: amateurs got caught up in
diving, jumping, making it look like something you'd

see on the Vids. Wasted effort—bad for your aim and your chances of staying alive. I raised my weapon calmly, sighted on the lieutenant, and squeezed the trigger, putting a surprisingly small hole in his forehead. Then I moved my arm and brought the cop behind him on my right into sight and squeezed the trigger again.

Thirty-five, I thought without pride, with just a dusty feeling, my whole body aching.

Then Happling was crashing into me, growling like an animal. The gun was stripped from my hand before I could bring it around, and my head did a little drumbeat against the concrete floor. His fist crashed into my mouth, breaking some teeth with a sharp, lancing pain and sending my head back into the concrete. The familiar taste of my own tired blood filled my mouth, and for a second I thought, *Do it, do it, you goddamn animal.*

Then I could hear Hense's voice, somehow cutting through Happling's wordless howling.

"Captain!"

One word, but Happling froze, his fist raised over me, my blood dripping off his fingers. His face, bloated and red, quivered as he hovered there, crouched above me. I tried to suck air and got a thick mass of blood instead. I burst into a spasm of choking coughs, spewing blood and snot everywhere as I twitched, little red spots appearing in front of me each time.

"You kill him, you kill all of us," she said, her voice expressionless. "You want to kill yourself, crawl over there and shoot yourself in the head."

Happling and I stared at each other. His whole body was shaking. Finally he tore himself away from me, rolling away and springing to his feet. He stood with his back to me and cracked his neck loudly, rolling his head around. "He doesn't keep the fucking gun," he said, biting off the words one at a time. I imagined hell, my final resting place, and saw Captain Nathan Happling, beating me forever.

"The fuck I don't," I gurgled, my words soft. "You still don't know where you're going, asshole."

He didn't turn around. "Eventually," he said, "I get to kill you."

I pulled myself into a sitting position, blood dripping from my chin onto Happling's coat. Hense stepped between us; I could feel her anger, but she was locked down and perfectly calm, her eyes dead and cold. I didn't like looking at her eyes. Every time I looked at her, I thought of cops I'd killed. I turned and looked at Marko, who was staring at me, eyes wide. I gave him my bloody grin and he looked away, finding the floor suddenly fascinating. My mouth ached in time with my pulse, pain fresher than everything else.

"Let's move," she said.

We moved. In silence we left the cooling bodies of the two cops behind and slipped out into the street. Which was nearly deserted, except for packs of Stormers hustling here and there, the occasional officer talking into the air and listening, badge exposed, to his earbud, and a civilian or two running for their lives. As we paused for a moment, dazzled by the gray light as fat hunks of yellow snow fell silently around us, a well-dressed woman ran full speed into Happling, bounced off him, and landed hard on her ass, staring up at us. She was pretty, of course, a blonde in a bright red, expensive-looking coat, her face sporting the overly smooth, expressionless look of the totally reconstructed, a rich girl who hadn't liked the face the cosmos had given her.

A moment later three Stormers skidded to a halt around her, gave us the once-over, and then took her by the arms and brought her to her feet. Hense and Happling had *cop* written all over them, and I guessed that was enough for the Stormers, who'd spent their entire adult lives getting their balls kicked by officers.

"Sorry, ma'am," one of them buzzed through his helmet speaker. "Emergency curfew."

They carted her off without another word, her blank face staring back at us until they'd turned the corner, where by the sound of it a hover idled, slowly filling with all the citizens who'd been too slow or too reluctant to get off the streets.

Hense started off east, heading up the block as she clipped her shiny gold badge to the front of her coat. "Keep your head down," she said to me in a tense whisper. "And resist...the...urge...to speak."

I was one solid ache, the rhythm of it mesmerizing. My heart would beat, and then my whole body would pulse with a muffled, diffuse pain, and as we walked I landed on my right foot with each pulse, imagining the whole side of my face inflating and deflating with each step. The empty streets were eerie. There was trash everywhere, just random things — paper, foam cups, a single black dress shoe. It looked as if there'd been quite a little dustup when the SSF had declared an emergency and ordered the streets clear. Hense set a killer pace, and I struggled to keep up; I hadn't eaten in a long time, a time spent getting acquainted with the System Pigs' newest interrogation techniques, which had turned out to be exactly like their old ones, only a little more enthusiastic.

The ruined building just off the river loomed up over us, big swathes of it nothing but gaping holes, exposed guts, all that glass that once made it shine in the sun shattered and jagged. It was like a huge box, thin and square, ugly as hell. It had taken a beating in the Unification Riots and no one had ever bothered to do anything about it. I stared at it as we ignored a hastily constructed checkpoint—so far no one had wanted to mess with a colonel—and crossed the last street, its pavement broken and uneven, before the river. The hover field was a small, fenced-in affair guarded by a couple of Crushers who eyed Hense in terror as we approached.

I looked over her at the field itself. It wasn't well populated; just a few sad-looking hovers, rusty and dented, remained.

"I'm sorry, uh, Colonel," one of the Crushers, an elderly gent of at least forty, his face gaunt and his uniform almost comically big on him, said. "We're under orders to keep these bricks on the ground."

To my surprise, Hense stopped and visibly collected herself. She glanced at me and then at Big Red Happling, and then looked back at the Crusher, who didn't enjoy her attention at all.

"By whose orders?"

The Crusher managed to look embarrassed. "Director Marin's, Colonel."

She nodded and took one step forward. "Director Marin is not here," she said in a cool, level voice. "And cannot hurt you. I *am* here, and can. Call it in. But don't try to stop us."

The Crusher looked at her, then at the rest of us, and then spun around looking for his partner, who had wisely retreated back into the little shack provided for them. "Shit," he muttered. "You won't even get out of the city, Colonel. I mean——"

"Excuse me!"

We all turned, startled. I saw Happling's arms twitch for his gun and then stop as we all watched an elegantly dressed figure crossing the street. He was a tall, broad-chested young man, his face chiseled and his skin clear—serious, serious surgery, I thought, with some genetic workups to boot. Expensive shit. His outfit, which was pink and white, was cut expertly and moved easily as he trotted up to us. The two cops, I thought, were too shocked to do anything.

"Please," he said with a smile. "I am willing to pay—handsomely—for a ride out of the city." He produced a credit dongle from his pocket. "Please—I have a family. There are rumors—disease, those animals downtown again. I am——"

Happling stepped forward, crowding him and making him step back. "Did you just offer to bribe us, you piece of shit?"

The man's confident smile drained off his face. "No! No! Of course not," he said quickly, putting up his hands. "I was just——"

The big cop slapped him across the face, moving so fast there was no time to react. The gorgeous man's head whipped back instantly, his lower lip split open, blood running in a weak trickle down his chin. His expression told me he'd never been hit before. In his entire life. He wasn't even afraid, he was fucking *amazed*. And I thought, *Who*

grows up without being hit? How rich did you have to be?
I wanted a number. I wanted *statistics.*

"You stupid fuck," Happling said, turning away.

He marched past us toward the field. The Crusher
stepped aside as the bigger man approached, and without
saying anything more we followed him onto the field to
a decrepit hover that had once been silver but was now a
charred sort of gray. It was a small, ancient model, but
designed for long trips over water. Happling climbed in
without a word, and we followed him, one by one.

"Ah, hell," Marko muttered as Happling and Hense
disappeared into the cockpit. "It smells like *shit* in here."

I had to agree with the kid's delicate nose, though my
own — probably broken — wasn't working too well. There
were seats, however, a great luxury, and I sank into one
with a snort of pain. Nothing seemed to be working right.
It was as if I had a million tiny fractures, all waiting for
the right moment to snap.

My hosts didn't waste any time. The hatch snapped
shut, the cabin pressurized, and the roar of displacement,
somewhat muffled, sprang up outside. With a lurch we
were off the ground. I turned to look out the tiny window
by my seat and saw the two Crushers standing there, paralyzed. I knew they were wondering who to be more afraid
of, Dick Marin, who they imagined was a single man in
an office far away, or these crazy cops who were right
there, who'd been close enough to touch.

"Mr. Cates." Hense's voice filled the cabin. "Where are
we going?"

I hesitated just a moment, but there was no margin in
keeping it a secret. "Paris," I said. "There's a beacon. In
my nanobots or some shit."

As we rose higher and higher, I heard Marko muttering darkly to himself as he got settled in, bringing out an endless array of devices and setting them up fussily around his seat. I kept my eyes trained out the window, watching as the city spread out below us. We floated over downtown, and instead of the serene emptiness we'd just left, there were masses of people, smoke, and other SSF hovers, most with the thin silver threads pouring out of them that meant Stormers being deployed. Downtown hadn't paid any fucking attention to any curfew and wasn't going to sit idly by while everyone died of some mysterious disease.

I wondered if there'd be anything left to save, if I ever had the choice.

XVII

DAY SEVEN: FREEZING OVER
THE WORLD AROUND US

Mentally I relaxed. After an hour or so, the world zooming past us at incredible speed, it was peaceful, and I had the opportunity to really analyze and enjoy each and every ache and cut I'd recently acquired. I probed each one carefully, savoring the pain. I pushed my tongue into my broken teeth, I pressed fingers against my broken ribs, I tried to pry my swollen eyelids apart. The dim, humming interior of the cabin felt like privacy, and I was so tired I almost dozed off in the seat. Then Marko cursed softly, dropping one of his tools onto the floor of the cabin, and I sat up with a jolt of pain through my back, cursing myself for falling asleep like a fucking rookie.

"So you're really Avery Cates, huh?"

I looked over at the kid. He'd connected a series of fist-sized black boxes together with cables, one of which ran to a small, handheld screen. He was staring at the screen while he manipulated some switches on one of the boxes, the sick green light of the screen making his face look rotten.

"Sure," I said, lisping painfully. "And you're no one I've ever heard of."

He didn't look up, his eyes dancing, his fingers moving gracefully, like independent creatures on the ends of his hands. "You really kill all the people they say you did?"

I looked out the window at swirling clouds. After a moment I said, "Maybe half."

"They all deserve it?"

I thought about it. There'd been a time when I'd been reasonably sure everyone I'd killed—mistakes aside—had deserved it, on some level. Now I wasn't so sure. It was different, somehow, when you weren't being hired for it, when you were doing it for your own agenda.

"Most," I finally said. "What are you doing?"

"Analyzing the signals from our friends the microscopic bots. Seeing what I can figure out, trying to reverse them." I had no peripheral vision left, but I felt his eyes shift onto me. "You really know Ty Kieth? *The* Ty Kieth? Who wired up Amsterdam six years ago?"

"I knew him. He's an annoying little shit, but then all you Tech boys are." I considered the persistent ringing in my ears and wondered if Happling had shaken something loose. "He did good work for me, though."

"He's a genius," Marko said without embarrassment. "A real-life genius. Up there with Amblen and Squalor, you ask me. Criminal, of course, beyond redemption, like every other pre-Uni genius, right? Squalor goes and starts the Electric Church, his pal Amblen's holed up in The Star, doing lord knows what." The Star was an island fortress off Manhattan, all that was left of some monument or statue or other waste of time. Rumor was that not even the SSF could get into it because of all the illegal tech Amblen had built into it, but I knew what those sorts of rumors were worth. "Kieth's number thirty-four on the SSF list, did you know that? Was fifty-three before he met you. You advanced his career quite a bit."

"Always glad to help."

"His name's all over this shit. It's like he *wanted* people to know it was him."

I turned my head to look at him, my neck making a gravelly popping sound. "Wanted you all to know it was him in the two days before you choke on your own blood and die?" I considered. "Why in hell would he do that?"

He looked back down at his little screen. "Mr. Cates, not *everything* will be dead. No vector for the Monks, you know." He leaned forward slightly, peering at his little screen. "There's another signal emanating from you, Mr. Cates. It's being touched right now by several encrypted fingers."

I closed my eyes in order to really revel in the aching that suffused my whole body. "Subdermal chip. My people use it to track me down if any of my fans manage to get the drop on me. Some of my friends in Europe are being notified of my approach."

"You're just that important, huh?"

If I'd felt any better, I might have leaped up to twist his nose a little, but I was too tired, so I let it slide. "Yen buys you a lot, kid. And I've got yen coming out my *ass,* thanks to your boss."

"Colonel Hense?"

I opened my good eye and trained it on him. He was serious though, and wasn't even looking at me, his piano-player fingers waving gently like grass underwater. "No," I said, closing my eye and sinking back down into the soft red ache that was my body. "Director Marin. We're old friends."

A noise from the cockpit made me open my eye again, and then Hense was in the cabin, a tiny black wind freezing over the world around us. She moved gracefully despite the vibration, and I admired her as she picked her way to the seat opposite mine, sinking into it and strapping herself in with one smooth movement. I kept my eye on her as she reached into her coat and pulled out her flask, liking her trim little figure and her soft, perfect skin. It didn't look like anyone had landed a blow on her in years. Some of the System Pigs, they were almost supernatural when they got going.

She poured a blast into the collapsible cup and handed it across to me. "Mr. Marko?"

He nodded without looking up at her. "I've got the signal and I can track it to its source. It's pinging the nanos in Mr. Cates about five times a second. I can't yet see what information it's getting back, but I can see Kieth's name pretty clearly. I can get us to the source of that beacon signal."

I stared down at the evil liquid in the little cup, thinking that some liquor would probably kill me in my present precarious state of health. And I wasn't a young man anymore. I was pushing thirty-three. I was ancient.

"Mr. Cates," Hense said, her voice as neutral and controlled as always. "This is fair warning: I'm considering asking Captain Happling to come in here and hog-tie you so we can carry you around like luggage. This will prevent you from acting against our wishes again, as you did back

in the loading bay. It occurs to me that your little germs
can keep us all healthy just as easily if you're bound and
gagged. In short, Mr. Cates, I think we need to renegoti-
ate our arrangement."

I was still eyeing the cup, my stomach already curling
up into a frightened ball at the thought of drinking its
contents, but I was onstage, in the unblinking spotlight
of Colonel Hense's regard, and I knew I had to start to
dance. Stomach flipping, I raised the little cup to my lips
and knocked the burning gin back, forcing my spasming
throat to accept it. My whole body flared up into sensible
protest, but I kept my eyes blank, my smile easy, and held
out the little cup for a refill, like the cold-blooded bastard
everyone thought I was. It was always better to be the
most terrible person in the room. Always.

She studied me for a moment, and then leaned forward
to pour.

"You don't look dumb, Colonel, so I'm going to assume the good captain has been giving you some really
bad advice," I said, snatching the cup back as soon as she
was done to conceal the way it shook in my hand. "Sure,
you can find Kieth. But Kieth never masterminded this.
Kieth is a hired hand. I needed you to get me to Paris, but
once we touch down, Colonel, I don't need you anymore.
You, on the other hand, need me. You need me to get to
the real architects of this clusterfuck, and you need me
just to stay alive for the necessary extra few hours it'll
take to sort all this out." I downed my second drink by
sheer force of will, swallowed my own stomach as it tried
to claw its way up my throat, and leaned forward. "I don't
need *you*. You can tie me up, sure, you can instruct that
gorilla you've trained to bop me on the head whenever I

get unruly, but in that scenario you've got me unhappy and determined to be rid of you the moment we hit Paris. Right?" I shook my head, hoping the cold sweat that had blossomed all over my body wasn't totally obvious. "No, Colonel, we're still partners."

She didn't blink or react in any overt way. I tried to remember if she'd ever blinked, and couldn't.

"Hey, Colonel?" Marko said suddenly.

She held up one small hand between them, not taking her eyes off me. I dug the nails of my left hand, hidden from her, into my palm to try and scare up a new jolt over the smear of steady pain that had enveloped me, trying to keep my head clear. She stared at me. I was getting mighty sick of the staring, which was Hense's prime tactic. I imagined a lot of people broke under that stare in Blank Rooms.

"Colonel," Marko tried again, tentative but determined. She flashed that hand out again, and he shut his mouth with a click.

We were all silent for a moment, the hover humming beneath us, and I thought I could feel her considering her options as she looked me over. I had her over a barrel in a sense, and she knew it. Maybe Happling and his big shovels for hands could hang on to me, but maybe not. And maybe if we worked together I'd shave valuable days off her trip. An extra couple of days roaming around might mean coming back to an entire East Coast eaten by these things. A week might mean North America gone.

She cocked her head and regarded me. I held her gaze as sweat dripped into my eyes, digging my nails in as hard as I could while she just sat there, completely still. Then, without warning, she straightened up. "Your terms, then, for *partnership?*"

I was ready. "Two things, Colonel, and that's it. One, I am going to kill every last person involved with this. Someone put this fucking hex on *me* and I plan to make them eat it, okay? No one is going to try and stop me from making whoever it is eat a bullet. Okay?"

She kept up the stare for a moment and then nodded. "As long as it doesn't interfere with cleaning up this mess, Mr. Cates. If I need someone alive in order to stop this from spreading further, your chances of killing them will be severely reduced."

I considered this, my whole body starting to shiver, my muscles twitching in a complicated dance that rippled through me on an obscure schedule. Gripping the armrest with my free hand, I sat forward, stiffening my body and hunching over to hide the reaction. "I can live with that, as long as it's understood that my revenge is deferred, not forbidden."

She nodded. "All right. Two?"

I shrugged my eyebrows. "I walk away after it's all said and done. We're probably going to die, Colonel Hense, but if by some miracle we *don't* end up watching each other be eaten alive from the inside out, I don't want a goddamn bullet in the back."

Her eyes shifted up over my shoulder and stayed there for an uncomfortable amount of time. Marko leaned forward urgently into the frame my working eye offered me.

"Colonel! There's a signal—"

"All right, Mr. Cates," Hense said, bringing her eyes back to my face and extending a hand. There was, to my surprise, a subtle smile in her eyes, and I had the bizarre feeling she *liked* me. "We have an understanding, and I give you my word that your wishes will be observed, assuming my stipulations. You help us track down whoever orchestrated this. You stick by us at all times to ensure our health and well-being. You get to kill whoever you deem responsible for this mess unless I ask you politely to wait, and you walk away if we happen to survive. Agreed?"

I took her hand, Marko panting in impatience behind us. Her skin was warm and dry, soft, the tendons beneath the skin taut and powerful. I liked touching her. You didn't touch anyone in the System, not unless you were trying to choke the life out of them or something, or at least not unless you were going to *try* and choke the life out of them. I was reluctant to pull away but let her extract her hand without protest.

"Yes, Mr. Marko?" she said, still looking at me.

"A signal, Colonel," he said, touching the brick. "It's SSF, encrypted, and there's a lot of traffic."

She frowned. "And your analysis?"

"I think—"

The hover shuddered, seemed to jump under us as if hitting an invisible bump in the air, and then went dark and dead, all the vibration gone, the three of us plunged into opaque, total darkness for a second. For one heartbeat it was like floating in a void, and Marko's voice drifted to me through the perfect silence, the perfect dark.

"—we're fucked."

XVIII

DAY SEVEN: LITTERED THE SPACE AROUND US LIKE SULLEN MONUMENTS

You never get the easy way, I thought as the emergency lights flickered on, bathing us in a weak green glow. Everything tilted wildly. Hense, too small for the restraints, flew up and around and saved herself from smashing into the ceiling by grabbing my arm, her grip a painful vise on my wrist as her weight yanked me against the chair's restraints, almost choking me. Marko grunted as he slapped against his own restraints, but his chain of black boxes flew up and dashed against the roof, making dull, heavy noises. From somewhere outside the cabin a tearing sound replaced the muffled humming that had embraced us. As Hense flapped above me like some sort of human kite, I could see flashes of her gold badge.

Happling's voice, tiny and small, buzzed from somewhere above me.

"Boss? You all strapped in back there? I don't know

what the fuck is going on. The stick's dead, I have no control. Repeat, no control."

"You're busted," Marko gritted out through clenched teeth, his hands white-knuckled on the armrests. "They remote-disabled the brick. Standard operating procedure when an SSF vehicle is stolen."

"Fucking hell," Hense said with zero emotion, her voice strained, her eyes on mine. "You hear that, Happ?"

"Copy. Tell Mr. Fucking Wizard that would have been fucking useful fucking *hours* ago, then send the stupid little fuck up here to see what he can do."

"Ever hot-wire a brick, Marko?" Hense said, her voice sounding calm and unconcerned, as if she experienced fucking free fall once a day to stay sharp.

The kid looked like he was smiling. "I can take this piece of shit apart and rebuild it," he spat, one hand working at the chair restraints. "How much time do I have?"

"Happ?"

There was a delay, during which Marko freed himself and almost went shooting off to a broken neck before catching himself. He began doggedly climbing upward to the cockpit, hand over hand, using the seatbacks. Then Happling's voice buzzed above me again. "Four minutes forty-six until we'll be too low and too fast to recover."

I heard Marko curse. "Tight ship you're running here, Colonel," I said.

"Shut the fuck up," she said, her dead mass making me feel like my arm was being pulled from its socket. "Do you have anything useful to offer?"

"My job description with this endeavor doesn't include flying the fucking hover, Colonel," I said. "Got any emergency packs on this tub?"

Happling's voice buzzed from her coat again. "We're over the fucking Atlantic Ocean, jackass," he hissed. "If you want to kill yourself and all of us with you, please find a quicker way."

The tearing noise was getting louder, and the vibration made everything jump and sizzle in front of me. I looked up at Hense. I'd never met anyone in the System who was that calm when death was all around—except Monks. I was terrified, holding my shit together by some thin miracle, panic like a bubble inside me expanding and pushing against my control. But Hense, she just hung on to me and looked down at me, her face serene. Suddenly I wanted to be that sure of myself.

The lights flickered and went out. I thought, *Fuck, not in the dark.*

The lights came back on, and then Happling's voice was barking again. "Hang on, Mr. Wizard here thinks he can get the displacers back online but I'll have to dead-stick, so it's going to be rough."

"It's *going to be* rough?" I muttered. I looked up at Hense. "You got a good grip?"

She didn't answer immediately, as if seriously considering the question, and then nodded once.

The tearing sound now became a scream that hurt my ears, and the sensation of being sucked up out of my seat was replaced by one of being pushed down into it by a huge invisible hand. Hense came crashing down, half on top of me and half in the aisle, letting a soft grunt escape. As if by magic, the normal gravity of the hover was restored. I celebrated by leaning forward, putting my head down between my knees, and puking up a thin gruel of stringy phlegm.

The vibration snapped back twice as bad, jittering me up and down in my seat and shaking loose anything not welded in place. Marko's bag of tricks started burping up its contents, which jumped around the cabin like living things. Hense pulled herself into her seat and strapped herself in again more tightly. Before I could say anything to her, the hover flipped over and I was being sucked out of my seat again, the straps cruelly digging into my shoulders, whatever rancid blood I had left inside me rushing to my head.

"Hang on!" Happling's tiny voice shouted. "This ain't gonna be pretty!"

Turning my head wasn't easy; the invisible hand didn't like it and pushed back, hard and smothering. Hense was being pulled out of the seat slowly but irresistibly, her body just too damn small for the restraints to be of much assistance. Slowly, fighting for each inch, I got my arm extended toward her and took hold of her lapel, digging my bony fingers into the material and trying to exert some downward force on her.

The noise became a wall of sound, impossible to discern individual parts, like god tearing the universe apart. My stomach started doing flips and I realized we were in a spin, gravity jumping from top to bottom over and over again. Something heavy and solid thunked into my head and I barely noticed, the new pain swept away on the river of my other discomforts.

Then everything went quiet and still. The cabin stopped shivering and resolved into a solid room again, Hense and I dropped snugly back into the seats, and aside from a tinny screeching noise, it was peaceful. I blinked, staring at Hense, who stared back at me with something close to amazement on her face.

I realized the screeching noise was Happling screaming in the cockpit a second or two before we smacked down into the earth.

It was common knowledge that the SSF had only one factory still building hovers. It was automated and dated to sometime just after Unification, located somewhere in fucking Indiana or some shit like that, the middle of nowhere, not a city left for hundreds of miles in any direction. Droids churned out hovers from raw materials, and the hovers were perfect—not a single seam, not a single loose bolt, 100 percent operational upon delivery and built to fucking last. Which was good, because the SSF had been hot-fixing that single plant for twenty fucking years, making repairs as needed but unable, or for some reason unwilling, to build a new goddamn plant. You had to admit, Droids took away every damn job there was, but they built some high-quality hovers.

We must have hit the ground going about three or four hundred miles an hour, the shock of it swirling up through me, shoving my organs into new configurations and smoothing my hair briskly, and then we bounced, everything going still and silent again for about five seconds, when we hit again. The shuddering resumed, along with a completely new noise that sounded like we were stuck in some giant's throat and he was trying to clear us, an almost wet-sounding roar in time with the brain-swelling shaking. But the goddamn hover held together. It went on and on, longer than I thought possible, longer than I could stand, until I realized I was screaming, too, just pushing my voice out so it could be swept away in that maelstrom as if I hadn't made any noise at all.

Slowly, things scaled back. The noise became merely unbearably loud, the shaking became just turbulence, my own scream became audible and I let it die, my throat burning. I could feel the momentum of the brick, a coherent force again. We were spinning lazily, grinding against the earth but slowing down steadily. My hand was still clinging to Hense's coat so tightly my knuckles hurt, and I looked at her. To my amazement she smiled, her teeth white and perfect, the product of decent medical care.

"Mr. Cates," she said, her voice for the first time a little unsteady, "you were fucking *useless* during that."

There was a crash and then Marko rolled into the cabin covered in dust and sporting a deep gash on his forehead that spat blood at an alarming rate. He stumbled to his knees and managed to stop himself more or less upright.

"Anyone alive back here? That man," he continued without waiting for an answer, "is a fucking maniac. He *laughed* the whole way down, like this was *fun*."

"Fucking pussy," Happling's tinny voice chortled from Hense's coat. "Fucking pussy was *praying* in here. To *god* or something."

With a loud groan and final shudder, the hover ground to a stop.

"Thank fucking *god*," Marko muttered.

Hense was up in a flash, striding forward. "Happ? You all right?"

"Fine," Happling shouted back. "I think the pilot's the only one *supposed* to survive a crash in this tub."

*   *   *

Paris. Like Newark a ghost town, except bigger, I thought. "I'm fine, too," I said, forcing myself to unstrap and stand up, my legs shaking and my head swimming. "Thanks for fucking asking."

"Mr. Marko," Hense said, "good work. Get a fix on our position, if you please, and scan outside and let me know what's waiting for us."

Happling appeared in the hatchway, arms hanging on the lintel. He looked fresh and unharmed, the bastard. "We're within half a mile of Paris, I'll tell you that," he said, satisfied. "I caught a visual before we ditched."

Marko remained kneeling on the floor. "Sure, sure. Give me a minute. I'm trying to swallow my lungs back into my chest." He took a deep, quivering breath and reached for his bag. I was happy to see his arms shaking as he moved. At least the goddamn Techie was as exhausted as I was.

I was content to watch the kid pull some of his equipment together and start waving weakly at it, his face once again bathed in the sick green light of his tiny screen. "I don't see any signs of life out there," he said. "Looks like we're within a mile of the city, like the captain said. I can get a fix on the beacon signal that ought to lead us straight to its source, which I presume will be Mr. Kieth." He let his arm drop limply to his side. He looked around. "I'm guessing we're walking there."

Happling leaned forward and clapped him on the back. "You can ride on my shoulder, like a fucking parrot."

Hense was all business, checking her weapon with a few quick, efficient moves and looking around. "We're all alive and uninjured. Let's move. We don't exactly have *time*."

Happling straightened up. "Right. Gather your gear, Marko." The big man looked at me but said nothing, storming into the cabin to retrieve his bag of guns, ripping it open and pulling one of the shredders out. He tore the huge clip from it, inspected it jauntily, and slammed it back into place. There was the almost inaudible whine of the rounds being counted, and then the readout on top of the rifle flashed green, and Happling grinned.

"Here come the boom stick," he said, slinging the rifle and bag over his shoulder and marching to the hatch. He looked back at Hense and waited for her nod before smashing the release with his hand. The hatch popped open with a hiss, and weak light filtered in. Happling crouched down with the rifle against his shoulder and did a fast turn, eyes wide and alert. Without putting the gun down or taking his eyes off the scene, he said "Clear" over his shoulder and then jumped out and down.

From outside I heard him shout back, "But very fucking weird."

Hense was out the hatch after him. I glanced at Marko, who was still slumped on the floor, and then I brushed past him, trying to force my body to move steadily. I still almost fell out of the goddamn hover, recovering sloppily in the damp grass. Hense and Happling hadn't gone more than a few feet away before freezing. I stopped immediately.

We were surrounded by Monks.

I hadn't seen so many of the Tin Men in years. Now and then a beggar or a crazy one wandered around bothering people, but after the Monk Riots most had been destroyed by the System Pigs in one of their rare useful moments, and aside from the small bands of them in the wilderness they weren't common, or much of a problem. Now there were at least fifty in the clearing, and they all appeared to be dead and posed in a variety of positions.

The hover had flattened some trees and emerged from a small wooded area bordered by a broad band of grassy land that maybe had once been a road. A circular clearing spread out around us, enclosed by a concentric ring of trees. The Monks were all mutilated—missing limbs, wires and boards spilling out of holes torn in their chassis, some burned or melted or plagued by rust, some bodies without heads and other heads without bodies. They littered the space around us like sullen monuments grouped in little tableaux, bent and fixed into position. Some had obviously fallen over, and a few appeared to have bird nests in their abdomens.

The three of us looked around. It was warm, the sun rising on the horizon, the air heavy with humidity. There was a lot of animal noise in the distance—birds calling, something crashing through the trees—but we remained silent, just staring, until Marko tumbled out of the hover, falling to the ground with a grunt.

"Well," Happling said, lowering his rifle, "welcome to Paris, shithole of the fucking universe."

XIX

DAY EIGHT: MEANWHILE I'M KEEPING CIVILIZATION GOING

"Hell, they're all nonfunctional," Marko said, spinning around slowly with one of his handhelds. "Been here for a long time."

"You're brilliant," Happling said from his perch on top of his bag of guns. "You needed a fucking mini-mainframe to tell you that?" He'd rolled up the starched white sleeves of his shirt, his muscles bulging as he gripped the shredder. He looked like a goddamn recruitment poster.

I was concentrating on not falling over as I strolled around the bizarre group of dead Monks. Hense was on her long-range scanner trying to raise SSF HQ for some obscure reason—personally, I thought the last thing we wanted was more *cops,* but I had to admit I was prejudiced, since most cops immediately started kicking and punching me when I met them. It was possible, being a cop herself, that she found them fun and interesting. I imagined she was trying to make contact to explain herself, or maybe trying to touch base with an informer who could tell her if any SSF were in pursuit: she'd stolen a hover, allowed two other cops to be killed, and made off with a prisoner who hadn't been entered into the database, after all.

The newly risen sun tinged everything gold, a soft halo of light clinging to everything. Despite the rust, the torn plastic skin, the torn-out wires and staring, dead camera eyes, even the Monks looked almost beautiful. I stared at one that had been posed with both arms in the air as if in a moment of triumph, and struggled down into a sitting position on the damp ground, pulling out my gun and popping out the clip. Counting the shell in the chamber, I had fourteen shots. I'd done plenty with less, but never in the middle of fucking nowhere, a Ghost City the only thing in walking distance.

I snapped the clip back into place and pocketed the gun. Squinting over at Hense, I watched her for a moment.

"Waste of time," I said.

She didn't look up. "Taken under advisement."

"It's a waste of time, Colonel," I said. "New York was on the edge of a fucking breakdown when we left. You think it got better? You think anyone's *looking* for you right now?" I shook my head. "We should be moving. We don't even know if the neat little suppression effect my pet nanobots have on us all is going to last."

"You're not in charge of this expedition, Cates," she said without looking at me.

I stood up, grimacing inwardly as I forced my way through the million or so separate aches that had coalesced into a single gauzy misery inside me. "When you all start coughing up blood," I said breathlessly, holstering my gun, "you can catch up."

I took two steps, forcing myself to move smoothly and confidently, and then Happling was in front of me, my nose pointed right at his chest. He had the shredder leaning against his shoulder, pointed at the sky. His face had gone dark red again as he pushed a fat finger into my chest.

"The colonel said sit the fuck down, Cates."

I looked from Hense to the behemoth. "Point of order, *boss*. She said I wasn't *in charge*. Fine by me, Big Red." I pushed my own finger into his chest, which was disturbingly hard and broad, the goddamn alpha male right there in front of me. "I'm *not* in charge. I'm not even *part* of it."

His finger became a fist, pushing me backward. "Sit the fuck *down,* you piece of shit."

I forced my stiff face into a smile. The cops were no different from anyone else in the System: you backed down, you gave an inch, they swarmed on you like fire ants and picked you clean. "What, you're gonna beat the tar out of me every five minutes forever, Happling? That's all you fucking pigs know how to do, huh?"

Happling's face seemed to fold in on itself, his fair eyebrows coming down toward his scruffy ginger beard. "You better watch your tongue. You pieces of shit piss on everything and we have to clean your shit up, and then you piss and moan about the manner in which we do so. Fuck you. I know you, Cates. You're a fucking parasite. You kill people for money, and meanwhile I'm keeping civilization going. If I'd killed you last week, the world would be a better place today."

He was breathing heavily through his nose, his whole body expanding and contracting with each breath. "I kill people for money," I said. I leaned forward, rocking off my heels. "I kill cops, too, but not for money, friend. Since you're so busy *keeping civilization going,* I'm gonna go ahead and assume you've never *killed* any *people,* right?"

His mouth kinked into an ugly smile. "I don't kill people," he said. "I kill *shitheads.* And I assure you, Mr. Cates, there is a goddamn *difference.*"

For a moment, we stared at each other. I had to crane my head painfully to maintain eye contact. "Do you think—"

"Enough," Hense said without raising her voice. She hadn't even looked up from her comm unit. "Let's get moving."

I looked back at Happling. He winked. I stepped around him. "Let's go save goddamn civilization."

We were farther than a mile out, but Hense set a bone-crushing pace, marching off in a swirl of black leather overcoat, broiling just to look at. We weren't far from major roads, either, encountering a weed-cracked highway in just a few minutes of panting march. Hense led the way with Happling taking up the rear, his massive gun balanced across his arms, his skin already peeling in the sun. Marko and I were herded between them, neither of us happy.

The silence was excruciating. I'd never been without the noise of a city around me—screams, threats, hover displacement, gunshots. All we had was the creak of our shoes on the ancient road and the wind pushing the weeds around, as close to total fucking silence as I'd ever experienced. The silence remained with us even as the city started to form up, shattered buildings and crashed hovers, occasional desiccated corpses and more rusting, dead Monks. Paris hadn't been much even before the Monk Riots, a shitheel city that had taken a beating during Unification, when half the populace had risen up and declared independence, repudiating the Unification Treaties. Six years Paris had burned, holding out. And then the System Security Force had been formed, and that was the fucking end of that. One thing the SSF always knew how to do was put down riots.

"Squalor's not dead, you know," Marko said suddenly.

Hense glanced back at us but didn't say anything. "Sure he is," I said. "I fucking killed him."

Marko shook his head. "Squalor's brilliant, man. Squalor could hack anything. You killed *a* Dennis Squalor. You killed a *version* of him. He's around."

I looked around. "Is he here with us, right now? Can only you see him?"

Marko looked at me as if he wanted to say *fuck you,* but thought better of it. I went back to sweating and aching and taking in the breathtaking scenery of broken buildings and melted asphalt. The city was firming up as we got closer to its core, old even before Unification came along to ruin everything. It had been the outer areas and suburbs that had flared up; the city core had seen little trouble, at least until all the Monks fleeing London had arrived and made Paris theirs.

We'd fought our way through new undergrowth to a roadway running roughly northwest by southeast, broad and broken up. Most of the old signs had crashed to the pavement, the red squares with A4 printed on them hanging limply from rusted bolts or pounded into the deteriorating asphalt like tiles. The sun was blazing down on us, and the muddy, shit-colored river was on our left, placid and low between its banks. It wasn't much warmer than New York, but the clear sky was what made it feel strange — to go from snowy, greasy New York to this sort of dry heat. These days you never knew what you were going to get.

The silence continued to make me queasy, and the air didn't smell like anything, a sterile kind of wind. There was no distant scent of smoke, or the close-up smell of terror, or even the acidic urine aroma of irritated people. It felt like we were walking through a void.

Hense marched without a moment's hesitation, directed from time to time by a word from Marko, who was tracing the nanobot signals beaming out from all of us every second, assuring themselves. She didn't look back at us, didn't nervously touch her gun or even seem to be sweating.

As the river curved slightly to the west, I could see a large building looming up in front of us. The road started to rise and curve into a rat's nest of half-collapsed thoroughfares, and we had to climb up then drop down a few levels to get back onto the riverbank, which Marko insisted was our best bet. Hense just kept going, confident, I supposed, that Happling — grinning, with his monster gun capable of cutting someone in half with a single second-long burst — would keep me and the Techie in line. Which was absolutely correct, since I had no intention of testing Happling's temper. I just took the dusty, rusted railings in my hands and swung myself over, biting my tongue against any urge to cry out or even grunt, dropping down onto broken pavement as lightly as I could. When Happling followed us down, I could imagine the fucking ground shaking.

The building in the distance resolved itself into a jumble of stone with spidery arms sprouting out of the sides as if holding up the walls. A tall, thin spire jutted out from the middle, and two squarish towers rose up on either side. As we got closer it became clear that it occupied an island separate from the east bank that had once been reachable by bridges now just stubs of stone and twisted metal. Around it, Paris consisted of short, square buildings, many blasted away yet some remarkably preserved. Still, nothing on the horizon was as tall or imposing as this thing.

I knew the answer before asking. "Hey, Marko," I said. "Where we headed?"

He pushed his chin at the island. "The church. There's a fucking *storm* of traffic coming from that church."

We made our way down to the river and stopped amid the ruins of one of the bridges, the old pylons jutting out of the water like teeth. A crumbling wall ringed the island, and we all stared at it for a moment, contemplating how hard it was going to be to swim across and clamber up, all without knowing what we were going to find there.

"Mr. Marko?" Hense said, squatting down and sounding just slightly out of breath. "See anything?"

Marko was already wandering the broken rubble at the river's edge with his eyes glued to his screen. "Aside from the digital traffic, I've got one heat signature that's in the right range for a human. I wouldn't see any Monks that way, though."

"Fuck the Tin Men," Happling growled, crumbling a cigarette in his hands and jamming the tobacco into his cheek. "The ones swam over here ain't going to give us any problems. That's why they're still *here,* in the shithole of the universe."

Hense rocked on her heels, staring across the water. "No one knows we're here. No one could be expecting us."

"Sure," Happling drawled, spitting brown juice onto the ground. "Because smacking a hover into the ground just a few miles away wouldn't have been noticed by anyone."

She cocked her head slightly back toward him but didn't say anything. For a moment she just stared off into the distance, the sun hidden behind scummy clouds. "Wait for night." She stood up and turned to face us, five feet and a hundred pounds, and I was pretty sure she'd make me hurt plenty if I ever tried to lay hands on her. "Mr. Marko, see what you can see, and find out what you can about that building. Nobody go more than a few feet from Mr. Cates."

Marko sat down where he'd been standing, staring at the screen and moving his slender fingers. "There's nothing there, Colonel. A minor heat sig, all the air traffic we've been tracking between it and the nanos, and nothing else. No hot wire, no cavities — just old stone and empty air." He snapped his little device shut and peered at us with squinty, screen-blinded eyes. "If there's anything over there, Colonel, it's one person."

I reached down and picked up a rock, chucking it into the water just to watch it be swallowed, the water like heavy oil, barely rippling. "All right," I said, heart pounding. "Let's go, then."

"Wait for night," Hense said from behind me. I could picture the tight shake of her head.

"No," I said. "What, you think night's going to make a difference? Anyone over there *expecting* us is expecting us. If Marko can't see them, then either they can't be seen or they aren't there. Either way, waiting doesn't accomplish anything." I shrugged off my coat and started going through the pockets, transferring anything useful to my pants. "I'm diving in three minutes, Colonel. What are you going to do? Shoot me?"

I dropped the coat to the ground and slid my gun securely into a front hip pocket. My arms were mottled blue and gray, but I felt better than I had in days, adrenaline coursing through me, the pain receding. I thought I might actually get to kill someone responsible for this, for Glee, for New York, and everyone else I'd just murdered without meaning to. I was almost cheerful as I picked my way to the water's edge and started taking deep breaths, my cracked ribs poking me with each inhalation.

"Fuck it," Hense said from behind me. "Lead on, Cates." She sounded amused.

I wasn't paying any attention anymore. I took three terrible, ragged breaths and then threw myself into the water. It was cold—surprisingly cold, a slap of freezing liquid against my body. My clothes soaked it up and got heavy, and after just a minute or so I was panting. Behind me, I heard them slip into the water, and pretty soon we were all making a lot of noise as we swam to the island. About halfway down the west side the retaining wall had been smashed up a little, and we were able to pull ourselves out of the evil river to stand dripping beside the massive building. I stood breathing hard and suppressing coughs, examining the structure. A grayish white, it was eerily preserved. I thought of the church in Newark and marveled at whatever ancient instinct people'd had to leave the fucking churches alone while they burned down the rest of the world.

We took a moment to check weapons and equipment. Marko did another scan and nodded wordlessly. Happling and I crept along the wall toward the front, where the two towers thrust up above us. There was a big open square right outside the church, the city silent and crumbling in the near distance. We paused to study the three huge doorways, curvy triangles with doors missing, darkness spilling out of them and fading the air around us. I glanced down at a circular stone set into the ground with words printed on it: POINT ZERO DES ROUTES DE FRANCE. I didn't know what it meant, if it had ever meant anything.

The doorways were empty, just black shadows. Happling pointed at the far one and I nodded, moving quickly to push myself against the wall and then creeping over toward it. We glanced at each other again and simultaneously stepped inside.

I took a moment to let my eyes adjust. My lungs were still burning, and it felt like I'd pulled a whole new set of muscles, but I stayed still for half a minute, letting my eyes find the light.

The interior of the church was a narrow hall, its rounded roof impossibly high over our heads. The rotted remains of what had once been benches littered the area directly in front of me, but far ahead the floor cleared and a raised platform sat under a row of empty, gaping window frames. I glanced right and spied Happling across from me. He looked around and shrugged. I didn't see anything either. I nodded back and took a step forward; he faded back a step and lowered his shredder to cover me.

I started walking, my feet making quiet, wet sounds. My heart rattled against my chest as if trying to break out, and everything inside me had turned to liquid, ready to spill out. My own breath sounded thunderous, wheezing in and out of my ruined nose, and sweat dripped into my good eye and every scratch on my body, setting me on fire. I kept my gun out in front of me, low, my finger alongside the trigger. I reminded myself that I had fourteen shots, I was exposed, and I was counting on a System Pig who hated me to provide cover.

As I got closer, I saw that the raised platform wasn't empty. It was made of polished stone with a checkerboard design, and it supported a large cube of clear material like glass. A man was sitting inside the cube, which was actually a small transparent room, complete with a small cot, a table and chair, and a bank of equipment hooked together by the usual black cables. The man was sitting cross-legged on the floor of his little cube, lazily waving at a Vid screen, the Vid's light flashing on his bald head and impossibly long nose.

I stopped, blinking. "Ty?"

Ty Kieth looked up sharply, sheer terror passing over his familiar face. Then he smiled, a huge, damp grin that looked a lot like mingled relief and happiness.

"Oh, fuck," he said, his voice raspy, rough. "Oh *fuck* is Ty happy to see you, Mr. Cates."

XX

DAY EIGHT: TY IS CONTEMPLATING THE END OF THE WORLD

All I could do for a moment was stare. Ty Kieth looked exactly the same as the last time I'd seen him years ago, when he'd left New York. As always he was bald—either something congenital or a procedure he'd had done, since I'd never seen him shave—and his ridiculous nose quivered in front of him, always a second or two in the future, waiting for Ty to catch up. He was wearing loose-fitting, colorless clothes that were obviously not tailored for him, and, of course, he was living inside a transparent cube.

"Ty," I said, feeling Happling behind me in the shadows, like an ember in the wind, "there's a big cop back there who wants very much to shoot you. You're going to have to give us a good reason not to, and fast."

Ty's face was almost comical in the way it collapsed in on itself, folding up into a rictus of horror. "You mean you're not here to *rescue* Ty?"

"Well, fuck," I said, frowning, my voice echoing off

the soaring walls, "why in hell would I be here to rescue you?"

"This is him, then?" Happling roared, stepping into the aisle behind me, shredder up and cords on his neck standing out like taut cables. "This is the fantastic genius Ty Kieth who created these goddamn bugs?"

I turned to face him, keeping my gun down but at the ready. Happling wasn't even looking at me. His bloody eyes were fixed on Kieth, as if trying to make the little man explode just with his mind. "It is," I said, stepping sideways to block his path. "And I need a moment to talk to him."

The big cop swung the shredder so it pointed directly at my chest and didn't slow down. "Step aside, asshole."

I'd seen shredding rifles cut through cement walls. I'd seen shredding rifles turn dozens of men into cheese. I stepped aside and spun back to face Ty.

"Told you," I said. "Ty, I'm afraid Captain Happling here doesn't respect my opinions. He might shoot you."

Ty reached up and rapped his knuckles against the glass. "Doesn't matter, Mr. Cates. The cube is bullet-proof." He looked up again. "Did Ty hear you say *bug,* officer?" He turned his wide eyes on me. "You're *sick?*"

Happling had stepped up to the cube and was peering at it carefully, running fingers over its surface, judging the veracity of Kieth's statement. I looked around. "No," I said, concentrating to avoid the lisp my broken teeth tried to give me. "Apparently I'm radiating some sort of suppression field. That's why we're all still alive."

Kieth put his hands over his face. "Oh my *god,*" he moaned. "You're the fucking *originator?*"

Happling tapped the muzzle of the shredder against

the wall of the cube. "Looks like he's telling the truth. Hey, Little Man," he shouted at Kieth. "How'd you even get *in* there?"

Ty lifted his face from his hands. His eyes were puffy, like he was about to cry. "Ty was sealed in, officer. Ty was *entombed*."

There was noise behind us, and Happling and I froze for a moment, cocking our heads, and then both came to the conclusion that the immense noise coming from behind us was Marko, stomping into the church in a lab-bound Techie's version of stealth. We both relaxed. Then there was movement at my elbow, and I turned and found Hense standing just inches from me. I started and tried to hide it with a shrug.

"This him?" Hense said. "This Ty Kieth?"

I nodded. Marko stampeded past us and walked right up to the cube. He stared at Ty's crumpled form for a bit. "I'm a *huge* fan of your work, Mr. Kieth," he said. "Although illegal, of course. But *genius,* nonetheless."

Kieth looked up with blank, red-rimmed eyes. "Ty doesn't give a shit," he said. "Ty is contemplating the end of the world."

I tucked my gun into my belt, carefully—SSF handguns did not come with a safety—and shouldered Marko out of the way. "Ty, are we safe here? Anyone coming to ambush us?"

He shrugged, nose quivering. "Ty doesn't know, Mr. Cates. Ty hasn't seen anyone in some time, but Ty cannot be sure."

I looked around. "All right."

"Captain," Hense said briskly, appearing at my side

again. "Take up a defensive position and patrol our perimeter."

"Yes, sir," Happling said, still staring at Kieth. After a moment's hesitation he turned smartly and marched off.

"Tell him not to go more than fifty feet or so for any extended period of time," Kieth said quietly, staring down at the floor of his cube. "If Mr. Cates is the originator, that would be the approximate range of his signal."

"Ty," I said, "why did you do this?"

He looked up at me, eyes glassy. "Ty was *forced*, Mr. Cates. Ty was offered a job, very lucrative. Ty was betrayed. Imprisoned. *Threatened*. Ty is not a brave man, Mr. Cates, and Ty chose to peck out a few more months of existence rather than resist." He raised one eyebrow and a faint ghost of a smile spread his face out a little. "But Ty is not *stupid*, Mr. Cates. That is why Ty is still here in front of you, preserved. Ty knew what he was designing, yes, and Ty built in a beacon system. An encrypted signal formed from a readout of Ty's own vital signs. The nanobots do their job. They manufacture themselves and spread out in several vectors — airborne, fluid transfers — and attack at a cellular level, destroying. A mechanical cancer."

"It's an amazing design," Marko said quietly.

Ty looked at him, frowning. "Ty thinks it may be the greatest work he has ever done, yes." He looked back at me. "And this is only stage one. Stage two — but Ty knew he would be dead the moment the work was complete — the Droids were designed to be self-replicating, yes? So why need Ty once the plague has been released?" He smiled more fully and tapped his bald pate. "Ty built in the beacon. If Ty dies, or if Ty's vital signs show any alarming changes, the Droids will shut down en masse and hibernate." He nodded. "Ty is confident the encryption is unbreakable by any current means. So Ty is *necessary,* yes? Ty cannot be killed or harmed."

I cocked my head. "Until everyone *else* is dead, at least."

The smile vanished and he ducked his head. "Yes. Ty is not proud, Mr. Cates. Ty fears death."

"Why is Cates special?" Hense demanded. "Why are the nanobots in his system putting out a special signal? Once the nanobots are in the wild, they will spread on their own, yes?"

Ty shook his head. "Ty does not know. Ty was given specific instructions, and they included an *originator,* a person to be initially infected, who would be the vector until the Droids inhabited the tipping point of subjects. The originator, it was specified, would not be affected by his own infection or anyone else's. The suppression signal was a dirty hack, but in the time allowed it was the best Ty could do." He looked at me. "Ty didn't know it was going to be you, Mr. Cates, Ty swears."

I smiled, showing him my bloody, broken grin. "Would it have made any difference, Ty?"

He looked down at the floor again. "No." He looked up. "They were very angry when my little deception was discovered, Mr. Cates. But they could do nothing to me, you understand, except entomb me here. Fed, watered, and allowed to live. But imprisoned while the world died."

"Who, Mr. Kieth?" Hense wanted to know. "Who hired— forced you to do this?"

Ty sighed. "The Monks."

A thrill went through me. "Monks?"

Ty looked up. "Monks. I was offered employment and

a hover was supplied to ferry me to my new employers for a meeting. It brought me here, to Paris, and I was met by a group of Monks. Only one spoke to me. He was...most persuasive."

I thought of the distorted voices in Newark — Newark, another Ghost City ruled by the last dregs of the Monk population that had survived the SSF purge during the Monk Riots. *Monks.*

Hense looked at me. "Mr. Kieth," she said, her dark, pupil-less eyes still on me. "Am I to understand that *Monks* of the former Electric Church forced you to do this? That they were coherent?"

"Yes."

"Armed?"

Ty nodded, his nose wagging up and down. "Oh, yes."

"Fuck," Hense muttered, turning away and starting to pace.

I squinted at Ty, my brain working furiously. "Wait a second. Wait a fucking second." I stepped forward and pressed my face onto the glass. "Ty, are you telling me that if you *die,* the whole fucking plague *shuts down?*"

Ty startled, staring back at me from an inch or two away. I could see the pores on his nose and the tiny, silky hairs growing out of it. "Yes, Mr. Cates."

We looked at each other through the glass for a moment. I'd never particularly liked Ty Kieth — he was irritating and had never taken orders well — but he was very good at what he did and had always done his job. As far as I knew he had never betrayed me. I brought the gun up near my cheek. "Then I'm sorry, Ty," I said slowly, something unfamiliar forming in my belly, acidic and heavy. "But I think we're going to have to kill you. Fucking immediately."

For a moment there was an almost perfect silence in the church as we all remained frozen, holding our breath. Inside me, the acid pellet burst and I felt tired and beaten. I didn't want to kill Ty. Ty was harmless, under normal circumstances. The universe had made Ty a threat, and now I was supposed to just execute him? I was disgusted with everything—the cops, the world, even myself.

Ty's eyes widened, and he tried to scamper back from the cube wall, tripping over himself and falling onto his ass, his skinny arms and legs moving anyway. He crawled in place for a moment and finally got some traction, pushing himself backward and knocking over some of his equipment. "Mr. Cates!" he sputtered. "Ty must protest!"

I looked away, ashamed. "Marko," I said quietly. "Think you can cut into that cube?"

Marko blinked rapidly and turned to look at me. "Kill Ty Kieth? The man's a genius. Are you, like, going to kill every genius you come across, Mr. Cates?"

I grabbed him by the shirt, pulling him in close, buttons popping. He let out a pained little grunt as I slammed him into my body, yanking him up so I could stare directly into his face. I put my gun to his temple, which was probably overkill for someone like Marko but I was in an overkill mood. I saw Gleason breathing in invisible monsters that set to work tearing and slicing at every cell of her body. I saw her burning. "Avery Cates, Genius Killer doesn't have much a ring, Mr. Marko," I said. "Can you get into that cube or not? Because if *not,* I don't have much use for you."

This time Marko's eyes, buried in the midst of his hairy, sweaty face, went wide. I felt the breeze of Hense moving and spun and ducked in time to evade her hand. I moved Marko roughly around between the colonel and me. She still managed to get in close, her piece jabbed into my stomach.

"Mr. Marko is SSF, Mr. Cates," she said evenly. "Release him."

I didn't move. If Ty's death meant the end of the plague, I was suddenly no longer necessary to Colonel Hense, and that meant it was more than likely that Happling's boots were going to be the last things I ever saw. "Colonel Hense, we have a deal, yes?"

She stared back for a moment. I knew she was thinking through the implications just as I had. Finally, she nodded curtly. "We have a deal, Mr. Cates." Her eyes shifted to Marko, who was vibrating in my arms, putting out sweat like someone was pumping water into him and it was coming out his pores. "Can you get into that cube?"

"F-f-fucking hell," Marko stuttered. "*Maybe*."

"Try." Hense looked at me again. "Let him go, Mr. Cates."

I waited another second and then nodded, springing back from Marko, who almost fell on his ass, staggering to regain his balance. He stood for a moment rubbing his chest, and Hense swept her gun toward the cube in invitation. "Try, Mr. Marko. People are *dying*."

"Get it open, Marko," I said, "so we can kill him."

Ty swept his bugged eyes from me to Hense to Marko and back again, his mouth open. Even in the darkness, I could tell he was about to say something to me, and I closed my eyes. I couldn't look at Ty, even for Glee. I *knew* Ty. I'd killed people I'd known before, but I couldn't look at him. Ty was fucking harmless. This wasn't fair. This was against the rules. I was supposed to break the only rule everyone in my world respected: you don't kill people who don't deserve it. Most of the people I'd known stretched the definition of *deserve* until you could barely recognize it, but I didn't. It was clear to me, and Ty simply didn't deserve to die.

"I'm afraid I can't let that happen, Avery."

It wasn't Ty's voice, and it came from behind us. Both Hense and I whirled and crouched down, guns in our hands. I stared through the gloom and for a second I couldn't move.

Standing just inside the rear of the church, his nickel-plated Roons in each hand, was Wa Belling.

XXI

DAY EIGHT: OLD MURDER INCORPORATED HIMSELF

None of us moved. "I heard you were dead," I said slowly. I remembered the stupid, fat-sounding voice on the radio: *He, too. He not here, the old man.*

Wa was growing a majestic silvery beard and mustache, but his eyes were as hard and flat as ever. "Hello to you, too, Avery. Did you shed a tear for me? Lower your weapons, please."

Wa Belling was possibly the best Gunner in the System—certainly the best in the room—and if I was going to be killed by maybe the last Dúnmharú left alive, I was going to go down with my gun in hand, giving what I got. I ticked my eyes over to Hense quickly and then back to Belling. The colonel just looked irritated.

"Wallace Belling, sometimes styling himself Cainnic Orel," she said. "I have to admit one piece-of-shit Gunner looks like another."

I opened my mouth to give Wa a smart response, but from behind us Ty started shouting.

"You absolute *cunt,*" he shrilled, muted slightly by the thick bulletproof walls around him. "You threw me this job. You brought me into this. You *shit,* you piece of *shit*—"

"Mr. Kieth," Wa said, a cold, unhappy smile on his face. "Calm yourself. You wouldn't want to pop a vessel after all the trouble you've gone to trying to extend your life."

"Wa," I said, resisting the urge to look for Happling, who had to be skulking in the shadows somewhere, inching into position. "Why?"

Belling didn't shift or look at me; he kept his gaze wide. "Don't be an asshole—they *paid* me. Are you going to pretend you're here for some altruistic reason? Saving the fucking world? Saving the *world,* Avery?"

I tightened my grip on my gun. "A lot of daylight between being a bad guy, Wa, and murdering the world. You did this for *yen?*" I was angry. I wanted to grab the old man and just beat my fists against him, make him yell. *You killed Glee,* I wanted to spit at him. *She was fifteen.*

"Yen?" Belling said, pursing his lips disdainfully. "Not yen, Avery. You of all people know there's more important things than yen. I'm an old man, and they made me an attractive offer. A funny thing happened while I worked with you in New York, Avery," Belling said, raising an eyebrow. "I got old, and I got tired of killing cops for free. I mean, hell, I—"

Belling spun, both guns burping at the shadows behind him as he moved toward the side aisle, seeming to glide into the darkness. I hadn't heard anything, but I didn't wait to figure it out; Hense and I had the same idea, fading backward and circling around, putting Ty Kieth's cube between us and the rest of the church. Ty whirled and stared at us, sweat beading his head and soaking his clothes.

"Mr. Cates! Ty reminds you of our past friendship!" he hissed.

I leaned forward and put my forehead against the glass. "Tell you what, Ty. Get down on the floor and stay there, and I'll consider it."

He stared at me until I motioned him down with my hand, and then he threw himself flat. Across from us, on the other side Marko stared at us with his mouth hanging open.

"Fucking hell," Hense hissed. "Mr. *Marko,* get your flabby white ass back here."

Shots, then, from the shadows at the front of the church, six or seven all at once. Marko jumped and scampered around, tripping and skidding on his knees as he tried to make the turn. Hense whipped out one skinny arm and hauled the Techie in like he was made of paper, depositing him on the floor between us.

"That really Wallace Belling?" Hense asked.

I nodded. "Old Murder Incorporated himself."

"He have any tells?"

I considered. I'd never actually gone against Belling; he'd made me look like a chump when we first met, but we'd never gotten wet against each other. Still, I'd run a dozen hits with him over the years. I'd seen him in action. "None. He's fast, he's quiet." I saw Glee again, as I would forever, eaten up. "And he has no heart," I said.

As four more gunshots exploded, this time with

muzzle flashes in the shadows, she said thoughtfully, "He's goddamn ancient, though."

I shook my head. "Don't fucking believe it. *I'm* old, Colonel. Wa Belling's getting younger."

She went back to watching the area in front of us, guns in both hands, her legs bent slightly at the knees, ready for action. I was just inches from her, and with all her attention fixed away from me, I thought, *Fuck, I could take her.* Happling was preoccupied, Marko was no goddamn worry—I could very quickly be rid of two people who didn't like me much and who kept me around mainly because I was some sort of magical monkey's claw against their own horrible death. I didn't need *them,* and my life might be considerably smoothed out if they disappeared.

All my problems, I realized, could be ended with just a few more cold-blooded murders.

I let my eyes linger on the smooth, dark skin of her neck, just below her hairline, where the elegant line of her ear was just beginning. Right there. It would take less than a second to move; I'd done it so often, in all weathers and all conditions. One hand across her body in case she tried to get her weapons up—the System Pigs were fast, and she was fast for a Pig—and the muzzle right under her ear, squeeze the trigger.

Something danced at the edge of my thoughts, some memory. Déjà vu, gone as fast as it came, and I was still just standing there like a chump.

Belling emerged from the front of the church at a run, vaulting over the remnants of a rotting bench with a smooth jump. As he landed, clips dropped from his guns, skittering across the smooth floor. Happling came tearing ass from the shadows, shredder slung around his chest, two coal-black guns in his hands.

"*Run,* you skinny old fuck!" he whooped. "You think you got an edge on *me?*" As he ran he took two potshots at Belling, but the old man was weaving drunkenly, and then made a sharp turn for the edges of the church again.

My moment had passed. Again, Hense and I moved as one. I *liked* her, the way she worked. For a System Pig, she reminded me of a Gunner; all business, and she just *moved,* just made it happen. There were none of the bullshit speeches most of the Pigs liked to make, one boot on your neck while they inspected their fingernails and rifled through your credit dongle. We each took a side, rolled out from behind Ty's cube, and sent lead after Belling, both of us pouring it on. The old man threw himself down like he expected the floor to open up beneath him, hitting with a brain-mashing thud and rolling as our bullets tore up the stone behind him, little geysers of dust, and the old man *kept* rolling, and then was gone into the shadows around the perimeter. I took off after him, hustling horizontally. I saw Happling doing the same up the aisle from me—a nice trapping movement—the big man moving pretty smoothly for a gorilla, and we hit the shadows at the same time.

The darkness of the side aisle blinded me. I skidded to a halt and instinctively dropped to one knee as Belling sent two shots where my head would have been if I'd been born stupid, muzzle flashes like lightning burning off the gloom for a second at a time. Cursing, I rolled back out into the main area, just as a thunderous series of gunshots erupted, going on and on long after I didn't think it was possible anymore, an unceasing cacophony that made you want to curl up and duck your head until it stopped. Those kinds of instincts were what got you killed. I'd learned early that whenever your underbrain wanted to hide, you had to do the exact opposite.

I got to my feet as quickly as my aching body would allow, gun in hand, and pushed myself back at the shadows. Happling and his two guns were putting the pressure on Belling, and maybe it was a chance to catch the old man occupied. Hense was at my side then, face blank, and as I looked at her she gestured toward the back of the church with a sweeping motion. I nodded, even though I had no fucking idea what she was getting at. I'd seen System Pigs have entire conversations using the complex hand signals beaten into them at Cop School, or whatever torture center they trained at after being tube-grown or snatched from their mothers by Stormers, but none of them had ever paused to explain the system to me. I didn't have time to protest, though. She took off toward the back of the church and I put myself against one of the archways that led to the side aisle, held my breath, and listened for a clue.

Fucking hell, I thought. *He didn't know Happling was there—we had the fucking* drop *on the old man, and we're still chasing our tails.* I put myself in that situation—surprised by a second System Cop I hadn't expected—and the result was easy enough to predict: me dead, three or four big holes in my back.

There was a noise behind me and I whirled, stopping myself just before I put a bullet in Happling's huge forehead. The big cop was sweaty and flushed, his automatics like little black holes in his hands. We stared at each other, and his face crumpled into an expression of irritation.

"Well, *fuck*," he hissed, and dived back into the shadows. A second later he was back. "Where the fuck *is* that old bastard?"

We were both scanning the church, trying to put our eyes everywhere. It was near dark; everything had gone a sort of blue-gray monotone. The empty windowpanes with their elaborate stonework were bizarre and alien; it was hard to believe human beings had built this. Such a fucking waste of time.

A crash and two muffled shots from the rear of the church, and Happling was on the move, two steps past me before I even turned. He pointed forcefully to our left, a fucking signal I could comprehend, so I took off at my top speed—currently a shambling shuffle—for the left corner. Before I'd covered half the distance, however, Belling burst from the darker shadows of the side aisle into the slightly brighter open area. For a second or two I had a good view of him as he ran, looking calm and energetic like one of the old duffers on the Vids selling tanning pills and other bullshit no one in the System needed. I couldn't believe my luck. It felt uncomfortable, like when you eat for the first time after starving for weeks and you get sick.

I shut everything out of my mind, picturing grass in the evening wind, swaying. I took a sighting on the space just in front of Wa as he ran and relaxed every muscle in my arm, squeezing the trigger as if it were made of glass.

The hammer dry-clicked.

Belling swung around at the slight noise, guns coming up, but kept moving. He tossed three or four quick rounds my way as I dropped hard to the floor, and then he was back in the shadows.

Cursing, I dropped the empty gun and took off, feet skidding on the smooth floor as I struggled to get traction. I had no weapon, but Wa didn't know that, and if nothing else I might herd him back toward my new best friends the cops. As I tore up the middle aisle, I caught a glimpse of Belling as he flitted from the sides out the front. Body burning, I put everything I had into running.

I knew better than to burst out into the night; I veered for the door on my far left and put my back against the wall between it and the middle door. Trying to control my breathing, I listened for clues, wondering what I was going to do if Belling surprised me. Insult him cruelly, I supposed.

"Avery," a new, strangely familiar voice called from outside. It sounded like someone was pushing molten metal through his voicebox instead of air. "Come on out, Avery. You're not going anywhere."

After a moment, I linked the voice with the memory—me, on my knees, in Newark. Just—what, a week ago? A shiver went through me. Slowly, I inched for the doorway and angled my head around the edge, peering into the square outside the church. I stared for a long time, frozen. The square was full of Monks.

XXII

DAY EIGHT: A FEW MORE INCHES
TO THE WILDERNESS

Dull rust spots were visible on the Monks' faces, they
were so close. The sound of a few dozen Monks being
perfectly still in the midst of a dead city was complete
silence. I remained hidden behind the doorway, peering
carefully around its edge. I was shocked; I hadn't seen this
many Monks—this many *fully operational* Monks—in
years. The ones you saw begging and stumping around
Manhattan were sad, pathetic jalopies you didn't think
twice about shoving out of your way. These looked to be
all original equipment, which maybe meant guns, but it
also meant they were all a little rusted, a little banged up.
I ran my eyes over them, counting the dents and tears in
their white skin, the rips in their clothes. They all held
themselves with that perfect, still confidence that hinted
at hardwired reflexes and nuclear cores ticking away their
half-lives, and they'd survived, but it obviously hadn't
been easy.

I hated them on sight.

Belling stood in front of them looking freshly pressed and relaxed, among friends, his arms at his side with gleaming Roons for hands.

"I'd like you to meet my benefactors, Mr. Cates," he said. He wasn't smiling.

A Monk stepped forward. This one looked so new I thought I could smell the fabric of its coat. In the darkness its face appeared to float above a faint outline of a body. For one horrible moment it smiled at me, a snapshot grin.

"Avery," it said. "You are as fucking slippery as ever. I never would have imagined I'd run into you here, although He told me it would happen. Come on out. We can see you perfectly well. Perhaps," it continued in a louder voice, "the System Security Force officers and their pet Techie would like to come out as well?"

I folded myself back against the wall, heart pounding. Fifty, sixty Monks. None of whom looked crazy. Digital sighting, laser guidance, reflexes by the fucking CPU clockspeed—and I had two unhappy System Pigs up my ass. And the one motherfucker I *wanted* to kill was locked inside a bulletproof cube. I thought I'd just stay pasted against the wall for a while, see what shook out. Let a few thousand more people die.

And then a slow lassitude stole over me, creeping down from my head through my whole body, a peaceful, easy feeling. *What the fuck,* I thought. I wasn't about to fight off sixty goddamn Monks—and Wa Belling, and what was the point, anyway?

Feeling strangely happy—just letting everything slip away, as if I'd been hanging from a rope for days and finally just let go—I rolled right and stood in the doorway. The Monk gave me that bastard grin again.

"Thank you, Avery. Ah, the police. Thank you, officers."

I was walking toward them, taking my time, all my worries distant memories. Turning my head, I was mildly surprised to see Happling and Hense emerging from the big middle doorway of the church. Hense was as tidy and tight-lipped as ever, guns held loosely by her side. Happling was soaked with sweat, his white shirt pasted against his huge chest, arms threatening to split the sleeves, the shredder still looped around him. His red hair looked black in the night, pasted against his forehead.

The Monk cocked its head at us. "Where is your Technical Assistant?"

Happling stumbled a little, a lopsided, stroked-out grin forming on his face. "Gone." He winked then, a slow-motion crumpling of one side of his face. "Yours, too, fucking freak."

The Monk stared, not moving, and for a moment anger swept through me, a flame of sulfur that singed me and was gone. It didn't say anything, but five or six of the Monks silently broke away from the group, moving past us so close I could hear the heavy thud of their steps entering the church. One limped, with an off-center, rolling gait.

The gleaming new Monk stepped forward and intercepted me, putting an arm around me. A million screaming jeebies broke out like sweat on my skin, but I just let it happen. Its arm was heavy on my shoulders.

"Walk with me, Ave."

It steered me away from the group, off toward the water.

"It's a fucked-up world, Avery, right?" Its voice was exactly the voice I'd heard in Newark, the same melted tone. It looked factory fresh, but it sounded like shit. "You know what? When I was flesh and bone, I was a fucking mess. I never realized it. Could never focus on anything. Always depressed. And the *headaches*. And then I'm Monked, you know? And I know *you* think that's a terrible thing, but for me, it clarified everything. I was a hundred percent better after that. And He has helped me stay in good condition, you know. To make sure I don't backslide."

We were at the edge of the crumbling retaining wall, and we stopped. The feeling of complete, terrible calm was still with me, and I stared down at the muddy water, where a watery moon stared back at me.

"I'd love to push you in, Avery," it said, voice low and easy. "You'd fucking sink like a stone and be dead in minutes. That's how fast things happen in this world. Minutes. *Minutes*. Do you know how long the brain stays alive after the body has died, Avery? A long goddamn time. A lot longer than you'd think. Long enough for a body to be retrieved and the brain extracted, placed in one of these Monks, at least. Minutes — it all comes down to minutes. Everything changes in just a few short minutes. How many people do you think you've left for dead, Avery? I don't think you can even count how many people you've stepped over so Avery Cates the Great and Terrible could go on living a few more miserable fucking weeks."

I listened and felt nothing. The water was strangely beautiful.

"I'd love to push you in," it repeated. "But you still have work to do. Things will take their course, of course. It's unstoppable now, and my sources tell me New York is quarantined and about to fucking burn to the ground. I want things to move faster, so I need you out there, spreading yourself around. I know you, you cocksucker. I know you'd never dream of sacrificing yourself. So you'll scuttle around like the roach you are and move things along, won't you?"

It spun me around and we started back toward the group, where the cops stood with Belling. The Monks emerged from the church silently.

"Mr. Kieth has escaped," the Monk said, its hand tightening painfully on my shoulder, "with the help of your pet SSF Techie, who is smarter than he looks. That is problematic. But I know him as well as I know you, Avery, and I know he'll stay alive, which is all I really need from him. We will, of course, search the city and find him. It isn't really a human city anymore, after all. It is *our* city, and I doubt Mr. Kieth will find it very hospitable. Very well. Officers," he said, stopping and letting me shuffle forward to stand with them, "I'd gladly kill you as well, but He has told me I need you to keep Mr. Cates alive. I fear if your colleagues arrive and find you dead and Mr. Cates here alone, they will simply execute him on the spot. So I need you to remain alive to vouch for him."

We all stared at him. I realized I didn't even mind the pain anymore. I felt *good*.

The Monks began to file away, falling into line and marching for the river. The leader spread its hands. "This is a mess, right? Fuck it. It's the System. It's always a fucking mess. Everything falling apart in goddamn slow motion, every moment. Look at this—Paris—a huge goddamn city. Lost. Lost and no one even trying to get it back. Every year they lose a few more inches to the wilderness, to the weeds—to *us*."

The Monks behind him were marching straight into the river, just walking into the water and slowly disappearing. In the distance, I noted with vague interest, I could hear hover displacement.

The Monk leaned in toward me. "Go home, Avery. Go home and scuttle about, spread yourself around. If they've managed to contain things, to set up a clean zone, that's exactly where they'll bring you, huh? And good-bye to that." It reached out and put its cold plastic hand on my face. "I'm glad, though, that I got to see you like this. Hurt, desperate. All that fucking yen you got for killing all those people—not even counting the people you left behind along the way—and here you are. It's *good*." It turned to follow the last of the Monks. "He told me it would be good. He whispered to me when I was reborn and promised me revenge. I didn't even know what the word meant until he spoke it to me."

I watched him go. "I know you," I said to the air, and then Belling was in front of me.

"Avery," he said, and then stopped, holstering his guns and shooting his cuffs. His face looked odd to me with his scum of beard and deep lines. "I *am* sorry our paths crossed like this. Even the best of us fear death. You, I know, understand."

Fuck you, I thought lazily, not really feeling it.

I watched, vaguely curious, as Belling was carried across the river by four of the Monks. He held the edges of his coat up out of the water and stared at the sky. I followed his gaze and saw the hover, a fat bug of light floating slowly through the sky, like a star crashing to Earth from a light-year away. At the sight of it, a hard kernel of anxiety bloomed in my chest, still smothered by a relaxed unconcern. I watched it slide across the sky, dropping lower and lower, displacement screaming around us, making us stagger backward. As it passed over the church it dropped to a few dozen feet above us and landed behind the building, shaking the whole island.

For a second the night was quiet and peaceful.

The kernel of alarm grew, like a pearl forming around a piece of grit, swelling and shunting aside the lethargic calm that had enveloped me. *Hovers were never a good thing,* I thought. *I should be worried. I should be moving.*

Shouts behind us, and then the familiar sound of boots in sync. We stood there admiring the night as Stormers formed up around us, moving stealthily and invisibly, detectable only by the blur of their motion as their Obfuscation Kit struggled to keep up with the terrain behind them. In seconds we were surrounded, the Stormers taking on the colors of the muddy water and the silvery sky behind them, their face masks empty space staring at us.

I shivered, alarm making my muscles twitch. Hense and Happling looked at me sharply, then around at the Stormers as if they'd never seen them before — which maybe they hadn't, not from this particular angle, anyway.

The Stormers didn't say anything. They didn't have to, since they were gathered together in the international symbol of *We will kill you if you move.* My mind was whirring along merrily, trying to figure out what the fuck had just happened to us, and in the near silence I heard boots crunching their way around the side of the church. This was standard operating procedure for the System

Pigs, of course; first the Stormers gathered, and then the officers in their brightly colored plumage came around to start the ritual ball kicking.

The footsteps turned flat and hollow on the flagstones, and I squinted at the approaching figure, looking for a clue to the exact type of ball kicking we were in for. As he drew closer, a chill stole over me, smothering my anger. I was no expert, but I was starting to think that every god-damned psionic working for the government looked the same.

He'd once had the ageless look I remembered from Shockley and his friends back in New York; this one still had the round face and big eyes, but a jagged red wound, dotted with pinker, smooth flesh, puckered one side of his face, a lightning bolt of broken skin. It gave him some years. As he walked I noted his left arm hanging down stiffly at his side. He stopped in front of us and squinted, his whole face scrunching up, muscles pulling skin into unfamiliar shapes.

"Mr. Cates," he said. "I hear you like to kill government employees. It may take more than a hover to do me." He looked around. "There is supposed to be one more? A Technical Associate?"

For some reason I wanted to laugh. I let a smile twitch my face. "The TA is AWOL."

Happling shivered. "What the fuck is this?" he said, his words firming up as he went, like he was coming back online.

"Howard Bendix," the newcomer said, his rainbow-colored ID suddenly held up for inspection. "Assistant to Undersecretary of the North American Department. Ah, weapons," he muttered, nodding his chin casually in our direction. As if a magnet had been turned on, the guns leaped from the cops' hands, their arms jerking forward. The guns skittered behind Bendix and stopped in a neat little pile. He glanced at them and then turned back to us.

"You've all been put under my discretion, Mr. Happling," Bendix said.

Happling studied the ID and looked past it at Bendix's young-old face. Then the big redhead turned and spat thickly onto the ground.

"Fucking Spooks," he said.

XXIII

DAY NINE: I CAN'T EVEN IMAGINE WHY YOU'RE STILL ALIVE *NOW*

Leering at Happling with my wrists bound behind me, I was snugly secured to the seat as we waited for liftoff, held in place so tightly I had to regulate my breathing to avoid choking myself. Happling, face almost purple, stared at me from the seat directly across from me, so near our knees were touching. I wondered if he was going to stroke out right before me. Hense was to my right, but I couldn't turn enough to get a good look at her. From what I could tell, she'd closed her eyes and gone to sleep.

The Stormers were seated all around us on the perimeter of the hover cabin, headgear off, smoking cigarettes. I didn't like looking at them, with their weird, ghostly bodies and their normal, sweaty heads.

My hands were going numb. I distracted myself by trying to figure out where Ty and Mr. Marko were hiding themselves.

I had no doubt they were on the hover—Techies

couldn't survive without their tech, their black boxes and endless, snaking cables, the guts of one machine soldered into another. Considering that for hundreds of miles in any direction there was nothing but creeping wilderness and some untamed Monks, when I put myself in Ty Kieth's huge, soggy brain it was pretty obvious he'd head for the one place where he'd be in control: the hover. For someone like Ty, wiring into a standard government hover was child's play. I wouldn't be surprised to discover he was already controlling the damn ship.

I looked back at Happling. His jaw was working feverishly, bunching and unbunching as if he were chewing something. His eyes shifted right and his face turned even darker, and then Bendix was at my elbow, holding a large digital clipboard in his good hand. He stood there staring down at us for a moment.

"Complaints, Mr. Happling?" he said. Happling's head jerked around and up, the cords on his neck bunching out as he fought against the tele-K's pull. "If you don't want your neck broken, keep your bullshit on simmer, okay?"

"Stop calling me *mister*," Happling growled. I could hear the straps on his wrists creaking. "I am a Captain in the System Security Force, you piece of shit. You don't have any authority over me."

Bendix flipped his clipboard around, the screen lighting up. "You have been released, dishonorably, from the SSF, *Mister* Happling, along with your friend here, and handed over to Undersecretary Ruberto's authority. This is a copy of Marin's memorandum, if you care to read it."

Happling stared at Bendix. The air around him had gone quite still.

"He burned you," Bendix went on, flipping the clipboard back around. "So quit your bellyaching. Unlike Mr. Cates here, I don't need *you*."

"Did they explain to you that you're a dead man, that you're dying right now?" I asked, smiling.

Bendix smiled back. "Yes, Mr. Cates, I am aware of the risks involved in contact with you. Unlike these two pieces of shit, these traitors, I am not going to kidnap you in a pathetic grab at a few more days of life. I am happy to sacrifice myself for the good of the System of Federated Nations."

"Holy fucking bullshit," Happling muttered. Bendix's eyes flicked to him, and then Happling screamed, his whole body tensing up as he struggled wildly with his restraints. The Stormers all shifted in their seats, watching.

"My training," Bendix said slowly, "has been very thorough, Mr. Happling. I can break bones without touching you, so *please* be *quiet*."

He turned to look at me as Happling continued to shiver and choke across from me. "Mr. Cates, I'm bringing you back to be *dissected* and *tested,* so we can solve this little problem and put it behind us. You probably won't survive this process. I know you were granted a pardon of sorts by Director Marin as part of your dealings with him, but the System has technically been in a state of emergency since the Monk Riots, and it is completely within Undersecretary Ruberto's authority to declare you property of the state."

I nodded. "We'll see how *patriotic* you are in a few days, kid."

Bendix smiled, his face twisting in various contradictory ways. Behind him, Happling's face had gone a shade of reddish blue that didn't look healthy. I had to hand it to the government—they apparently knew how to train their tele-Ks.

"I think you'll be dead before me," Bendix said, tucking his clipboard under his arm and turning away. "New York isn't a secure area at the moment," he said as he strode away. "Once we're in the air we'll be heading for Washington, where a team has been assembled to analyze you, Mr. Cates. So you know that no remnants of your organization will be on hand for any bullshit."

I watched him exit the cabin, the hatchway popping open as he approached and snapping shut as he stepped through it. *Showy bastard,* I thought. Happling slouched forward, sucking in an endless, shocking breath as his face returned to an almost normal color.

I leaned in so close I could have licked his ear. "We have to gain control of this hover."

The big man was sucking in air desperately, his chest heaving. "Are you fucking crazy?" he gasped. "We're restrained. Disarmed. Surrounded. By Stormers. With a goddamn. Spook."

"And if we end up in Washington on this hover, we will be *dead*. Shit, *you* will probably be dead somewhere over the fucking Atlantic. I can't even imagine why you're still alive *now*."

Hense spoke, her voice rough and blurry. "Because we're surrounded by SSF, and even a jackass like Bendix is afraid to kill two cops in cold blood in front of them."

I flashed back to a Vid show announcing that the civilian government was resurrecting the military, and suddenly thought it made sense. Every branch of government needed to be able to kill the members of the other branches. It was how things got done.

"Hey." I lunged forward and hit Happling lightly with my head. "Pull your shit together. We have to gain control of this hover." I had no idea how we were going to do this, but knowing for a fact that you were a dead man if you didn't move soon was a great motivator.

He glowered at me from under his eyebrows. "Fucking hit me again, and—"

"Kill me later," I said. "Kill me *after.*" I glanced at Hense. "I think our Techies are stowaways."

Her head twitched slightly, the tiniest movement toward me. "How do you know?"

"I don't *know,*" I said. "I *think.* Ty Kieth is the key to our survival. I think he's hiding on this hover. Now get your heads out of your asses, *officers,* and help figure out what to do."

I didn't think Hense was going to respond, that maybe she'd had the fight kicked out of her. Then she nodded curtly, looking me in the eye. "All right, Avery," she said. She held my gaze for a moment. "You never give up, do you?"

I shrugged my eyebrows, picturing Glee and thinking I'd *love* to give up. For a moment it was just Hense and me, and I knew she understood at least one thing about me, because she was exactly the same: we knew only one way. She scanned the cabin, looking at all the Stormers, who looked back at her expressionlessly. Finally she oriented on one, a round-faced veteran, maybe twenty-five, receding hairline shaved close, his face pale and glistening with sweat. A crappy filterless cigarette dangled from his lower lip, burning, forgotten.

"You," Hense said, her voice suddenly the clipped, projected colonel's voice she'd perfected. "I know you."

The Stormer looked down and took the cig from his mouth. After a moment he nodded. "Yes, sir. Was on the team in the Bronx a year ago. Beatin' on the Kabeer Gang in the bowling alley."

Hense nodded. "Your name's Kiplinger, right?"

The Stormer didn't look menacing anymore. He looked embarrassed. "Yes, sir."

"Don't fucking talk to her," a round-faced girl snapped. She was red cheeked and healthy looking, a big girl who was comfortable in her skin. She spoke in a stretched drawl, as if she liked tasting the words. "And don't call a busted ex-officer *sir,* eh?"

Hense waited a few beats, keeping those terrible eyes on Kiplinger and ignoring the girl completely. "You know this is bullshit, trooper. You know you're being played by the Spooks. We're SSF. We're *cops.* You're going to side with the fucking *Spooks?*"

Kiplinger studied his cigarette as if the secrets to the universe were contained in it. "We were assigned by direct order of—"

"*Fuck* the direct order," Hense said, her voice rising in volume. All the Stormers were staring at us now. "This is bullshit. We are SSF. That freak in there is *not a cop.* You don't think this shit *stinks?*"

"Fuck you," the round-faced girl said, taking a breath between the words, looking right at Hense—which I could personally attest took *balls*—and blowing a strand of her limp brown hair from her face. "You were burned by the Worms, eh? You're not cops any*more.*"

Hense turned her head with a birdlike, precise move-

ment, her eyes on the girl, who tried to stare back but
looked away after a moment. It was hard, I guessed, to
forget that Gold Shield. "We were? We *were?* What's
your name, trooper?"

The girl studied her fingernails. "Name's Lukens," she
said, visibly stopping herself from adding *sir* to the end.
"You want my digits, too, *Colonel?*"

"Trooper," Hense continued, "if the King Worm
burned us, *where are the Worms?* You really believe Internal Affairs decided to fuck us and then sent the fucking *Spooks* to collect us?" She looked back at Kiplinger.
"Use your fucking heads. You're being played. And when
Marin finds out what's going on here, none of you are
going to survive the encounter. If nothing else, he's going
to have to delete all of you to keep this sort of *embarrass-
ing* bullshit quiet. Police, helping the fucking civvies fuck
with *police.*"

Some of the Stormers were looking at each other.
They didn't like this. I could feel a new tension in the
room—hell, *I* was starting to feel outraged, listening to
Hense's clipped, commanding voice. I glanced at Happling, and he was sitting up straight, breathing loudly
through his nose. He looked like a man who could burst
through his bonds with a shrug.

"Kiplinger," Hense barked, "get the fuck over here and
release Captain Happling and me."

The Stormer was looking at the floor miserably. "Colonel, I—"

Hense sat forward as if willing him up. "Trooper, when
this shit hits Marin's desk, the King Worm is going to be
angry. He is going to be *pissed off,* and if you think any of
you are going to survive the experience, you are fucking

sadly mistaken. This is fucking treason. We are *police,* and that freak up front is *not,* but you're taking his orders like a fucking faggot because he has a *scan of a fucking memorandum?* Are you seriously that stupid, trooper? Fuck you, then. Once we handle this situation, I'm going to personally break you and ship you off to Chengara, trooper, where I'll keep you on ice until shit settles down and then I'll take some goddamn vacation and spend a few weeks there pulling your teeth out and breaking your fingers." She turned her head to the Stormer next to Kiplinger, a younger woman with frizzy black hair and a bad, greasy complexion. "You, what's your name, trooper?"

"De Salvo," the Stormer stuttered, dropping her own cigarette.

"You know what's happening in New York, trooper?" Hense demanded. She was perfectly calm and still, her eyes the only part of her that were animated.

De Salvo blinked, her face slack. "Disease. A plague, or something." She shifted in her seat. "It's turned up in Philly, too."

"Baltimore," one of the other Troopers rumbled.

"Fuck, I got a sister in Baltimore," someone else muttered. My mind tripped over that. I'd always assumed the System Cops were assembled somewhere, soldered together.

"Forget that," Hense snapped, raising her voice. Everyone went silent. "This is fucking treason. This is *civil war,* troopers. This is the Spooks setting shit on fire and making us chase our own tails. We're not the only officers in hovers right now, being carted off on phony orders. They're making their move against the SSF. If the SSF is pacified, who's going to stand between them and the

System? This is a *coup,* De Salvo. You know what a coup is, or did your education end with handjobs and *yes, sir?*"

The whole cabin was silent. The Stormers, including Kiplinger, were all looking at Hense. Some were even nodding. My own heart was pounding, thrilled at the fantastic, huge lie Hense was spinning. It was a piece of goddamn *art.*

"You have a choice, trooper," Hense said, her voice going low, almost friendly. "You can be stupid and just go along with this bullshit, in which case you're about as useless a fucking cop as there could be, or you can think for yourself and figure this shit out, and stand up for the Force." She shrugged. "Your fucking choice. You're all *cops.* Act like it."

Shit, even *I* was pulsing with patriotic fervor. A few moments of absolute stillness passed; I thought I could hear the cigarettes burning. Then Kiplinger stood up, dropped his cigarette on the cabin floor, and cocked his head to one side until his neck popped.

"Fuck it," he said, striding forward. He straightened one arm out with a sudden gesture, a blade sliding into his grip. The other Stormers just watched in silence as he stepped behind Hense. He was close enough for me to smell him, rancid sweat inside that smothering ObFu. He paused to look around at his patrolmates. "We're cops," he said, and sliced through Hense's restraints, pausing to stare down at the round-faced trooper.

She put a cigarette between her chapped lips and shrugged. "I spoke my piece," she said, sending a cloud of heavy smoke into the air. "Y'all gonna take their orders, I'm not gonna be a bitch about it. And shit, maybe y'all are right. Even a blind hog can find an acorn once in a while."

Hense was up immediately. "Thank you, trooper," she said. I blinked. It may have been the first time in history an officer had thanked someone. She rubbed her wrists as the Stormer cut Happling free, and then she nodded at me.

"Him, too," she said. "He's in our custody, and he's important. We can't have him getting killed because he's tied down."

The Stormer hesitated, but then nodded curtly and with a jerk I was free, my own wrists burning. Hense and I looked at each other. I was still throbbing with patriotic fervor, my heart racing, and I smiled at her. To my amazement she smiled back, and for a second or two looked young, like a kid. Then Happling, his hands curled into permanent fists, took up position behind her and on my right, glaring around, and she blinked.

"All right," Hense said in a low voice. The whole cabin went silent. "Form up. De Salvo, you're on weapons detail for the captain and me. Trooper," she said to Kiplinger as the rest of the squad stood and began pulling on their stifling ObFu face masks. "Give me the rundown: who besides the Spook is up front?"

"Just Bendix, sir." As Kiplinger started giving her a terse, professional briefing, I stood up and put my hand on Happling's shoulder, grinning. When the big man turned to scowl at me, I winked.

"Congratulations, Nathan," I said. "You're criminals, now."

XXIV

DAY NINE: AND YOU CAN GO QUIET, OR YOU CAN GO HARD

I watched the Stormers form up outside the cockpit hatch, shredding rifles in their hands, straps wrapped securely around their wrists. There was a strange, thick silence smothering the air, the humming sound of twenty-five men and women working hard at not making any noise. None of them had their face masks on, so their heads appeared to float in the air whenever they stopped moving for any period of time, all of them greasy, sweaty heads, puffy and unkempt. Two of them knelt by the hatch, pressing your standard-issue blue putty explosive into the hinges while the rest were poised for the cockpit invasion. The rest occasionally muttered to each other, and two near me exploded into inappropriate, barking laughter, earning them a glare from Happling. They sobered up fast, but I'd learned that System Pigs did indeed laugh.

Hense and Happling were back in charge as if nothing had happened. It was amazing what a few Stormers could do for an SSF officer's self-image and what the gibbering fear of death made people do. So far we hadn't had any indication that Bendix was aware of the mutiny—he was a telekinetic, after all, not a fucking Pusher. He could toss you around like a rag doll, but he wasn't able to poke into your brain, see what was going on, make you do things you normally wouldn't do.

I paused, something tickling the back of my brain. I thought back to my previous interaction with a tele-K, with Shockley, trying to kick-start the feeling, but I couldn't get hold of it, so I let it drift away.

"Standard infiltration formation," Hense snapped. "Captain, take Mr. Bendix seriously. Do *not* terminate. Incapacitate. Render him unconscious, Captain, and keep him that way."

Happling, sweating again and gripping his new shredder tightly as he tossed wide grins around the cabin, nodded once. "Incapacitate. Unconscious." He slapped the back of the nearest Stormer. "Ready, kids? Let's show this fucking *politician* what the System Security Force can *do*."

This with an enthusiasm I considered insane, but I kept my mouth shut. I'd conspicuously not been armed; I wasn't being paid much attention, but Hense seemed to have changed her mind about the relative threat level I represented after our romp in the church. When the colonel turned away from the operation being organized up front and approached me, I pushed my tongue into the painful bloody gaps of missing teeth and kept my expression neutral.

"All right, Cates," she said, stopping in front of me

with her tiny hands on her hips, looking fresh and clear. "What next?"

I noted her rock-solid assumption that her new squad would be able to contain and control Bendix but said nothing; I'd been in a crashing hover with a government tele-K and wasn't so sure. I also wasn't sure anymore — at all — that my assumption that Ty Kieth was on board and wired in was going to prove out. It made sense, but I was living in a world where invisible robots were eating people, where System Pigs followed my suggestions and turned to me for direction, where just about everyone I'd known was dead or turned against me. I wasn't counting on anything.

If Kieth *was* hidden aboard and wired in, he obviously wasn't trusting anyone. I had to proceed on the assumption that I was being spied on by the bald-headed little prick, so I couldn't say anything to alarm him.

"I suspect, Colonel," I said slowly, "that once we have Mr. Bendix under wraps, a direction will present itself."

She narrowed her eyes and stared at me. Then she shrugged her eyebrows and looked away. "Since I can't go more than a few feet away from you without dying, Mr. Cates, I am forced to consider your opinions on things while you're ambulatory." She looked back at me with a raised eyebrow. "Of course, if you weren't ambulatory, I could strap you to my back and solve the problem."

I nodded. "But—"

The putty on the cockpit hatch detonated, a muted explosion that seemed to suck all the air and sound out of the cabin for a second. Several of the Stormers slipped into the forward cabin silently, their little duckwalk smooth and creepy, low to the ground. For a few seconds there was no sound at all as the majority of the Stormers, Happling, Hense, and I just stood where we were, waiting. After a few seconds I looked back at Hense.

"But—"

Shouts erupted from the cockpit, overlapping voices melding in a cacophony impossible to dissect into individual words or phrases. A Stormer came hurtling through the still smoking hatchway, cutting through the air as if aerodynamic for a moment and then hitting the floor with a bone-cracking jolt, dissolving into arms and legs and grunts of pain. He rolled to a stop right at Hense's feet, and the colonel glanced down, stared at him for a moment, and then kicked him lightly in the head.

"Up," she said fiercely. "You're not hurt. Get the fuck up."

The Stormer moaned but slowly sat up and climbed to his feet, limping off to rejoin his mates, where Happling was issuing a flurry of hand signals as he shouted into the cockpit.

"Listen, Mr. Bendix," the big man said in a reasonable tone of voice. "We are placing you under arrest. No one here wants to hurt you, just because you're a soulless paper-pushing hack who likes to order cops into hot zones even though he's never carried a weapon in his life. We are taking possession of this hover, Mr. Bendix," Happling finished with a closed fist and a wide grin, "and you can go quiet, or you can go hard."

Through the clearing smoke, I made out a figure framed in the hatchway just as the Stormers wriggled into formation under Happling's cheerful direction.

"Ah, *fuck*," I managed, and then my feet flew out from under me and I was being pulled through the air. The cops ducked and scattered like a single living thing, a body undulating, and as the narrow hatch rushed toward me I tried to tuck my head as close to my body as I could manage. My legs smacked into the wall as I was sucked through, something shattering deep inside with an oddly numb pain that filled my whole leg like jelly, insulating and smothering, squeezing its way up into the rest of my body.

Once through the hatch I dropped to the floor hard, and before I could react fingers laced into my hair, yanking me up and tearing half my scalp off in the process.

"Hense, I suggest you *back the fuck off,* unless you want to risk Mr. Cates and his little Helper Robots, and—"

I was getting sick and tired of being everyone's prisoner. I planted my good leg solidly on the floor, reached up over my shoulders, and in a smooth movement that tore my back to shreds I leaned forward, knelt down, and rolled Bendix off-balance and onto the floor.

There were no rules for dealing with a telekinetic psionic, so I made up one on the spot: once you got him down, don't let up. You had to keep him from getting his balance and sending you flying.

I turned as fast as my lame leg would let me and dropped on top of him, letting gravity pull me down onto his chest hard enough to crack a rib or two. He howled, really getting his lungs into it, kicking his legs and trying to flail his arms. I lifted my heavy arm and brought my fist down onto his face, aiming for his half-healed scar. I was rewarded with another scream, so I did it again. It wasn't fun; unlike some Gunners, I didn't really enjoy kicking the shit out of people—I'd been on the receiving end of too many kicks. Every time I punched Bendix, my whole chest burned as if some bone spur in my rib cage were scraping and tearing at the pulp of my body, blood leaking inside me. I remembered Happling and his purple-suited pal tuning me up just a few days before.

It was just business. Bendix was a psionic and would have me bouncing off the walls if I paused for breath, so I didn't pause. I mashed my hand down onto his bloody face, and kept mashing as long as he kept moaning and wincing. When he stopped I paused, fist in the air, breath burning in the back of my throat, blood dripping from my damp hand.

A second later Bendix dropped away from me as if the floor had given out beneath him, except it was gravity sucking my lungs out through my mouth, and I smacked into the top of the cockpit so hard my teeth clicked together, reigniting every broken or missing tooth and sending stars into my eyes. Something invisible and heavy pushed me up against the ceiling as Stormers swarmed him, four throwing themselves across his battered body as Happling strode in, veins on his neck and arms pulsing. The redhead glanced up at me as he unslung the shredder from his shoulder. With one well-aimed shot of the butt Bendix twitched and went still, and I dropped back to the floor as if gravity had just realized I was there. I landed on my bad leg and swallowed a shout so hard I didn't breathe.

"Sir," Happling called back into the cabin. "The subject is unconscious and incapacitated, as ordered. He's, uh, a little worse off than you envisioned, I guess. What do we do with him?"

"Blindfold," I managed to gurgle, lying back on the floor and just breathing for a bit. "If he can't see you, he can't toss you." I wasn't entirely sure this was the case, but I remembered Kev Gatz and his limitations as a Pusher. It made sense.

I lay there aching while the cops bustled around me, barking orders and getting shit done. The ceiling of the hover was only sheet metal bolted onto the frame, and it looked beat-up, dented and with flecks of rust here and there. I wondered how long the hover had been in service. It felt good to not move, to not keep myself standing through willpower alone and just let gravity hold me down for a while. I had a fluttery, nervous feeling in my belly, as if I'd start shaking and laughing if I let myself.

Hense's face appeared over me.

"Cates," she said, raising one eyebrow. "You okay?"

I blinked up at her. "You afraid I have internal injuries? That maybe I'm going to die and take you with me, all quiet and shit?"

A faint smile imposed itself on her face. "Something like that."

I shook my head slowly. "Broken leg, I think. Broken ribs, but no punctured lung. Everything hurts, thanks to your gorilla boy over there, but nothing fatal."

She nodded. "Then get the fuck up. I need to know what the part B of your plan is."

"Plan?" I laughed, pushing myself into a sitting position and then pausing there, dazed. It seemed a nice compromise between the bullshit Hense was demanding and the more sensible plan of remaining on my back that I'd been entertaining. "Holy shit, are *you* confused," I said with a laugh. As I suspected, once I started laughing, my whole body began to shake.

"Cates," Hense said, voice pissed off. Then she stopped

and said nothing. It made me laugh harder, because she didn't know what to do. She had nothing left to threaten me with.

Finally, I swallowed some of the shivering and looked around. "Ty!" I shouted. "Mr. Kieth, I assume you've been monitoring our activities, right, you smart little fuck? It's all right. I think it's time for a parley, Ty, so we can come to an understanding. We've taken Mr. Bendix down and we're in control of the hover."

Hense and I waited, staring around like morons. Happling and the Stormers were dragging Bendix back into the cabin. I was considering the effort involved in sucking in enough air to make another shout when there was a click and a blast of static, and then Kieth's nasally voice in the air.

"No, Mr. Cates," he said. "You're not. Ty is."

I smiled and slumped back down onto the floor. It felt fucking *good* to be right about something for a change.

XXV

DAY NINE: INVISIBLE THINGS INSIDE ME STARTING TO SWELL AND TURN BLACK

Kieth spoke with confidence now that he was hidden. "Ty advises everyone to stay still. Ty has wired into the security systems on this hover and Ty will be *overzealous* about defending himself."

Shit, I didn't blame Ty for not trusting anyone. The hover was crowded with cops and a known killer, all of whom would solve half of their current problems if Ty Kieth were dead. If I were Kieth, I'd stay hidden, too.

I pushed myself up again, fighting against gravity that seemed to have become thicker and more insistent since last I checked. I looked around, trying to figure out where in hell Ty'd hidden himself. The hover was a big one, capable of transporting thirty or so people plus their gear, but where could a Techie—even a skinny piece of shit like Kieth—hide himself and still have access to the hover's systems?

"Mr. Kieth," Hense said loud and clear as she stood in

the cockpit, looking at the bank of controls, "is Mr. Marko with you?"

There was no response. I chuckled a little and she gave me a sour look. "Of course he won't tell you," I said. "Ty's *smart*. The more information you have, the more likely you'll figure out where he *is*."

"If I wanted to know where he *is*," she snapped, "I'd order Captain Happling to tear this hover apart until he found him."

Happling nodded. "And I *like* taking shit apart."

Kiplinger, his face mask off again, was suddenly at my side, cigarette dangling from his mouth. He shook one out of his crumpled pack and I leaned forward to place it between my lips.

"You really Avery Cates?" he asked, flicking his lighter on, the soft orange glow giving his sweaty face an unattractive gleam. He had a way of smiling without looking at you, like he was shy. "*The* Avery Cates?"

I nodded, sucking in smoke. "The gweat and tewwible," I advised.

He studied his hands for a moment, then smiled a little as he bent to light my smoke. "I was on a raid once, we were supposed to scoop you up. Some Gold Badge had a hard-on for you something serious, marching up and down in the hover, telling us what he was going to do to us if we missed you." He smiled again, shaking his head. "We missed you all right. Shit, I'll never forget the look on that asshole's face."

"Quit kissing his ass, trooper," Happling bellowed from across the cockpit. "Last week that bastard would have shot you dead without hesitation."

Kiplinger nodded, grinning at the floor as he stood up.

Then he paused and looked at me long enough to wink. "That's okay, sir. I would have shot *him,* huh?"

With that he stepped away, one of those eternally happy bastards. Hense looked from Happling to me as if she was waiting for us to cut out the grabass and get down to business. "Mr. Kieth," she said clearly, her flat eyes on me. "Since you are in possession of this hover, I'd like to ask politely what you mean to do with it."

After a moment's pause there came the staticky click and then Ty's voice. "Ty hadn't gotten that far in his thinking, to be honest."

"Heck, Ty," I said, taking my time with the cigarette, "how in hell do you end up here? Who the hell *is* that Tin Man? I'm sick and tired of him calling me by my first name."

Another long pause, but this time the buzzing static remained, the line held open. "Ty doesn't know. He calls Ty by name, too. It was Belling, that cunt. Came around talking about brokering a big job, needing the best, throwing out round numbers. *Big* round numbers. Ty admits it: he got greedy. The cunt arranged a meeting, and next thing you know, lights out, and Ty wakes up on a hover headed for fucking *Paris* for fuck's sake. Ty spent some time hiding in Paris when things got hot a few years back—right before you found Ty, in fact—and Ty was not happy to find himself here again. Ty was less happy when he found out what was expected of him here."

"Very touching," Happling muttered. "When they mark your tombstone, Mr. Kieth, it will say Murderer of the Human Race, Wasn't Happy about It."

"Ty had no choice!" Ty's voice was warped with feedback. "Ty didn't even realize what it was, at first. They compartmentalized it, gave it to Ty in pieces."

"That's a sad fucking story," Happling said, leaning on his rifle. "You're a real goddamn hero."

"Ty," I said, ignoring the cop. "Ty, you're in charge here. What's our next move? We should find that cocksucker. Neutralize him." I was tired of being on the defensive, tired of being tied up and beaten up and talked to. I wanted to get on the offensive, be moving. Hense gestured at someone in the rear cabin and the round-faced female trooper came trotting in. Hense pointed at me without looking my way and the trooper nodded, unslinging her rifle and producing a small medical kit as she stepped over to kneel next to me. She smelled...good, considering she'd been simmering in her own juices for hours and hours. Her smell reminded me of Glee a little, that sort of naturally clean smell.

Without looking at me she grabbed my fractured leg roughly, making me bite my cheek to stop from crying out, and began cutting open my pant leg.

"Don't be a baby," she drawled, her vowels all stretched out. "You look like the dog's been keepin' you under the porch."

I held my breath and resisted the urge to grab her nose and twist. Her face had a secret little smile on it, like she knew what I was thinking.

"Mr. Cates," Ty replied. "Ty is of the opinion he should be brought to a secure lab facility in New York or someplace nearby and be allowed to develop a workaround for the plague."

"Plague, huh?" I said, sucking in breath sharply as the Stormer ran her competent hands up and down my lower leg, feeling for the break. After the past few days, it felt like a hug. "Ty, why would we go to New York? Our Tin Man is here. And if we drag you someplace while he's still prowling around, he'll just come after us with his merry band of Monks."

With a jerk the Stormer set my leg, and I passed out.

When I came to, everything was warm and numb and words were in the air, people talking, but nothing made sense for a moment. I silently thanked my new best friends the police for whatever synthetic narcotic I'd just been given and looked up lovingly at the brown-haired Stormer playing nurse to me. She gave me a flat, disinterested look back and dug into her little bag, bringing out a short stick; with a flick of her wrist it extended into a perfect splint. I wearily admired her compact, efficient movements—a girl who knew what the fuck she was doing. I felt sorry for anyone she'd start sleeping with—they wouldn't have a chance.

"Mr. Cates," Ty said, the words slowly taking on meaning again, as if it were being pumped up from a deep well inside me, "we *must* go to New York. That is certainly where the Monk is headed, and he expects to find you there. He did *instruct* you to go back, didn't he?"

I nodded, feeling woozy. "Yes, Ty, he did. Which is why I shouldn't do it. The Tin Man wanted me to go back so I could keep spreading this shit around. I guess it hasn't reached critical mass for an unstoppable infection yet."

"Mr. Cates, if the Monk expects you to go back, you have to go back. If you don't your usefulness to him ends. And he will shut you down."

I winced as the splint was expertly fastened in place,

tight enough to restrict whatever blood was left inside me. "What the fuck are you talking about?"

"Your suppression field, Mr. Cates. It's remote controlled and can be disabled at any time, effectively turning *your* nanobots into the same deadly ones that are killing everyone else. You and everyone currently surviving in the waste of your suppression field will die, just like everyone else. The Monk is leaving it on because he wants you to keep spreading it — why, Ty doesn't know, because there are a dozen more effective ways to reach a tipping point on this — but if you don't do as it expects, what's to stop it from simply flipping the switch?" There was a tinny sigh from the invisible speakers. "Mr. Cates, you *must* return to New York as instructed. You must appear to be following its orders while I work on a solution."

The Stormer finished fixing up my leg. "No need to thank me, eh," she said primly, gathering her equipment and exiting the cockpit. For a few seconds we all just sat there, silent. In the rear cabin there was a sudden commotion among the Stormers.

"Balls," I muttered. I looked at Hense. "Any facilities in New York you think we could use?"

She looked back at me. We were all thinking the same thing: dragging Ty Kieth around the world so he could spend hours or days trying to hack his own creation was a waste of time when one bullet to the back of his head would solve the immediate problem nicely. I hated even thinking it — in a way, Ty was still part of my team. We'd parted on good terms; he'd always played fair. He'd gotten screwed, betrayed by Belling, and rewarding him with a bullet in the head because it was the easiest solution tasted like bullshit in my mouth. But I thought of

Glee again, and millions of people—everyone I'd ever known—dying, and it was hard to argue with the cosmos on this one. While Ty was hidden away, we had to watch how we conversed, though.

"There is an emergency bunker in Manhattan," Hense said slowly, staring off into the rear cabin. "But I can't know if it's still in use or in SSF hands, or if I'd even have access since..." She let that thought drift, frowning, then strode back into the cabin without another word.

"Mr. Cates," Ty said quietly, "how does Ty know you won't simply execute him when the opportunity comes? How does Ty know you won't kill him?"

I bought some time by struggling to my feet, making it look harder than it was. The splint was excellent, and I found I could pretty much put weight on the leg with only a modest, throbbing pain for my troubles. I wouldn't want to sprint anytime soon, but I figured I could clump about pretty effectively. I was still trying to lawyer up a noncommittal response when Hense stormed back into the cockpit.

"You mobile?" she snapped.

I nodded. "Not very graceful, but I was never much of a dancer anyway."

She held up one of her own shiny Roons by the barrel and pointed the grip at me. "Take it. We're going to need every bit of talent we can lay our hands on, I think. We're under siege."

I blinked, accepting the gun and several spare clips. "Siege? By whom?"

Her withering look indicated it was the dumbest question she'd heard in a long time. "Who the fuck else? The Monks. They're back."

The gun felt good in my hand, comfortable. Roons weren't manufactured anymore, but they were still the best handguns in the world, barring a few ancient pre-Unification models. It fit perfectly. I dropped the clip and inspected the chamber, reloaded and snapped everything back, surprised at how much better I felt armed.

"Told you," Ty said. "You're supposed to be over the ocean by now. The Monk's pissed."

I grimaced. "Or they're here for *you,* little man."

A curious feeling stole over me, a creepy-crawly kind of sensation, as if I could *feel* all the tiny, invisible things inside me starting to swell and turn black, spikes sprouting from their delicate, molecule-thick skins. As if I could feel death polluting my blood, poking holes in my vessels. I tried to ignore it, swallowing hard.

"Let's go," Hense said, turning away. "Mr. Kieth, let's get this brick in the air."

She'd turned and made it to the hatchway before Kieth's small voice stopped her. "That presents difficulties, uh, Colonel."

Hense stopped but didn't turn around. "Why is that, Mr. Kieth?" she said, cocking her head to the side.

"I am unfamiliar with the exact systems on this hover," he confessed slowly. "In my haste to secure my position, some systems were offlined."

"Systems," she repeated, her little hands curling into fists, "were *offlined.*" I remained where I was, waiting, all of *my* systems up and sniffing the air, because the scent of violence was in the air. After a moment she relaxed. "I would suggest, in a purely advisory function, that you get them back *online* and get us into the air soon, Mr. Kieth, unless you want to end up back inside that box."

She stepped through the hatchway. I started to follow, but before I'd gone two steps Ty's voice crackled through the air, warping and melting.

"Mr. Cates!"

I stopped and closed my eyes. I saw the nanos, like tiny little spiky fish, floating in the darkness. "Yes, Ty?"

"How does Ty know you won't kill him?"

I swallowed. "Ty, you have my word. You know me, Mr. Kieth. I keep my promises. You have my word. We will find another solution."

"Your word, Mr. Cates," Ty said.

"You have my word, Ty," I repeated, and stepped quickly into the main cabin. I kept my eyes on the floor and didn't look at anyone. Because I was lying.

XXVI

DAY NINE: THE REST OF THE WORLD WAS A BONUS

Eyes down, I dropped my extra clips into my coat and hobbled into the cabin. The Stormers were all assembled, back in their full ObFu kit, in standard formation for a drop. The drop in this case was just a few feet, since the hover was sitting dead on the ground. The big drop-bay doors were shut tight, leaving the cabin gloomy and claustrophobic. The whole place smelled of soured sweat and oiled metal, and I knew I was pumping self-loathing and a good bit of fear into the atmosphere, too.

If Kieth could get the hover into the air, we didn't have much to worry about: the hover's bottom-mounted turrets would chew even Monks into small, digestible pieces in short order, and Monks still couldn't fly, as far as I knew. Until that magical moment when the displacers roared into life, however, we were basically sitting in a shiny metal box that had never been designed to repel boarders.

The closed Vid screens above the drop bay lit up

suddenly, showing the dead city around us. "Ah! Found the visuals," Kieth chirped, sounding pleased with himself.

Onscreen, I could see the Monks outside, dozens of them surrounding the hover, more emerging from the scummy water of the river. I watched them arrange themselves and tried to imagine what they were planning to do. They didn't know the hover was incapacitated, and if it took off with them underfoot it wouldn't be pretty. The sight of them in grainy, pixilated color—white faces, dark coats, some still wearing their standard-issue sunglasses—made my whole body tighten up in dread.

Ooh, Avery's afraid of Monks, I heard Glee say. *Avery's got a* phobia.

Happling appeared at my elbow, two autos slung into crisscrossed holsters under each arm, his huge humming shredder in both hands. His red hair was standing up in bizarre, dirt-crusted directions, and he was smiling. I kept my eyes on him without moving my head, resolving not to speak to him because I didn't want to hear what he was thinking. Happling looked like the sort of berserker who got you killed. He was enjoying himself.

Hense produced her flask from some hidden pocket but didn't bother with her dainty little cup. She unscrewed the cap and took a blast, then walked over and handed the flask silently to Happling, who took a superhuman gulp, liquor dribbling down his chin. Smacking his lips, he handed it back to the colonel.

"All right," he said, and I braced myself for crazy. "We dealt with these freaks once," he said loudly, to the whole cabin. "Some of you were with the force, I know, when we had to clean up these Tin Men during the Monk Riots. They're fast. They have digital filters on their visual and can switch between visible spectrum, heat sig, or motion sensing. They don't like bullets any more than you and me, but they can shut down individual systems if damaged and don't exactly feel pain. They're fucking murder. But a shot to the head puts them down, and inside that freak show is a stupid shithead brain."

I stared at the multiplying Monks on the screen and felt Happling next to me. I couldn't decide where I'd rather be. All the cop testosterone in the air was suffocating. On the other hand, I had this weird feeling that I was watching civilization in action here—the line between order and chaos—and it was manned by the Nathan Happlings of the world.

"Order it up, Captain," Hense said in a low, controlled voice.

"Listen up!" Happling shouted immediately, as if her command had been a coincidence. "This is a Scenario B4 situation. Rumor has it you faggots have had some training, so I'm expecting a clean execution. Watch your crossfire! Hey, fat girl," he snapped, jabbing one huge hand in the direction of the round-faced, slow-talking Stormer. "You're on Intrusion Detection. I want you humping it up and down this fucking hover and anything you see, feel, hear, or fucking *smell* that seems unusual, you make a fucking ruckus, right?"

I had this weird urge to defend her. She managed to make her salute simultaneously crisp and mocking with just the slightest curve of her lips, and I thought I might be falling in love with her. "On it like a duck on a june bug, *sir.*"

Happling stared for just a second, then obviously decided he didn't have time for ass-kicking and nodded, sweeping his gaze back around the cabin. "This group here," he said, dividing about a dozen of the Stormers with a knifing motion of his hand, "you are on the hatch. That's our weakest point. Watch your fucking *crossfire,* but when they rip that shit off—and they will—you pour murder into it and you don't let a single one in here. Do *not* deploy your shredding rifles in this enclosed space. If I see any of you unslinging a shredder, be sure the next sensation you feel will be me shoving that hunk of metal up your ass."

"You," he said, turning to look at another Stormer, this one a big, square-headed guy apparently made out of a single slab of beef. Beefy looked at Happling as if he wished he'd remembered his suicide pills that morning. "You're on the drop-bay door panel. See it? Do I have to go piss on it so you can find it, trooper? We don't have time for this, Nancy—okay, open that up. If it looks like they're going to force those bay doors, trooper, cut those wires. The fail-safes will kick in and snap that mother-fucker shut tighter than your asshole right now. This is your discretion, trooper, don't make me fucking dig you up later to reprimand you."

"The rest of you," he continued after a moment, in a lower voice, "you just wait for people to die. Someone goes down, you get in there and take their place. Do *not* fire from a rear position, you'll just fucking kill your own people."

From above came three or four dull thuds, but I was the only one to glance up.

"Here they come!" Happling shouted, pulling his guns from their holsters and grinning. I thought to myself, *Every cop in the fucking System is batshit insane.* And then, with a shivery feeling as if someone had dumped cold water directly into my bloodstream, I thought, *Where the fuck is Ty?* If the Techies had found a way into the hover, it stood to reason the Monks would manage it too, eventually.

I looked around, but a bell-like metallic clang and the groaning noise of metal fatigue sounded as the hatch door was grasped by something outside and pulled outward. With a rattle of metal all the cops leaned forward. I ran my eyes over the whole cabin and stepped back, suddenly sure that we'd just fucked up in a massive way but completely unsure how to rectify the situation. I didn't have plans for the hover and couldn't even begin to guess where two Techies might be spending some quality time breathing each other's farts and whispering about security protocols.

The hatch popped off the hover with a loud cracking noise, and immediately three Monks were climbing into the cabin. The Stormers opened fire as one, and for a second or two the cabin was solid sound, the noise almost a wall that squeezed the breath out of me.

I stepped quickly toward the cockpit. "Ty!" I shouted. "Ty, can you hear me?"

In the cockpit I could barely make out his voice. "Ty is a little goddamn busy, Mr. Cates!"

"Ty, where are you?"

There was no response. In the cabin, the roar of gunfire grew impossibly louder, and then added to it was more hollow pounding from above as Monks worked their way in from the top. I made fists. "Ty, goddammit, we're being *invaded,* and you're sitting in a spot that took you about fifteen seconds to get into! Where the fuck are you?"

I waited another moment. "Mr. Cates...we have an understanding, yes?"

I struggled to stay still, to keep my face blank. "Ty, you have my word."

After another moment of listening to the Monks hammering at the hover, Happling's gleeful voice roaring above it all, a panel in the floor almost at my feet slid away in a smooth, mechanical motion, and Ty's bald, gleaming head appeared, nose twitching nonstop. We stared at each other.

"Redundant manual repair module," he said with a shrug. "Almost no one knows these exist, since most of the work is done digitally or by Droids."

I kept staring at him. Here he was, the living kill switch to the little devils eating up the human race, floating around inside me and biding their time. I had a gun in my hand and every other living and not-living thing in the area distracted. My arm wouldn't move, though. I'd made a promise; I'd given my word. As I stared at Kieth I thought, *Fuck my word.* This wasn't about honor. This was about *living,* and not just me.

I checked that, tightening my grip on my gun. Why lie to myself? It was about *me* living. The rest of the world was a bonus.

My arm twitched and started to bring the gun up but then I paused, a blurry feeling of calm, pleasant buzzing seeping over me. A much better idea, I thought, was to investigate the entry point, see if it posed a threat of infiltrating Monks. A grin, crooked and loose, formed on my face. "Shove over," I suggested, stepping forward and jamming the gun into my coat. "Show me how you got in."

Kieth blinked in surprise but did what he always did when you moved toward him—backed away. I followed down into a cramped space where we had to almost embrace, crouching over the prone shape of Mr. Marko, who stared up at me as sweat streamed down his face from every pore, and Kieth gestured at a dark crawl space behind me barely wide enough for someone my size to fit into. I dreaded it on sight. Once inside I would barely be able to breathe, much less move myself along.

Still, the curious feeling of cheerful laziness filled me, an oily, viscous sensation that coated every thought I had. Should I report this to the Pigs? The feeling said no, too much trouble. Should I squeeze myself into the crawl space and hump to the entry point, make sure of it? The feeling said emphatically yes, that was an excellent idea. I gave Kieth the same crooked smile.

"Stay here," I suggested. "I'm going to check it out."

Kieth jumped as if he'd been stabbed with a pin. The banging noises, carried by the hull, were just as loud in the hole as they'd been up above, but with extra echo, as if they were happening deep below the earth. "Mr. Cates! I can assure you—"

I didn't stop to listen. Without hesitation I pushed myself into the pitch-black tube and began wriggling forward. I felt fine. I was calm, almost happy, and perfectly sure of my actions. It was a familiar feeling, and as I wriggled through the greasy ductwork toward a slowly growing pin of watery light, I wondered idly why it seemed familiar. It wasn't an urgent worry, just a mild curiosity I was confident would resolve itself eventually.

Sweating and gasping, I managed to slide the last few feet down to a thin wire grating that separated me from the outside world. Peering through it, I had a good view of the muddy ground beneath the hover and could tell the grating was hidden inside a surrounding well of metal not easily seen from anywhere but directly below. I could see the mechanism that snapped a protective plate over the grating when the hover was pressurized. The Monks would likely not discover it for some time yet.

I watched, bemused, as my arms reached out and smacked against the grating, easily knocking it out of its clips. It fluttered to the ground and didn't even make any noise I could pick out amid the din. As I let myself slide forward, I realized I was still smiling, the expression stuck on my face. I decided I would worry about it later.

The ground jumped up at me and I landed awkwardly, tumbling out onto the wet earth. I lay there for a moment, staring up at the scorched, riveted underbelly of the hover, its landing gear looking monolithic, like trees made of metal and cable. The noise around me had swollen back up to full size, but I wasn't concerned. Sitting up, I stared around for a few moments before struggling awkwardly to my feet, hanging on to the bottom of the hover for balance, my head ducked uncomfortably. I stumped out from beneath the hover and found myself in the middle of a battlefield.

The Monks were everywhere, clinging to the hover like barnacles. I staggered forward, smiling around, feeling at peace as I watched the Tin Men pounding their alloyed hands—some without any skin covering the chromelike fingers—into the hover's hull while a constant stream of them assaulted the narrow hatchway, getting chewed up by the Stormers within for their troubles. None took any notice of me as I limped toward the river, where their leader stood with its arms folded across its chest, looking like a new penny. Wa Belling stood next to it, and for once didn't look particularly pleased with himself. It was such a new expression for the old man that I was momentarily startled, the whole world seeming to rush back into me for a heartbeat, and I remembered when I'd felt this way before: years ago, in New York, before everything.

I studied the Monk as I approached. It still seemed like a good idea, and I didn't worry about it because I knew I didn't have much choice. My decisions were being made for me.

When I was right in front of the Monk I stopped and gave it the benefit of my loopy smile, cocking my head to one side. After another heartbeat all the calm burst inside me, bitterness and fear rushing in to take its place, my whole body shuddering with suddenly remembered pain and anxiety. I kept the smile in place, though. I was Avery Cates. I smiled at everything. Even ghosts.

"Hello, Kev," I said. "You've looked better."

XXVII

DAY NINE: IT'S WHAT I DO

Long ago I'd been Pushed by Kev Gatz, my old, dead friend, and I knew the feeling, I knew the print of his mind on mine. He was better at it, more refined and more in control, but now that he'd lifted the Push off me I recognized it, and recognized it from earlier at the church, too. I stared at him and my carefully maintained cool started to melt away as he smirked his plastic Monk face at me, trying to smile.

Kev and I had rattled around New York for years. He'd always been a little cracked, a little strange, and the only thing that had kept him alive was the Push, the psionic power he'd been born with. Somehow he slipped under the SSF's radar and hadn't been disappeared like every other kid who showed any kind of mental talent—kids who grew up to be the Shockleys and Bendixes of the world—and had managed to become a minor criminal, a bottom-feeder. And when I'd gotten the Squalor job, when Dick Marin had rammed the Squalor job hot and glowing up my ass and told me to kill the founder of the Electric Church or be killed, I'd taken Kev

Gatz with me as my psionid ace in the hole. He was the only reason my plan had worked, and it had cost him his life.

I remembered him slumped against the wall. I remembered I'd been hiding behind a cart when he'd been killed.

"How——?" I started to say, and then found I hadn't actually formed a coherent question.

"Thanks for showing us where Ty is hidden," he said as three Monks detached from his retinue, retracing my steps and ducking under the hover. "Avery, do you know how long the human brain remains viable—and functioning—after death?"

I shook my head a little, the most movement I could manage.

"I know. *He* told me. Long enough," Kev said. "You *left* me there. You left me. Good old Avery, my only friend. The only person who ever gave a rat's ass about poor old weird Kev Gatz. You bullied me into helping you, Avery. You bullied me and you hit me and you treated me like *shit,* and I took it because I thought you were my friend. And then I saw your boots walk off and just leave me in that fucking hallway. Just *left* me there like trash."

His face had gone blank again, and with the sunglasses I couldn't tell if his little camera eyes were on me or not. "They came for me. A few minutes after you left me there, they came for me. Know how long it takes to process a corpse into a Monk, Avery? I do. Twelve minutes, once the body is strapped in. Twelve fucking minutes. And then there was no doubt. No headaches. No trouble thinking. Just a wonderful voice, Avery, telling me he'd made me and I was his son, and telling me what to do. Telling me how to keep myself in repair. Telling me how to find other brothers who'd survived, who were *functional.* Telling me to have my revenge."

I worked my mouth once or twice, and finally got enough saliva into it. "This is *revenge?* Against *me?*"

Kev leaned forward slightly, and I felt the numb touch of his mind on mine, holding me perfectly still as his stiff, molded face pushed close to mine. "This is revenge, Avery, against *everyone.*"

From behind I heard Kieth's ragged voice as he shouted incoherently. I couldn't move, but I knew how he probably looked in the grasp of a few Monks, being dragged from his hiding spot: eyes wide, nose vibrating, head glistening with sweat. After a few beats he stopped shouting and started calling my name.

"Cates! Mr. Cates! What's happening!? Mr. Cates!"

My head was held stiffly in place, staring back at Kev.

"This is a course correction, Avery," he said, his voice modulated to be calm and pleasant, as if we were discussing drinks after dinner at the fucking club. I had the feeling these weren't Kev's words. "This is a controlled burn. One thing I can say about what happened to me, Ave, is that I found clarity. You know what being a Monk is, Avery? Why it's so *hard* to stay in *control?* It's pain, Ave. It's been pain, pain flowing through me like fucking blood. It just *hurts,* all the time."

Kieth was dragged past us. The Techie had stopped shouting and just stared at me as he was pulled along. I managed to move my eyes enough to follow him.

"But I have *Him,*" Kev continued. "Helping me *clarify.* That's what we've all done. And we decided it would simply be easier if there weren't so much meat around."

Meat. I struggled against his Push. Kieth and him within feet of me, a gun in my pocket, and I was standing there as if someone had cut my spinal cord.

Kev reached out and put a dead plastic hand on my shoulder. "Go, Avery. Go home, or as close as you can get, and spread yourself around. We want you to be *directly* responsible for as many people as possible. Okay? Go home and scratch out a few more days, and then I'll collect you, and then—*then*—you will be punished. You think the System Pigs are bad, Avery? So bad you've spent your whole life like a roach, scuttling away from their terrible light? Listen, my old friend: just wait till when they're finally gone and you must worry about *me*."

He lifted his hand and pushed me in the chest, oddly gentle. Again I had the impression he was quoting someone. "Go," he said, and I went, against my will.

As I walked slowly back toward the hover, the Monks retreated, trading fire with the cops in a perfunctory way. Bullets sizzled past me once or twice, but I couldn't make myself move, not even to duck or dodge. I cursed up a storm as I was propelled toward the hover, praying the fucking cops didn't mistake me for something else and decide to snipe me just because of Best Practices and shit. About halfway there, a Monk veered across my path, running silently, smoothly, and as it passed a few feet in front of me its head exploded in an off-white mist and it dropped to the mud. My puppet body just stepped over it, calm and steady, while I bit off a stream of *Fucking hell*s and tried to clench my fists. I might as well have tried to pop my eyes out of my skull. Kev had me in his grip.

When I was within a few feet of the hover, Hense appeared framed in the hatchway, wind moving her hair around. She looked tiny, like the wind might just pick her up and send her sailing off. Her eyes were as flat and steady as always, but I had the nervous feeling that if I hadn't been absolutely necessary for her survival, I'd already be dead.

"What the fuck," she said slowly, "was *that* bullshit?"

My leg ached, a deep, steady ache without a pulse, without relief. I wanted to cut it off myself, just tear through the bone and tendons and rip it off, replace that bottomless ache with some real pain, something sharp and satisfying. Something I could pick at. I deserved it. Knowing she couldn't kill me yet, I pushed past her and pulled myself into the hover. "We're old friends."

I paused in the hatchway, hip touching Hense's hip and liking the way it felt. The hover cabin was a fucking charnel house. Five or six of the Stormers were dead, their ObFu flickering, torn up and bloodstained. Another half dozen were getting field dressings, one of whom, expert appraisal told me, was a waste of time and resources.

"Hell," I said, looking around, "you fucking had *guns*, right?"

Something the relative mass of a planet hit me in the chest, and I was lifted off my feet and sailing through the air. I landed in the mud and Happling was on top of me, his face almost as red as his hair. His hands were on my throat, and like *that*, I couldn't breathe. I bugged out my eyes and pushed feebly against him. He was like a goddamn boulder on top of me. One of his hands slipped away from my neck, allowing me to suck in a quick breath, my mouth opening wide at the unexpected opportunity. Which was a mistake, because suddenly Happling's gun was jammed into it, knocking a loose tooth out. It landed in my throat, making me gag.

"The Spook missed this," he panted. "This is a modified M nineteen eleven semiautomatic. Not standard issue, but we all have to have our fucking vices. It's fucking ancient.

Pre-Unification. You can't even get ammunition for it. I have *three bullets left,* you piece of shit. I've got dead cops in there. And you *know* that fucking monster? You *give* the fucking Techie to it?" He panted a few breaths, warm against my face. "I've been saving these three shots. Right now I'm considering giving all three to you, as a fucking gift."

I gagged on the barrel, making wet noises around it.

"Yeah—kill you, kill me. *Got* it, you fucking asshole. Got fucking it. How many times you gonna say it? I should have killed you back in the Rock, you fucking cop killer."

"Captain Happling!" I heard Hense bellow, amazing volume for such a small woman. "Stand down!"

I wondered idly how often Happling was almost going to kill me. His eyes were the brightest green I'd ever seen, like rot beaming down at me. Bloodshot and bright white, too, dilated. The man was insane. I considered, tonguing the metal, and after a contemplative snort of phlegmy oxygen through the narrow aperture that had once been my nose, I decided, Fuck this asshole. Like an amateur he'd left my arms free, and I knew he wasn't going to shoot me, so I snaked one hand down between us and grabbed his balls like they were mine. He froze for a second, and I smacked my forehead up into his nose and scissored my legs, flipping him over like dead weight and letting his momentum carry me on top of him. I pushed his wrists into the mud and put all my weight onto them. Happling was roughly six times my size, so I didn't doubt he could flip me off if he wanted, but for a moment we just stared at each other.

"Captain Happling!" Hense shouted again. "Stand the fuck down."

Happling blinked. "Yes, sir," he said in a barely audible whisper, eyes locked on me. I released him and rolled over, and just lay there in the mud for a moment, dragging in breath. Then Hense was kneeling over me, looking surprisingly clean and coiffed.

"Cates," she said in that flat, disinterested voice, "you got a story to tell us?"

"The Monk, the leader—I knew him when he was… before he was a Monk." *I watched him die. I got him killed.* "We have history."

Her face didn't shift. "So maybe you weren't a completely *random* choice to be patient zero?"

I squinted up at her. "Maybe." Groaning, I sat up, forcing her to stand up awkwardly. "He was—is—a psionic. A Pusher. It doesn't matter. Nothing's changed. We need to track down Kieth. We need to figure out where they're going. Your Mr. Marko still alive?"

She nodded, holding out one pleasantly dry hand and helping me to my feet with surprising strength. "Yes. He's terrified, but I'm getting the impression that isn't an unusual state for him." For a moment she kept hold of my hand. "We have an agreement," she said, and we stared at each other.

I nodded and let go. "Then get your gorilla in line. Let's dump bodies and get that hover in the air, and maybe Mr. Marko can help us figure out where we need to go."

She gestured at Happling, who immediately climbed to his feet and holstered his ancient gun, silently falling in behind us as we returned to the hover, which now looked as if it had crash-landed. "And what do you plan to do once we get there, Mr. Cates?"

I didn't look at her. "Kill people. It's what I do."

XXVIII

DAY NINE: WAVE HIS HANDS IN THE AIR AND RAIN DEATH FROM THE SKY

Afraid and too exhausted to do much of anything, Marko took longer to be coaxed out of hiding than to get the brick into the air. Sweating and jumping at every noise, he picked up the boards and cables Kieth had left behind and in a few moments a shudder passed through the hover, and we were in business. Talking in low voices among themselves, the Stormers finished pushing bodies out the drop-bay doors. Kiplinger had taken a bad shot to the chest, a sucking wound that wheezed with every shortening breath he took while his squad shouted around him, trying every useless trick in their field medical kit. He finally turned blue and died as they all shut the hell up, staring down at him and then looking at me. I just stared back, and they said nothing, dragging his body over to the doors and pushing him out with the rest.

I kept my eyes on the opposite wall, thinking back over the past week and farther back, to Westminster Abbey and Kev getting killed. He'd been *dead,* and an hour later so had Dennis Squalor. I'd ended up with Wa Belling as a partner. It should have been Kev. I realized that after all those years I didn't really know what Belling's motivations had been. With Kev I would have *known,* I would have had a friend at my side. And none of this shit would have happened.

I wondered how many people were dead now. How far it had spread. Kev—or the voice he kept talking about—had wanted me to be the source, and eventually to know it. To torture me with the idea that I'd killed *everybody.* The whole fucking *world.* I stared at the bare metal cabin wall, dented and perforated by bullet holes, my hands tight on my knees, scabs on my knuckles cracking and oozing blood. There wasn't any point in keeping up my list anymore. I'd never even know most of the people I'd hustled off to death now.

Appearing quietly at my elbow, Hense sat down next to me and produced a small plastic canister. Making it rattle in my ear, she said, "Hungry?"

The moment she said it, I was. "Starving," I said. I eyed the tiny box. "Ah, nutrition tabs. Breakfast of kings."

She didn't smile, but there was perhaps a tiny softening around her eyes that might have indicated mirth. I held out one scabby hand, noting with surprise that my pinky was bent in the middle in what looked like a painful way, and she shook three white pills into my palm. I dry-swallowed them and cursed them, my still hungry stomach clawing at itself.

As usual, the nutrition tabs made me nauseous almost instantly.

"I was Pushed once," she said suddenly, her voice low.

"Years ago. We raided an apartment in the Bowery, little shits selling homemade guns to the brats, causing us more fucking trouble than you'd believe from goddamn seven-year-olds with plastic single-shot peashooters. I bust into the bathroom and there's this kid trying to wriggle through the window, but it's a little too small for him and his clothes are so goddamn big his pants are being left behind and it's just his bare ass staring at me. I yank him back and decide to throw a scare into him. I flip him over and I have this little speech prepared, but he looks at me and next thing I knew, I was letting that little shit walk right past me and feeling pretty good about it for a minute." She shook a pill into her hand and popped it into her mouth. "I never saw that punk again, and I'll tell you this: I'm glad, because that shit scared the hell out of me."

I licked pill grit from my jagged teeth and thought, *Hell, I've hit rock bottom. I'm being pitied by a System Pig.*

Marko saved me from having to reply, shambling into the cabin looking sweaty and greasy, wiping his hands on his shirt. "We're ready to go," he said, his voice low and stretched out. "If anyone has any ideas about *where*." He remained standing, and after a moment I looked up. To my sudden horror, he was looking at me, chewing his lip. "Mr. Cates," he said. "I heard what Mr. Kieth said. About them just turning you off. A kill switch."

I could smell more pity, pity from a man who would be dead just as quickly as me if things went in that downhill direction. To put a stop to it, I cleared my throat. "New York," I said. "We have to go to New York."

"Are you fucking *insane?*"

I turned sharply at the voice. Bendix had been tied

securely to the safety netting in the rear of the hover, his arms and legs bent uncomfortably back, a thick blindfold wrapped around his eyes. If the hover crashed — which was entirely possible considering the damage the Monks had done to it — I put my money on Bendix being the only one of us who survived, he was so securely restrained.

Hense gestured, and two Stormers took a bead on Bendix, ready for the order.

"New York is a *graveyard*," Bendix said forcefully. "I doubt anyone's left alive there. There's no government. We have no presence there. You might as well land in the fucking ocean and let us sink."

"Mr. Bendix," Hense said, standing up. "I advise you that you are being covered by two randomly placed troopers who have orders to shoot you at the first sign of any psionic activity. Am I understood?"

He grinned, that puckered face twisting up, but he said nothing else. I looked at Marko.

"New York," I said. "That's where he wants me to go anyway, and I can't risk the kill switch. Besides, that's where he'll be."

"But why would he take Mr. Kieth to the same place we're going?" Marko said, scrubbing his face with his filthy hands, leaving dark streaks on his cheeks.

I glanced at Bendix. "Because the Spook's right — New York's a fucking Ghost City. There's no safer place for Kev and his merry men to hole up."

From my right, Bendix's congealed laughter filled the cabin. "Monks? Kev? Kev *Gatz?*"

I stared at him, my right eye giving a twitch. "You know him?"

He moved his head around as if sniffing the air. "Mr.

Cates, the government naturally keeps track of all known terrorist organizations. Kev Gatz and his fellow cyborg refugees have been on our radar for some years now. His file is admittedly thin; we have almost no record of him prior to the Monk Riots." His face twisted up again. "Our usual agents had tabs on his organization up until two days ago, when our usual agents...died."

For a few seconds we all sat there in silence. Finally I licked my cracked lips. "Mr. Bendix, do you have a point?"

He nodded, opening his mouth as he did so and waggling his eyebrows under the blindfold. "Oh, yes, Mr. Cates. Three days ago our last official report on Gatz had his group seizing Bellevue Hospital Center with little resistance, the complex having been abandoned and occupied by itinerants of deteriorating health. You would have heard the report, officers, except you'd been burned off the force by then, of course."

"Well, hell," I said. "We get a fix on Kieth's signal like before, you can call in a fucking missile strike or whatever. Kieth's dead, this whole mess goes away." A thin kernel of hope bloomed inside me, and I almost welcomed the idea of having to worry about getting away from Hense and Happling or whichever System Pigs stepped in to take their place.

I felt Marko looking at me, and I knew he'd heard me make my promise to Ty. I kept my eyes off him, but I still felt his scrutiny.

Bendix nodded. "Certainly. But you would have to put me in touch with my office."

"Uh," Marko said slowly, raising his hand, "there is one problem with that. When I got the hover going I tried a scan for Mr. Kieth. I can't find him anymore." He shrugged, an incredibly slow, lazy movement. "I think they're shielding him."

I closed my eyes. The Kev Gatz I'd known had been a burnout, a man who could make you dance and sing if he bent his mind to it but who sometimes didn't seem capable of forming sentences. Now he was a goddamn cyborg mastermind. "All right, but I think Mr. Bendix is saying we know where they're headed—Bellevue. Just take the shot. We'll know soon enough if we hit the mark."

We all looked at Bendix. His smile got even twistier, but he shook his head. "No."

I almost jumped to my feet. This was *it,* this was a solution. This was burning out an infection. This was *easy,* and I wanted to squeeze an answer out of the goddamn assistant to the Undersecretary. Before I could find my voice, Hense spoke up.

"Why the fuck not?"

"Ms. Hense," Bendix said, shaking his head. "The whole eastern seaboard is in turmoil as this spreads, and we're starting to see flare-ups of the infection elsewhere in the System, probably spread by System Security Force personnel moving from place to place. We've lost huge numbers of assets and resources, and we're struggling simply to maintain control in North America right now. Intact assets in the rest of the world must be preserved to guard against what is at the moment an inevitable spread of chaos and loss of life." His smile faded a little. "We're stretched thin as it is. You expect me to arrange for military assets to be transported to New York and expended for the *chance?*" He shook his head again. "No. Show me where Mr. Kieth is, and I will issue such an order. Not before."

"Motherfucker," I hissed, looking up at Hense. "Call the cops. Call your people." The cops didn't hesitate. The cops killed everything first and asking fucking questions later.

Hense didn't look at me. "No, Mr. Cates," she said quietly, looking at the Stormers around us. "We're burned. No one will talk to us. We won't get through to anyone."

I stared at her, then at Happling, who looked like he was chewing his own tongue. "You're fucking kidding me."

She shook her head. "You don't understand. You're not police."

I stood up, the action intended as dramatic but ending up slow and pathetic. "I'm not *insane*," I said, turning to Marko. I hated him because he knew what I'd said to Kieth. "New York. We find Kieth and then Mr. Bendix will wave his hands in the air and rain death from the sky." I looked around. Hense, Happling, Marko, and the Stormers were all focused on me. Except for Marko, they'd all wanted me dead not so long ago, but they were looking at me calmly, expectantly, as if I knew what our best move was.

"Fuck it," I said, turning for the cockpit. "We do it the hard way. As fucking usual."

XXIX

DAY TEN: SEND THE VIP ON DOWN

Zooming toward the coast, the hover rattled and shook violently, but I barely noticed. It had been shuddering and lurching through the air, the displacers roaring with a sour, off-center noise that was painful to the ears, ever since we lifted off. Marko handled the brick like he was riding a dead elephant, and by the time we were halfway across the ocean he'd made four of the surviving fifteen Stormers puke into the safety netting.

I was sitting in the copilot's seat. Wires snaked from the maintenance duct on the floor between us directly into the dashboard, which made me nervous. Any sudden, un-planned move by Marko would more than likely result in some disconnections, and I had a vague but heavy cer-tainty disconnections would result in us smashing into the Atlantic.

"Things must be bad," I said to Hense in a low, careful voice. She crouched on one side of me, awkwardly folded into the space between the copilot's seat and the dashboard. Happling was behind us, grim and silent, all his crazy cheer gone for a change. I'd liked him better laughing. "You hear Bendix? Assets, resources: translation is, they've lost the fucking East Coast and have nothing to throw at it."

Hense nodded. We'd all been out of touch for too many days; we were working from hints. "That explains a fucking civilian Spook leading a team of cops," she said. "A week ago that would never have happened."

I'd sketched out a primitive map of Bellevue Hospital Complex in a mixture of blood and grease on a piece of cloth torn from one of the Stormers' underuniforms. It wasn't pretty but it gave the general idea. I'd been there only once, eight or nine years before, on a job. Three doctors, all rich and under guard, all had to be dead on the same day. I remembered the job well: a challenge. I'd been forced to take some pains with the grounds; next to The Rock, the hospital was one of the most heavily guarded areas of the city. After all, they couldn't let in the assholes without medical chips.

Nine years was a long time. Buildings went up or down, security configurations changed, floors were abandoned or populated. Still, my hazy memory was all we had to go on until Marko dug up something more useful.

"We're on a schedule, too," I said. "From what Kev said, they're just waiting for enough people to die off, and then they won't need Kieth or me anymore."

"And they shut you down," she said, giving me that steady stare.

"Shut us *all* down," I reminded her. "I don't know when that moment is going to be. But if the whole East Coast is gone in a week, it can't be long. Give me a cigarette," I said. She didn't hesitate, snapping open her little case and offering it to me, then adroitly manipulating case and lighter with one hand, managing to snap the case closed and the lighter open without dropping either. Admiring her tidy movements and enjoying the feel of her leg against mine, I sucked the bitter smoke in and stared down at my crude little map. "The hospital complex is like a goddamn fortress to keep out folks like me who don't have a med chip. But it's nothing complicated—it's walls and electronic gates and motion sensors and a lot of private guards. Okay, let's assume the private guards are all dead. Let's also assume they've been replaced by Monks. That's an upgrade. Is the power grid still up?"

Hense shook her head. "According to Bendix it went down two days ago. Apparently a large part of Long Island isn't there anymore."

I nodded. "Okay. So the electronic perimeter can be discounted. So what we've got is a few dozen Monks guarding roughly a mile of concrete and barbed wire. But it's a hospital, right? So it's designed to let people in and out."

Happling's huge arm moved past my face, a thick finger pointing at my diagram. "Your map's a little out of date. I pulled bodyguard duty on some asshole doctor there three years ago. Fucking prick. Acted like I wasn't even there, wouldn't even say fucking hello in the morning. I must have walked all over that place. It's a goddamn maze. Every corridor looks exactly the same. They've got these colored lines painted on the walls that are supposed to show you where everything is, but I'd swear they just loop around."

I sat and stared at Happling's dirty finger for a moment. "Think you could draw a floor plan?"

The finger was retracted. "Nah. I've got no head for that shit. But your best bet for getting in is the front door, plain and simple."

I twisted around to squint up at him. He was still caked in dried blood and dirt, his eyes bright white and green in the middle of it. "That doesn't make any sense," I said.

He shrugged. "They wanted to keep the shitheads out, sure," he said. "But there were always big shots coming by, for treatment or just to walk around and give each other handjobs about how great the hospital was, whatever. The front door had to be *grand,* you know? Impressive. Security's boring, ugly." He shrugged. "You try wriggling in through the ass of that complex and you'll get squeezed—that's how every chipless asshole in the city tries to get in. You want an easy in, go through the front like you're selling cookies. No matter how many goddamn Tin Men they got, it's still just unreinforced glass and non-load-bearing columns."

I turned to look at Hense, but she just stared back at me. If she was going to stand up for Happling, I was prepared to accept his assessment. "All right, through the front, then." I looked at Marko. "How close to the hospital can you set this tub down?"

"The way the nav systems are fried, combined with the shudder I've got from peeled back plates, I'd say I can get us into the goddamn city of New York," Marko said, his eyes locked on the dashboard readouts. "I'm going to aim for the Madison Square Airpad. Plenty of room to crash there."

I considered saying something, but the Techie was

sweaty and had the deep-focus stare of someone struggling not to scream, so I opted to look back at Hense. "All right, so we walk."

She looked at me for a moment, then shifted her gaze past me. "Mr. Marko," she said, "how's your stick? Think you can maintain a deployment position?"

"Can I make this hover *hover?*" Marko asked, blinking sweat out of his eyes. "Sure. It won't be pretty. Your boys know how to drop with a little bit of yaw?"

"I don't know," Hense said, turning to Happling. "I've never seen them drop before. Captain, get set for a drop and form a security ring. We can't have Mr. Cates taking any more chances."

Happling nodded and spun out of the cockpit. "Mr. Marko," Hense said, looking back at me. "When we arrive at Madison Square, give me fifty feet and let me know when you're as steady as you can manage. Mr. Cates," she said, raising an eyebrow. "I'm sending my men down to have a look before we risk our magic talisman. Any objections?"

I shook my head. "As long as it's understood that when we reach the hospital, I'm the one that kills Ty Kieth."

Silence greeted this. I looked at my cigarette coal, feeling dirty. They thought I was being bloodthirsty. And a traitorous bastard who killed friends after promising them he wouldn't. But Kieth wasn't Glee's revenge—that was Gatz. Ty Kieth's death was the cure. Someone would end up pulling the trigger on Ty; it was unavoidable. Might as well be someone friendly. Ty deserved to have someone look him in the eye and speak to him when his time came, and there was no one else. Once that was taken care of, there would be time for revenge.

"Very well," Hense said, standing up. "Mr. Marko, let us know when you're ready."

She ducked out of the cockpit, leaving me alone with the Techie. I heard him open his mouth to suck in a deep breath.

"If you say a fucking word to me," I said to the cigarette, "I will tear your goddamn tongue out. It has to be done."

I heard his mouth click shut. I didn't feel powerful, or smart. I felt like a piece of shit. I put the cigarette back into my mouth and drew in smoke. It tasted terrible, stale and bitter. We sat there for a few minutes, the shouts and thumpings of the Stormers as they geared up for a drop coming to us through the bulkhead and filling up some of the space. Finally I couldn't take it anymore, the silence, Marko knowing this about me, so I stood up, dropped the red-hot butt onto the floor, and pushed into the cabin.

I'd never seen a Stormer drop up close. From the ground, where I'd usually watched them while cowering in some hole, gun in sweaty hand, praying not to be noticed, they always looked like something from a nightmare: half invisible in their Obfuscation Kit, gliding to the ground on beautiful silver threads, raining down murder on us fearlessly, wordlessly.

Up close, their ObFu was stained and torn, and some were having technical difficulties, flickering on and off. The Stormers didn't have their cowls on yet, and their faces were sweaty and unshaven and blotched with dirt and blood. They stank—the whole cabin smelled like marinating humans, powerful enough even for me to notice, and I'd spent far too much time cowering in holes with other people to ever really notice body odors again.

The silver drop cables were old and worn, some a little rusted at the connectors, and snaked from the drop poles to their belt clips in a jumbled mess on the floor. They shuffled and rearranged themselves as Happling barked orders, and chattered loudly, making jokes. They looked like a lot of unhappy, overstressed people instead of silent death machines sent to kick our asses. I leaned against the wall and watched, feeling my leg throb in time with my pulse.

Hense glanced at me. "You gonna be able to keep up? You look pretty banged up."

I shrugged. "I've been worse. I've been *dead*." I never got tired of that line.

She nodded and put a hand on my shoulder. "Fine. But you can't be killed, understood? Don't make me take extreme precautions."

"You're two officers and fifteen exhausted Stormers with low ammunition and no chance of resupply," I said, liking the weight of her hand on me. "You need my gun." I studied her as she turned away, thinking this was someone I could work with. I *liked* her.

Happling was crushing two cigarettes in his massive hands, a small, eager grin pushing through the gloomy expression on his face. "All right, faggots, listen up: we're treating this as a VIP drop, got that? Hold your fucking formation on the way down and I want to see a *tight* pattern when you hit the bricks. Keep in mind this tub is damaged and is being piloted by some idiot who hasn't been outside a lab in decades, so there's gonna be some English on the cables. Establish the situation and radio up a report right away. You have *full fucking discretion* when on the ground. Dumb Shit," he said, pointing at one of the Stormers, "the word *discretion* means *unrestrained exercise of choice,* which means take whatever action you deem necessary, which means shoot anything that fucking looks like a threat, got that?" The Stormer didn't say anything, which seemed to satisfy Happling.

"All right," Marko's voice crackled over the comm. "I'm *hovering.* It's not a pretty sight, so be prepared for some corrections."

"You heard the man," Happling said, stuffing the crushed tobacco into his cheek. "Fat Girl, open the bay."

Without hesitation the Stormer standing nearest the bay controls flipped them open and mashed a big green button. As the bay doors split open and rapidly shrank into the skin of the hover, the Stormers went through a flurry of tugging and slapping, checking each other's hookups and pounding each other's shoulders to confirm the checks. The wind came pouring in, roaring and pushing around us. Then, wordlessly, they formed up into lines three rows deep, the first row crouched low, balanced, while the back two stood ready.

From my vantage point in the back I could see the skyline but not the ground below us. Columns of smoke rose into the air, some white and fluffy, some dark and ominous.

Hense nodded silently. "Go! Go! Go!" Happling roared, brown spittle spraying from his mouth, and the first row of Stormers leaped out of the hover, followed immediately by the second row and then the third, drop lines humming as they spooled out. One second they were outlined against the gray sky, the next it was just wind racing around the cabin and Happling looming in front of me, arms akimbo, like a goddamn titan observing the mortals. We stood there waiting for a few moments.

"Cap," one of the Stormers' voices crackled around us, thick with a musical accent. "Cap, this is Team Leader."

Happling spat tobacco juice onto the floor. "Go ahead, Team Leader," he boomed, then turned to look at Hense. "No gunfire."

"Cap, send the VIP on down. No threats identified. Hell, we got nothing but bodies down here."

XXX

DAY TEN: I WAS PRETTY SURE BULLETS WERE NO LONGER GOING TO BE ENOUGH

"All clear," the round-faced Stormer said to me, her cowl dangling behind her head. "Watch your step, now. They're all pretty soft." She sounded like she'd stepped on plenty of softening corpses in her time.

I imagined the smell around me like a green haze, it was so thick and heavy. We were just a block away from the remnants of the Pennsylvania Hotel, but I felt I'd arrived in a strange new city—a city of silence, of smoke. A city of dead bodies rotting in the cool June sun.

They were everywhere, looking a little better than I would have expected, a little fresher. The airpad was past me behind its cinder-block walls and security checkpoints; the empty space around it had always made me a little itchy, all that air around you. I preferred the tall canyon walls of ancient, crumbling skyscrapers or the bursting pipelines of downtown, flesh pressing against you. The big open square felt like eyes on you.

We'd landed, rough and shaking, just outside the air-pad, crushing a few dozen festering corpses beneath us. The bodies fanned out from the airpad in a crush, swelling in their clothes, luggage piled around them. They all looked like they'd been eaten alive, their chests and necks pulpy wounds, bones showing through ravaged skin. I stepped carefully through them, staring down and picking out details — good clothes, jewelry, clean fingernails. These people were *rich*. Their eyes were all open, and most were untouched, staring at us.

"Fucking hell," Happling muttered next to me. "This shit is disgusting." He pointed. "Entry wounds. Shredders. I don't know what's *eating* these poor bastards, but what *killed* them was good old-fashioned guns."

We both glanced over at the airpad walls. The gates were shut but it appeared empty, and Marko hadn't gotten any response to his hail. I scanned the crowd again. Every now and then I had the sense that the mass of bodies rippled, but I couldn't catch it to be sure.

"Poor bastards," Happling said, turning away. "Just trying to get out."

I lingered on the closed gates for a moment. Fucking cops. I didn't doubt for a moment that Happling would have given the order to shoot, too, if he'd been in charge of the airpad with a crush of desperate people trying to get in. I stood there for a moment with the sour wind pushing against me, listening to my own coat flapping. There was a muffled burst of gunfire in the distance, there and gone just as suddenly. Happling and I looked at each other, the big man grinning at me as he chewed tobacco.

"Not everyone's dead," he said, sounding happy. He

spun away. "Troopers! Form up! I want to see a fucking humping formation in thirty seconds!"

I remained where I was for a moment, staring at the crowd of corpses around me, just to ram home the point that I wasn't one of Happling's troopers. As I turned to follow him a hand shot up from the jumble of bodies and grabbed my ankle in a slick, loose grip.

I stumbled backward as one of the corpses seemed to pull itself toward me, a jowly man in an impressive suit, his lower jaw missing, his throat a wet sore, blood oozing from the ruined skin. His tongue, fissured and blackened, writhed in the open space above his neck like a worm.

Panting, I tried to flee backward, and stomped my free foot down onto one of the inflating bodies around me. It went right through the softened chest as if I were stepping into half-dried mud, a spray of jellied blood, black and chunky, splattering me as I lost my balance and fell back onto my ass, the jolt sending a shock of pain through me that made my vision swim.

The jowly guy, flesh jiggling loosely, peeling away from him in spots, continued to feebly pull himself toward me, tongue working like he was trying to talk and hadn't yet noticed that his jaw was gone. He had no eyes, just scabby craters in his face where they'd been eaten away. I bottled up a scream—Avery Cates did not scream—and searched for my gun, hands trembling. For a moment I couldn't find it, panic swelling inside me, and then I felt its familiar hard shape in my pocket and pulled it out, pointing it down at the ghoul clawing toward me, its soft hands on my thighs. I stared at it for a moment, hands shaking. *I'd* done this. This had started with *me*.

I pulled the trigger and the shot was fucking thunder,

the loudest thing you'd ever heard. The ghoul's head exploded, the torso dropping down onto my legs and disgorging a thin gruel of fluid from the neck that soaked into my clothes. Out of the corner of my eye I saw the Stormers drop into combat positions and then slowly relax.

"Fucking hell," Happling bellowed.

I continued to stare at the ghoul's torso for a moment. A mercy killing, I told myself. Poor bastard was better off dead. As I stared it twitched and I hurriedly pushed the gun back into my pocket and climbed painfully to my feet, walking as briskly as I could toward the group of cops, wincing every time I stumped onto my fractured leg. Bendix, still blindfolded, with his arms bent painfully back behind him, stood calm and still among them. When I was a few feet away, a noise to my right made all of us whirl and drop, the metallic rattle of readied guns echoing off the street. A block south, a small crowd of people sprinted across Eighth Avenue, just shadows against the sky, and disappeared past the corner.

For a moment, we all just crouched, ready. Bendix stood without moving, smirking.

"All right," Happling said, "don't get your panties in a bunch, kids. Form up, weapons check, give me a D-nine formation, and let's move out."

I kept moving my eyes from point to point and holding my focus, searching for any sign that someone was holding back, skulking around a corner, waiting for us to turn away. As I watched, a second group of people burst into the intersection, running full speed across the street, and were gone.

"Avery?" Hense said from behind me.

I stood up, joints popping, gritting my teeth. Turning your

back on a possible threat was suicide—you learned that right away when you were a kid—but the whole city was a goddamn three-sixty threat, so it didn't matter. I stumped over to Hense and nodded, moving past her. "This is my city," I said. "Follow me."

Her hand fell on my shoulder, surprisingly strong, and pulled me off-balance, forcing me to stop and turn. "Avery," she said, expressionless, "you are the only reason any of us are still alive. You will not march out in front like a goddamn *target*."

I smiled. "Your concern is touching, Colonel."

She took me by the arm and pulled me toward her troopers, most of whom, I was pretty sure, would gladly put a bullet in my head themselves. "You let us form up around you, and you *duck* when shooting starts, understood?"

I shook my head. I wanted to use her name, but it stuck in my throat. "Stop thinking like a fucking cop protecting some ass-hat VIP from up the Mountain. You want to get me killed? Then parade me around in the middle of a brick of Stormers. You want me to make it down this street alive? You've got fourteen Stormers, the gorilla man, Marko, and Bendix, who'll tear your head off the moment he can see you. You really think you're going to control this situation? I need to be fluid."

She glanced at my splinted leg. "Fluid?"

I bunched my jaw muscles and swallowed. "Let's get moving." There was a scrape behind me, followed by a soft grunt, and her eyes flitted over my shoulder and then back to my face. I resisted the urge to whirl around, the urge to whirl and just dump a whole clip into the empty space I knew would be there. New York was a Ghost

City. I was pretty sure bullets were no longer going to be enough.

"All right," she said. "All right. But I'm detaching a trooper to shadow you at all times." She turned and scanned her little unit. "You!" she barked, pointing at the round-faced trooper Happling always called Fat Girl. "Here."

She trotted over, equipment jangling. "Sir."

Hense didn't look at me. "Shadow Cates. Take his orders, within reason. He is your CO until I say otherwise. Do not obey any order that risks his life unduly, understood? And keep him alive."

The Stormer's face remained blank, but she looked at me for a moment before nodding and sighed a little. "Sir."

Hense stepped past her. "Captain, let's move out. Mr. Marko, stick by the captain. Nathan, keep Mr. Marko out of trouble."

I checked my gun. "What's your name?"

Fat Girl just stared back at me. I gave it a couple of seconds and then hit her with my most insincere grin, polished in a hundred deals downtown. "How'd a nice girl like you end up kicking balls in the SSF?"

At first I thought she wasn't going to answer me, but then she turned a little to scan the horizon, squinting. "I made a living cutting cow throats back when," she said, her accent making everything sound exotic. "Then they fucking Droided the whole fucking combine and there ain't too many other jobs out there, eh?" She looked back at me and spit a little to the side like she had the memory of chewing tobacco. "Besides, beats being *you*."

I nodded and thought *I bet it does*. I turned and

rejoined the rest of the squad, and Fat Girl followed me one step behind. Happling glanced back and I nodded, and with a gesture he set the group in motion. Nothing felt right, and I resisted the urge to spin around as I walked; I felt off-balance, like no direction was safe. The cops felt wrong, too—they weren't moving like System Pigs, like they owned the street. They were moving like they were scared, as if they were in enemy territory. Only Bendix, tethered to a Stormer by a short leather strap, appeared confident, even as he stumbled and staggered along.

We moved up Thirty-first Street, heading east. About a block from the airpad the bodies ended, the street suddenly clean, empty. A few scattered possessions spilled out from the crowd, blown about by the wind, but once we'd passed that perimeter it was just pavement and the fading light, like everyone had gone inside, like pigeons, wanting a cool dry place to die. The Stormers moved in eerie silence, half crouched, shredders in hand; I could hear my own breathing, a painful hitch in my chest making me twitch with every inhalation. Now and then there were sounds off in the distance—gunfire once, shouting a few times, an explosion at one point that sounded huge and distant, like something we imagined. The cops didn't pause or break formation, but I did, stopping at each noise to scan behind me and squint up at the dead buildings. Fat Girl stopped with me each time, saying nothing, her cowl pulled back into place so she was just another faceless cop like all the ones I'd killed over the years. I felt hot and grimy, a trickle of sour sweat down my back.

At Fifth Avenue we turned south and encountered more bodies, just a few scattered here and there, torn up, looking like they'd been lying facedown on top of a hand grenade when it had gone off, but otherwise relaxed, sitting with their backs against walls, arms down at their sides. All of them had bloody craters where their chests had been, deep, open wounds that went up their necks and onto their faces, drying blood caked everywhere. They appeared to be shouting at us but not making any noise, their lower jaws either gone or melted into a pulpy goo, yellowed and cracked teeth grinning. Eight or nine blocks south I could make out Twenty-third Street, where smoke rose in a haze over what had to be barricades. I knew if we went down that far we'd find a lot more bodies.

I was staring at a corpse still wearing a luxurious blond wig as she slumped forward against an old Vid installation when movement in front of us sent the cops instantly into a battle pose, the main group on their knees with shredders trained while four or five flyers headed for the sides of the street to press against the walls. As Fat Girl stepped protectively in front of me, I turned just in time to see four people shuffling out of a skyscraper lobby and moving toward us.

"Police!" One of them gurgled. "Finally!"

They weren't in good shape. Their faces had a blackened, bruised look, their necks swollen up like balloons, each sporting several wet-looking sores. They were all men and, judging by their weight and clothes, they'd been prosperous enough until a week ago, when prosperity stopped meaning anything.

"We were okay until a day ago," croaked one of them, his pale face scummed with beard, yellow bags under his eyes. His voice had a molten quality, and he cleared his throat constantly as he shuffled, making a gagging noise as if he had a large beetle trapped in there. "I knew you'd be back to secure the city."

Happling made two sharp gestures and the Stormers flicked the safeties off their shredders in unison, the humming noise each made collecting together into a mild roar.

"Turn around," Happling bellowed, arms akimbo, "or we will fire."

The four men slowed down but didn't stop. "Are you fucking insane? We're citizens!" the guy with the molten voice said, hacking out the phlegmy words, a trickle of thick, black fluid spilling out the corner of his mouth. "You're worse than those psychopaths across the street."

I glanced past him to the midsized old building he'd pointed at, half a block away. It looked like every other old pre-Unification structure in upper Manhattan, blind window glass and stained old gray stone, worn down by pollution and time. It seemed as deserted as every other spot we'd passed, except the windows had all been boarded up from the inside.

Happling's face was impassive. "You are ordered to step back to your previous location, citizen," he said, managing to make the word *citizen* sound like an insult, "or we will kill you." He paused and then raised both eyebrows. "Got that, shithead?"

For a moment I thought maybe they were going to turn back, to crawl into whatever stuffy hole they'd been hiding in to continue rotting out. Then the beetle-throated one shook his head and kept coming.

"Fuck it," he warbled. "I'm dead if you leave us behind anyway. We're all dead."

I watched as Happling raised his hand slightly and held

it there. Feeling hot and gummy, I was moving before I'd formed any conscious thoughts, pushing past my personal Stormer and through the thin ranks of Hense's little army, putting a hand on Happling's shoulder, intending to spin him around.

"Fuck this—they'll either be dead or cured in a couple of hours, you goddamn—"

The big man moved fast, almost like a jump cut in my brain. One second I was standing behind him, reaching up to grab his shoulder, the next he had my hand in his, bending my wrist back painfully with inexorable pressure that forced me onto my knees. With his other hand he somehow produced his ancient automatic, pushing it against the back of my head, forcing me to stare down at the cracked pavement. I blinked down at the street, sucking in breath that tickled my chest and brought on a spasm of thick coughs. I hadn't been handled that easily in *years*.

"Mr. Cates," Happling said, not at all out of breath, "don't get in the fucking way."

A burst of ear-splitting shredder fire erupted as I twitched at Happling's feet, hacking up what felt like a lung onto the street. Silence followed; I could hear the faint sizzle of the shredders' muzzles as they cooled. Happling released me and stepped away but I remained on my knees, staring down at the glob of bloody phlegm I'd just produced.

Guess Kev knows I'm here, I thought. *And he's not happy.*

XXXI

DAY TEN: RICH BOYS WHO'D ACTUALLY SURVIVED

Reeling, I pushed myself up, scrubbing my chin clean and placing my foot over the bloody glob. I didn't know what had changed Kev's mind about keeping me going, but I knew without a doubt how long I'd be allowed to live once the cops realized I was no longer necessary—or even beneficial—for their own survival, deal with Hense or not. I squinted through the sunlight, my cheeks hurting, as she walked forward with her handgun to toe the four newly dropped citizens and make sure they were dead, her face blank. I didn't think she would actively betray our deal; she might even make some effort to uphold it. I didn't know why, but I felt I could almost trust her. But Happling, her huge red gorilla, he wouldn't hesitate, and without her captain's support it wouldn't be long before an unfortunate accident occurred.

Hense nodded to herself and then at Happling, retreating back into the loose crowd of Stormers. Next to me, Happling started booming out his orders, and the troopers scrambled back into line. As we started moving down Fifth again, stepping over the bodies we'd left in our wake, I struggled to contain the twitching irritation in my chest that wanted to explode into a fresh coughing fit while I moved my eyes over the block, trying to gain some advantage.

I knew where we were, of course, and I was pretty sure I'd been in the building on our left that the unfortunate citizen had indicated. None of the other options raised any sort of memory, so I stole a long glance at the building on the corner. I remembered that it had an open lot or something in the back, a patch of dead earth with a huge sewage drain in the middle of it, rusting and fucking dangerous. I was burning through my memories of the place, trying to remember if the drain hooked into the main sewage system, trying to remember how you got from the front of the building to the back. If I could get into the sewers, I could get anywhere in Manhattan, including Bellevue. When a single shot churned up a divot of asphalt right in front of Happling, the cops stopped as a body.

Without hesitation I kept moving, slowly, edging my way toward the side of the street.

"Far enough, Chief," a voice called from somewhere within the building. "Now turn and go around."

I scanned the facade as I moved. The sun hit it on an angle, giving each worn, dusty brick a deep shadow. The windows had been boarded up sloppily with gray, rotten wood that looked ready to disintegrate and stared blindly back at us. There were a million gaps and cracks where a sniper could be holed up. I saw the Stormers drop their cowls back into place, instantly becoming one faceless blob of cop, scanning the place, switching between heat and infrared scanners, trying to isolate the voice.

Hense stepped forward, and a second report tore through the air. The Stormer Bendix was tethered to suddenly did a whole-body shake and crumpled to the street in silence. I blinked in shock as Bendix reached down and smoothly unclipped himself, taking off in a blindfolded, handcuffed run down the street. Hense looked back at Bendix as if committing him to memory while I wondered why they'd chosen *that* trooper, of all the targets on the street. Before I could linger on the subject or even examine the body, another shot cracked out, echoing off the steel valleys of Manhattan, making us all hunch down in instinctive, useless ducking motions.

"I said, go around," the voice called out. It was a pleasant male voice, deep and gravelly. He managed to make it sound polite. I was about ten feet from the wall, moving carefully. The front door was shut tight and probably barred on the inside, but I knew another way in. Midtown wasn't like downtown Manhattan; there weren't countless Safe Rooms and hidden tunnels—but there were a few secrets.

Hense peered up at the building. "Did you just fire on System Security Force officers?" she asked in disbelief. "*Twice?*"

"We're not sick in here," the voice responded, sounding not at all impressed. "It's proximity that does it. We're not taking any chances. Now, all I'm saying is, go *around*. Go one block west, cut down south, and then turn back east. You do that, we don't need to have any goddamn trouble."

I forgot about Bendix; this was my chance. As I slowly sidestepped my way to the wall, keeping my eyes on the cops, my chest flexing with another spasm, I saw one Stormer suddenly straighten up and put a hand to his ear. My eyes flicked to Happling, who cocked his head a fraction and then nodded. They'd gotten a fix on the sniper, and I figured he was about to find out how well the SSF—even defrocked SSF like Happling and Hense—liked being shot at.

Hense looked at her captain for a moment and then nodded, turning back to the building. "I don't know who you are—"

"Who I *am?*" the voice interrupted. "Shit, five days ago I was a stockbroker who hovered upstate once a week to hunt," he said.

"—but *we* are police, and we don't fucking *go around.*"

Without a command, five Stormers swung their shredders around in unison and opened up on the windows, the roar pushing all other sound out of the way, forming a wall of earsplitting noise. This was my cue, and I took off, pulling my gun from my pocket and throwing myself against the building, flattening my body as much as I could. I took a moment to let my coughs rack me, an explosion that sent more bloody phlegm jetting onto the pavement, and then I pushed off and sprinted for the corner. At the base of the building, the snipers above couldn't even see me, and the Stormers' attention was directed upward. I was at the corner, skidding into a sharp turn to my left, when some bright thing noticed me and belatedly tried to cut me down, shredder shells slicing into the facade next to me as I disappeared behind it.

I didn't stop. At ground level sat a long, narrow window that five or so years ago I'd been just able to shimmy through. It had been boarded up from the inside with the same gray wood. Running, I leveled my gun and shattered the window with two careful shots and then dived for it, wincing in anticipation of a dozen deep gashes from the jagged glass. I wasn't disappointed. The wood gave like cardboard, tearing from the inner wall with a high-pitched squeak, and I managed to get my head and neck through without tearing open something vital, wriggling through more easily than I remembered, cutting myself deeply on my arms and thighs. It seemed to take forever to pull myself through as I envisioned being shot in the ass—a perfect way for me to go, I thought: *Avery Cates, world's greatest Gunner, shot in the ass while running away from his enemies.*

Dropping farther than I remembered to the cold concrete floor, I lay there panting, a gurgling chuckle that mutated into more coughing. Something damp slowly soaked into my pants.

Shit, I thought, *I'm fucking dying.*

It didn't matter—the real question wasn't how long I had to live, but how long I had before I was too sick to do anything. I rolled over and pushed myself up onto my feet. It was dark, and I felt gritty as concrete dust stuck to my bloody wounds. Outside I could hear a firefight—shredders mixed with the sound of high-powered hunting rifles owned by rich boys. Rich boys who'd actually survived and gotten ruthless. And here I was inside their perimeter, about to shove these nanobots right up their collective asses.

There wasn't time to look the place over, to recollect

floor plans and memorize exits. I saw stairs in the gloom and I ran for them, every breath painful, like razors inside my lungs. Moving as quietly as I could, I took the steps two at a time, the old wood groaning under my weight. At the top I didn't even have time to ponder the soft-looking wooden door before it was torn open and I brought up my gun in an automatic response. A fat, puffing bald man appeared in the door frame, dressed in some ridiculous outfit that approximated combat armor: a dark, heavy vest; tough, thick pants tucked into heavy-duty boots; an ammo belt slung jauntily across his shoulders. He stared at me in red-faced shock for a second, his rifle—a nice, expensive item, but semiauto and too slow on the refire for practical use in my world—pointed lazily at his feet.

I gave him a second to make a choice. It had been a long time since I'd been a free agent, and to celebrate not having any dead friends to Push me or angry cops to compel me, I waited until his hand twitched the gun up at me. Then I squeezed the trigger and shot him in the face, knocking him backward into the opposite wall.

I ducked my head into the hall for a quick look, but there was no one else. Stepping over his legs, I moved quickly, gun held low and away from me. It was a long hall, stretching from the back to the front of the building. A frozen escalator led upward to my left as I coasted forward in the gloom—all the windows had been diligently boarded up—the dust drifting around me making everything hazy and making my chest heave with the urge to tear itself up again. I sorted my dim memories of the place and knew I needed back access, second or third floor, although I had to assume all windows had been blocked.

I heard feet on the upper floors, pounding down toward

me. *Amateurs,* I thought as I glided around to the base of the escalator, crouching and peering upward. I didn't take any joy in it. Killing assholes who thought picking up a gun made them tough guys was an occupational hazard and always had been, and besides, I was killing them just by being there, and in my opinion a bullet to the head was a lot more humane.

Waiting patiently, gun poised but held down a little to make me take a second before unloading, I contemplated the dusty gloom above and wondered what their plan had been. Just survive for as long as possible, see if their luck changed? Maybe the plague would burn itself out, maybe the government would find a cure, come flying in on rainbow-colored hovers, calling its children home. Rich folks usually thought the System would take care of them, but a funny thing happened when all that yen became worth approximately zero: you became dead weight.

Dust undisturbed since the start of time crowded the air around me, giving it texture and choking me. Two men, beefy and sweating in their cobbled-up combat uniforms, swung obliviously around the handrail onto the dead escalator. I shot the first in the chest, taking my time, and as he tumbled down toward me I sighted on the second guy, who'd stopped cold on the fourth step, looking almost comically shocked. He moved to turn back as I squeezed the trigger again, and my shot must have split some hairs on his neck as it missed, forcing me to come halfway out of my crouch and squint up at him, nailing him in the back as he reached the top of the escalator just as his buddy crashed into me, knocking me back, stumbling to keep my balance.

The second man thumped down the steps and onto his

buddy with a soft moan. I put another shell into the top of his head, ending it. I thought about adding him to my list and then wondered how I'd account for the people who'd died from this so far. Did it matter anymore? I'd killed the world. Individuals didn't make any difference.

Chest burning, sweat dripping down my back, I crouched between the bodies and peered up again, listening. I could hear a lot of noise above, but it was muffled by flooring and drywall. Trying to control my breathing, I took the escalator steps two at a time. Outside, the firefight was still going on, but in bursts as the Stormers patiently waited for the snipers to reveal their positions.

At the top of the escalator, I ducked down behind the low railing and chanced a quick look around. No one was on the other side, and I heard nothing on the next flight of steps. I allowed myself one mighty cough, a powerful spasm that brought another glob of rusty-tasting snot up through my throat with a searing jolt of pain, like I was dragging chunks of my lungs up into my mouth. I looked toward the back of the building, where two widely spaced windows had been boarded over pretty solidly, no light creeping in through gaps or cracks, the wood in pretty good condition. Three doors faced the escalator on the opposite wall, none particularly forbidding, all tightly shut.

I crept around the low divider and backed slowly down the hall until I had a good view of the next escalator, which had a rise about twice that of the first and disappeared into a worrying gloom. While I stood there contemplating my situation, the middle door to my left groaned open, comically loud, and I brought my piece to bear on it just as a short, bearded man poked his head out, looking away from me with such exaggerated care that some leftover sense of honor prevented me from nailing him in the back of his head. Seconds ticked by, the distant gunfire a comforting background noise while I stared at his bald spot, a wide circle of pale flesh in the midst of his thick black hair. I just wanted him to look at me. Shooting an idiot in the back when he didn't even know you were there wasn't right, even if you knew he'd happily kill you if given the chance.

The other two doors opened almost simultaneously. I blinked and made myself wait an extra two ragged heart-beats for both doors to be mostly open, and then I put a bullet into that bald spot, thinking I'd done what I could to satisfy useless honor. I spun into the nearest door and put another shell into some old man's neck, forty if he was a day, who stumbled backward into shadows clutching at his bloodied throat, rifle clattering to the floor. I leaped across the hallway into the room behind him, following him as he spluttered backward, stumbling over his own feet and dropping to the floor.

Two more were kneeling by the front windows, pretty impressive sniper rifles mounted on the sills, the barrels moving through narrow slits they'd cut into the boards. The wood didn't give them any armor protection, but by kneeling on the floor they had a decent field of vision, weren't very exposed, and could rake the street below with their careful, sissy shots. Seeing me, they both flopped around squawking. With their rifles bolted to the fucking windows and without any backup weapons, they were a couple of chumps. I knew it was a sloppy move, but I dropped my arm and ignored them. They weren't a threat. Throwing myself back against the wall just inside the door, with a tearing pain in my splinted leg, I waited a moment, forcing myself to listen, my breathing loud and raspy.

Three breaths, and I ducked out into the hall. A shot sizzled over my head and *thunked* into the wall above me. I put a quick shell into the kneecap directly across from me, dropping the figure into a ball that squirmed and screamed. The hall was clear, so I tossed my clip and fished out a fresh one just as a boot edged out of the far doorway. I pushed off and rolled back into the front room, slammed my clip home and racked a shell into the chamber, then rolled back out. This one was a big round guy, a fucking blueberry in a tight black bodysuit—the latest fashion, I supposed, for facing Armageddon with the *best people*. I was afraid a bullet in the gut would just be absorbed and processed, so I ticked upward. The blueberry had his rifle slung over his shoulder, and the pistol in his hand shook terribly. As I moved my arm up he fired, the gun jerking in his hand, sending another shell about a foot above me. I held my breath, chest heaving, and showed him the right way to do it.

I opened my mouth and sucked in air, my chest heaving, and as I struggled to my feet, face feeling tight with blood, I coughed uncontrollably, spittle drooling from my mouth as I stumbled forward, pushing myself into the middle room long enough to see five empty cots and a lot of trash. I whirled and stumbled back out, turning around to sweep the hallway as I stepped into the final room. The spasm passed, and I gulped in mouthfuls of hot, stuffy air.

The room was empty. In the back were two more windows covered by thick boards, one with a sniper rifle bolted into place, the other hinged, a large padlock holding it shut.

"Fucking hell," I muttered. I shot the lock off and staggered for it, pulling the boards up and staring out into the back garden, the huge storm drain exactly as I remembered it, open, yawning.

Pushing my gun into a pocket, I climbed out onto the rusted fire escape and slid down the steep ladder, dropping the last few feet and landing on my ass to spare my splinted leg, teeth rattling in my head. Behind me everything had gone ominously quiet, so I kept moving, pushing up onto my stiff leg and hobbling over to the drain. The silence behind me was worrying, and pushed me along like a sour wind, urging me along. At the edge of the drain I sat down and slid my legs over, easing myself down until I was hanging from the lip. Bracing myself, I dropped the last few feet into a familiar damp sludge, pain shooting up from my fractured leg.

Everything was starting to make sense again: I was back in the sewers.

XXXII

DAY TEN: THIS IS A CONTROLLED BURN

Unconcerned with Best Practices—coughing up sewage and my own blood, I was ready to take a head shot and be done with it—coming up was like being born again. Covered in blood and grime, I pushed my way through a narrow shaft, oozing out onto the damp floor of a sub-basement far below street level. It was cold, and I lay there hacking up loose, rust-flavored phlegm and shivering, feeling sorry for myself. I should have been at the top of my game by now, rich and happy. Instead, here I was buried underground, dying and alone. I'd wasted the past five years on petty revenge, and for what? A few dead cops, the System still alive and well, Dick Marin still immortal and everywhere.

Me, dying alone and underground. The game had been stacked against me, and I didn't like it. I intended to find some way to shake it up.

After a minute or two of gasping on the cold concrete like a fish out of water, I felt my chest ease up a little and the burning gashes on my arms and thighs subsided. I got to my feet and tried to get my bearings. I knew the sewers, and finding Bellevue through them hadn't been so hard, but I'd never been on this level, and my memories weren't very helpful. Bellevue was a huge complex, and wasn't designed for internal defense—there was no easy way to close off sections of it. As I crept around the gloomy space, feet squishing inside my tattered boots, leg aching steadily, I imagined the Monks spread thin, concentrating on the perimeter in order to defend against an external assault, the interior of the complex empty and cavernous.

The floor sloped upward, the room growing brighter as I walked, until I was standing at the bottom of a softly humming escalator, the illuminated edges of the steps gliding upward in a steady, mesmerizing rhythm. *Hell,* I thought, *the Monks have power.* The rich assholes had been in one small building and they'd been sleeping on cots, eating nutrition tabs, and crapping in a fucking hole in the floor. Maybe the Monks were going to inherit the earth after all.

Thinking about the rich assholes, I decided maybe that wasn't the worst-case scenario.

I stepped onto the escalator and enjoyed gliding up silently through the darkness. I drew my gun and held it loosely against my hip, trying to bounce on my feet as best I could. Remarkably, I felt pretty good, aside from my aching leg and the way each breath made me wince. I felt loose and calm. Things had narrowed down to a familiar and happy point: I had to kill someone and go through hell to get to them.

At the top an automated door split open, disgorging me into an open, dark area of sloping, cracked pavement and dusty steel. Ancient paint marked out areas on the floor. Whatever the space had been, it was underground and long abandoned, though a few yellow lights gleamed weakly here and there. My wet boots echoed as I walked, leaving tracks in the dust behind me. But the smooth, settled look of all that grime made it pretty clear that no one had been down here in years, maybe decades.

I picked a direction and stuck with it, squinting through the dark for signs or any other info. After I'd gone a few dozen steps a mechanical hissing from behind stopped me with my bad leg in the air. The automated door I'd just come through had opened.

I knew I was probably well concealed in the darkness, unless these were Stormers with their vision filters or someone with a night-vision Augment. The thick silence meant that any kind of move would give my position away, but just standing in the middle of the room was a surefire way to get sniped. I let my foot sink slowly down to the pavement and then eased down until I was kneeling on my good leg, my bum one stretched out stiffly before me. I crouched, trying to make myself small, a shadow, and turned around just as slowly, swallowing my flexing chest and keeping my gun up and ready. I could hear two sets of steps approaching.

I squinted, pushing my aching eyes to see something, and nearly jumped when she spoke. "Mr. Cates, please don't shoot at us."

The voice was all round edges and endless vowels. I kept my gun up. "Fat Girl?"

"You can call me Lukens," she replied, her voice sort of irritated. "We have *names,* eh?" A pair of dim figures began to resolve. "I'm here with Mr. Marko. I'm not threatening you, so quit moonin' at me like that."

I considered this. "Marko?"

"I'm here," he said, sounding miserable. "I've been kidnapped. Again."

This with an air of acceptance, as if he'd finally realized that his purpose in life was to be pushed from spot to spot by tormentors — among which, I assumed, I numbered. He paused, and Lukens shoved him from behind, a little harder than I thought necessary. I let them get closer, but kept them covered. The Stormer had her shredder looped over her shoulder and her sidearm holstered, sure enough. Marko wasn't armed either, though he carried his black duffel and his handheld, fingers of one hand flying in complex gestures as he walked.

"Close enough," I said when they were about ten feet away, visible in the shadows, two binary people, all whites and blacks. "Tell me why you're here alone." Somewhere in the darkness water was dripping.

They stopped. Lukens didn't move or change expression. She was really a pretty girl, baby faced with a fine, long nose, that same strand of brown hair hanging in her face. She stared at me unblinkingly. "I was ordered to keep you alive, Mr. Cates. That order was not rescinded or altered. I saw you break away, and I saw one of those hard-case boys disobey orders and try to terminate you. I decided the best way to comply with my orders was to follow you. Since you left the first two floors of the building pretty clear, it was simple enough."

She sounded *sleepy*. I made a mental note to ask her the secret of napping while the whole fucking world died around you. I looked at Marko. "And you?"

He opened his mouth without looking up, but Lukens interrupted. "I requisitioned Mr. Marko as a member of this detail because your chances of survival here are much higher if a Technical Associate is available."

Marko shrugged without pausing his gesturing. "What the she-hulk here said."

Lukens's eyes shifted to Marko for a moment. "Shrimp," she muttered.

I considered my options. I could handle the Stormer—I'd handled dozens of fucking Stormers—but I wasn't sure I could afford to waste a resource. She wasn't under my orders, but if she was going to watch my back while I encouraged Monks to shoot at me, that would be useful. And Marko doubly so, since they'd powered up the complex and the electronic locks, sensors, and security systems it contained.

"All right," I said, lowering my gun and grunting my way up to a standing position. I hesitated, considering, looking from her frozen face to Marko's absorbed one, bathed in greenish light. "You both should know that I'm sick," I finally said. "I've been coughing blood for an hour now."

Marko's hand stopped, but he didn't look up at me. Lukens didn't flinch. She stared at me with that flat, cop stare I'd come to know so goddamn well. Like I'd just told her the time. Like I'd just told her *nothing*. Fucking cops.

"Gatz shut you down," Marko said, his voice flat, hands still.

I was watching Lukens. She was still staring at me as if she were doing sums in her head. "Looks like it," I said. "I think I broke some invisible rule. Kev was never…

normal, you know, and now he's fucking batty. Who knows what I did. Or didn't do."

Slowly, Marko's hand resumed motion, gaining speed. "You're further along than us," he said. "We'll be showing symptoms in an hour, maybe two, depending on when exactly the suppression field was deactivated. I'd estimate you've got thirteen hours before the damage done by the nanobots is irreversible."

I smiled. "Thirteen *hours?*" I said, chuckling, my chest burning and trying to slip the reins again. "Mr. Marko, I could kill the whole damn *System* in thirteen fucking hours." I started to cough, sputtering and flinging spit everywhere. "If...I can't...kill...one goddamn *Techie*...in thirteen...hours..."

Marko finally raised his eyes from his handheld, staring at me for a few seconds. "You've no doubt noticed that this complex is powered. Sixteen generators, by my count. There may be more offline at the moment, coming into play as others fail. From what I can tell, this complex is about sixty percent bright, which is amazing, since I'm scanning just fifty-three Monks in the vicinity. They're pulling an amazing load right here."

I looked around. "You got any plans of this place?"

He nodded. "Sure. We're one level below street level here—there's a retrofitted escalator over *there*." He pointed off into the darkness. "But I'd recommend against it, as it'll be the obvious choice if anyone's waiting on us. There's an ancient elevator shaft over *there,* and despite the structural concerns of such an ancient element, it would be a less obvious entrance."

I looked in the direction he indicated but couldn't see

much. "You're helping me?" I asked. "You know why I'm here, right?"

He shrugged without looking back at me. "You're coughing blood, right? That means *I'll* be coughing blood soon."

I nodded. Everyone was just scrambling to stay alive. We started moving in the direction he'd indicated, me on point and Lukens bringing up the rear, shredder back in her hands.

"Why the hell do they have this place so bright?" Marko mused as we walked. "I can see firing up whatever bullshit security tech this complex has, but they've got this thing *burning*. I don't get it."

I swept my useless eyes this way and that as we walked, making more noise than I liked. "Fifty-three Monks, you said."

"Yeah," Marko agreed. "That I can see."

Controlled burn, Kev had said to me. *This is a controlled burn.* "Fifty-three Monks who expect to pick up the pieces of the System in a few weeks when this is over. And this complex is a hospital."

"Yeah? And?"

The elevator loomed up in front of us, rusting doors covered in faded, ancient graffiti, the two call buttons missing, disconnected wires spilling out of the wall. I stepped forward and ran my free hand along the seam between the doors, dust spilling down onto the gritty floor. "They're not going to run the whole world with fifty-three fucking Monks, Mr. Marko. They need the power because they're making more Monks."

XXXIII

DAY TEN: IT WAS LIKE LIVING UNDERWATER

━━━━

Screaming rust, the elevator doors split open in response to some not-so-gentle pressure, revealing an empty, shadowed shaft, a damp-smelling breeze blowing gently against us. I leaned in and peered down into almost total blackness and then up, where enough light was filtering in from various sources to outline the dim shape of the elevator car hanging several floors above us. Realizing I was sweating freely, I pulled myself back and looked at Marko.

"Any juice in there?"

He leaned into the shaft with his handheld and stared around for a few seconds, then pulled back and nodded. "Yep. Either they're using this elevator — which would be insane, considering the last time anyone serviced it — or they didn't have the time or knowledge to route the power selectively and just juiced the whole place. But that shaft is hot." He frowned. "I've also got a lot of nano traffic...but nothing like what I was seeing before. There's been a—"

He trailed off to a low mumble, talking to himself, and I stopped listening. I considered, taking quick, shallow breaths. I'd identified the threshold where my lungs rebelled and spasmed, sending up chunks of myself in bloody packets, and if I stayed just shy of that point I could control the urge to cough. It was like living underwater. "I don't suppose you could get that elevator to come down here?"

The Techie cocked his head. "I might, Mr. Cates, but I'm not sure that would be such a good idea, actually. It'd be noisy and would probably attract attention, and as I thought I just pointed out, that car has been hanging there for *decades* at *best*. The chances that it would drop us to our deaths are pretty even."

I nodded, swallowing blood back into myself, a light fever film all over me. "Excellent." It was always the fucking Hard Way. Even when I'd just been a street-level Gunner, popping shitheads in a crowd for five hundred yen at a time, it had always been the hard way. Too many people, too many bodyguards. A mark who traveled underground all the time. A mark who wore body armor head to toe. A mark buried inside Westminster Abbey. A mark guarded by a System Pig on the take.

I paused, something tickling my brain again, a memory. Before I could pursue it, a horrible grinding noise came from the opened shaft and a shower of quickly fading sparks danced downward inside it. Before I could form a question for Marko, I watched in curiously delighted horror as the ancient lights inside the shaft banged on one after the other, most of the bulbs immediately exploding in a flash of soured light. The ones that survived gave the shaft a sickly yellowish glow.

The slow screeching began descending. *Kev knows we're here,* I thought. I didn't feel him on me, no Push that I could detect, but I was disinclined to move. Kev was coming, or Kev had sent some of his minions to finally kill me off, and I was relieved. I was tired. Exhausted. I turned to spit blood onto the ground while Lukens circled behind me, the climbing whine of her shredder filling the air, to cover the elevator doors when it arrived.

The car made terrible noises as it lowered itself, rust on rust. Dust shook down the shaft in front of us, and when the cab finally came into view it did so slowly, hitching and shaking like a square box being rammed down a round hole. It sank a few feet past the floor before shuddering to a stop, and then—silence. I could hear the rain-like sound of sprinkling dust and then the low, keening sound of complaining metal filling the cavernous space around us.

After a moment a booming noise came from within the elevator cab. Marko jumped and quietly moved farther back, his eyes locked on his little device. The Stormer didn't flinch. She just stared at the elevator doors, one short finger resting lightly on the trigger of her rifle. The booming repeated twice, and then the cab's doors parted about half an inch as the tip of a pry bar appeared between them. With a warping, grinding noise the doors were slowly forced open, centimeters at a time, with a jerking motion that hinted at great effort. One more inch, two inches, and I could see movement. Three more, and I could see hands. As the doors split open enough for someone to shoulder through, I finally raised my gun, which shook in front of me embarrassingly.

With a final wrench the doors slid all the way open as smoothly as they'd been designed to. A single figure stood in the shadows within. He dropped the pry bar, which made a metallic rattle, and put up his hands.

"Don't shoot. I'm an old man."

"Fucking hell," I spat out, keeping my gun trained on him. "Wa, you're a goddamn virus."

He stepped slowly from the elevator, hands up, looking a little less pressed and neat than I was used to. Even his motion was less fluid, a little more brittle, as if Wa Belling had grown old over the past few days, a lifetime catching up with the old man. "From what I hear, Avery, *you're* the virus, yes?" He gave me a raised eyebrow, an expression that used to convey endless disdain and amusement. It looked tired and forced now. "At any rate, I've come to throw myself on your tender mercy."

"He's not emitting any signals," Marko announced. "He's not carrying any devices, aside from four guns and some ammunition."

"Of course not," Belling said, smiling. "I've come to surrender."

"Fuck you, surrender," I barked, coughing. "You did this to me. You fucked me, Wa. You fucked everyone." I staggered forward, pushing my gun at him and making him retreat, raising his hands higher. A part of me thrilled at making Wa Belling retreat. "You killed Glee, Wa," I hissed, my whole body shaking. "You had her chewed up and fucking *digested*." I knew that if he'd come here to kill me, he'd have an excellent chance of doing so. One Stormer and a rusted-out Avery Cates weren't a match for the man who'd successfully posed as Canny Orel for years. I felt like I'd turn to dust if someone so much as used harsh language on me.

"I fucked everyone," he admitted, his hands still up in the air. "And I got fucked in return."

I struggled for control. I wanted to make him suffer. I wanted to *hurt* him. But I had a job to do, and Belling could help. "How'd you locate us?"

He waggled his bushy white eyebrows. "I tracked your nanos, Avery. They *all* know you're here. You're filled with transmitters. You can't take a piss, the Freak up there doesn't know about it."

I considered this, fighting the urge to start coughing again. "Then why isn't he down here?"

Belling looked at me, a hint of the old bravado smile on his face. "Because, Avery, the Freak doesn't consider you a threat. What with his Wonder Boy brain and all, you see. Also," he continued, looking away and making a show of examining his surroundings, "I have gotten the impression he wants you to die of this plague, slowly. He wants you to suffer. Or rather, the voice in his head does."

When it is over, you will be punished again, I heard Kev saying not so long ago. I gave Belling my best hard-assed stare: emotionless, cold. I was a little surprised how easily it came back to me. "So what's changed, Wallace? What's happened in the past two days that brings you to *me?*"

Belling's expression changed, all the humor going out of it, rage lighting him up and filling him, peeling back a few dozen years instantly. "Avery, I made a deal—you can cry about it if you want, but you and I, we didn't have a *deal*. We had an informal arrangement."

I almost pulled the trigger right then and there, the words *informal arrangement* like acid in my ear. The gun shook in my hand, and I told myself it was pure, corrosive anger. I wanted to shove our *informal arrangement* up his ancient ass.

"I made a *deal* with the Freak. A deal," he added, "that no longer exists." He looked away, finding something over my shoulder to study. "He fucking *reneged*. On *me*. On Wa Belling."

A smile flashed onto my face. I almost felt good. "You got fucked in return," I said, feeling some small part of the universe click back into alignment.

The old man's eyes latched onto me. "You can be amused, Avery," he said icily, "at least for the remaining few hours of your life. As for me, I am not happy. I was going to be immortal, Avery. And now I am *dying*."

I squinted at him. "So? Just kill Kieth. Kill Kieth and the whole nano network crashes, right? They'll just become bits of silicone and alloy in our bloodstream, and we'll piss 'em out."

He nodded. "That asshole Kieth is a *clever* asshole, yes — his little back door in the nano design is the only reason he's still alive. But Avery, it isn't that simple. Every time I do something Kev doesn't like the look of, he *tells* me to stop, and I stop, yes? And he is under ... *guard*." He shrugged, suddenly looking small. "And I've grown old, Avery. I need your help."

I snorted at this ridiculous situation, which set off a chain reaction of coughing I couldn't stop. I was laughing and hacking my lungs up simultaneously, face going red, sweat pouring down my back. I bent over, putting the gun flat against my knee, trying to suck in enough breath to respond.

"Where the fuck were you a day ago?" I gasped. "I'm fucking dying *now*."

Belling had recovered some of his old fire and was grinning at me as if we were all sharing a little joke. "So am I! The metal fucker put me on the list. I've never been so fucking screwed in my *life*." Then he sobered. "I don't wish to die, Avery, but I want to make that Freak *hurt*." He cocked his head at me. "You and I come from the same place, in some ways. You know what happens when someone screws you out of a deal." He nodded as if that was all that needed to be said. "We were an excellent murder team, Avery. *Excellent*."

I spat a glob of red phlegm onto the floor and stared down at it, still doubled over, gasping shallowly. I was slowly getting myself back under control. I put my gun on him again. "You can say what you want, Wa, but *we* had a deal, you and me. I should shoot you in the belly. Shoot you in the fucking belly and leave you here to bleed and be *eaten*. To feel what she felt. And you want me to *trust* you?"

"You have a choice?" He laughed, lowering his hands with a glance at Lukens. "My dear, feel free to shoot me if I make any false moves. That will be *our* deal."

She nodded and spat on the floor as if chewing an invisible wad of smoke. "All right."

He looked back at me. "You're half the man you were yesterday, Avery, and sledding downhill. You have one System Pig here who is *not* taking *your* orders, but we'll list her as an asset on the assumption that since she hasn't killed you yet, she probably won't, and may even kill your enemies in the meantime. You—what the hell is your name?"

Marko blinked. "Ezekiel Marko," he said, sounding confused.

"*Ezekiel?*" Belling repeated wonderingly. "Well, Zeke, my friend, what are you bringing to the operation?"

"Uh." Marko frowned in thought for a second, then held up his little device. "Uh, this."

"Ah," Belling said with a sour twist of distaste. "A Techie. My favorite people. Very well; I assume you are skilled?"

Marko nodded slowly. "Uh, according to my OFS of you, you're fucking Cainnic Orel."

Belling waved him aside. "Optical facial scans are notoriously unreliable," he said, "and the database you are pulling from is an official SSF one, yes? Years out of date, I assure you." He looked back at me. Somehow he'd filled up again, swelling until he was Wa Belling again, bouncing on his feet and speaking in that subtle brogue I knew so well, maybe the last living member of Canny Orel's old Murder Incorporated. "You have no *choice,* Avery. You and I, even at half speed, can take down any mark, I think. And we have more resources here than we've had at low times in both our careers."

This was true. When I was young, I'd pulled off some high-profile hits, just me and my gun. It took years of crawling the streets to develop contacts, to get in with someone like Pickering for information, to cultivate the reputation that got you loans, information, extra hands when needed. I pulled myself upright and pushed my gun into my pocket. "All right, Belling. You're right: no choice." I needed his gun, and I wasn't sure I'd succeed if I tried to kill him. If I put him on the run — well, fuck, I didn't need Wa Belling in the fucking shadows in addition to all my other woes. I held out my hand. "We have a deal. But only until Kieth is dead. After that I plan to make you suffer."

He eyed my hand warily. "You're a man of your word, Avery," he said, stepping forward, "and I am not. But for what it's worth, I promise this: until we're done here, you can trust me absolutely. As for suffering, I expected nothing less. We're each making deals with the devil."

I almost believed him. *You're a man of your word,* I repeated to myself and thought of Kieth, upstairs. *Shit,* I thought, *you're thinking of last week's Avery Cates.* Hating him, I pumped his hand.

I took a slow, deeper breath, taking my time with it in order to avoid triggering more coughing. "All right, what intel do you have?"

"Little man," Belling said over his shoulder to Marko, "do you have floor plans of this complex on that delightful little device?"

Marko nodded, rushing forward. "I do!" he said briskly, thrusting the screen toward Belling. "I have floor plans, wiring networks, plumbing, air ducts — none big enough for a person to crawl through, however." He was sweating lightly, whether from excitement or the first stages of his own nano invasion it was hard to tell. Based on the way he was looking up at Belling, as if he'd found god, I decided it was excitement.

Belling nodded, turning to me. "I know where they're holding Kieth, and I know the basic deployment of the Mutant Freak's fellow Monks. We know their strength and resources, Avery."

"Do we know their strength? Isn't Kev up there making new Monks right now?"

Belling blinked. "Making *Monks?* No, not exactly."

I frowned. "Then why a hospital complex? He wants Monks to take over once we're all dead, Belling. That's the whole idea."

Belling shook his head. "You're behind the curve as usual, Avery," he said in a fatherly tone that made me want to split his lip. "Monks were five years ago. You think that was Kev Gatz designing this nanotechnology? Kev *Gatz?* I've seen melons with more mental energy than that asshole. This kind of tech comes from a genius, Avery. Someone with a pre-Unification degree." He raised an eyebrow. "You must have heard Mr. Gatz talk about *Him,* yes? The voice in his head? Didn't you wonder who that *was?*"

"Holy fucking shit," Marko said suddenly, sucking in breath. "You're talking about Squalor. You're talking about *Dennis Squalor.*"

Belling's eyes stayed on me, but he nodded. "Avery, Kev's got Squalor in his ear, telling him what to do, *how* to do it. Monks? Squalor's lost his manufacturing base. His corporeal body. His political clout. He's *personally* keeping Kev Gatz from flying apart at the seams, from what I can tell. The rest of the Monks, Kev's followers, look like the rarities who survived the destruction of the suppression signal — strong minds, I'd guess. Crazy, sure, but crazy in a focused way."

I shook my head. Something was roaring inside it, making it hard to think. This shit wasn't *fair.* "I *destroyed* Squalor," I said slowly.

"Avery," Belling replied, "Squalor was a digitized intelligence. You destroyed his *server.*" He fluttered his smooth, unscarred hands in the air. "He's in the air. And he's looking for a way to rebuild. Monks were yesterday's tech. The way Mr. Kieth tells it, what Squalor's doing now is, in Techiespeak, *utilizing the available resources.*"

I turned, keeping my eyes on Belling, and grabbed Marko by the collar, pulling him in close. "What the fuck," I said slowly, "does that mean?"

Marko swallowed, his wide eyes on me, hands limp at his sides. I felt I could have lifted him off the floor. "I think it means all these dead people aren't going to *stay* dead."

Belling smiled and shaped one hand into a gun, poking it at us. "Bingo."

XXXIV

DAY TEN: I AM VERY IMPRESSED, MR. BELLING

I followed Belling as he enjoyed his voice some more. "Come along, Americans, we've got some deep shit to wade through before we even get to kill the incredibly annoying Mr. Kieth." He whirled and walked backward a few steps, looking almost fucking ebullient. Americans—Belling was old, and he remembered the world before Unification. Who knew where the fuck he'd been born, but I hated that he knew more than me, that he'd known the world before Unification. I hated Wa Belling. I'd never liked the man but I'd respected him. Now I could hardly wait to kill him, the one person, maybe, in this whole mess who fucking deserved it.

Deserved. I pictured Kieth, just trying like hell to stay alive. I didn't doubt he'd work like a demon to reverse all this if given half the chance, but there didn't seem any choice: if it took him a week to do it, there might not be anyone left to *save*. It wasn't fucking fair, and it was making me angrier every time I thought about it. I'd never liked Kieth, either, but we'd worked together for years, and I knew the Techie had never screwed me on purpose. He didn't deserve this. I didn't deserve to have to *do* this.

"Are you serious?" I asked, staring into the rusty interior of the elevator cab, my mind still trying to process what I'd just been told. "You came all this way to commit suicide by elevator?"

"As I may have mentioned when you were perhaps light-headed from coughing up your innards, Avery, your presence here is no secret, and trying to skulk about when your old friend can scan your location anytime he pleases—can have your location beamed into his brain at will, in fact—is just human folly. Gunners avoid folly, or so I've always believed. We are a hard-bitten, realistic breed, although you've always been a sensitive type, apt to go blubbery at the sight of sunsets and butterflies and good-looking women."

We stared at each other, and he grinned.

"The elevator got me down here. It will get us back up. Stealth is wasted effort at this point. Go straight at them, Mr. Cates, and never mind the maneuvers."

He was right. We might waste hours creeping around looking for a secret way up, only to find Kev waiting for us. If our arrival was news, well, at least we knew the odds: fifty-four against four, although I wasn't sure I should count Marko as a whole person.

"Mr. Marko," I said suddenly, "you're a *cop*, right?"

He looked up from his little screen, surprised. "I'm a *Technical Assistant*."

I nodded. "For the SSF. Do you know how to handle a gun?"

He stared at me like I was speaking some bizarre language, and then Belling strode over to him, producing one of his shiny custom-made Roons from somewhere within his coat and proffering it to the Techie. "Here," Belling said impatiently. Marko regarded it dumbly, so Belling leaned in and pressed the gun into his hand. "You pull the trigger and it goes boom," the old man said. "Just point it away from yourself. And me." Belling looked back at me and raised his eyebrows. "Satisfied? Come here, let's get organized. Zeke, show us the main floor, right above our heads."

Marko continued to stare at the gun in his hand, worth more on the black market—at least the black market that had existed a week ago—than he probably cleared in legal SSF pay in a year. He slid it gently into one of his pockets, as if it might explode if he held it too tight. Which, I decided, was the preferred attitude of useless Techies when handed a gun in my presence. It was the ones who started pointing it at things and squinting that you had to worry about.

"Okay, this is where I think we are," he said, slowly at first and then with increasing speed as he got back to his comfort zone, voice bouncing off the ancient pocked cement. "This subbasement level *here*." I leaned over Belling's annoyingly broad shoulders and saw that he was zooming in on a large, square-shaped area on the plans, all load-bearing columns and ramps. "Which is, as we all know, more or less closed off from the main complex at this point, used only as a bridge between the main levels and the mechanical rooms, which they never bothered shifting upward. It's directly below the core of the complex. The lobby is...here, and...here's the main offices."

Belling stabbed a long, elegant finger at the screen. "Here's where our boy is, Mr. Cates."

I stared down at the plans. "That's an operating room."

Belling nodded. "That is the Mutant Freak's office."

"How many in there?"

"Just Kieth and the Freak."

I waited a beat. "What's the catch?"

Belling seemed amused, like his old self again. "Aside from the fifty-three other Monks that are patrolling the space, the fact that the Freak knows you're coming and that he's not only a fully functioning Monk but a psionic as well? Why, Mr. Cates. I know you've come up in the world over the last few years, but I think those are catches *enough,* don't you?"

My chest spasmed but I managed a thin smile. "No, Wa, after the last few weeks, in all honesty, I don't."

"As always, Wallace Belling aims to please," he said, still grinning. "You will note that in order to get to the Freak's office, we will have to go through this rather large area here."

"The general admission area," Marko said, nodding, "and the emergency room processing area."

"Wa," I said, "what the fuck's up there?"

"Walk and talk, Avery. There's no time to waste." The old man spun and strode purposefully for the elevator, producing two more guns from inside his coat. I limped after him, pulling Lukens and Marko along in my orbit.

"Your man Zeke here can probably shade in the fine points, of course, but what you've seen so far—this plague—is just the first stage of the nanobots processing. Once the body has been killed and allowed to, well, *marinate* or something, reach some level of early-onset rot that is somehow magically necessary, they take over." He stopped to sweep his hand toward the yawning elevator cab. "They *reanimate*. The bodies."

I stopped in front of him. "They come back to life," I said slowly.

"No," Belling corrected, putting a hand on my back and pushing me gently into the elevator. "They *reanimate*. Except better."

We all entered the cab and turned to look out into what appeared to be perfect darkness, Lukens sweeping the field with her shredder as Belling plucked his rusted pry bar from the cab floor and used it to pull the doors shut. As they clicked into place, a double row of circular buttons lit up to one side. I'd thought the basement had been quiet, but inside the elevator we'd found a new level of silence.

Belling reached over and jabbed one of the buttons near the top. The cab lurched disturbingly, making us all stumble and reach for the walls, and then nothing happened for several seconds as we gently swung there in the dark. With a lazy grinding noise the cab began to shudder, which I took to indicate movement.

Marko's face was so close to his handheld I thought he might swallow it. "This is some *thick* code, Mr. Cates. I can only see the packets being transmitted, but there's some serious shit going on nearby. I've got signals burning off the nanobots like crazy." He looked up at me and licked his lips. His beard had gotten a little tangled and crazy. "I'm guessing at some of this, based on papers

Squalor published in his youth and some of the work I've seen Kieth do in European cases—we study some of them in training—but I think...I think the nanobots are remaining functional after biological death and taking over respiratory functions." He stared at me for a second and then ticked his head. "They're *breathing* and *pumping blood*. People get sick, they die, and then the nanos...bring them back."

A full-body shiver swept through me. "Why?"

"Mr. Kieth," Belling said, his voice melodious in the darkness, "called it Phase Two. Squalor cannot fabricate Monks anymore. Even if he has a handful of intact, unused chassis around, even if he searches the dumps of the System for burned-out chassis that can be reused, he no longer has the ability to acquire new converts. As I understand it from Kieth, the nanos kill you—brain death, at least—then keep you upright and walking, and start to link together to form a brain." I heard his coat rustle as he shrugged. "And there you go: breedable Monks."

Lukens muttered, "Fucking hell."

For a second we all stood there in silence. I understood why Belling had cut and run—things must be getting pretty hot with Kev and his merry band of Monks, and it didn't sound as if the immortality he'd been offered was what he'd been expecting.

The cab shuddered again, and I felt a distinct gravitational drag as a metallic screech filled the air. We lurched up and then settled back, lurched up again and finally stopped dead, flat silence rushing into the tight space. We waited, looking around for some sign of progress.

"Aw, hell," Marko muttered.

"Baby," I heard Lukens mutter.

"Patience," Belling whispered, waving a negligent hand in our direction.

I thought, *If this is a trap, if this is Belling fucking me in the ass* again, *then this is when it comes.* I resisted the urge to check my gun's action, to check the chamber and feel it move in my hands, and settled for tightening my grip on it. I was hot and my head swam, and the constant, maddening itching in my chest had taken on a burning edge I didn't care for. I pictured the tiny little bastards inside me, tearing, ripping, filling me with my own blood. I straightened up, reached out my arm, and put the barrel of my gun against the back of his head. "Wa, I'm having a crisis of faith back here. And I swear, if you've — "

With another lurch the cab squealed into motion again and shuddered upward for several seconds. I left my gun where it was, and Belling ticked his head toward me slightly. "Patience, Mr. Cates."

"Fuck you, patience. We are being *eaten alive.*"

"Mr. Cates, I was in Kampala thirty-three years ago with Mr. Orel. A young man. We'd been hired by the Americans to assassinate three Germans, because the Americans — well, *those* Americans — were trying to derail the Unification process. On entering the country our documents were questioned, we had some trouble escaping, and I was shot in the back. Bullet lodged in the muscle. Pain like you've never imagined. Every movement felt like someone was cutting me open with a dull blade, and there was a chance of paralysis. I did not complain. I did not recuse myself from the operation. The bullet was there when we were finished, and I had it taken care of then. I was *patient.*"

I tapped the back of his head sharply. "I am very impressed, Mr. Belling."

There was a soft *ding* and the elevator stuttered to a halt. Belling grinned in the dim light, picked up his pry bar, and snapped the doors open with one grunting heave.

Horrible yellow electric light flooded our little space, making me wince. Belling turned back to us and drew one of his guns. Behind him was a blank white wall pockmarked with large jagged holes and an unbelievably wide blood streak that disappeared behind Belling's smiling face, continued past him and off into infinity, clotty red turning a dull, crusty brown. The smell was sudden and monolithic, something so terrible and rotten that it defeated any attempt to break it down into its component horrors. I gagged and immediately convulsed, unable to breathe as my lungs heaved. I went down to my knees and puked stringy blood from my own lungs, my vision going black, little red dots dancing in front of my eyes.

I started to stagger out of the cab, but Belling placed a hand on my chest.

"Avery," he said, standing there backlit and terrible. "This is going to be hard. On you."

I breathed shallowly and the red dots in my vision pulsed with my ragged heartbeat. "Why?"

For the first time I could remember, Belling looked unhappy. "Because some old friends are waiting for you."

XXXV

DAY TEN: LIKE BREATHING DEATH ITSELF

───────

"Explain it to me," I snapped as I followed Belling into the hall. I was getting sick and tired of mysteries.

"It takes a bit of time," he said conversationally, as if discussing the action on his gun or the juice rates on illegal loans off the Bowery. "First they have to die — that varies, as you've no doubt noticed. Some go right away, some linger for days while their chests collapse and they cough blood. Once they're dead, there's that *marinating*. They look dead. They *are* dead. But those tiny little buggers inside them are doing something."

"Repairing damage," Marko said without looking up from his handheld. "Bringing the physical shell of the body back into basic operating shape. Sealing off and rebuilding broken vessels. Taking cellular material from the portion of the body they won't need anymore — the brain — and modifying it to create stem cells, which are used to repair arteries and destroyed organs."

"Thank you, Zeke," Belling rumbled, stopping outside a pair of swinging doors and turning back to us. The square panes of glass set into the doors showed a darkened room beyond lit only by a scattering of signs suspended from the ceiling, a rainbow of cheery colors in the gloom. "Whatever it is, people pop up after a period of time—hours sometimes, days mostly. They come *back,* Avery. They're not who they were. They're not even human anymore. They've got blood pumping through their veins, they're breathing, but the nanobots are directing things. They're like biological robots." He looked at me. "Your people, Avery, were the first ones to go down with this. They're the first ones to come back." He jerked his head over his shoulder. "Kev's got himself a couple of bodyguards. And more on the vine."

I stared over his shoulder at the doors, feeling a slow anger filling me like syrup, steady and thick. I'd spent my whole life trying to walk the line—for *this* bullshit? This was my reward? I didn't have people anymore; they'd been stolen from me. My city was gone, a shell filled with corpses, corpses that would, it seemed, soon be up and dancing to Dennis Squalor's tune. I'd played by the rules for years, and I'd been beaten and shot at and thrown around like a fucking rag doll. I was sick and fucking tired of waiting for my reward.

"More on the vine," I said dully.

Belling raised his eyebrow again, and I thought that one of these days I would hold the old man down and shave that fucking eyebrow off. "A few days ago, Mr. Cates, New York reached a tipping point. Most of the population was sick or dead, our friends the System Pigs, like the useless tubs of shit they are, were getting scarce—no offense, my dear—and things were going haywire everywhere. People had even stopped *looting,* Mr. Cates, if you can imagine it, because there was no longer any point. Thousands, packed into the hospital like logs. Five days ago they started accepting patients without Health Department Underskin Chips, and about three days ago there wasn't any staff left to stop people. People just kept coming. Didn't know what else to do, I suppose. Most are dead now, of course...for the moment."

"For the moment," I repeated. I felt like my latent psionic powers were bubbling up. If I just waited a moment or two, I'd be able to set people on fire with my fucking *thoughts.* This shit was unfair, and I wasn't going to play along anymore.

"Last I checked, there were three operational in there," Belling said. "I'm not sure if any others have come online. Avery"—he looked down and made a show of checking his gun as he spoke—"they're not who they were, anymore. They're robots, really. Just biological robots. Don't forget that."

I looked at him, suddenly feeling burned out, emotionless. I was just feet from putting an end to this, and I was ready to get it done, one way or another. "Monks?" I asked. "Old-school Monks?"

"On the roof, guarding the perimeter," Belling said immediately. "Kev knows the cops are still out there."

"Spooks, too," Lukens drawled.

I looked at her, feeling cold, calm. "What?"

She tapped her ear. "Command's shifted to Mr. Bendix again," she said flatly, with her long vowels. "A government hover found our team. Colonel Hense is still field commander, though." She looked at me for a moment, her round face pink and damp. "No one's bothered to issue me any new orders, though, so I'm here, ain't I?"

I nodded, looking back at the doors. "Let's go."

As he snapped his gun closed again Belling studied me for a moment before nodding and looking at Marko and Lukens.

"Zeke, keep that hand cannon pointed away from me. Dear, how many rounds do you have for that shredder?"

"Thousand, Grandpa," Lukens said in her lazy tone, blinking her eyes like a cow, "plus fifty in the deck."

Belling considered. "Not much. But I assume you're trained on the weapon and will not waste ammunition. Three reconstitutes in there, guarding the way to our quarry. There were a few dozen incubating corpses, however, and some of them may have ripened."

I grimaced at the word.

"So there may be several people to get through. These are human bodies. They will bleed and can be crippled, but I don't think they feel pain, except as a data stream, and from what I've seen they have taken human reflexes to the limit of their capabilities." He paused. "I have seen them do...amazing things."

Belling looked serious and grim—all bullshit, though; Belling would look however he thought we expected him to look. I could see now why he'd come down to meet me. Cut loose by Kev, he saw his fate in the next room: an animated corpse. And while I had no doubt Wa would be able to handle three or even five of these things in time, *time* was exactly what he didn't have, and when he fought his way through he'd still have Kev's Push to deal with. Belling needed a *distraction* for Kev. I shrugged and twisted my neck until I was rewarded with a satisfying pop. The old man and I each reached forward and pulled the doors open, stepping aside as Lukens smashed a nova lamp against her thigh and tossed it inside. It skidded along the floor and stopped near the center of the room, its clear white light bringing the whole room into being. It was a big, square room, and looked like a little riot had passed through not too long ago. The ceiling was high, the walls rising up to tall windows that let in light, pipes and ducts snaking around in a complex pattern. It had once been filled with rows of plastic seats bolted into the floor, but most of these had been torn up and strewn about, some still attached to their metal brackets and intact, some broken up into chunks of brightly colored plastic. The Vid screens that had been bolted onto the walls had all been torn down and smashed on the floor, along with big chunks of drywall.

In just about every intact chair sat a corpse. It might have been a goddamn town hall meeting, except for the blood and the huge, concave wounds on people's chests and necks. Bodies were scattered around the floor, too, some leaning against the walls. All looked as if a huge blood-filled pustule had formed and burst on their chests; some with the perma-grin of a lost lower jaw. Across the room stood a high counter where the staff had once lorded it over the patients, with a solid-looking security door to the left. It was through the door or over the counter. As I stared into the room, trying to memorize the layout and regulate my pained breathing, the nova lamp brightened sharply and then began to flicker on and off rhythmically, throwing the mausoleum into gloom and then painfully bright light. I looked back at Lukens, who blew the loose strand of hair out of her face and spread her hands. No more lamps.

"Well," Belling said after a moment, "let's get moving. We should split into two groups."

I nodded. Two groups, creep along the perimeter, keep a wall on one side. Assholes burst into a room and let space build up around them—you could get sniped, you could be attacked from any direction. If you had a fucking wall, you *used* it.

"I stay with Cates," Lukens drawled. "He's my asset."

"Your asset is going to break one of your thumbs soon," I muttered, shaking my head. Belling would throw Marko on the fire the moment it was convenient. "You go with Methuselah here." She began to protest and I put my open hand over her mouth. "I am not your asset," I said. "Unless you're prepared to shoot me, go with Belling."

I took my hand off her mouth and reached behind me, pulling Marko forward roughly. He let out a soft squawking sound. "You, on the other hand," I said, "are *my* asset." I leaned in close to his ear. "Stay between me and the wall. Keep that cannon Belling gave you in your hand, but keep your fucking finger off the trigger unless you're so desperate you're not afraid of *me* anymore, okay?"

He stared a moment, then fished the gun out of his pocket and held it awkwardly, his finger along the barrel. "Okay," he said, trembling. I felt sorry for him then. He'd spent his life in a lab and never looked for this. This was the universe being unfair to him, too. I patted him on the shoulder. "Look, I need you. I'm going to try to keep you alive."

It was as honest as I could be, and he seemed to appreciate it. It didn't matter, of course, if one more person died because of me; the list had gotten endless. But I didn't have to sit back and let the fucking world shit on me, shit on *everybody*. Something had to start making sense again, and soon.

Wordlessly we all crept forward into the room. Belling and Lukens hugged the wall to the left, and I put Marko between me and the wall on the right, my gun in hand, eyes everywhere.

The smell crept up on you. The first few steps I was concentrating on the first row of seats still bolted into the floor, each one filled with a half-eaten corpse. In the flashes of light from the broken lamp, I could see they weren't in as bad shape as I'd thought. A lot of their chest wounds had skinned over with puckered, pink flesh that looked healthy and new. I couldn't be sure, but it almost looked as if a few of them were breathing in slow, unhurried movements. A skinny blond girl had been so eaten away her head had sagged over the back of the chair at an unnatural angle, and the huge wound had skinned over to hold her head permanently upside down against her back. As we moved along the wall it was as if I'd crossed an invisible line, and the smell was all over me like oil. It was something I couldn't identify, something my whole body instinctively wanted to crawl away from. It was like breathing death itself.

We made our way toward the corner. I kept one hand on Marko's sweaty back, urging him forward, and my eyes on the bodies we passed. *Ripening,* I thought. One moment we'd be lit up bright as day, everything sharp edges and deep shadows, the next we'd be in darkness, only the cheerfully colored signs suspended from the ceiling casting a ghoulish watery light. I could hear my own loud wheezing and Marko's frightened panting next to me.

"Do you still need me, Cates?" he gasped in a stage whisper.

I kept my eyes on the bodies we passed. Their seats had dissolved into wreckage and they were sprawled in a pile on the floor, limbs entwined, crusty gore everywhere. "Every time you speak," I replied, "I reevaluate."

I knew how it would come. If I were ambushing someone in a darkened room filled with decoys I'd be in among the bodies, lying still, picking my moment. I'd be positioned far enough in to draw my quarry away from the doors, and I'd create a bottleneck to make them change course or slow them down. In one of the lamp's flashes I saw a spot just beyond the corner where a trash can and a pile of intact chairs appeared to have been tossed together haphazardly, and I thought, *There. That's where I'd be waiting.*

Tensing, I forced myself to keep moving at the same pace, raking my watery eyes over the jumble of bodies around this spot as they vanished and reappeared in the flickering of the lamp. They all looked dead to me. I was vibrating with adrenaline and wanted to breathe, really *breathe,* so much I thought it might be worth it just to let the whole fucking world die so I could get some air.

As we drew close to the trash can, past a jumble of moist-looking bodies, there came the tearing snarl of the shredder followed by half a dozen shots from one of Belling's pistols, an extra flash twenty feet away. Out of the corner of my eye I saw a blur of movement and then a hand was on my ankle, the grip strong, painful. With a jerk it pulled me off-balance, and I had to take a handful of Marko's shirt to keep myself from being flipped onto the floor. I fired twice into the mass of bodies and then a figure was rolling away, jumping to its feet with eerie grace and in silence as the nova lamp flickered off. I fired twice more where it had been, but light, slapping steps told me my attacker was barefoot. I shoved Marko behind me and put every neuron I had left into my ears, listening, but another burst of fire across the room briefly muscled all the other noise out of the way for a moment. When it faded I held my breath and heard two soft slapping noises right in front of me as the lamp flickered back on.

I swung my arm up and froze, squeezing the trigger out of reflex and shooting her in the shoulder almost by accident. She was just a foot away, her shoulder a sticky mess of blood and bone, her neck and chest just a fused wrinkled mass of new pink flesh. For one second her blue eyes—perfect, preserved, and every bit as flat as when I'd last seen them—stared into mine.

"I told them," I whispered hoarsely, "to fucking *burn* you."

Without expression Glee spun around, shot her arm out, and sliced a deep gash down my face.

XXXVI

DAY TEN: ON A RAIL MY WHOLE LIFE

Night fell as the nova lamp flickered off again, and I heard the soft sound of her bare feet against the floor for a second or two and then another burst of terrible shredder fire from across the room. I sank onto one knee, yanking Marko down with me, and felt the breeze as her blade sailed through the air above me. I had a decent shot—in the dark, but I could sense where her body had to be—but I didn't take it. It was *Glee*. It wasn't Glee, but it was, and I kicked out with my bad leg, using my good one for support, and knocked her off-balance. In the darkness I heard her hit the floor but there was no grunt, no intake of breath—nothing.

I could feel blood on my face but didn't feel the cut. Coughing something salty and chunky from deep within my chest as the nova lamp came on again, I was amazed to find Glee on her feet already, as if she'd immediately and perfectly flipped up off her back like some sort of fucking undead gymnast. Her face wasn't mottled with bruising anymore, although starting at her jawline, the new flesh that had covered her wounds was tight-looking and unnatural. Her red hair had been cut raggedly down to a spiky minimum and she was still wearing the oversized suit I'd given her the day we'd headed uptown, but it was her eyes I couldn't stop looking at. They weren't hers. They were flat and steady, and she didn't blink. There was nothing of Gleason left in them.

"Mr. Marko," I coughed, razors in my lungs, "you might want to run now."

"Fucking hell," I heard him mutter, and then I forgot all about Mr. Marko, because the lights went out again and I heard the tiny slaps of Glee's feet. I jerked back and felt her blade slice the air just beyond my nose. I ducked again and she sailed over me, her blade carving down my back as she went over. I jumped up and threw myself to the right, diving awkwardly and landing on a jumble of limbs that were soft and disturbingly warm for corpses.

The light bloomed again, and through the red spots in my vision I saw Glee sailing up into the air again, her murderous dead eyes locked on me without a hint of recognition. For half a second I could only stare at her. Whatever demon this was that had taken her shape, I still couldn't shoot her. I rolled a second too late and she landed square on my left arm, pinning it under her surprising weight. I coughed a trickle of bloody phlegm onto the dusty floor, feeling hot and shaky, took a firm grip on her loose pant leg, and rolled again, pulling her off-balance and letting her drop to the floor, head bouncing once, while I rolled another few feet and pushed myself up, gun in hand.

She was already coming at me so fast I fired three times without thinking, instincts kicking in. She seemed to change direction in midair, rolling up into a ball and crashing into a mess of broken chairs as my hand trailed her, my bullets a second too late. Just before the lamp went dark again I saw her flip backward onto her feet and whirl around to face me. I thought, *Little Gleason's going to kill me, right here and right now.* She didn't even look winded—hell, she didn't seem to be breathing. When the lamp died again I was almost relieved.

Head fuzzy, the back of my coat wet with my own blood, I pushed myself into motion, running toward her. Running away was suicide, and I needed an advantage.

I smacked into her after a second or two of breathless staggered running, easily knocking her out of the air—it was still Glee's body, and it weighed nothing. I let my momentum carry me toward her landing spot, based on the sound, and the lamp snapped back on as I landed on her. If I'd wanted to, I could have aimed my boot for her neck, but I couldn't. She was half twisted around for another gymnastic leap when I landed on her, putting one knee into her back and pushing her down onto the floor with prejudice, getting an involuntary gasp of air forced out of her lungs as my reward. Before I could consolidate my position she bent an arm behind her impossibly and slashed blindly with her blade, making me jerk backward to avoid it, giving her just enough leverage to push herself up with her free arm and spill me off her.

I kept her in view and got my feet under me as she cartwheeled away, the lamp shutting off again. Listening to the alternate slaps of her hands and feet on the floor, I drew in a damp, ragged breath of rotten air that tasted slick and yellow. I pictured my sky—silent, a soft wind blowing, peaceful and quiet. I pictured the clouds and that electric feeling that rain was coming, and I listened to her flesh slapping against the cold floor, picturing her moving through the room, sailing over debris and bodies and circling back around to me. When gunfire erupted to my right I ignored it, made it distant thunder on the horizon, a rainstorm that wasn't going to affect me.

The lamp flickered back on, and she was closer to me than I expected, still moving head over heels in a rapid cartwheel Glee would never have managed when she was . . . still with me. I barely had time to register her approach before she was on her feet in front of me, slashing savagely, her face completely expressionless, empty eyes locked on me. There was nothing there — not hatred, not anger, nothing. I stumbled backward and knocked her blade aside with my gun. She leaned low and slashed at my belly, missing by a molecule. I was off-balance; with each stagger I deflected the knife—from my face, my chest, my abdomen—sometimes with a well-placed slap of the gun, sometimes just with my arm, taking deep cuts for my trouble, since my coat offered little protection from her diamond-sharp blade. Red spittle exploded from me with each painful hitch of my chest and my legs seemed the heaviest things I'd ever lifted. My gun was just a weight in my hand. Even if I could have beaten her reflexes, which I wasn't sure about, I couldn't shoot Glee. I couldn't shoot something that *looked* like Glee.

There was a quick pattern — head, belly, chest, head, belly, chest — so I took a chance, and after knocking a chest thrust aside I ducked low and barreled forward, butting my head into her belly as hard as I could and putting everything I had into pushing her back, keeping *her* off-balance.

She twisted away and I stumbled several steps before getting my balance back. As I ran in a wide circle I caught a glimpse of Belling and Lukens backed into a corner and pouring fire at three leaping figures. It was like a tableau, everyone frozen, muzzle flashes and ragged bloody people suspended in the air, Belling's face squinted up in concentration, Lukens looking like she was going over her laundry list, bored.

When the lamp shut off again I decided it was high time I ran away. I wasn't going to shoot her and I wasn't going to beat those nano-sharpened reflexes. I oriented on the back of the room and sucked in as deep a breath as I could manage, my chest twitching into convulsions. I ran with a heavy, uneven tread. When the lamp flared up I didn't need to look to know she was right on me: her slapping feet were thunderous. I threw myself up and around, my back protesting with searing pain, just in time to knock her blade aside once more. My thrust didn't have any power behind it, though, and she immediately righted herself, diving forward. I knew at once that I didn't have the traction or strength to get out of her range this time. This time was going to end with my guts spilled on the floor.

Then I was yanked backward, landing hard on my ass and skidding a few extra feet while Glee belly flopped onto the floor. Hands gripped my shoulders, and for a second I was floating back, staring at Glee's red hair, my gun pointed at the center of her head out of habit, my finger on the trigger. A tiny bit of pressure and that would be it, but still I couldn't do it. I couldn't kill her again.

Marko was looming over me, a trickle of blood leaking out of his nose. He looked used up and shiny. "*You're* the

most wanted Gunner in New York?" he asked, panting.
"You're getting your ass kicked by a kid!"

"You touch her," I hissed back, "I'll kill *you*." I pushed
him away and climbed to my feet—slow, too fucking slow.
I felt like I'd aged a thousand years, my insides cheesed
out, my blood poisoned. I saw myself dying, eaten away,
and then getting up again a few days later, repaired, my
eyes flat, my brain consumed and used as spackle for the
rest of me.

And then Glee was crashing into me again and slicing three times deep across my belly as I stumbled back
toward the counter. Entirely on instinct I shoved my gun
into her stomach and fired twice, knocking her little body
back onto the floor just as the lamp flickered off again.

I stared into the darkness where she'd been a second
before. From my right I could see flashes of light as Belling and Lukens handled their own problems, but I tuned
out the gunfire. I'd killed her again. Just like I'd killed
everyone. Everyone I'd ever known was dead, or would
be soon. Except Dick Marin, the eternal, smiling Richard
Marin, Director, SSF Internal Affairs. And, it seemed,
Dennis Squalor, the ever-fucking living. Those two
roaches were going to kick each other around the dead
world when it was all said and done.

It was always the big shots who started this shit up. I'd
been on a fucking rail for the past week, going from point
A to point B, a fucking puppet. I get pinched and dragged
here, I get plucked into the air by a fucking Spook and
dragged there. I'm pushed into a room and there's Glee,
and I have to kill her because that's what the fucking universe dictates. Then I have to go into another room and
kill Ty Kieth—*betray* Ty Kieth—because that's the next

thing the universe wants. I'm on a rail. I'd been on a rail my whole life.

The lamp flickered back on. When I saw her there, gasping like a beached fish, dead eyes locked on me, I was almost surprised. She was bleeding heavily and obviously couldn't breathe, but there was no writhing, no sign of pain—just those eyes, staring at me. I ran my eye over her wound and figured I'd hit an artery, and estimated she'd be dead...again...in about five minutes. Her chest spasmed, her hands clenched and unclenched, her mouth was working, but she just stared at me. I forced myself to meet her eyes and watch. I felt like I had to watch.

Dimly, I could hear gunfire. I felt Marko tugging at my coat. I ignored it all and just watched her die, the rhythmic fountains of blood getting weaker and more random, her spasms subsiding. I watched as her hands went still. I watched as her chest shuddered and stopped twitching. Her eyes didn't change. I knew she had to be dead but her eyes remained open and on me, just as flat and empty as before. Marko's tugging became insistent, and the gunfire came rushing back into my ears. As I stared at her, she twitched and made a horrible sucking noise. I blinked as she started to breathe again, horrible shuddering gasps as if an invisible fist were pumping her chest up and down.

The nanos were repairing her again.

I rushed forward and stood over her, pointing my gun at her head, hand trembling. But it wouldn't do any good. A head shot wouldn't kill her, and how many bullets would it take to damage her so much the fucking nanos couldn't fix her? I stood there trembling—it wasn't *fair*. It wasn't fucking *fair,* and I wanted off the rail.

Then Marko was in my ear, pulling me away.

"Goddamn it, Mr. Cates, there's no fucking *time!*" he shouted, his voice warped.

I jerked around and then froze. Behind Marko a trio of corpses had opened their eyes and were looking at me. I spun and saw that all over the room bodies were twitching, coming to life. I turned to Marko, opened my mouth, and the lamp died again.

For a second, there was complete silence. Then, a crash of shattering glass and shouts, crash after crash, light stabbing into the room in weak, watery shafts that outlined Stormers, their tether lines like spidery tails. I closed my eyes and thought it was probably the first time in my life I was happy to see the fucking System Pigs.

XXXVII

DAY TEN: CALM, SERENE HAPPINESS

I opened my eyes and looked around. With deadly speed the Stormers, still hanging from their tether lines, scrambled up to stand in the smashed window frames, rifles hooked into belt straps, efficiently leveling their weapons and running a fast check. Painful, flesh-ripping coughs tore through me, my eyes lighting up red with each twitch as I envisioned delicate tissues ripping silently apart, bloody clouds filling the spaces between my organs.

The bodies around us were moving, slowly, like they were learning to move each muscle individually. I saw Lukens looking almost relaxed as she lay against the far wall staring up at the ceiling, her belly torn open, her intestines leaking out in loose coils. I started to look for Belling when a familiar booming voice filled the cavernous room.

"Cates, you piece of shit," Happling shouted from above. Framed in shattered glass, he looked a little rougher than I remembered, with some new scratches bleeding on his face. He held on to a duct for balance with one hand, his other hoisting his ancient gun. "Did you really think you were going to betray us and get away with it? We knew where you were *going,* you asshole. You're a walking *transmitter.* How stupid are you, exactly? Don't answer." The big cop stepped into the air and leaped down, crashing into the cracked tile of the floor with a grunt, bending his knees and putting his free hand out to steady himself as if he'd been practicing jumps like that for years. Standing, he cocked his gun and trained it on me as he stalked through the room, ignoring the twitching, stretching bodies piled up haphazardly around him.

I still had my gun in my hand, but it seemed impossible to lift, as I watched the gorilla come closer.

"I've never had to wait this fucking long to execute a shithead before," Happling shouted, grinning. "The Spooks have taken back command—a fucking *hoverful* of the freaks showed up and were kind of irritated to find our Mr. Bendix leashed like a *dog*—and they'd probably order me to leave you alone, because you're on the fucking *Person of Interest* list, but fuck 'em. They're not here; hanging back like pussies until we clear the area. Looks like we don't need you anymore, Mr. Cates."

I just watched him, a bubble of reddish mucus expanding and shrinking at the end of my nose, my stomach tightening in expectation. When the big man was just a foot or two away his eyes suddenly flicked over me and he dived, *fast,* to one side as shots boomed from behind. Right where the cop had been the floor exploded into little plumes of dust. I twisted around to stare back at Belling, who stood pristine and ageless in front of the low counter that separated the waiting area from the offices, his custom Roons in each hand. The familiar smile on his face was like the universe clicking back into shape.

"Captain Happling," he said with a raised eyebrow. "Don't they teach you about threat analysis in Pig School?"

I heard Happling's snarl and watched as Belling whirled into motion, streaking to his right as gunshots trailed him. The old man launched himself toward the remnants of a dividing wall that had once held a large Vid screen. As he sailed behind it, his body elegantly stretched out for a rolling landing, a whining burst of shredder fire cut into the wall just above him, carving out chunks of heavy stone.

After a moment, the Stormers all poured it on, shredder fire thumping into the wall, the noise almost palpable in the air, the wall shuddering under the onslaught. I just sat there, twisted around, watching. Happling appeared from behind me, silently padding in a wide arc until he had a view behind the wall. Face red, he turned and made a sharp cutting gesture. The shredder fire stopped immediately.

I watched as Happling crept toward the wall, holding his gun ready, down low, arms extended. My eyes were locked on the big cop. I wasn't worried about Belling; the old man was slippery and couldn't be trusted, and if he'd just saved my life it was for his own reasons. But I didn't want Belling—or any Gunner, any one of *us*—to go down to a fucking System Pig. I watched him step lightly over two entwined bodies, a man and a woman who looked like they'd died in each other's arms, and then they both unfurled like flowers blooming, arms curling up almost lazily and taking hold of Big Red.

Happling grunted and looked down with an almost comical expression of surprise. He swung his gun down and oriented on one of their heads, putting two shells into its skull. The body twitched from the impact but otherwise didn't seem to mind, and kept pulling at the big man relentlessly, staring up at him as blood rushed out of the wound and over its face to form a slick mask of red.

As Happling's expression took on a more desperate, worried tint, he staggered a little trying to remain upright while the two figures more or less climbed up him. Suddenly Belling streaked from his hiding place, running at full speed and then slowing in astonishment as he took in Happling's situation. The captain looked up, face reddening, and managed to right himself long enough to throw a quick succession of shots at the old man as he ran. As Belling passed between us, barely ahead of Happling's awkward fire, he turned his head and looked right at me.

It was time to move. None of the cops were paying any attention to me. As I watched, Belling faded behind a jumble of ruined chairs and Vid Screens. A second later the junk exploded as the shredders turned them into dust, and with a roar Happling swatted his gun down at his attackers, savagely beating them off his body inch by inch, and then he was on the move again, his shirt more or less one huge sweat stain as he sprinted toward the spot where Belling had disappeared. I knew Belling wouldn't be there. The old man had mapped out the hiding places and could keep them on the run forever, if need be.

I started for the desk at the front of the room, my broken leg aching and protesting. I saw movement off to my right and turned my head in time to see Belling appear atop one of the metal ducts that crisscrossed the room. I paused to suck in air as he fired nonstop for a few seconds, pouring shells into the Stormers. Before they could react he'd thrown himself backward, disappearing the same way he'd gotten up there. Like any Gunner who lived beyond his teens, Belling had done the most basic thing: get to know your venue.

I kept moving, feeling that if I didn't look at the cops, they wouldn't look at me — some sort of low-rent psychic invisibility. When I reached the counter, I took two painful breaths and gathered myself, pulling myself up and over it in one clean move and letting myself roll and drop to the floor on the other side, the sound of my landing masked by the cacophony.

I rolled onto my belly and scanned the area beyond the desk. My only option was a flimsy-looking wood-and-glass door marked SERVICE ROOMS, no more than a fancy divider. I wriggled toward it staying low, sweat streaming into my eyes. Behind me things sounded hairy, and the still-hot shredders began to whine again. I dimly wondered whether even a dozen Stormers could take down Wa Belling, who so far seemed immortal. I kept crawling. I was used to crawling. When I reached the door I flipped over onto my back and reached up to try some standard gestures at the lock, but as I put my weight against it the door leaned inward, spilling me into a hallway.

I pulled my legs tight against my chest and rolled over, letting the door slide shut and pushing up onto my knees. Recalling the floor plan Marko had displayed for us, I started down a wide white hallway, a green line painted on the wall to my right. I took a moment to straighten up and force a long, painful breath, rubbing a hand over my bristly head and wiping a sleeve over my mouth. Speed was going to be key. I needed to get Gatz into my sights and get my shot off immediately, faster, the moment I entered the room. Any delay and I'd be Pushed, I had no doubt.

I gripped my gun and launched myself forward, my leg stiff and awkward.

As I turned a corner, the noise behind me dropped away and I was left with my own ragged breathing and the wet sound of my boots on the floor. After the gore of the waiting room, everything was amazingly clean; the floor looked like it had never been walked on. The air — the little of it I could suck in through my swollen nose and ruined throat — even smelled antiseptic, devoid of life. It was a relief. I'd had my fill of bodies, of their smells, their heat, their touch.

Around another corner I saw what had to be my door. It was marked only with the number 655, but Marko's floor plan and Belling's intel said this had to be it. I raised my gun and forced myself to move faster despite the pain and my body's calcification. Breathing hard, I threw myself at the door, smacking into it and then swinging my gun up as a shadow slammed into the wall next to me. For a second I stared at Marko's bearded face without recognition.

"What the fuck is wrong with you?" I rasped.

He was on his knees, fishing in his bag. "Door's locked, Mr. Cates," he said breathlessly. "I think you saved my life back there." Without another word he pasted two leads against the door's electronic keypad while I lay there, sucking in air as best I could, blinking rapidly.

"You Techies," I wheezed. "Think we all need you."

He nodded as the door lock disengaged with a soft click. "The way things are going, Mr. Cates," he said, "we're all going to be Droids with brains. And someone's gonna have to wind everyone up, right?"

I nodded, pushing him out of the way and putting a hand on the door. "You ever try to *wind me up*, kid," I promised, "I will blow your hands off." I paused and looked at him. "Stay. Out. Here," I instructed, and with a strained breath I pulled the door open and rushed inside.

I tried to put my eyes everywhere. It was incredibly bright inside, and my eyes burned and watered. I saw a Monk standing near an examination table, standard issue white face and dark coat. I put the gun on it, thinking *Fast, fast, squeeze the trigger.*

"Stop," Kev said.

I drained out of myself. I went numb and stopped in my tracks, my momentum almost pulling me down onto my face. Calm, serene happiness floated into me like gas, and I hovered motionless.

Ty Kieth was strapped on the examination table, professionally gagged. His nose quivered and his eyes rolled spastically, but I noticed he didn't struggle against his bonds. He just lay there.

"Shoot yourself," Kev said.

Smiling, I turned the gun and pulled the trigger.

XXXVIII

DAY TEN: A GODDAMN SUPERHERO

I didn't even feel the bullet smash into the meaty part of my broken leg. Kev hadn't specified where to shoot myself, and some primitive instinct inside me that still wanted to live chose my nearly useless limb for sacrifice. The leg buckled immediately and I crashed onto the floor, teeth rattling, but there was no pain — my pain circuits, I guessed, were maxed out. For a moment I was a goddamn superhero, impervious to physical suffering.

Blood spurting from the wound alarmingly, I wondered if I'd outsmarted myself by nicking an artery, and feebly raised my gun again, squinting through a strange yellowish haze that had inserted itself between me and the rest of the world. As I searched for Kev again, lead seeped into my arms and they became incredibly heavy.

"Avery, stop."

I froze, arm shaking. The familiar feeling of peace sank into me, and I was happy and thoughtless. A Monk resolved out of the haze around me, one I thought I recognized as Kev because it was so new and clean. The Monk crouched down in front of me; my gun was almost thrust into its abdomen. I stared into its expressionless white face without feeling, without thought.

"Avery, you were always persistent. Did you think I wouldn't expect you here? I forgot, you think I'm stupid. Always have. *He* told me you were coming. When I woke in this fucking Monk costume, Ave, it *hurt* so bad, I just howled and howled and prayed. I fucking *prayed,* Avery. And then I heard His voice. In my head. He said He'd created me, and that I was His son, and told me what to do." His creepy plastic face settled into a smile that made my skin crawl.

It was still fascinating to watch a Monk talk — the fluid movement of its artificial face, the modulated, pleasant sound of its voice. If you paid attention it had a limited array of expressions, and it got boring — and creepy — when you'd seen them all. But it was still amazing.

"I didn't expect the two-pronged invasion, actually," he continued. "You caught me a little off guard there." His face split into a wide smile. "Do you remember, Avery, that time you needed me to help you with those fucking kids? The ones kept nicking your credit dongle from your pocket while you were mapping sightlines for the — the — whatever job you had. You sat there on that wall taking sightings to make sure you could hit everyone you'd been hired to do, and the fucking kids would sneak up on you and lift your dongle. They did it, what, like four times? You asked me to Push them a little." The smile snapped off. "You didn't ask. You pushed me around and ordered me to. You *always* pushed me around."

I remembered. I nailed four people in less than thirty

seconds, earned one hundred and forty-five thousand yen. Took me five days to get the sightings mapped. When you worked out the hours, I got paid shit.

The smile popped back. "It's good to see you, Avery. I don't have any friends."

Closing my eyes, I thought, *Kev's gone crackers.* Sadly, this probably increased my chances of being killed within the next few minutes, a possibility I observed with clinical detachment. There had to be a way off the rail. There *had* to be. The universe could *not* be this fucking unfair. I felt weak. The only thing keeping my arm up and the gun jabbed into his gut was Kev's Push. I opened my eyes with some effort, and Kev's face had transformed again, glowering at me, a ridiculous mask of hatred.

"Avery," he said.

I looked down and there was a gun in Kev's white plastic hand. It was black and charred looking, original Monk issue. He turned it toward me, the barrel a black hole, like death itself. I stared at it and wondered if my calm was because I was such a hardcore bastard, or because of Kev's Push. "He says your usefulness has passed."

The door to the room exploded inward, slamming against me with concussive force that knocked me onto my side. Two gunshots knocked Kev off his feet and he went sliding, face twisted into something that wasn't even a coherent expression, pursued by a blurred figure. I saw Kev raise one hand, an old legacy gesture still stored in his rotting brain.

"Stop," he commanded.

She didn't stop. She leaped on top of the Monk, swinging her gun down in a wide, sloppy arc I attributed to excitement—the Colonel Hense I knew would never pull such a shitty, sloppy move out of her ass—which gave Kev plenty of time to shove her off with some force, spraying white coolant everywhere as he did so. Hense's little body went flying, her shot barking into the ceiling, and before I could wonder why Kev's Push wasn't working on her, Happling roared into the room. I could have sworn he was *grinning* as he ran, pumping shells at Kev. The Monk flipped onto its feet and dodged, moving too fast to keep track of. Happling continued to chase Kev with his gun, emptying a clip while trying to catch him. Then Kev twisted around and made the same bizarre gesture.

"Stop!" he shouted.

Happling froze, and the Monk immediately shot the big man twice in the chest, dead center. Happling tottered a second before crashing down. I was suddenly released, my arm going limp, my gun slipping from slack fingers. I remembered when he'd been human, Kev always had trouble with the Push, trouble having more than one person under his control or keeping people Pushed for long periods. Clarity of mind hadn't broadened his range much, I supposed.

More gunshots, and Hense rolled out of my view. Kev was a whirlwind, scampering up the walls and back onto the floor in a blur, then leaping into the air as Hense scrambled past me, dropping an empty clip. Before she could reload the Monk crashed into her, knocking her into the wall a foot or two away from me, the whole room shaking with the impact.

"Stop!" Kev screeched, his modulated voice distorted as the circuits tried to compensate for an emotion they'd never been programmed to run. Hense didn't hesitate, smashing one fist into Gatz's face hard enough to jerk his

head around. For a second we were staring at each other.
Then Kev looked back at the colonel and started to swing
his gun on her. Hense reached up and grabbed his wrist
in her tiny dark hand, and they sawed back and forth, the
gun veering this way and that.

Hense wasn't sweating. I squinted at her to be sure.
Then, feeling empty, I turned my head to focus on Ty
Kieth. The Techie was right where he'd been left, tied
down to the examination table, his gag slick with spittle
and pushed partly off his mouth, his tongue working free.
Our eyes met, and he froze.

Taking a deep, agonizing breath, I hacked up bloody
phlegm, spat it out onto the floor, and pushed myself back
into a sitting position. Kieth continued to stare at me, eyes
wide, nose still for what I imagined was the first time in
his life. I got one foot under me and slowly climbed to
my feet while the Techie watched, and stood there swaying while my vision swam again, everything going hazy
and then gradually clarifying. I blinked as Hense went
hurtling through the air in front of me, smashing into the
far wall and leaving an impact crater in the drywall as she
bounced back onto the floor. A second later she was up
on her feet again, bounding behind Kieth as Kev splashed
bullets after her. The colonel wasn't even breathing hard
as she hovered there with the Techie between her and the
Monk, sliding a fresh clip into place while Kev considered how to shoot her without accidentally hitting his
prized Techie. I stared dully, wondering how it was that
Hense could go through this, could fight a *Monk* hand to
hand and be bounced around the room like a fucking rag
doll and just stand there looking as fresh as the day I'd

met her. I knew System Pigs were hard-core, but this was ridiculous.

As I stared at the colonel, Kev flashed through the air, coat fluttering behind him like the dirty tail of a comet. Hense ducked at the last moment, firing almost directly into the Monk as he sailed over her. A white hand snaked out and grabbed her shoulder with hydraulic strength, tearing the cop from the floor and dragging her with him as they crashed into a bank of medical instruments piled up against one wall.

I put my eyes on Kieth, who'd succeeded in pushing his gag completely out of his mouth, but he continued to stare at me in silence, mouth open, chest heaving. He remained frozen until I was a step away; when I languidly racked a shell into the chamber of my gun, it was as if someone had pressed a button inside him.

"Mr. Cates!" He hissed, forcing a squeamish smile. "Mr. Cates, Ty is glad to see *you!* Rescue at last!"

Behind me, there was more gunfire, and I sensed movement, harried and desperate, but nothing was left inside me to produce alarm or urgency or fear. I stared down at Kieth with my gun held waist-high, almost forgotten, and felt only a tired sadness.

Kieth licked his lips. "Rescue at last," he repeated more quietly.

My whole body tightened as I looked down at him, and I brought the gun up. His eyes flashed to it and he convulsed on the table, struggling madly against his bonds, whipping his head back and forth.

"Ty had no choice, Mr. Cates! Ty had no choice! Please, please, Avery—Avery! You know me! You *know* me! Please!"

I nodded. "I know you, Ty."

He nodded back eagerly. I felt like the world's biggest asshole, making him squirm, making him beg. "Ty can work on this, Mr. Cates. We have some time. Ty *designed* this; Ty can hack it under control. Mr. Cates. *Please*."

I could feel the universe pushing against me like wind in a sail, pushing me inexorably, gently toward its preordained destination—which was, unfortunately for Ty, a bullet in the Techie's head, everyone linking arms and singing as we all got well again. Or some bullshit like that. My city gone, even if they repopulated the buildings. Glee gone. *Everything* gone.

And I decided, Fuck the universe.

Feeling weak, I jerked my arm and my blade snapped into place, the one thing left in the world that was still working properly. With a slash I cut through Ty's bonds and then stood there wobbling a little. I let the blade slide back into its holster on its spring and brought the gun up, shuddering a breath into my ruined lungs.

"Ty," I said raggedly, fighting an epic coughing fit that was beating its way up from my chest. "I'm going to get you out of this building."

Fuck the universe. I was off the rail, and for the first time in a week felt normal again. I was probably going to die—it was a wonder I wasn't dead *yet*—but for a while now I'd known I'd outlived my time. It felt all right. It felt *natural*. I was going to get Ty out of here, and he'd do his best.

Ty struggled upright, nose quivering, eyes damp and glassy. "Mr. Cates," he said hoarsely, "Mr. Cates, Ty doesn't know—"

"Ty," I said tiredly, waving my gun toward the exit,

"you're not going to kiss me or anything, are you? We don't have time."

He smiled, convulsing into an unexpected laugh, radiating relief. As he opened his mouth to say something, the back of his head exploded, splattering a sticky mess of blood and bone onto the wall behind him. As if a supporting thread had been cut, Ty flopped back down onto the table.

I whirled, a push of adrenaline giving me a last burst of energy. Belling stood in the doorway, sweating and pale, one gun still outstretched toward me. His eyes shifted to me, and I squeezed my own trigger, getting a dry click in response.

Belling nodded, keeping his gun on me but not firing. "You never could go that last bit, could you, Avery?" he said, and in his mouth it was a curse. Wordlessly, he turned and strode away.

There was no moment of salvation, no feeling of disease evaporating. I felt as shitty as I had a second before. Whatever damage the nanobots had done to me had been done, and whether that was enough to kill me remained to be seen. A molten, distorted scream filled the room, and I felt Kev's Push, harder than I'd ever felt before, crashing into my head like a boulder, flattening everything that was me. Before I could blink I'd bent my arm up and put my gun against my own forehead and pulled the trigger. Another dry click sounded like thunder in my ear. Behind me, I heard a volley of gunshots, and Kev's Push vanished as suddenly as it had hit me, my arm dropping, the gun slipping from shaking, numb fingers. My legs disappeared and I hit the floor softly, just sort of sagging down onto it, feeling like every nerve ending I had left had been pulled to the surface through my pores, screaming and raw.

I heard a soft rustling behind me, and then Hense's boots appeared near my head. She stood for a moment staring down at Ty, hands loose at her sides, one still gripping her automatic. Her hands were spotless: not a nick, cut, or bruise. I wondered if Colonel Hense was even human. I shifted my eyes and studied her upside-down face, and with a surge of adrenaline I remembered where I'd seen her before.

Hanging upside down from the ancient fire escape, guns still clutched in her hands. I'd killed her. Years ago. She hadn't been a lofty colonel back then, and she'd shown up moonlighting as a bodyguard for one of my jobs. I hadn't expected a bodyguard, and I remembered barely surviving the encounter.

I never actually killed the target.

Without a sound she turned and disappeared from view, and then those perfect tiny hands were sliding under my arms and pushing me into a sitting position with my back against the examination table. I looked up at her as she knelt before me. She stared at me. She wasn't sweating. She wasn't breathing hard. Why would she? She was a ghost. Her face was cocked at me like a bird or a cat examining prey, just like Dick Marin, and I thought, *Fuck me, she's a fucking avatar.*

If Marin had started making avatars out of the cops, we were all completely screwed. You'd never be able to stop someone who could just pull another body out of the fucking warehouse and return to kick you in the balls again and again.

She put one of her small hands on my cheek and looked

at me, her face almost soft, a slight smile in place. A tiny flare of hope sparked inside me. I *liked* Hense, cop or no cop. "I am a woman who keeps her word," she said softly. "Mr. Kieth is dead, and in your way you brought us here. I could quibble about details, but I see no reason to kill you, Avery."

She wiped something off my face in a gentle, almost affectionate gesture. "Because the Monks will almost certainly do it for me," she said quietly, patting my cheek and standing up. I watched her walk out of the room without another word as I struggled to suck air into my ruined lungs, too tired to even mind the pain.

For a moment Marko regarded me from the doorway, hands clenching and unclenching in indecision, and then he whirled to follow.

I heard the remnants of the cops pulling out, a few ragged shouts, Hense's voice clear and unfatigued. A ghost. As they faded, silence crept in behind them, and for a while I just sat there, staring at Happling's corpse. I thought of Gleason and tried to imagine what she'd say about this, what wise-ass remark, but I couldn't think of anything. Then the distant sound of heavy boots running.

XXXIX

DAY TEN: I SHOULD HAVE BEEN KILLING *MONKS*

━━━

Right, I thought, *that's goddamn fair*. For a few moments I sat and stared blearily at the door, happy to not move. This was fitting. After all that, I was going to be torn to pieces by the last of Kev's Monks, fifty or so still in the complex. We'd slipped past them and they'd arrived too late to save their boss, but here I was, the consolation prize.

In a strange way, I thought it was only right that Kev have his revenge. I'd led him down into Westminster Abbey and he'd died sitting on a bare concrete floor, one of Dennis Squalor's digital avatars grinning down at him. Now I was sitting on a cold floor, high up this time but close enough. I sat there immobile. My arms weighed a hundred pounds each, useless lengths of bone and flesh, and the thought of moving them made my head ache.

Doors were being slammed open, glass shattering.

My eyes found Happling. The big man was staring at

the ceiling, eyes wide open, mouth drifting. Blood had pooled around him, black and shiny, like oil. His hands were still curled into loose fists—the motherfucker was pissed off even in death. I thought of Hense again, and wondered if Captain Happling would show up again someday, grinning and asking me if I felt fast.

I wondered if all the cops I'd killed were going to come back one day.

I could hear the Monks approaching. As I stared at Happling, my heart unexpectedly began to pound in terror. They were going to crowd into the room with their blank, white faces, put their plastic hands on me, and tear me apart in silence, in *complete* silence.

Glancing at the door, I lunged forward and started dragging myself toward Happling. Sputtering bloody spit onto the floor, I slapped my hands onto him, pushing into his clothes and prying his Roon from his lifeless fingers. I flinched, with every movement expecting him to surge up and grab me, laughing and grinning blood. I found three extra clips in his front pocket, his body still warm beneath the clothes. I checked the chamber of the gun as I pushed myself as far back as I could get, opposite the door but on a slight angle, so when they came in I wouldn't immediately be in their field of vision—though the Monks had heat vision and night vision and every fucking digital bell and whistle the tech of five years ago could offer, so I wasn't sure how much my old tricks would help me. I'd never actually beaten a Monk in a fight, much less a squad of them. It didn't matter. I racked the chamber and laid my extra clips in my lap and tried not to do the math that told me I didn't have enough ammunition for fifty-four Monks. Trembling, I raised the gun and waited.

Time had stopped. I struggled to hold the gun up and stay ready while the echo of approaching steps seemed to get louder but never arrive. There was no talking, no shouting or other sounds. Just boots clicking on the hard floor, slowing as they got closer. I assumed they knew exactly where Kev was: his brain had been killed but his chassis still hummed with electronic life, sending out beacons, scanning frequencies. An immortality of deaf and dumb.

Doors slammed in the distance, and then there was total silence. They were just feet away, creeping toward me, probably scanning my heat signature and suddenly getting cautious. You could put a brain into billions of yen of technology, but you couldn't improve the *brain* — put an asshole into a Monk chassis and he was still an asshole. Still, these were the assholes who'd survived. Through their initial conversion, through months or years of involuntary servitude, screaming endlessly inside, and then through the Monk Riots and the SSF's steady attempt to wipe them out, they'd managed to remain sane enough to function.

I cleared my mind. I saw a line of trees at night, a dark wall of rustling leaves in the wind. I had no idea where I'd ever seen trees, but there they were. I felt everything drain away as I imagined it, just the soft sawing of the branches in the breeze, nothing else, no sound, no light, just me. My hands steadied, my breathing slowed, and my vision narrowed to the door, excluding Happling's symmetric corpse and Gatz's twisted form in a heap against the wall. Gatz's white face was staring at me, and it took all my concentration to ignore it.

When they came, they came fast, two at a time materializing from thin air and bursting through the door. I fired once on instinct and the first Monk's face exploded in a spray of white coolant. It crumpled to the floor as if it had just remembered it was a fucking ton of alloys and plastic. The second one leaped over the first with a graceful, silent move that was almost beautiful. I tracked it upward with a small tick of my wrist and put two shells into its face while it was still in midair. The range was about six feet. You'd have to paralyze me for me to miss at six feet.

By the time I reoriented on the door two more were through. I managed to knock down the first one with a shot into its nose, but the second swerved around it and was on me from the side. I swung my arm around just as it landed next to me and fired three times into its abdomen, knocking it back, but before I could make a kill shot two more were diving for me. I rolled, screaming in tearing pain, and slammed myself into the corner, bringing my arm up as a Monk with horrible, cancerous rust welts eating through its latex face landed with a earthquake-like jolt nearly on top of me. As I pulled the trigger it batted my arm aside and the shot took off its molded ear and part of its face, the ruined fake skin torn away to reveal the corroded alloy beneath. It grinned as it lashed out a hand and clasped my wrist painfully.

"Too slow, Meat," it hissed, the words melted and ruined in its rusted, damaged mouth.

It squeezed my hand open and my gun dropped to the floor with a dead-sounding thud, and then another Monk was at my opposite side and a third was between them. The blank, identical faces peered at me, one pair of scratched sunglasses and two pairs of whirring, delicate camera eyes. Up close, I could see how time had treated them—their fake skin scratched and pocked with collision damage, the little servos of their eyes sounding labored and sluggish, their clothes filthy and tattered without any attempt at repair. So much, I thought, for immortality.

Two more leaped in behind them, and I knew I was dead. There were too many, and they were too fast. A lot of noise suddenly welled up outside the door, hard to identify. An off-rhythm pounding vibrated through the floor, as if someone were lazily hurling cannonballs at the building.

The Monk's hands were on me, tightening.

"All this time I was killing cops," I said, panting, "I should have been killing *Monks*."

Rusty smiled down at me. "Your turn, Meat. Your *fucking*—"

The Monk jerked upward as if an invisible thread had been drawn taut. Everything paused for a second, and then Rusty leaped up and backward, sailing away from me and smashing into the far wall hard enough to shake the room and bring chunks of drywall down onto the Monk as it slid to the floor. The Monks around me whirled as one and then all four rose into the air stiffly, arms dropping to their sides, and smashed into the concrete ceiling, dropping back to the floor in front of me in a broken heap.

I didn't try to move, certain I wouldn't be able to anyway. Standing there, pale and haggard but calm, was Bendix, his terrible scar torn open and bleeding, one arm hanging loose at his side. He looked back into the corridor and then at me.

"Mr. Cates, you are one lucky bastard."

He crossed over to where Ty Kieth's body lay and stood

there a moment, staring down at the Techie. Four more people entered the room behind him, young, round-faced kids in spiffy suits and long coats, three men and a woman. They were all binary, like the triplets I'd killed a week before—pale white skin and black hair. They hung back and watched Bendix like he was the Big Dog in the room. "Well, that's done, at least," he said. "It's a waste, of course. Kieth should have been working for us. *With* us. A brain like that could have been accomplishing amazing things, properly funded. Properly channeled."

I snorted and was amazed I had the energy to be amused. Properly fucking channeled. That was hilarious.

He glanced at me, and at once I found myself paralyzed by an invisible fist, almost unable to breathe. *Just do it,* I thought savagely. *Just get it over with and fuck all this bullshit.*

"You are a lucky man, Mr. Cates," he said, turning and walking toward me. "You have a guardian angel. When I was dispatched on this mission I was given very specific orders, and I was given discretion to kill you if it seemed necessary for the survival of the human race—that's a technical term, you know, SHR. In any scenario wherein I deemed your death *not* to be necessary for the survival of the human race, I was directed to leave you alive. You're a Person of Interest, Mr. Cates, at least to Director Marin, and for the time being we are still taking Director Marin's requests seriously. Though the time for that is fading, I think."

He leaned in close, his open wound wet and puckered near my nose. I imagined I could smell him, but the fact was I couldn't push enough air through my ruined nose to smell anything. His eyes were a little yellowed, dry and used up.

"You do not," he said as I dropped back to the floor in a heap, "seem all that interesting."

Turning, he waved his good hand in the air as he walked away. "The human race will, apparently, survive," he said. "And the King Worm can fucking collect his own trash." He spun out the door and his fellow psionics turned without looking at me, without saying anything, and followed. I lay where I was and watched him go, and then it was just me and my old friends. *Nothing's changed,* I thought. *It's still assholes in nice suits running the world.*

XL

EPILOGUE: THE MOMENT WHEN I ALMOST SHOT YOU IN THE HEAD AS A HIGH POINT

Enduring the ache in my leg that never left me these days, I sat at the bar in silence. I pushed some of the trash onto the floor with one hand; the place had been ransacked at some point, like every other place in Manhattan. The doors had been torn from their hinges, the windows smashed, and just about everything carted off. I imagined the thieves enjoying their booty for all of three days, days in which they coughed blood and spat out their own lungs, days in which the city fell apart around them. I sat on the last stool left intact in Pickering's and felt the heavy dust I'd disturbed settling on me, seeking to reclaim the surfaces it had come to think of as its own.

Outside, the constant blaring of SSF loudspeakers was distant and tinny, official voices stepping over each other. New York was sick with cops and government—there were more Pigs and kids in suits crawling around the wreckage than citizens. People had survived, and more were arriving every day to pick over the carcass of the city. The city was dead. I'd lived in it my whole life, and I could smell it decomposing around me. The new people were maggots who'd infest it, tunnel into it, make it into something new. It would still be here, but it wouldn't be my city anymore.

I was thirty-six. I had nothing.

Scratching at my beard, which I'd let grow into an unruly, tangled mess of gray and black, I stood up and stumped down the familiar length of the bar, my bad leg stiff and painful. It might still heal some and get some movement back, but I'd never dance again. It didn't matter.

I paused by the door where, years before, I'd sat with Kev Gatz and Nad Muller, drinking Pick's gin and plotting grand things. All of them worm food, the schemes only the dust they were buried in.

Somewhere outside there was an explosion and a jumble of shouts.

The SSF and the government were at each other's throats, Undersecretaries claiming authority over the cops, Dick Marin telling them to shove their authority up their pencil-thin assholes. Word was the government was pouring yen and matériel into the new Army, and that the System Pigs would have bigger worries very soon. I believed it. The Pigs were, in the meantime, chasing down every last motherfucker they saw as a possible threat or a possible resource. I'd heard rumors from all over the world—Mexico City, Vancouver, Kinshasa—that people were being rounded up and shot in the head in record numbers, the fucking cops just hammering and hammering without any of the old rules or traditions. Rumor was you couldn't even bribe them anymore, not that yen was worth shit anymore anyway. They came with high-end brass running the show, fucking colonels and up, kicking their own troops in the balls, fucking famous criminals, good people lined up in alleys and shot in broad daylight, and screw the citizen who saw something and complained. The cops weren't even hiding you in the shadows when they executed you these days.

I'd seen it in Manhattan, too. I'd heard Marcel had been taken away from his little throne room and left alive—rumor was the fat fuck had walked on his own dwindling legs for the first time in five years, weeping. I'd been by his little hotel the other week, just out of curiosity, and it had been a morgue, the rotting bodies of Marcel's little court all dead with their SSF straps still around their wrists, the Stormer cables still coiled up where the troops had hit the ground. There was no sign of Marcel, and he would rot for goddamn *weeks* before he disappeared, so it might even be true.

My days were numbered, and I didn't care. If Marcel was on their list, so was I, and I had a feeling that even if I'd somehow been left off— maybe a remnant of my old deal with Marin, which had cleared my old record—there were a few cops who'd be happy to put my name back on it. A couple of weeks ago I'd seen Hense busting out an old apartment building on Jane Street, standing there impassive and shiny, her dark hair tied back in a tight bun, her skin perfect, eyes hidden behind pitch-black glasses. The lower floor had blown up, fire and brick blasting out into the street, and she'd just stood there, unconcerned. I'd ducked into a doorway and limped through the building, keeping my head down, and never looked back.

I didn't hide, though. My leg had healed crooked over the weeks and I had headaches all the time, but I hadn't died, and I could breathe normally again. I'd been forced to kill four people over the past few weeks, all punks. Two who'd recognized me and wanted to be the ones who took out Avery Cates, two fucking infants who didn't know me from any other old man tottering around with worthless yen in his pocket. I'd taught them a lesson, but it had been rote, mechanical. Put a gun on me and I'll put a gun on you, but I didn't take any joy in it. If I'd had his address I would have gladly pointed them at Wa Belling if they were looking for reputations, but Belling had faded away. The Old Man wasn't going to live forever, maybe, but he'd been breathing last time I saw him and was one person I'd gladly kill with my bare hands, on sight.

I stared at my hands. Two fingers were bent in unexpected ways and ached on cold nights.

Swinging around, I limped behind the bar, kicking chunks of the wall out of the way. I crouched down and searched the floor, smiling faintly when I found the hidden trigger, a secret panel popping up smooth as silk. Stupid fucks hadn't done a very thorough job of searching the place, but then it was probably hard to concentrate when you were coughing blood and fighting off a million other looters.

Two dusty bottles of cloudy liquor greeted me, along with two gleaming handguns—cheap pieces of shit, meant for emergencies—and a scattering of credit dongles and health chips. Looking at the chips, I reached up and fingered the deep, pus-filled scab on my hand where I'd gouged out my tracking chip. Why I'd done that if I didn't care if I lived or not, I wasn't sure.

I picked up one of the bottles and slumped down onto the junk-strewn floor. I held it up to the weak daylight streaming in and squinted at it. It looked deadly, but I was going to drink it anyway. I twisted off the cap and smelled the old, familiar reek of homemade gin.

Outside, I heard hover displacement approaching. I paused with the bottle halfway to my mouth and then put it down. I shifted my weight and reached into my coat, pulling my gun and tossing it onto the floor with a thunderous crash. I was ready. If they were finally coming for me, I decided I would be drunk. Thirty-six was old enough. Too old. I tipped the bottle and took a long swig of the burning liquid, feeling it edge its way down, turning from knife blade to warm ball in my stomach. For a few moments I sat in relative silence and peace, sipping from the bottle and not thinking about anything. It was just me and the booze and my aching bones.

When they came, it was almost funny, Stormers crashing in, shouts and smoke, a fucking army invading the empty shell of Pick's until it was crowded with cops. They found me immediately, of course, kicking my gun away, slapping the bottle onto the floor where it shattered in a spray of booze, and jerking me to my feet.

"*Sulle vostre ginocchia!*" one of them shouted. I laughed. They were pulling cops from all over the System, trying to man up New York again.

"*Fuck,*" he muttered in a heavy accent. Hands took hold of me and I was flipped around and shoved to my knees, my bad leg barking with a shaft of white-hot pain.

A silicone strap was looped around my wrists and pulled achingly tight. As my hands went numb I was thoroughly frisked, but I had nothing else, and they came up empty. My head was pushed down until I was staring down at the dirty floor, and a gun barrel was positioned against the back of my head. It was a familiar feeling.

"Belay that!" someone shouted, and the whole room went still. The gun was immediately gone.

"Flip him around. We need an OFR scan."

I was pulled up roughly and spun around, two Stormers holding me in place. Two officers had entered the bar. One was a tall, skinny man in a ridiculously pristine black leather overcoat that gleamed in the dim light. He was tanned and shaved close, his dark hair combed back and perfectly barbered. The other was short and my age, maybe even a little older. He looked out of shape, with a belly not quite hidden by his long overcoat and his hair a thin ring around the edge of his skull. He had a long, ugly nose that had frequently been broken, and carried a digital clipboard that reflected a ghoulish green glow onto his chubby face.

The tall one stepped close to me with sinuous grace, giving the impression of having choreographed the movement the night before, and thrust a small black box into my face. I was partially blinded by a bright red flash, and he snatched the box back, peering down at a tiny Vid screen.

"Cates, Avery," he announced. Looking up at me, he grinned. "Well, shit, Mr. Cates, it's a fucking honor to execute you!"

I grinned back. "You're not executing me. I'm committing suicide by cop."

He winked, drawing an impressive-looking chrome-plated automatic and cocking the hammer back jauntily. "Happy to be—"

"Wait," the bald guy said quietly, and the Grinner stopped, glancing over at him. Baldy looked up at me, face blank and his eyes empty pools. *This* was the guy to worry about in the room, I realized. The Grinner was more concerned with the cut of his coat than anything else. Baldy would cut your balls off. Baldy didn't look at the Grinner, just tilted the clipboard at him. "He's on the list."

"Ah, fuck," the Grinner moaned, glancing down at the clipboard. "So you are, Mr. Cates. Fuck, that's *Marin's* fucking sig block." He looked at Baldy, face flushing red. "Do you know how many cops this piece of shit has killed?"

Baldy looked back down at his clipboard. "Doesn't matter. He's POI, and if you kill him I will make you a personal project, understood?"

The Grinner's face drained of color as quickly as it had reddened. "Yes, sir. Of course, sir. I didn't mean—"

"Fuck what you meant, Colonel," Baldy said, turning away and gesturing delicately at his clipboard. "Get him loaded up and let's clear this building for demo."

Baldy stalked out of Pick's, and we both watched him go. Then the Grinner turned back and looked around, flushing again as he stuffed his piece back into its holster. He stepped up to me and ran his blue eyes up and down my body.

"All right, shithead," he said, finding his grin again. "Chengara it is for you, you lucky, lucky bastard. Give it a few weeks. You'll think back on the moment when I almost shot you in the head as a high point in your life." He paused to study me again, his mouth smirking. "Shit, you don't look like much, Cates," he said.

Avery Cates, the gweat and tewwible, I thought. *Avery Cates, Destroyer of Worlds.* And I started to laugh.

APPENDIX

EXCERPTS FROM AUDIO DIARY OF TRICIA AMBER POLLOCK

Joint Council File #668RF9
Reviewed by: C. Ruberto, Joint Council Undersecretary

Background: This is a transcript of audio files found on a handheld device recovered from a stairwell at 435 East Fifty-second Street in Manhattan during postepidemic sweep and demolition operations. The later entries were very muddy and required a great deal of lab cleanup in order to transcribe, and accuracy cannot be guaranteed. Most background noise and bodily functions are not recorded here, but in later entries notation of pauses, coughing fits, or other unintelligible sounds have been included in order to show that nothing has been censored by this department, due to direct request of Director Marin's office regarding transcribed artifacts shared between our divisions.

It should be noted that no body was found near the handheld that contained the audio entries. Ms. Pollock did maintain an apartment in that location, but to date she has not been located.

<BEGIN TRANSCRIPT>

never going drinking below Twenty-third Street again. I don't know why Gerry likes slumming it down in those places, playing tough and drinking that paint. None of the animals around us is fooled, I am sure—I can see their looks as Gerry plays his little game. I am so tired of Gerry. I may have to give him the slip, try on someone new for a while. I felt frail and dried up when I finally got home and had to take four e-tabs to get to sleep, and this morning I feel even more dried up and need four a-tabs to even get out of bed. Thank goodness for tabs.

Wednesday, 3:33 a.m.: *Only because the universe hates me, my shell is acting strangely. Quoting fucking poetry at random moments. Like ten minutes after I go to bed. I've reset and restored the damn thing a hundred times, and it behaves for a few days and then starts quoting again. Today I got a gem about an endless trail of sunsets. I put it into shutdown mode for my sanity—I can make my own Vid calls and order my own meals for a while, I suppose. Like Daddy used to say, I'm full of pluck.*

Wednesday, 1:33 p.m.: *Really, Gerry is simply disgusting. I think I might hate him.*

Wednesday, 8:22 p.m.: *Old pal Vincent asked me out to drinks tonight at Umano, the new place in the Forties. Supposedly they don't use Droids or mechanicals at all, just people. Though what kind of people would be willing to serve food I'm sure I don't know, and I don't want to. Why are all the men I know so interested in thrill seeking and slumming?*

Today I'm supposed to meet with Carol whatshername about the finances. I don't feel up to it. I've been a little hot and achy all day long. There's always more money. Hearing about it piled up here and there just makes me sleepy.

Then again, I can't just sit in this apartment all night, watching the story Vids and making my own cocktails. I'm going to take a few x-tabs to perk up a bit and put on this divine new coat I acquired—bright red and cut to order, six hundred thousand yen. It's almost time for another visit to the loathsome Dr. Killicks, but I think I look all right for at least a few more weeks, and the coat fits so well it won't matter.

Thursday, 12:34 p.m.: *Oh baby, there aren't enough a-tabs in the world to wake me up today. Vincent—who knew he was such a lush? I feel terri-*

ble today, worse than yesterday. Maybe it's too many tabs. They say there's no harm in them, but I have been pushing it lately. I'm just so bored. When I'm not out I want to sleep, and when I wake up I want to get going! But it might not do a girl any harm to lay off for a while, eat healthy. Nothing but nutrition tablets and that nice imported water for yours truly, starting today. The moment I can get Vincent out of my bathroom, and have it cleaned. Or perhaps just bulldozed and completely replaced. On top of everything else, I'm coughing up a lung.

Thursday, 11:00 p.m.: *Unstoppable Vincent dragged me out again. He can be pretty persuasive when he wants to have some drinks, and I was feeling a little better, and a few a-tabs took care of the rest. I wasn't looking for a long exhausting night, though, and we went to a little bar on Fifth, one of those unmarked places all the plebs and strivers are always trying to get into. There were barely any people there, but Vinnie tells me this is the way it always is, that's it's pull — you don't have to be crowded in like everywhere else in fucking Manhattan. It was nice, I have to admit, except for this ridiculous girl staggering around on these lengthened legs telling everyone that she was just in from Tokyo on the long-haul and the new rage out there is bald. Bald! Of course, she was* *bald. Telling us that next year every woman worth her salt would be decorating her head with paint and sparkles, diamonds. Of course, she may be right. I've made a note to talk to Dr. Killicks about it.*

Considering I had no stamina, I made Vinnie take me home early. He's out again, of course, and I probably won't see him for some time. Once you let little Vinnie out of your sight he tends to get lost. I thought about calling Gerry but didn't really feel like it. I'm tired, and I've got a cough that hurts every time. I might have to see Killicks tomorrow anyway, just to get something for this tickle in my chest. What a bore!

Friday, 4:30 p.m.: *Hell, what a strange day. I am feeling sick, really sick. Coughing and spewing up the most disgusting things. I woke up feeling like I'd had another rib removed, and when I looked at myself in the mirror, I almost screamed. Killicks guarantees his treatments last a minimum of three years, but I looked almost my age in the mirror and I decided I had to get down to his office and let him know what I thought of his fucking "procedures" and get him to give me something for whatever's taken up residence inside me.*

Exasperated, I called for my hover but the hover guy wasn't answering, so I had to fire him, which is a huge pain in the ass. You'd think these people would be glad for a job, but they treat it like an inconvenience. I end up firing everyone eventually and I am starting to think I should just replace everyone with Droids where I can. Monique went all-Droid a few years ago and says she's never been happier with the service.

So I had to go down to the fucking street and catch a pedicab. Horrible. The streets weren't as crowded as usual, at least, but nothing beats sitting upwind from a man whose diet is no doubt on a par with cockroaches and rats—it may, based on the smell, be cockroaches and rats—but who also seems to like the scent so much he refuses to bathe. Ever. While my smelly driver huffed and puffed in front of me, coughing almost as hard as I was, I was barely able to keep my new red coat out of the slush in the streets. Killicks's is almost seven blocks away—it was an eternity. Then, not only do I have to walk in through the ground lobby like some piece of trash from downtown, I have to pay my fat friend for the privilege of smelling him for seven blocks.

My goodness, Killicks's office was crowded, everyone coughing. Something must be going around. One man in an absolutely gorgeous Silvio Martini suit—million yen if it was custom-cut, which of course it had to be—actually passed out and slumped onto the floor. This was after I'd been there for some time, and people whispered that he'd been there for almost an hour! An hour! Whatever Killicks is thinking, he'd better stop thinking it. I don't care how popular you are, you have to treat your customers with respect. An hour! I'd be passing out, too. Though the poor gentleman looked pretty badly off as I left, and I think I saw blood.

Friday, 9:33 p.m.: *Exasperated again. Someone is shouting in the streets down below. I popped the police up on my Vid screen but there's a static graphic there instead of an interface, complaining about the volume of complaints. Complaints about the service, no doubt. I have been in bed for hours, sweating, coughing. Every breath feels like someone put a knife inside my chest. The last thing I need is some wretched subhuman from downtown—and no one in my building would wander the streets, screaming—keeping me up all night when I need rest most. I look twenty years older, dark circles under my eyes and on my throat.*

Now, I may have to swallow my pride and go wait in Killicks's office no matter how rude success has made the man. And I might have a little tightening done here and there while I'm in there. The skin under my chin seems a little loose these days.

Saturday, 2:09 a.m.: *Okay, the man has finally stopped shouting. The last hour or so he was almost unintelligible, as if he were gargling thick oil when he spoke. I haven't been able to sleep. I can't breathe through all this phlegm and I feel hot, so hot. I can't believe the police let him shout like that all night. They must have their hands full. I wonder if those animals downtown have set the city on fire again.*

Saturday, 11:03 a.m.: *Really, I didn't feel too bad this morning, and I thought maybe I'd gotten past it, slept through it. I felt okay until I got to the bathroom and looked in the mirror. I almost screamed. My throat is bruised and looks kind of swollen. The moment I saw it, it was like all of a sudden I felt awful.*

Determined, I called around for a hover, but no one answered. I think most everyone got out of the city last night, but no one thought to tell me. Feeling weak, I went out onto the street for the second time in two days. Big mistake. No pedicabs. Not a single fucking pedicab anywhere. I would have paid one of those sweaty slobs a million yen to drive me seven blocks, but there were none to be had, so I had to walk. In my sixty-thousand-yen Pierre Olivier stilettos, which fell apart about three blocks along, one heel just snapping like a twig. By this point I was sweating and gasping, coughing, but no one would help me. In fact, every-

one kept away from me, crossing to the other side of the street. Some had these ridiculous masks on, white pieces of cloth strapped to their faces.

Oh, the punch line? Killicks's office was closed. Fucking closed.

Saturday, 7:33 p.m.: *Even getting home was hell. The city feels empty—there are people everywhere, but for some reason it feels light and thin. And every third person has on one of those masks, like that's going to do anything. I finally got around to watching the Vids, and according to them this is just the flu, the regular old flu. And I'm late to take my position down on the street to hold hands with everyone else in New York and start singing. The flu. I know the Vids aren't worth much, but do they really think we're that stupid?*

Sunday, 12:45 p.m.: *Shit, I think it's time to get the hell out of the city for a while, go travel a bit. I'm worse than ever and it's got to be this rotten city air, poisoned by all the lowlifes I have to rub shoulders with. Besides, I can't raise anybody—it's like the whole town has skipped. I'm wheezing my way down to the street again, because of course again there are no hovers to be had, and*

Sunday, 12:53 p.m.: *Right here in front of me, there is a dead man in the street.*

Sunday, 1:09 p.m.: *Unbelievable. A Department of Public Health hover has arrived. They're scooping him up using Droids, and they're all wearing protective clothing—rubbery suits, masks, gloves. They won't talk to any of us, though most people are just avoiding them, crossing the street. He's...disgusting. His neck is like a balloon, and crusted blood is all over his front. It looks like his whole jaw is just...gone.*

Shit, I'm not feeling well at all. I think it might be time to get out of the city. A little vacation. I'm heading home to make a few Vid calls. Vinnie has a small shore house somewhere in the Caribbean, he's told me. If Manhattan is about to go all redline again, with another riot and police everywhere, it'll be nice to ride it out somewhere far away.

Sunday, 2:35 p.m.: *Total washout—no one is in. I thought Vinnie answered—the Vid screen jiggled and I thought I saw a flash of his apartment, but it might have been just a dropped connection, and he didn't pick up when I retried. I even tried Father, which tells you how desperate I am, but the old bastard wasn't picking up, either. Probably out in the fields whipping the Droids. I think Daddy wishes he*

*still had people working for him instead of robots, just
so he could go out there in those fucking boots and
inspire them a little.*

*Well, looks like we're dipping into the trust fund.
I'm going to see if there aren't a few cops willing to
stick me on an SSF manifest heading somewhere better. Oh, but I look like hell. My neck is all black and
blue and I'm red and shiny. My hair! Oh, my hair is
a fright. Thousands of yen and it looks like a wig. I'm
going to have to spend some time getting myself into
shape, and then my new red coat and we'll see if we
can't charm some lieutenant or captain into slipping
me onto a police ride.*

Sunday, 5:46 p.m.: *Insane, fucking brutes. Just
as I step outside, wearing flats for a change since
apparently we'll all have to spend the rest of our
lives walking everywhere, all the Vids go fritzy and
there's a goddamn lockdown. We're all ordered into
our homes. I've been through this bullshit plenty of
times — every time those assholes set downtown on
fire again, they lock the city down and order us into
our homes and no one pays any attention.*

*Toddling on my sore feet, I made my way over
to The Rock, where all the cops hang around looking tough. All I needed was a friendly young man
with a gold badge and clearance to sign me onto a*

hover. I saw a likely-looking group—three men and a woman, one of them looking a little beat-up and weathered, but I'm used to my police looking worse for the wear—and hurried over. It had started that scum-yellow snow again, bad for the skin, and I guess I lost my footing and ended up stumbling into one of them, a nasty-looking giant with red hair. I went down on my ass, feeling dizzy, feverish, my chest seizing up into a painful fist. And then there was a team of those hover monkeys they toss out, the ones that never speak to you. I was dazed, and they just plucked me up, called me ma'am, *and took me away.*

*No way—*ma'am! *I felt a hundred goddamn years old. By the time I got my lungs working again, I started coughing until I almost blacked out while they loaded me into a big, smelly hover that fucking ruined my new coat. By the time I had the strength to protest, they were all gone with a vague promise that an officer would be around to check our IDs and decide what to do with us. Half an hour later some fat asshole in a leather overcoat, hacking and wheezing like there was a smaller, much sicker man inside him, showed up and did brain scans on each of us, grunting your fate. He told us he could arrest us for violating an emergency instruction, but he'd just send us home and expect us to stay there. Fucking assholes.*

Excellent. I feel like shit. Feels like someone put a razor blade in my chest. I'm taking e-tabs until I pass out.

Monday, 10:44 a.m.: *So, I feel like someone's cut me open, removed a few pounds of necessary materials, and closed me back up. I don't dare look in the mirror. There was blood on my pillow when I woke up. I'd rather not see what I look like.*

Shit, the city is quiet. I tried to go downstairs, but they finally got around to setting the building shell, and the elevators are locked. My own shell won't boot now. It's like living in an empty, hollow building. I can't even get my own front door open. I don't have any food in the apartment—who keeps food in the apartment? If this emergency goes on much longer, I won't have to worry about coughing up my own lungs. I'll be dead.

Think I have a few n-tabs here and there, some older than fucking I am—or parts of me, anyway.

Monday, 7:48 p.m.: *Oh crap, I slept for a long time and feel worse than ever. Everything is so quiet. There's plenty on the Vids, though you'd never know anything's going on from it. Serials, those half-minute dramas everyone's so nuts about these days, but no news. Well, news, but nothing local. They're dem-*

onstrating in Tokyo again because they're so terribly happy, and the police have caught some murderer who was very much wanted in Cardiff of all fucking places. But the fact that I can't leave my own apartment? That I'm coughing up my own lungs? Nothing. Not a peep. I

Monday, 9:33 p.m.: *You keep thinking the worst has come — there were shots outside. One minute everything is so quiet I can hear myself wheeze, the next it's like a war outside. Just a burst, gone just as fast as it started, and then it was silent again. Then more shots. I'm frightened. I've turned off all the lights by hand and I'm just sitting here in the dark, and every time there are more shots outside I jump and want to scream.*

Monday, 10:21 p.m.: *Okay, I keep falling asleep. Or passing out. Shots keep waking me up. It's so hot in here. I can't breathe.*

Tuesday, 6:09 a.m.: *Unbelievable. There is a man <unintelligible> outside my window. He is <unintelligible> walking along the narrow ledge, slowly, picking his steps with great care as he is twenty-seven stories up and there is barely room for one foot at a time on the ledge. He doesn't look good . . . oh, shit . . . I*

*bet neither do I. His neck is just a huge open wound.
I wonder how he got out there, and if I should try to
get out there, too. But this seems like a lot of work. I'm
so tired.*

Tuesday, 9:15 a.m.: *Right. I woke up unable to
breathe* <unintelligible> *like there was a mass of
soggy cotton jammed down my throat. I took some
a-tabs, but I barely feel them.* <unintelligible> *I'm
going to have to get out of here or I'm going to . . . die
here. I don't know what I have or what's going around,
but I know I need to leave this apartment.*

<unintelligible>

*Damn. Getting out of the apartment's no bother —
just pull the manual lock override. Getting out of
the building is another matter.* <unintelligible>
*Emergency lockdown means the building shell won't
budge. I'm not even sure the elevators will run.
I . . . don't know*

Tuesday, 10:55 a.m.: *Excel — Oh, shit* <unintelli-
gible> *I don't even think I can walk. I tried to stand
up and just fell over. And that was . . . an hour ago.
There's a big bloodstain on the rug where I was, too.*

*Ah, it's fucking unbelievable. I'm going to die. That
quack Killicks kept telling me they were doing won-*

ders in Europe about death — pushing it off, making it more of an inconvenience, but where the fuck is he now?

<unintelligible>

There's finally something on the local Vid spectrum. Not much, just a grim-faced DPH asshole telling us to remain indoors and not panic. It's a loop — he talks for five minutes and then starts again. Stay inside. All is well. DPH is scooping up the bodies as they fall from your ledges and keeping our city clean. Downtown is certainly not on fire again, and you are all not going to die. Ever. Fuck.

Hey

Tuesday, 3:02 p.m.: *Yikes. The power's out.*

<unintelligible>

Outside, far away, something exploded — my windows rattled and everything in the place jumped — and then <unintelligible> dead. It's stuffy as hell in here, and I can barely breathe. I wonder what the battery life on this handheld is? I'm <unintelligible> set it to sound-activated to try and stretch it. Though I don't know why I'm <unintelligible> gasp into it. Habit, I guess. And shit, aside from cataloging the spongy red shit I'm <unintelligible> all over the place by size and weight, what else do I have . . . to do?

Tuesday, 3:05 p.m.: <unintelligible, coughing>

Tuesday, 4:33 p.m.: *Unreal — this can't be allowed. Isn't* <unintelligible> *wondering about all of us? Or am I the only one trapped in here? I've been in bed for hours,* <unintelligible> *puking myself up onto the sheets. I'm so hot. This can't be. This can't, I mean, I have* friends, *I have money — did every single other person just up and leave the city? I can't even get out of my own building now. I could maybe drag myself down to the lobby,* <unintelligible> *every third floor, but then what? I don't even know if the doors will open with the power out.*

<unintelligible, heavy breathing>

Right. And if I can get out of the building, so what? There's no one to take me anywhere. And it's not like there's some magical hover to take me somewhere.

Tuesday, 5:05 p.m.: <unintelligible, coughing>

Tuesday, 5:15 p.m.: *Exit Tricia — shit. I should try to get to Bellevue. What the fuck is wrong with me? I've been chipped. There have to be doctors at the hospital, don't there? Better than just dying here.*

Tuesday, 6:15 p.m.: *No ... I think ... I think I'm on ... Twentieth ...*

Tuesday, 6:21 p.m.: <unintelligible, coughing>

Tuesday, 6:23 p.m.: <unintelligible, coughing>

Tuesday, 6:34 p.m.: *Daddy always* <unintelligible> *I guess... trying to walk... down... so... many... fucking stairs... when you... only... have... half a lung left... wasn't...*

Tuesday, 6:45 p.m.: *don't want... don't want*

Tuesday, 6:47 p.m.: *<unintelligible, coughing>*

Tuesday, 4:23 a.m.: <unintelligible>

<END TRANSCRIPT>

ACKNOWLEDGMENTS

When the government asked me to write this book, I wanted to refuse. I had planned a busy summer of drinking beer on the deck and watching my cats hunt sparrows, and writing a book would, I knew, take up precious hours of my day. The scientists sent by the government were adamant, however—something about the space-time continuum, me being my own grandfather, and avoidance of future events so terrible they shuddered every time the subject was returned to. Eventually they got around to mentioning huge advance monies and nationwide promotion, and since I was getting sleepy by that point, I hastily agreed.

When my lovely wife, Danette, found out, she didn't believe me about the government scientists and whatnot, which didn't bother me because in the movies the noble hero is always doubted, made fun of, and mildly beaten by his wife before he's revealed as, well, the hero. But she remained my biggest supporter and fan throughout the process, and it could not have been done without her. Every time I made her read a draft of the book, she would hit me on the head with her shoe and shout, "Better! You can do better!" And then she'd dry my tears and I'd revise, and it *would* be better.

My agent, Janet Reid, and my editors, Devi Pillai and Bella Pagan, are three women who can probably kill a man from across the room, just thinking about it with their huge, pulsing brains. Every time I sent a draft of the book to one of them the ideas and suggestions they returned to me were humbling in their genius. It was a privilege to receive sternly worded Edit Letters from each of them.

My sainted mother was interested in my writing even before there were huge advance monies to be contemplated, and also she brought me into this world and somehow ensured my survival until I was able to care for myself, at approximately age twenty-eight. When, coincidentally, my wife took up the job.

As always, Jeof, Ken, Misty, Cassie, Rose Ann, clint, Karen, and a host of other disreputable people served as inspiration, in very strange and indescribable ways, for this and many other stories. Most of them won't be pleased to read this, and there are probably lawsuits in the works right now.

And no acknowledgments would be complete without a shout-out to Lilith Saintcrow. Lili, you took a bullet for me in Berlin and joked through the entire back-alley operation, my flask of bourbon your only anesthesia. As soon as the State Department closes the investigation and I get my passport back, I'm taking off for Panama to collect our bounty.

extras

orbit

meet the author

JEFF SOMERS was born in Jersey City, New Jersey. After graduating from college, he wandered aimlessly for a while, but the peculiar siren call of New Jersey brought him back to his homeland. In 1995 Jeff began publishing his own magazine, *The Inner Swine* (www.innerswine.com). Find out more about the author at www.jeffreysomers.com.

introducing

If you enjoyed THE DIGITAL PLAGUE,
look out for

THE ETERNAL PRISON

by Jeff Somers

My Russian frowned and pushed his hands back into his pockets. From below his collar a smudge of ink was visible—a star atop what I assumed was a crown, the symbol of high rank. I reached up and scratched my chest where my own prison tattoo still burned. Prison had been good for me. I didn't like to think about it too much, about Michaleen and Bartlett and the others. It hadn't been a good time, an *enjoyable* time, but it had been a *necessary* time for me. It boiled me down and I'd come out of it the better man.

He saw me looking and smiled. "You know what it means?" He suddenly jerked his sleeve up, revealing two and half of the blurry skull tats on his arm. "And these?"

"Prison work," I said, keeping myself still, feeling the bodyguards' eyes on me. "Where'd you get the art?"

"You know what it means, my friend?"

I smirked, figuring that would annoy him. "I know what it's *supposed* to mean, Boris. Anyone can slap some ink on you."

"My name is not *Boris*," he complained. Maybe he wasn't as smart as me after all. I wasn't used to being the smartest guy in the room. "And where I come from, they kill you for false emblems like that. Buy you a drink somewhere and slit your throat, you fall back onto a plastic sheet, five minutes later it is like you were never there."

"Yeah," I said. "How many? Five? Ten? You think *ten* is a big number?" If I'd had a skull for every person I'd killed, I'd be a fucking shadow, I'd be nothing *but* ink.

"Numbers do not matter. You New York boys, always counting." He peered at me. "You are sure you did not work the Brussels job? I heard your name, very clear."

"Then someone is lying to you," I said. I'd been sucked into Chengara Penitentiary and hadn't made it too far away since getting out. "The last two times I made it to Europe, things didn't go so well for me." The two big boys behind me hadn't moved, not even to loosen up their coats.

He nodded, crimping his lips as if to say, yeah, okay, whatever you say. "You know my people?" he said suddenly, voice soft and casual, like he was asking me if I liked his shirt. I didn't. My own shirt was white and scratchy and a little tight around the neck, like it'd been made for a different man. "You know who I work for?"

"Sure," I said, nodding. "You're connected. You're a high roller. You run this town—for your boss. You live in this fine suite in this ancient hotel, you go from an air-conditioned room to an air-conditioned mini-hover—it's fucking cute, like a little toy—to an air-conditioned room every day and probably haven't sweated in ten years."

He chuckled, nodding and stepping around me. *"Da,"* he said jovially. *"Da!* And you were sent to kill me. It is funny. Now, if you will excuse me, I must have my dinner. Lyosha and Fedya will finish your conversation."

I turned to watch him walk back into the restaurant, the door shutting behind him as if on a motor of some sort. I looked at one of the big guys, and then at the other. They were slightly different in the shape of their rounded heads and the angle that their mouths hung open, but were essentially the same person occupying different space. I wondered idly if there would be an explosion if they accidentally touched.

The one I was looking at—I thought he was Lyosha but wasn't sure why I thought that—grinned. "You break my finger now?"

I sighed, feeling tired. "Sure, why not," I said. I could do the math: two of them against one of me, alone in a back lot, their friends inside and everywhere, fuck, the whole damn city. They hadn't frisked me or tried to take my own gun away. I chose not to be insulted. I reached up and took my crappy cigarette from between my lips and held it carefully between my thumb and forefinger.

Lyosha flicked his own cigarette into the air and exhaled briskly, shrugging his shoulders, getting loose. The butt fell limply to the ground as if the air was too thick to travel through, the coal bright on the dark, shadowed ground. For a moment we all stood there, hands hanging free, each of us waiting to see who would move first. First move was a losing move—it telegraphed your intentions, and when you had more than one person to deal with it, guaranteed at least one gun was going to find its way onto you and make some painful alterations. The air around us was completely still, like hot jelly, and I was reminded of the yard back at Chengara, where I'd gotten a free but excellent education on how to fight when outnumbered.

Rule number one was sometimes making the first move made sense.

I launched myself at the one I'd decided was Lyosha, tossing my cigarette into his face with my left hand as I pulled my gun with my right. He cursed in Russian, all consonants and fucking phlegm, waving his hands in front of his face and dancing back. As I crashed into him I brought my gun up and fired twice into his belly, falling down on top of him and rolling off to the side. I wasn't worried about the noise; my Russian expected a few shots. A few more and he might send the waiter out to see if we needed anything, but not yet.

I came up into an unsteady crouch and fired three times, quick, where the other bodyguard had been a second before. He was still there, for a moment, and then toppled over, hitting his knees and then falling over face-first. I stayed low for a moment, listening to the sudden silence, feeling the heat on me, straining my senses.

Rule number two was to never assume. It wasn't nice, but I turned and found Lyosha, put my gun against his head, and made sure he was dead. Then I stepped over to his buddy and did the same, warm blood spraying me lightly. You assumed people were dead, they had a habit of coming up behind you at the worst times. I'd learned that in Chengara, and it was a hard lesson to unlearn. And I wasn't sure I wanted to unlearn it.

I turned and jogged back toward the door in a wide arc, approaching from an angle, taking soft, easy steps. I knew I didn't need to worry about getting the door open—I had magic. By sheer force of will the door was going to pop open. After five steps it did just that, and a big, thick-necked woman with a goddamn shotgun held across her body, a streak of absolute darkness, stepped halfway out into the yard. She peered out into the lot, muttering to herself, not seeing me coming at her in the dim light on an angle. I just kept approaching, holding off; you couldn't shoot someone in the back. I wasn't a big believer in justice, but everyone deserved to at least see it coming.

I was just a few feet away when she suddenly turned, hissing something I couldn't make out and swinging the shotgun around, slow and clumsy. I squeezed the trigger and she whipped around, sending one blast from the shotgun into the night air and falling awkwardly against the open door, propping it open with her body. I leaped forward and plucked the shotgun from her loose grip, studied the wet, ugly wound I'd created in her chest, then looked into her open, staring eyes. With a quick glance into the bright, empty kitchen, I broke open the shotgun and let the shells drop out, then tossed it away to my right, the shadows swallowing it. Stepping over her, I edged into the humming kitchen, going from the heavy darkness to the brittle cold light, all the crank air of the restaurant rushing past me like someone had opened an airlock out in the desert. I stopped right inside and wasted a moment or two, listening, watching the swinging doors that led to the dining room.

As I stood there, the doors swung inward and admitted a pair of serving droids, skimming along the floor bearing dirty dishes. As the swinging doors closed I caught a glimpse of the busy dining room, all reds and browns, plush fabrics that looked heavy and old. My Russian was sitting back toward the front of the place, laughing and holding a drink up as if making a toast. I looked straight at him as the doors swung shut again, gliding slowly on their tiny motors, but he never looked up at me.

I raised my gun and let the clip drop into the palm of my hand; it was difficult coming by hardware these days, most of it coming out of scavenge yards down south, Mexico generally, where the SSF's grip was getting a little sketchy under pressure from the Army. For six yen a week kids sorted bullets into calibers and hand-filled clips, which were then sold to assholes like me for a thousand yen a clip. I wasn't sure where the fucking bullets came from, loose and sometimes ancient as hell, and I generally expected my gun to blow up in my hand every time I pulled the trigger. It kept things exciting.

I exchanged the old clip for a fresh one and snapped it into place as quietly as I could. I wasn't paid to scamper around waiting for the safe moment — I was paid for results, and now that my Russian was aware of me, there was no better time than the present, before he called his people and brought the hammer down — a wall of fat guys in leather coats, a team of idiots with garrotes in their pockets with my picture on their little handhelds. Besides, my instructions had been pretty clear: my Russian had to die *tonight*. I'd agreed to terms, and terms had to be upheld. I took a deep breath and racked a shell into the chamber gently, deciding that the best way to do it would be fast — no wasted movements, no wasted time. I didn't want anyone else to get hurt, no matter how rich — they'd just come out for a nice dinner; if they were willing to leave it between me and my subject, I had no reason to include them on my bill.

I put the gun down low by my thigh and pushed my way into the dining room. I walked quickly and steadily toward my Russian, my eyes on him the whole time. Momentum was the key — no one paid me any attention as I crossed the room, just part of the blur of motion around them.

When I was halfway to his table, my Russian glanced at me, then looked away, his face a pleasant mask of polite enjoyment. Then he snapped back to me, his expression tightening up, his hands jumping a bit on the table like he'd thought about doing something and then killed the idea. It was too late, by then; I was at his table. I should have just brought the gun up, killed him, and walked out. But I stood there for a moment with my gun at my side. I wasn't sure he could see it.

"Lyosha and Fedya will have some explaining to do, yes?"

I shook my head. "No. And neither will the kitchen help." I gave him another second, but he just sat there staring at me, his hands balled into fists. Macho asshole, no gun because he was *tough*. Fuck tough. Tough got you killed.

I raised the gun and there was no reaction at first — I'd expected a hubbub from the crowd, some noise, chaos. But I'd been away from civilization for so long I guess I'd forgotten the rules, how it worked. I raised the gun and put it a few inches from my Russian's face — not close enough for him to grab it easily, or knock it aside — and nothing happened. There were people just a few feet away, eating their dinners, but no one was even looking at me.

My Russian stared at the barrel. "You know who I am, my friend," he said slowly, licking his lips. "Maybe you wish to be rich?" His eyes jumped to my face and then tightened up. "No, I see you do not wish to be rich. Perhaps you don't wish to *live*, either. You are not a young man. You know who I work for. This will not be forgotten."

I nodded. "I know who you are. You're organized. You draw a lot of fucking water out here. And now it doesn't matter. I don't know what you did, but you pissed off the wrong people, and here I am." Talking was for amateurs, but I wanted to give him his say. When you killed a man, you had to let him have his last words, if you could.

He was shaking now — with fear or rage, I couldn't tell. "You do not care who I work for, then? But you do not understand. It is not like the old days, where we run from the fucking cops and they chase us behind the furniture. We are *part* of things. We are *partners*. You do not fear *us*, but do you fear Cal Ruberto? Ruberto, the Undersecretary."

I blinked. Now there was a shout from across the room, and the whole place got quiet for a second, followed by a hissing wave of whispers. Cal Ruberto was Undersecretary for the North American Department and, nowadays, a Major General in the New Army. The Undersecretaries had been running things — as much as Dick Marin and the System Cops would let them — since the Joint Council had gone senile years ago, but now they had some muscle. Ruberto wasn't just an Undersecretary anymore. He was a fucking *general*.

"You do not fear my boss," my Russian continued.

"But maybe you fear Ruberto. Maybe you fear the whole damn System behind him."

I stared down at him a second longer, then cocked the hammer back. "Cal Ruberto," I said, "is *my* boss."

I squeezed the trigger, the gun making a thunderous crack, my Russian's face imploding as he was knocked backward, spraying me with a fine mist of brains and blood. I stood still another moment, thinking that I was almost at the point where I felt nothing when I admitted that.

Then I spun around, bringing my cannon with me, and stood there dripping blood, running my eye over the crowd. Most of them ducked down as I covered them, crouching in their seats. There were some shouts, but no one was moving. I let my gun drop to my side again and stepped quickly toward the entrance. There would be no cops, but you didn't kill a man with a crown on his chest in this town and just walk away, whistling.

I crashed through the doors and into the hot, empty desert night, slipping my barker into my pocket. I imagined my Russian's blood baking onto me, turning into a shell. The street was busy, crowds of people who made up the infrastructure of the Russians' private city out for the night. I just pushed through bodies, looking up at the dark, hulking shapes of the ancient hotels on the horizon, huge complexes rotting in the sun, marking the outer edge of a rotting city slowly filling with sand and choking sunlight. A man could get lost in the darkness there forever, if he wanted. In the heat, forever was a lot shorter than you might imagine.

Walking steadily toward the horizon, I wiped my Russian's blood out of my eyes and heard him asking me,

How many men have you killed, for yen? I shook a cigarette out and placed it between my lips. I didn't know. I'd
lost count. I was dead. I'd died back in prison. As I leaned
in to light up, there was a deafening boom behind me,
and I was lifted up off my feet for a second by a warm
gust. I staggered forward and steadied myself with the
street, lying there for a moment, my cigarette crushed into
my face. When I flipped over, the restaurant was on fire,
pieces of its roof sailing down in fiery arcs from the night
sky.

Well shit, I thought, sitting up on my elbows. *That's
fucking strange.*